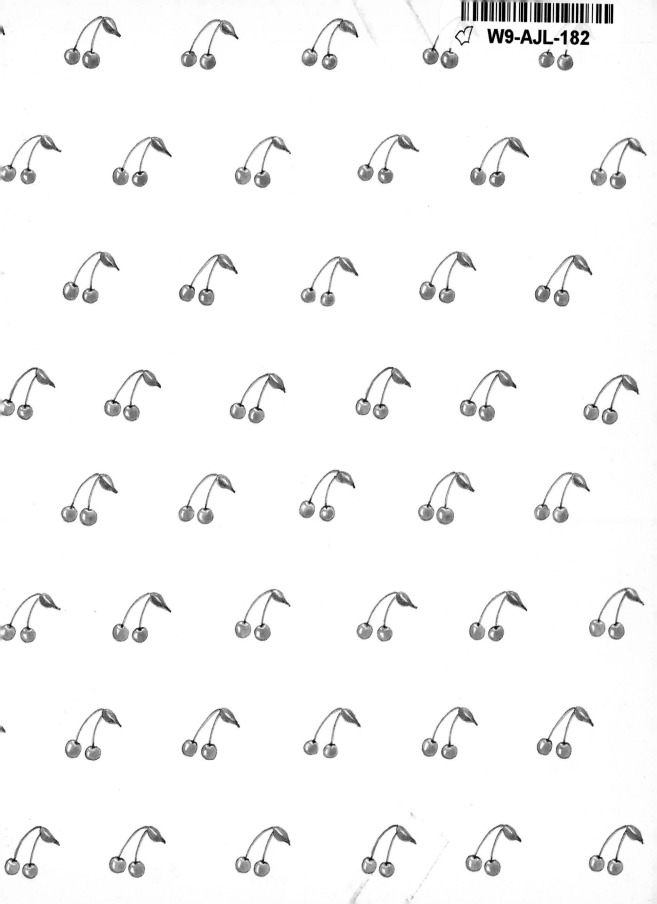

FLORENCE AND ERIC
TAKE THE CAKE

FLORENCE AND ERIC TAKE THE CAKE

Jocelyn Wild

Dial Books
for Young Readers
New York

For Granny and Grandpa
Wild

First published in the United States 1987 by
Dial Books for Young Readers
A Division of NAL Penguin Inc.
2 Park Avenue
New York, New York 10016

Published in Great Britain by
William Heinemann Ltd.
Text and illustrations copyright © 1987 by Jocelyn Wild
Printed in Great Britain
First edition
OBE
1 3 5 7 9 10 8 6 4 2

Library of Congress Cataloging in Publication Data
Wild, Jocelyn. Florence and Eric take the cake.
Summary: A brother and sister lamb
accidentally cause a major mix-up between
a delicious cake and a beautiful hat.
[1. Sheep—Fictional.] I. Title.
PZ7.W64573F1 1987 [E] 87-639
ISBN 0-8037-0305-8

This is Rosemary Cottage where Granny and
Grandpa Mutton live. It's summer vacation
and Florence and her little brother Eric have
come for a visit.

This morning Granny is very busy. The ladies from the Little Nibbling Knitting Circle are meeting here and Granny must tidy up.

Florence and Eric want to help Granny get ready.
Mother has told them to make sure they
do everything they can for Granny and Grandpa.

Just then the telephone rings. It is Miss Lavinia
Bleating. She's made her heavenly angel food cake
for the Knitting Circle this afternoon. But now
she has come down with the most frightful cold
and can't come.

"Oh, take care, my dear," says Granny. "What if
I send Florence and Eric for the cake? It's about
time they had some fresh air."
"Good idea. I'll leave it in the hall," Miss
Bleating replies. "Tell Florence to walk
straight in. The door will be open."

Miss Lavinia has spent all morning icing the cake with her favorite marshmallow frosting. At last it's finished!

14

She leaves the cake in the hall and goes upstairs
to lie down. Poor Miss Lavinia doesn't feel well at all.

A moment later Lavinia's sister Muriel comes home. She has been out shopping for a new hat to wear to *The Baa Baa of Seville*, her favorite opera. Muriel is going to town to see it this evening.

Muriel loves the opera and has a very fine voice herself. She keeps it in perfect pitch by practicing in the bathtub every day. So when the front door opens, she doesn't hear it.

Florence and Eric have come for the cake. Eric sees the box on the hall table, lifts it down, and takes it to Florence.

Florence checks to make sure the cake's inside
and puts it in her basket.
She carries it herself – Eric might drop it.

Promptly at four-thirty the taxi arrives to take Muriel to the train station.

In two shakes

she is dressed

and ready
to go.

There is just her hat to put on.

And what an
elegant hat it is.
Why! Those cherries
look almost real!
She puts it firmly
on her head.

Oh, no! What a mess!
This isn't her hat at all!
It's a *cake!* A horrid
sloppy sticky cake!
Muriel lets out a
very loud scream.

23

Meanwhile the ladies of the Knitting Circle have been very busy all afternoon knitting sweaters for poor orphan lambs and now it is time for some refreshments.

Everyone is looking forward to a nice cup of tea
and a slice of dear Lavinia's cake. It looks almost
too good to eat.

But, oh dear, how tough the cake is! How dry!
Mrs. Woolly-Jumper has just broken a tooth on
one of the cherries. And Mrs. Scrag is choking.

26

There's no doubt about it. The cake is uneatable.

But Florence thinks it makes a lovely hat.
And Eric agrees.

Pack up the Moon

Pack up the Moon

Mary Anne Kelly

Thomas Dunne Books

St. Martin's Press 🐦 New York

THOMAS DUNNE BOOKS.
An imprint of St. Martin's Press.

www. thomasdunnebooks.com
www.stmartins.com

Library of Congress Cataloging-in-Publication Data

Kelly, Mary Anne.
   Pack up the moon / Mary Anne Kelly.—1st ed.
        p.   cm.
   ISBN-13: 978-0-312-34208-1
   ISBN-10: 0-312-34208-X
      1. Breslinsky, Claire (fictitious character)—Fiction. 2. Americans—Germany—Munich—
Fiction. 3. Europeans—India—Fiction. 4. Documentary films—Production and direction—
Fiction. 5. Caravans—Fiction. 6. India—Fiction. I. Title.

PS3561.E3946P33 2006
813'.54—dc22

                                                                                                           2006042917

First Edition: December 2006

10   9   8   7   6   5   4   3   2   1

For Michael

Acknowledgments

With love and thanks to Ruth Cavin for her help and guidance; to Toni Plummer for her keen insight; to my Tommy, my love, for everything; to Osse and Tereza, Hilde, Helen, Annie, Marcia, Dorothy, and dear Mom for their encouragement and support; to my friends Barbara, Jeanie, Claudia, Ann, and Teresa; to Patricia for being, imaginative honor, my best friend.

And in memory of sweet Melissa Willy Castro.

All we in one long caravan

Are journeying since the world began . . .

Bhartrihari

chapter one

*P*aris had been exciting, but there'd been the nagging threat of dwindling finances. The unhappy face of my booking girl and the disappointed tone of Francoise, the agency owner, told me that perhaps it would be best if I try Milan.

I'd gone right away. Milan had plenty of paintings. I wasn't just another photographer's model. I was an artist. Or I would be one day.

Milan *was* better. The booking people there were almost gay as they informed me I'd completely run out of lire.

"But what shall I do?" I gaped stupidly at the booking girl.

"Enh," she shrugged, "you might try America." She returned to her phone.

I wasn't going home. My brother was dead and I wasn't going home.

"Hold on a minute," I said. "What about the money due me from those last three jobs?"

"There was a bill from the New York office," she said. "You had a thousand Sed Cards made up."

"No," I said, "the agency did that. I never ordered them."

She gave me the now familiar shrug. "Look. You can't work unless you have Sed Cards, photographic calling cards. How can clients book you if they don't know who you are? Someone has to pay."

I was dismissed. It was only by chance that I ran into a German agent in the agency waiting room. She grabbed hold of my portfolio, crossed her booted legs, flipped through and looked hard at the pages.

"You'll work in Germany." She frowned knowingly. "They'll like you there."

I could hardly believe this after months of barely scraping by, the endless rejections because I was simply too short, but I didn't say a word. There had been the odd job here or there; lawn furniture circulars for the Italian Sunday supplement, but never the full day rate. Of course I still imagined it was romantic to be poor in Europe, with the certainty of happy endings to sustain me.

Hadn't my father marched across the continent in army boots, crept into villages to deploy bombs, and then returned home intact? He'd led a charmed life. So would I. I straightened my posture to give the appearance of added height. I was not beautiful, but my teeth were white and my smile captivating. Once the shots were developed, mine was the face you were drawn to. The camera loved me. And I had that one other precious commodity: nerve.

The German agent offered me an airplane ticket, scribbled out her agency's address and one of a magazine she thought would book me.

I went back to the apartment on via Gardone and told my roommates I'd be leaving. They made the appropriate expressions of dismay but I could tell they were relieved. They were kindhearted students. Each one had proudly taken me to sketch his favorite vista or painting throughout Milan. It had been fun to

have an American model to stay but, *porco!* who would have
known such a skinny thing could eat so much?
To celebrate, we would go to Luna Park. This was an amuse-
ment park on the outskirts of Milan. We went, driving past the
roadside *puttanas* and their fires. I couldn't believe it when my
friends told me they were whores. I'd never seen anything so
beautiful. I stuck my camera out the window and snapped their
pictures, knowing I would want to try to re-create the scene on
canvas.
We had a fine time at Luna Park. I knew I'd overstayed my welcome. But my roomates had been so happy with me at first. *"Foto
modella.* Click Click," they would say. I'd met them through Massimo, a university student who had modeled with me for the cover
of *Panorama,* a sort of Italian *Time* magazine. I'd been sitting in
the studio bathroom weeping when he'd walked in on me. So I'd
told him about my brother and he brought me back home with
him. He and his friends convinced me to give up my expensive,
ballroom-sized hotel room and come live with them. I'd screamed
in my sleep at the hotel the night before that, and had awakened
the other guests. I was happy to go live with Massimo and his
friends. They were communists, but this, I realized later, was in
name only. It was that or fascist. At the time, all Milanese university students were communists—the way even self-serving hedo-
nists from America like myself were considered hippies.
I slept on a cot in a room beside the kitchen. There were always
people there, studying or getting drunk. One night they took me to
a demonstration. "Take care," Angelo warned me severely. "The
fascists have lead bars in their gloves. If they hit you, they can kill
you." But it hadn't been a bad demonstration. The fascists seemed
trustworthy and the communists alarmingly well dressed. We'd
maneuvered down antiquated passageways to a white and wood-
beamed restaurant where Angelo played his guitar and they'd
watched me, disapprovingly, eat cheese. "No," they'd protested,

"not-a like that." They'd pushed away my fork, drizzled the chalky stuff with thick green olive oil, fastidiously crushed oregano, salt, pepper, and rosemary. Then I was permitted to continue.

At Luna Park that last night, we spent a lot of time in the bumper cars. Relieved of the necessity to translate, we laughed uproariously. We returned to the apartment and went to bed. I woke up before dawn and packed my things. Only then I realized my purse was missing.

"*Porco*," Massimo declared. "It's gypsies that run that place. You'll never see your money again."

"No, I've got to." I sank onto the kitchen chair. "My passport was in there. My ticket."

"Forget it." Angelo came up behind him, rubbing his long lashes. "Gypsies! Gypsies steal for a living."

They saw the anguish on my face, weighed it against the emptiness of the refrigerator. "I'll-a tell you what," Massimo decided. "We'll drive out to the *aeroporto*." He shrugged. "Maybe by then, some-a-body turn it in."

He wanted to be rid of me. I didn't mind. I wanted to go. We piled into the *macchina*. On the way to the *aeroporto* we passed Luna Park. The fog went this way and that in ghostly scarves. Deserted, the Ferris wheel spun. Baroque wrought iron gates stood alone without a fence in the empty field, without a road, just this elegant entrance to nowhere. Massimo, on a whim, turned in. We jostled and lurched up the dust and gravel to the far-off circle of caravans huddled behind red and yellow rides. You could see the rust in the morning light, hear the garish hinges creak forlornly without any music. Thugs in black leather skulked about. We asked around but no one knew anything. They didn't speak English. They didn't even speak Italian. They were in fact Romanians. One fellow kicked the tent ties again and again. He wore shrimp-colored nylon socks. I went up to him. "Listen," I said, my shoes sinking in the mud, my shoulders giving in, "I know you can't help us but maybe you know someone who can. I've lost everything here last night. My passport. My purse. Please. Can't you help us?"

He went on kicking his tent tie.

I gave up. "Come on. Let's get out of here."

But he stopped my companions, signaling them to go with him. I followed them. We went up to a yellow caravan surrounded by the others. He banged a secret, backhanded knock on the door. A smooth-skinned, heavy-armed woman opened. Her hair was shoe polish black and parted white in the middle sharp as a scar. Her cheeks hung in soft wabblebags. I think the fellow was her son. He talked. Massimo talked. Angelo talked.

I stood behind them looking at the sacred hearts on velvet, the plastic white lace doilies. There was tea on an electric ring. The woman kept looking at me, searching my eyes. She pushed the others out of the way and brought me into her caravan. It was warm and smelled of sleep. I don't know why I wasn't frightened. She sat down at her table. It was a hideaway table, the kind that could be snapped up against the wall in a hurry. A manila envelope lay there. I looked at it. Then I gaped at it. My name was on this envelope: Claire Breslinsky, care of the American embassy. I sank onto an electric radiator. She dumped the insides of the envelope onto the table. My plane tickets slid out. My passport. There was no money. But there'd been little to begin with.

My friends at the door let up a shout.

It's so long since this happened, but I recall it as though it were this morning. I can see her face, her intent eyes. I can feel the rigid strips of heat seeping through my damp clothes. Nobody speaks badly about gypsies around me.

Massimo, Angelo, Beppe, and Guido drove me speedily away to the airport.

"What did she say to you?" I pressed Massimo. "You were talking for a long time."

"The usual rot. You are going to meet a handsome stranger and go on a very long journey."

"Well, I'm on that." I grinned.

Massimo frowned. He looked away. "No. She meant something else. A 'special' journey, she kept saying—like a necklace—no. Like a string of beads." He let it go.

But I couldn't help feeling that he was holding something back. That there was something he wasn't telling me. I said so.

He pressed his lips together as if he was coming to a decision and then he let go, saying, "I dunno. She said that if you were a tree, it would be the pistachio tree." He shrugged. "Whatever that means. But she said you are 'protected.'" He downshifted. "She was queen, you know. Queen of the gypsies."

I digested this pronouncement with a thrill.

"She also said you go in and out of trouble," he frowned, not liking my delight, "like a teabag. And," he added ominously, "that you will be in great danger on this *journey*." He said "journey" demeaningly, the way you would say "cockamamie scheme."

But he couldn't take away my joy. Her words were like winning a prize. I'd never won a prize. Everything I had I'd clawed through disapproval to get. I opened the passport and looked at me. I thought of my brother. If a gypsy queen said I was protected, I thought, it might be so. I began—testing the waters like a reprieved fish thrown back in—to breathe.

"Bunch of crazy people," Massimo muttered about gypsies in general.

I defended her. "She *was* sending me my passport."

Angelo said, "They stole a chicken from my *nonna*'s yard."

"Of course," Guido said. "They're thieves."

"But they brought back the bones," Angelo pointed out. "Buried them in the yard."

"Enriches the soil," Beppe said.

We were silent.

"A circle," Angelo summed up. He was the poet.

Nobody cried when we said good-bye. I thought one of them would slip me some money when I went through the gate but nobody did. Well, I hadn't slept with any of them. I imagined this had something to do with it.

"Look." Massimo held me back by the crook of my arm. "Germany is famous for murdering innocence." He stopped, glanced over his shoulder. "Just, ah, never change, okay?"

"Okay," I lied into his dark, kindhearted eyes. A lump formed in my throat as they shuffled, trench-coated, away.

I put my straw hat on and adjusted it with a fearsome-looking hat pin. It was a wide-brim straw, soft and floppy, a preposterously romantic bridesmaid's hat, saved from my sister Carmela's wedding. One slender brown ribbon circled the crown and streamed twice down the center of my narrow back.

I stood at the boarding gate and could not imagine why everyone was looking at me. In my long straight hair, bell bottoms, and jeans jacket ensemble, my wide-brimmed hat, I'd just beat the hippie look across the Atlantic. The Brownie camera hanging from my shoulder might have been cheap, but I so loved looking through that lens and capturing moments to draw later on. It didn't matter to me that it was unprofessional.

A well-heeled, conservative-looking couple, sun drenched and merry, hurried up to the gate. They hadn't checked their baggage and were laden with suitcases and baskets of duty-free bottles. I just happened to turn and knocked the man's ticket to the ground. We both knelt at once.

And that was when I saw him. I looked into the liveliest, handsomest pair of green eyes I'd ever seen. Inside me I heard, "This is the one!" We stared at each other for a captivated moment, then, shaking ourselves back to normal, stood. The woman clicked her tongue in annoyance and harrumphed the both of them away.

I'm a Catholic schoolgirl at heart, and anything attached at the other end gets no attention from me. But while we waited for the Alitalia flight to call us on board, in a crowd of a hundred or so people, I felt myself being watched. You know how it is. Suddenly you look up as though someone has called your name. I turned. It was him. He was scrutinizing me. I looked again into the eyes of destiny. Still, he *was* part of a couple. I snapped my head away.

When I landed in Munich, it was 1972. I wasn't yet twenty. I had only the airplane ticket and those two crisply written addresses. Imagine, I remember thinking, going to Germany on purpose! Oh, I knew a lot about Germany, all right—all from black-and-white World War II movies. The Germans, I was about to find out, had seen none of them.

chapter two

*I*n Munich's tiny airport, propeller fans spun overhead. I retrieved my trunk—more suited to ocean liner travel than this—and lugged it out onto the road.

It was only November but already the curbs were heaped with dirty snow. One white Mercedes taxi after the next sped from the small international building. I looked around for the handsome couple and saw them shrugging into a taxi. I wasn't dressed for such cold. I looked over each shoulder and, in desperation, stuck out my thumb.

Almost immediately a private car stopped. The driver helped put my trunk into his and we went toward town. I took out the crumpled address I had safely in my pocket and pressed it into his hand. He scrutinized it in a despairing way that let me know it would be far out of his way. But, bless him, he drove me there. There was an American station on the radio, Armed Forces Radio, and Richie Havens was singing. I could hardly believe my good fortune. I was living the faraway life I had yearned for, but I was lonely and homesick by now.

He stopped outside a glass and steel building. I watched nervously as he drove away. I brought my great trunk inside and onto the elevator with me and rode up to the room on the note. Someone was summoned to the front desk who could make something of my English. A plump lady in a thrifty gray suit trotted out. She put on the glasses hanging on a brass chain and waited skeptically while I explained.

"*Fräulein,*" she informed me, "this is not a model agency at all but a fashion magazine."

I realized then I'd given the driver the wrong address of the two I had. My horrified expression must have struck her as funny. That and the sight of my enormous trunk, because she doubled over with laughter.

The receptionist had had enough. She used the internationally recognizable eject finger and pointed toward the exit.

"*Halt!* Wait! Come with me one moment," the gray-suited lady broke in, and she ushered me to the office cubicles behind the reception area. "Try this on," she said, handing me a yellow ski suit.

I slipped out of my jeans and put it on. My heart sank. Once again—as usual—it was too big. I was too small.

"I'm sorry," I said. "Thank you for trying to help." I gathered my clothes from the ledge. "This was what always kept me out of all the runway work I tried for in Paris and Milan."

"No, *Liebling.* That's not it. Nobody can get in this and we must shoot it by Friday."

"I don't understand."

"*Na!* This is not the runway business." She clothespinned the back, took a step away from me, and looked me up and down. "For photography it doesn't hardly matter what the back side is looking like. We were afraid we would have to cut the back open to shoot it. Perfect!" She beamed at me. Just then, another lady arrived wearing a bracelet of pincushions. She shoved me around inside the snowsuit and I joggled back and forth. *"Endlich! Gut,"* she said. Finally. Good. "We'll need you for two days. Which agency?"

I dove cooperatively into my messy bag and came out with my other paper. They bent over it and nodded approvingly. I guessed the agency must be all right and I left, lugging my trunk. At least, I hugged myself, I would have work.

This time it took a long while to get a ride and by the time I got to the agency—a cozy pink house on a canal out in the outskirts of Nymphenburg—they were about to close. The booking girls left me sitting on a red leather sofa while they drank their hot chamomile tea. Although there were bar stool–type chairs, they stood. They manned the phones.

One girl finally noticed me. *"Was ist?"* She frowned and jerked her chin at me.

I suppose I looked pretty bedraggled at that point. I skulked unhappily over and asked to see Gita Ratleman.

Gita Ratleman, the booking girls informed me in harmony, was still away in Italy on a business trip. They seemed like very stupid girls to me. I didn't like them. They were as arrogant as the French, but without the sharp, high style. One girl I'd been watching had switched from rapid-fire English to Dutch and then French. I directed my plea to her.

"Excuse me, miss, but Gita Ratleman, your boss, gave me my ticket and," I shrugged, "here I am. Do you think you could advance me some D-marks, so that I might get a hotel?"

She snorted disdainfully and turned her back, saying, "You must come again in the morning," and returned to her telephone call. She had seen girls like me before, girls who smoked pot and played the guitar. She had a very smart Mary Quant sort of hair-cut and the heels of her olive suede shoes were not worn down on each side the way mine were. I waited humbly, by now very tired.

"Look," I tried again when she at last got off the phone, "at least you could advance me enough money to get a meal. . . ."

Scornfully, she looked me up and down. "Do you mean you have no money at all?"

I looked out the clean expanse of window into the twilight. The air over the yard was dense with empty branches. "Yes," I admitted.

"Oh, come," she scoffed. "No one changes countries without *any* money. Not even rootless photomodels." She delighted herself with her grasp of the language. The disdain in her voice dripped with her true feelings for the models she booked. And there was a horror there, underneath. She'd made her choice, this girl. Hers was a safe, humming office and health insurance. No gallivanting around the world for her.

"I don't have a single mark," I protested, knowing I must sound pathetic and realizing what she said was certainly true, yet here I was. I'd come this far. If I was ever in this snippy little office worker's place, I promised myself, I would behave in a more char-itable way. I would be darned if this small-minded *Fräulein* would play any role in thwarting my destiny. Suddenly I didn't care what she thought. "Listen," I said in a harsher tone, "Gita Ratleman is your boss, isn't she?"

Like most bullies, she had little spine when bullied herself. She unpursed her lips.

"I don't think she would have paid for a flight for me from Milan if she didn't think I'd work here."

She gave a hard laugh. "Gita takes a chance on a lot of girls. That's what she does. Tickets are tax deductible. Only one of ten will work, though. She makes money either way."

I uncrumpled the paper I still held in my hand. "But this fashion magazine, *Freundin*, booked me for two days starting tomorrow. At least you'll be assured to get your advance back."

She really saw me for the first time.

"I went there first, by mistake," I explained.

Her eyes widened at the signature on the paper. Suddenly, she became almost courtly. "I'll tell you what," she acted as though we'd been chummy all along, "I'll advance you twenty marks from my own pocket and book you a pension near the Leopoldstrasse. The Franz Joseph. It is cheap and clean. And it's in Schwabing."

Even I knew that twenty marks was hardly anything, but I was so tired and hungry now. All I wanted was to get away. Laboriously, she wrote out the directions for the trolley but as soon as I was out of sight, I stuck out my thumb. There wasn't much traffic out this way. Swans glided up the canal, hoisted up their skirts of belly and waddled across chunks of ice, then plopped back in the water and continued gliding down the canal. They eyed me as they passed.

This was so different from Italy's dark, narrow canals, its lives behind groaning shutters. Out here were spacious lawns of clean blue snow. The twilight had turned the water a shimmering purple. I wished I'd thought to open my trunk and find a thicker sweater. Far off, stout ladies and men played a serious game of *Eisstockschiessen*—bowling on ice. The people were all twice the size of Italians—and I could hear the pins clacking in the crisp air where they played. I could see right into kitchen windows edged in white lacy curtains. Farm lamps twinkled. Families ate their supper. I thought of my mother and father back home. The newspapers open. The smell of food. A car came down the lane but passed me by. It didn't matter how long it would take. Twenty marks would not go far and who knew what tomorrow would bring? Eventually, a car did stop and I hitched a ride to the Pension Franz Joseph. It seemed hitchhiking wasn't done, but the fact that I'd transported this great trunk with me struck them as jocularly original. Each of my drivers had laughed and laughed at my plight, but each one had driven me to exactly where I'd had to go.

The pension was in a dark, gated *Hof*. The stones on the ground were worn with the centuries and shone with moonlight. I lugged my trunk through the yard and up the stairs. The stout woman behind the heavy wooden door spoke no English but it didn't matter because everything she said was drowned out by the shrill barking of her four vicious dachshunds. Together, they showed me to my tiny room. I shut the door. The window looked out onto a medieval stone courtyard. I had never seen a bed so soft and high or linen so white. Cherishing the thought that this would be mine tonight, I took from my trunk my sketchpad and charcoals, a heavy sweater—my brother's varsity football sweater from St. John's University—put the wrought-iron door key in my pocket, and went out to find some food.

This place didn't look so bad, I thought. I went into the Pschorr Brauerei on the Leopoldstrasse, where huddles of university students sat smoking cigarettes and drinking coffee. No one troubled over my sketchpad here. I could sit and draw to my heart's content. I ordered a goulash soup and a glass of milk, the only dish I could decipher on the menu. I can taste it still. The milk was odd tasting and not cold but the soup was delicious, hot, greasy, and spicy. I wiped the bowl with the last crispy roll and sighed with renewed hope. The next day I would begin to work. Work! I calculated my expenses. Why, I could live for weeks on one day's paycheck, if I scrimped. I began to draw the smoky room.

"Excusez-moi?" A young man stood at my table. I looked around, meaning to indicate another table, but the restaurant had filled. Before I could answer, he sat down and stuck his straggly head of long hair behind a menu. He wore a Greek sweater tied around the waist and raggedy clothes. He introduced himself. "I am Chartreuse."

"I'm Claire Breslinsky." Nice, I thought, eyeing the acoustic guitar slung over his shoulder. Like Angelo, my friend in Italy.

"Student?"

"Always." I smiled. "But not matriculated." I apologized, "I just model, I'm afraid."

"Ah." His eyes glittered. He actually rubbed both hands together in leering appreciation.

"You are French?" I asked shyly.

"I am . . . shall we say . . . intercontinental."

"Oh," I said, impressed. I was so happy to speak English. "Are you a student?"

"Mais non." He eyed my sketchpad. "I am an artist." He did look like an artist; his long, lustrous hair down to his shoulders, his dirty fingers, his handsome nostrils flaring with sensual abandon. He could have been a rock star.

"Imagine," I gushed naively, "the first person I meet in Germany is an artist!" I blushed. "It's what I hope to become!"

We smiled at each other. He glanced over his shoulder. "Joint?"

"Sorry?"

He held a hand-rolled fabrication of hashish and tobacco— complete with filter—up in the air.

I looked around. "What about the police?"

He laughed. "This is Schwabing. Student territory. What you would call the Left Bank of Munich. No one weel bother you here."

"Oh, not tonight, thanks," I hedged. "I've got to be up before dawn tomorrow. We're going to Austria. To Kitzbühel."

"Ah! Keetzbuhel! I love eet! Which mountain?"

"They didn't tell me that. It's for some magazine called *Freundin*." Little did I know that in my country that was like saying 'some magazine like *Glamour* or *Mademoiselle*.' Chartreuse's eyes opened wide.

"Would you do me a favor?" I asked. "I just want to pay my bill and I don't speak German."

"But, of course." He snatched the twenty-mark note from my hand and signaled the waitress. In one deft movement he slipped the rest of the rolls from the breadbasket and smuggled them into the Nepali bag he wore across his chest. The waitress arrived, counted up how many rolls were gone, and added them to the bill.

Chartreuse paid with an elegant flourish. He had beautiful eyes. Yellow. Rimmed in kohl. Then these long silky eyelashes. He, too, was short, I realized when I stood.

I can't tell you why I liked him. I believe now that the attraction happened because I was at that time still innocent. It was before anything untoward had happened. Perhaps my goodness was drawn to his wickedness. But there was something very sweet about him, too, something of the small boy alone in the desert hankering for Westerners and all they brought with them. And he looked at me as though I were made of gold. He seemed romantic to me. Not in a sexual way, certainly (I remain aghast at dirty fingernails) but as a pal, another artist. I held out my hand firmly for the change he'd so cavalierly pocketed. He gave it back. We grinned at each other.

We walked outside together and then back to my pension. I wasn't sure I could have found my way and I was glad for the company.

"So long!" He gave me a peck on both cheeks as I fished for my key. His breath smelled of sen-sen, which I learned later he kept at all times in his pocket. "See you soon!"

"How will I find you?"

He gave an easy shrug. "I am always at the Café Münchner Freiheit."

There, I thought as I slipped the lacy key into the gate, one day in town and already I've got a friend. I went to my room, washed up, and climbed into that scrumptious bed. Then, for some reason, my eyes would not close. I turned over. I thought I'd crack open the window a bit and rolled out of bed. But before I could open the sash I caught sight of a figure below in the dark. People still hurried down the tree-lined avenue but someone stood there in the shadows looking up. The ember on his cigarette had captured my attention. I took a step back and peered through the drapes. Why, it was Chartreuse.

I left the window shut and stole back to my bed. I lay there, contented in the assumption that he'd fallen for me. I felt idiotically proud. But you know what they say about pride.

The next day I began to work.

A caravan of oversized Mercedes taxis arrived in the still-dark morning. I climbed aboard one of them. They were full of sour, sleepy, grumpy Germans—they were so big! I think I was half the size of every one of them. They dozed with their heads pillowed against windows and I was forced to wedge myself into a middle spot of the last car—low man on the totem pole as I was. Still, I was excited. We were headed for the Alps. The Alps! I sat up straight, the driver and I the only ones awake. We chatted convivially in English. He was happy to point out the sights.

My hungry eyes devoured the picturesque countryside.

We drove and drove. I was beginning to doze off myself. At the Austrian border we were jostled awake, our passports reviewed by humorless, armed agents, then waved through.

At last we arrived. The muddled gray sky and the bitter air were not very inviting. I just let myself be pushed along with my group. The men were all impossibly handsome, I noticed, and effeminate. They minced along. The women, more masculine, were bleary-eyed and their hair was done up in rollers. They stomped along carrying "falls"—great manes of pretend hair that they would later anchor with combs to their own.

We were hustled into a large gondola, where, standing, we were wedged like sardines among early morning skiers and photographic equipment. I felt my stomach drop as we became suspended onto a cable and lifted, airplane-like, upward. Breaking through clouds is always a thrill, I don't care how many times you've done it. Suddenly we were bathed in morning light.

Nothing the Germans like more than sunlight. At once they awoke and began to chat. Outside, the sky was crisp and blue. The other passengers, used to this sort of thing, were prepared in their own ski clothes and boots. It became manically cold. I wriggled over to the side and took a peek down. We glided above what looked like miniature villages and pines. Cars and trains the size of toys slid by and then, stuck in a cloud, the gondola hesitated, then swayed. It jigged an interrupted little dance, sending the passengers into one another. My heart was in my throat. I could feel the sweat on my back. We lunged higher still. I began to tremble. The others, however, were as casual as New Yorkers on the el train. There was the smell of suntan lotion and the happy sound of loud, guffawing bliss that is the German in unrestricted sunlight.

We landed, sliding along an icy embankment, and were jostled into a herding gate. I was glad to see some sort of rest house of glass and wood built into the mountain. It was rimmed with broad balconies and slanted, magnificent skylights. One steward swept away the snow and behind him another went about setting up leisure chairs. I could smell coffee and the promise of food. Coming from New York as I had, I'd never tasted air that sharp and fresh. It practically bit you.

"Hey!" One of the models nudged me with her huge tote bag. *"Mach' mal! Beweg' dich!"*

I imagined she meant, "Get a move on!"

"Sorry!" I said, pulling myself together and moving along more quickly. She looked vaguely familiar although I couldn't imagine why. I supposed it was because she and I were the only redheads—I was auburn, she had the I-love-Lucy red. That sort never quite trust my naturally dark brows and lashes. She was of the pale-lashed, pinkish-eye variety. She wore an awful lot of jewelry for so early in the morning, I thought to myself, but I quickly dismissed her. There was so much going on.

The photographer and his assistants were already out on the mountain ledge beside the T-bar, setting up for the shots. We were led to a makeshift dressing room in the building; it was at the end of a tile corridor near the cold passageways. I looked longingly through the windows at the steaming pancakes on trays in the canteen-like restaurant but there was to be none of that. Everything was, *"Komm! Komm! mach' schnell!"* "Hurry hurry," the stylist would cry, for though there wasn't a cloud in the sky, there were bundles of outfits to be got through and the weather this high up could change in an instant. There were so many trunks of clothes, I couldn't see how we would ever get done in a day, but, carefully, systematically, the assistants lined everything up on portable-hanger trolleys and we were soon under way.

There were six female models and six males, the men up and ready first. We women had a part of the balcony cordoned off and we applied our makeup from handheld magnifying mirrors. I remember not being very impressed with the models. To me they all seemed old. They looked as if they were almost *thirty*, for heaven's sake. But these were catalog models, the kind with whom I'd not had any experience. They were "girls" who were no longer girls but who, on every roll of film, never lost the photographer a shot. They knew all the tricks, how steadily one must hold a smile, how not to move too quickly but in rhythm with the camera—just enough movement to give the outfit another angle, but never so much that the texture of the cloth might blur. In every shot the hands were extended and held with the grace of a ballerina. These were the pros. Their complexions might look spackled in person, but in the catalog or the weekend circulars they graced, they glowed like young brides. They also made a lot of money. The girl with the pink eyes, for example, in a gloss of mascara and black liner now, looked extraordinarily glamorous.

BoBo, the stylist, instructed us that we must not make use of the skis. There would be severe repercussions if anyone tried.

"Es heisst wir werden nicht bezahlt,"—It means we won't get paid—wisecracked one of the girls and everyone laughed. I turned to get a better look at her. She was a wild stallion sort of girl with lots of unkempt, mahogany hair—not like the others with their sleek heads in varying shades of blond. She stood out.

But not only because she was dark. I noticed that everyone chuckled then shook their heads in fond indulgence when she said anything in her deep, attention-getting voice. For the first time I wished I understood German. She moved unhurried and panther-like, comfortable in her own skin. This girl carried an edge of danger. I was just thinking that I'd love to paint a girl like that when she hopped the fence, flung herself down on one of the sunlit chaise longues, and presented herself to the sun.

"Hey! Isolde!" the photographer shouted at her. *"Bleib' mal genau so!"* Stay just as you are! Quickly, he disassembled his camera and refocused in her direction.

"Isolde." I said her name out loud to remember. Stalking about like a panther—that's the only way I can think to describe her.

She was as old as the rest of them but she gave off a sort of spectacular charm. They were all a good six foot but this girl had something special besides.

Suddenly she sprang from her languid pose, heaved herself away with a pair of poles, and took off down the slope. Everyone leapt to their feet and leaned in one movement over the fence to watch. Obviously an excellent skier, Isolde gave us all a good show, skimming to a stop in an arc of snow at the bottom of the hill. Not missing a beat—she *was* supposed to be up here working with us— she hopped onto the ascending T-bar.

I'll never forget the way she looked. She was wearing a china red ski suit and as she glided toward us in the crisp morning sun with the blue sky behind her, every eye was upon her. She waved. Her dark mane of hair shone with good health and her agate eyes glittered with mischief. I looked at the photographer to see how he was taking her hijinks, expecting fury. Oh, boy, I thought, who's in trouble now! But everyone seemed instead to be filled with admiration. She carried it off. She had a threat about her, something carefree and a make-my-own-rules kind of ruthlessness that you had the feeling if you went against, you'd be sorry.

Or maybe it was what I'd overheard one of them say—Isolde was a noble, a countess.

We all had a smoke. Everybody smoked in those days. Just then, the client arrived. He emerged from the gondola to see his high-priced models lollygagging at the viewing fence, puffing away. His outrage set the photographer on a tirade and we tiptoed back to work.

"No monkey business, you!" BoBo, the stylist, surprised me by wagging her pointer finger at me.

"Don't worry about me," I assured her, stretching my neck out and peering down the treacherous ravine. "I'm terrified of heights."

Eyeing a threatening scarf of clouds in the east, the photographer shouted instructions to BoBo and she took me back to the dressing area. They had to make sure they had this outfit photographed. I was jiggled into the yellow ski suit and propped up on three telephone books piled on the snow. I stood there trying to look like I knew what I was doing.

After a while, though, I could tell from the expression on the photographer's face that this wasn't working. He shot a roll without much enthusiasm. My heart sank. I knew I was wearing an important suit or they wouldn't have gone through so much trouble to book little me. I remembered the look of pure relief on the face of the woman in the gray suit at *Freundin* when she'd found me, as if something more than a couple days' booking depended on it. I had to do something interesting and I had to do it fast. The trouble was I had nothing to work with. The highest up I'd ever been was the top of the Empire State Building. All I had to go on was a yellow suit. Maybe I was inspired by Isolde's saucy caper or maybe it was my natural competitive-sibling spirit kicking in, but I knew I had to take a chance to make things less stale.

I proceeded to ham it up. I built an imaginary trampoline and sprang from it. This was either going to get his attention and hold it, or he was going to get rid of me. And that would be the end of Germany. Where these girls had moved like statues on lazy Susans, I jumped up into the air, threw my arms akimbo, and gave what I thought was a crazy rendition of a trick skier flying down the mountain.

As luck would have it, the sun broke through. The photographer rose from his crouched position, unscrewed the stable camera, and resorted to his handheld Nikon. In this brilliant light even a 64 ASA film could catch movement without blurring. Wonder of wonders, he loved it. *"Mach das nochmal!"* he cried. "Do again. Same! Same thing!"

"Sehr gut!" the photographer actually congratulated me after he finished not one but three rolls. He was perspiring, I noticed, but I think he'd been having fun. He showed me the Polaroid. There I was suspended in blue sky, the yellow suit dazzling, my head thrown back, laughing. *"Spitze!"* I could tell it was high praise. Beaming, his assistant helped me down from my perch.

"Ja!" the stylist called out to me.

As I hobbled, trembling, on my skis past the other girls, they were all looking at me. Isolde came over, and if in the headiness of the moment I imagined she, too, was going to pat me on the back, I should have known better.

"Hey," she actually poked me with her ski pole, "where are the rest of your legs?"

"They're home," I answered, disappointed, without looking. Then I added (lying for spite), "Holding down my fat bank account."

Americans can take care of themselves. I should have known all along she'd come gunning for me. But I could handle her. I had my own beautiful and insulting older sister back home.

That only stopped her for a moment, though. "I see." She narrowed her eyes, one provocative eyebrow up, showing off her English, catching the eyes of the others with collaborative derision. "And so you will build your career standing upon telephone directories . . ."

"That's right," I sallied, "*and* I've still got years and years to do it."

That stopped her. I knew where to hit. I don't normally like to go below the belt but when it's needed I'm all set; I'm not part Irish for nothing. It sent her back to speaking German. I was pretty sure she didn't translate *that* word for word. I went and changed into my next outfit.

Fast-moving clouds dashed across the sky. The light was beginning to fade and the tempo changed to quick. While the photographer and his assistants moved lights into the restaurant, one of the other models approached me—the one with the bright red hair. Her skin, I noticed, was sunburned under her makeup.

Suddenly I realized where I'd seen her before. This was the other half of the man of my dreams at the airport. She was much prettier than I, but, I reminded myself soothingly, only after a thorough application of makeup. She narrowed her eyes. I thought she was going to say something like, "Hey, I saw you at the airport," but, "We don't care for foreign girls here," was what came out of her mouth.

"Excuse me?" I said. I couldn't believe I'd heard her correctly. And people were listening.

"No, I don't excuse you," she went on in her heavy Teutonic accent. "You take work from the rest of us. You should go back to your own country and find work there. That would be better. Much better. That's right. You heard me right. We don't need you here."

At first I thought she was joking. I was at a complete loss for words. She turned on her heels and stomped away. I stood there with my mouth open, watching her go.

Now Isolde, the magnificent dark one, walked across the canteen toward me. She placed herself next to me and the two of us watched the redhead leave. I suppose I was still visibly trembling. I didn't know what this one would do. But Isolde lit two cigarettes and put one in my mouth. She didn't smoke the regular ones. She carried a black package of pastel-colored, gold-filtered Vogue cigarettes. I'd never seen such things before. She gave me a peach-colored one and herself a purple, and ripped the filter off hers. She hadn't liked me before but it seemed she liked the redhead even less and so I was, by demotion, promoted.

"She your welcoming committee?" I tried to sound casual.

"Ach. Don't worry about her. That's just Arianna Weiss. She won't give you any trouble. She's on her way out." Isolde flicked a piece of tobacco from her lip. She did this all the time, like a hooligan in a film noir. "That was quite a show you put on," she said.

"Oh," I gave a wry shrug, "in New York all that jazzy stuff is nothing new. I used to stand on the sidelines—you know, poor, dejected me—and watch the working models do all sorts of contortions. This is the first catalog job I've ever had. I thought I'd try it out."

She looked at me with interest. Self-effacement was something new. At this point, however, I was growing weary of who thought what of me. My ankles ached and my nose felt burned.

"Where are you staying?" she asked. "Which pension?"

"The Franz Joseph."

"How much are you paying for your room?"

I told her. She snorted and the way she sucked in the fat smoke of her cigarette informed me it was too much.

"I am Isolde."

"Claire Breslinsky." I shook her outstretched hand. Its touch was capable and solid, more like a good strong peasant woman's than my idea of a countess's, but there was a warmth that drew you in.

"Where did you learn to speak English so well?" I asked.

"Boarding school. England." She sniffed. She was even more dazzling up close. Isolde had brunette skin, like a good rare roast beef with the pink in the middle and brown around the edges. Her mouth was broad and generous and she had those dazzling-with-good-health and twinkling, mischievous, but shrewd brown eyes—the whites of which were almost blue.

"I'll bet you gave them hell," I said.

She threw back her head and, just as she was about to laugh, she stopped. At any moment with Isolde, you got the uneasy feeling she was about to run off. She pulled in her chin and frowned. Her eyes became dull. "It was dreadful," she admitted. "They were sadists."

"Oh," I said, a little taken aback by her sudden black mood. To change the subject I said, "So I'm paying too much for my room, eh?"

"Why don't you move in with me," she suggested. "I've got a lovely little apartment in my house. I've got the au pair in there right now. She can move in with the children. She won't mind. I sometimes rent to foreign girls like yourself." She leaned toward me and said in a confidential tone, "You'll make a fortune here."

"You look more German than the Germans, with your sweet smile." She looked me up and down, shrewdly evaluating my earning potential. "You're curvy enough, but you're too skinny.

You're lucky you have that big mouth. That's what they all want now."

Not sure I'd ever been described quite that way but liking the description for its blatant mercantilism, and impressed with the bold way Isolde ordered everyone around—including the photographer—and although it hadn't occurred to me first, I suddenly asked myself why shouldn't I stay awhile in Munich.

"Anyway," she shook out her long mahogany hair, "I'm in the middle of a divorce. You'll keep me company. My only prerequisite is that you speak English. It's something I insist upon for the children."

"I must tell you," I warned her, wanting to be fair, to set things straight and give myself an out if I needed it, "I'm actually not sure how long I'll stay." I lowered my voice. "I'm really an artist. My dream is to make enough money to travel to the East. I'm not much of a model at all. Well. Obviously. You can see that." I cleared my throat and adjusted my spine. "But nothing will interfere with those plans. That's my dream and I'm determined to have it."

She gave a little "sure, sure" snort. But then she said, "All the better. You can sketch the children. I'll deduct it from your rent."

"Well," I drawled, still imagining I had some say in the matter, "I'll think about it."

A man came running toward us. "At last!" he cried and threw his arms around Isolde.

His clothes were beautifully made. I assumed this was her husband.

"Harry!" Isolde pushed him off her. He was heavyset but light on his feet. His mustache was wispy and unfortunate but he had these startled eyes—blue and light. He was flushed—he had lovely skin—and out of breath.

"Oh, Mr. Harry Honeycutt, this is Claire . . . what?" She turned to me. "What *is* your last name?"

"Breslinsky," I said.

"What a ride!" he puffed. "But I'm here at last." Harry wiped the snow from the rim of his elegant Donegal walking hat.

Isolde turned coldly from him. "Yes," she said, "it was kind of you to come all this way. But I'll have to stay with the group."

He looked panic-stricken. "But I've come all the way from Munich just to take you home!"

"Dear Harry! You're so good. But no one asked you to come. It wouldn't be professional of me to just run off with you, would it?"

"But you said—" He looked bewildered. "You told me I should come. You told me where—" Isolde barricaded herself with a haughty I-don't-know-what-you're-talking-about look and he gave up. "Yes, of course," he blustered. "Idiot me. Thinking of myself . . ." He swatted his knees with his hat. But you could see the disappointment in his eyes. I felt sorry for him. You could tell that was how she was. Everything was a trick.

"I'm sure no one would be upset if you went home with him," I whispered.

"Tch. I wouldn't go with him anyway. He's been drinking."

"Oh," I said, and we went back to work.

Eventually we finished and packed up to go home. The photographer was herding the rest of the models onto the next gondola. There was only room for so many passengers. Harry waited for Isolde. Isolde pretended to hop in the car and just as the doors were closing, she jumped out beside me and said we would wait for the next. She stuck her tongue out at him. Poor Harry Honeycutt glided away with a marooned expression. Laughing, she jumped into the next car and I followed. There was a sweep and a roar of metal and we were off. I joggled back and forth with the rest of the shivering passengers. I hardly felt the dangling height on the way down. I wasn't afraid anymore. Although there were other models in the gondola, it was to Isolde everyone spoke.

That was the effect she had on people. I noticed she'd forgotten to return the pale pink cashmere turtleneck she'd worn with her last outfit. Well, I reasoned, there'd been so much going on. Filled with admiration, I watched her.

She felt my look. "It's too ghastly to spend the night alone. You'll come home with me now."

"Oh, no," I said. "I couldn't impose. And your friend Harry . . ."

"Nonsense. You'll sleep in Daisy Dahlhaus's apartment. She's the au pair. She's used to being bullied about."

"Well . . ." I drawled, more interested to see where such a prima donna lived than tired of being alone. That's how I am: curious of the rich. It comes from being raised in a big family without money. We weren't poor. We just never had money.

"If you don't love it, darling," Isolde picked up a lock of my hair and rubbed it between her fingers as though she were examining a leather wallet she thought she might buy, "you can go back to your overpriced pension tomorrow."

"All right," I agreed. "Sounds fair. But I'd better let the pension know."

"*Liebling*," she scoffed, dropping my hair, "they could care less."

It was a long drive back to Munich and dark when we got there. They let us off somewhere and I groggily followed Isolde into a stately *Hof*, then up a Biedermeier stairwell with worn wooden foot furrows and wrought iron railings. Just the thing. You huffed and you puffed but you knew you were in Europe.

"There are ninety-seven steps," Isolde called over her shoulder as she briskly took the stairs, "or ninety-eight. They vary according to how much you've drunk."

Drinking, too! I calculated excitedly, trudging along behind. Ah, to be a boarder in a German household at the top of the stairs! I'd read too many books about this sort of thing—romantic thrillers starring potentially courageous young women on their own in continental garrets—not to be impressed with my good luck.

As I climbed along behind, though, trying to keep pace, I had a premonitory glimpse that this would be the way of our relationship: Isolde confidently dashing on ahead and I struggling unsuccessfully to keep up. But I followed her willingly—delightedly, even—because I knew instinctively she held the key to what I yearned for. Privilege.

chapter three

*A*t Isolde's, the days passed quickly. The months dropped away like calendar pages, snowy scenes of villages I watched from the cozy insides of taxis, trains, and airplanes. It was work that kept me busy, gave me credibility and money. The studios were all the same. You can get used to the cold gray winter when you're working every day. Time passes. You keep plugging away and then suddenly you're walking home after work and you notice that flowers have sprung up everywhere. You raise your chin to the sun and there is still warmth. You can't imagine where the time has gone.

One fine evening in April, I cut down the Hohenzollernstrasse and into the lush green of the Englischer Garten. This was where I would go when I was feeling moody. I'd often pause on one of the stone bridges and look out over the rapid green Isar. It was narrow but swift as traffic. You had to be careful never to drop anything into it or you'd never see it again.

I always felt safe behind the sturdy, moss-softened railing. I'd crouch down and put my chin on the velvety stuff and soothe my eyes with the rushing water, giving in to my feelings of homesickness for my parents, my sisters, the dog, my brother, Michael, who'd died. I couldn't help being touched at the thought of Michael. My throat closed and I let myself cry. Michael had been a cop. At least he'd had that. At least he'd lived his lifelong dream. Very short was his life, though. And violent at the end, shot to death by a useless, weeping junkie.

Just the day before I'd telephoned. "Claire!" my father had cried out with delight. "You're not in Asia, are you?"

"No, Dad, still in Germany."

"Germany," he'd repeated with distaste. He'd blown up plenty of swastikas in Germany. "When are you coming?"

"No, Dad." I'd spoken with jocular volume to disguise my sorrow at not bearing the news he'd hoped to hear. "I won't be coming home this month. I've got to stay. There's so much going on!"

"Oh," he'd said, his disappointment final as a child's.

"Dad," I shouted into the post office phone, "you wouldn't believe the flowers here! I've never seen such flowers!"

"Richmond Hill is filled with flowers, too," he'd said with no guile, just loss.

"I'll come home soon," I promised, my throat suddenly tight.

"Make it sooner," he'd said. Then, "I love you," always gentle, always kind. "Here's Mother."

I could see it all, the *Daily News* unfolded on the kitchen table, the cups of endless tea, the dog alert to who was on the phone but really only caring how it would affect his walk. And then my mother, loving me, too, but unhappy at the thought of my being over here having fun. Fun! When I ought to be home taking sensible courses in college. I was spared a sermon because long distance intimidated her. We hung up quickly, before the operator intervened. I was glad now to be gone, glad to be spared the shelves of Mass cards my mother kept like literature to be read and reread, glad not to hear her stifled moans of grief in the night. Or my father's military posture wane when he thought no one could see.

I pulled my hair back, hard, until it stung. I wiped away my tears and presently I felt better. I needed voices and happy faces, I told myself. I would stop off at the Riding School café. That would do it. I hurried.

I climbed the stone steps, skirting through the busy tables and chairs until I made it to the quieter corner of the stone balcony.

I fumbled around in my sack and came up with my charcoals and pad. I steadied myself, snapped a shot with my old camera as a backup for details, ordered a *Kaffee* with milk, and lost myself, finally, sketching the faces and figures around me.

"Claire!"

I glanced up, my teeth gripping a pencil pirate-knife style.

"Hi, Chartreuse. Sorry." I pulled the pencil from my mouth and patted the chair beside me.

Chartreuse didn't have to be asked twice. He rubbed his unshaven chin, leaned over, and made the slightest thumb smudge on the edge of the horse's mane, pushing in the direction behind the horse, giving it the immediate impression of speed.

"Brilliant!" I sat back and beamed up at him. "You're too much. Now, see, why didn't I think of that?"

"Eet is not in the thought but in ze immediate response, chérie. And . . ." He paused and I had the feeling he was trying to say something important, "You must try to capture, to convey, what is *not* seen. What I mean is, the atmosphere is as urgent to communicate as the view. Eh? Do I say it right?"

"Oh, yes, Chartreuse. You say it very well. Tell me. Why did you ever give up painting?"

"Me? I never gave anything up in my entire life. There are so many wonderful ways to spend one's time." He shook his head.

"You Americans! You think life is lived from one category to the next!"

"It's because we watch television stories between the commercials and we think that's us."

He swung his guitar around onto his lap and strummed it softly. "Anyway," he added in his thick French accent, "I can't afford the paint."

"Yeah, sure. Maybe if you stopped dealing for a couple of weeks, you'd have a little energy and space."

"Just a leetle hashish." He shrugged. "Eet hurts no one."

"No one but you, you dope."

He looked at me with his lion yellow eyes. The picture of innocence. "You are not paying attention to me," he admonished.

Across the room, Isolde's husband, Vladimir, got up, lit a cigarette, and walked across the restaurant with a young pretty girl. He was a big man, with hands the size of hamhocks. A sculptor. Aristocracy from Denmark and Japan had had their heads done by him. And politicians. So you knew he was well thought of. Isolde wouldn't let any of his larger pieces out of the flat. She claimed to be so attached to them, although I suspected it was the money they represented. And Harry Honeycutt, the fellow I'd met on the mountain that day, thought so, too. He was always warning her not to let them go. Harry knew about those things, Isolde confided. He was a well-respected arts and theater critic in London, although I found it hard to believe (he was always such a mess around Isolde).

I knew Vladimir and Isolde were still scheduled for a divorce, although the plans to part seemed to be going on longer than the marriage itself. I also knew that Isolde, despite her bravado, was still in love with him. I waved. Seeing Chartreuse, he raised one disapproving brow and kept walking.

I couldn't help liking Chartreuse, although I knew well enough he was usually up to no good. One day I'd caught a glimpse into his guitar case. Sterling silver forks and spoons glittered dully from the pocket. I'd not dared wonder where they'd come from. I'd looked away. The truth was, I liked him despite my better judgment. He made me laugh with his irreverent jousts at authority and the establishment. He entertained me with his songs. And he spoke English. It didn't occur to me until much later that the thing I liked most about Chartreuse was his admiration for my drawing.

"I don't suppose you could lend me some money?" he said now.

"I've already lent you some! Pay me back and you can ask again. Not before."

"I could sell you my van as collateral. It's in superb condition."

"That van again! You don't *sell* as collateral. You give."

"Oh," he said, not at all offended.

We sat there, me sketching the colorful, unusual faces, he strumming his beat-up acoustic guitar. "This is the life," I said.

"You are quite sure you are not interested in a leetle rendezvous? At my place? This evening?"

I laughed happily. "I've got to give it to you, Chartreuse. You never give up."

I went ahead trying to capture the leisurely gonging kirk bell, the too blue blue sky, and the nearby bright drone of a well-poised and resolute bee.

chapter four

I walked home with a feeling that life was good. The au pair's apartment, a cozy little knotty-pine appendage, was so comfortable and suited my needs so well that I knew I would remember it with regret wherever else I would live for the rest of my life.

It had a bookcase and a waterbed and a hot plate on a white marble slab that had been placed on a wrought iron sewing machine stand. A dramatically eaved bathroom was papered old-fashioned beige with tiny pink blossoms. There was an easy chair and a comfortable claw-foot tub with an oval window overlooking balconies and lines of clean clothes. At all hours the delectable aroma of bread wafted from the bakery below. It was from this idyllic covey that the children's au pair had been coldheartedly ejected overnight and made to go live with the children, but at the time I'd imagined one didn't have to pay at all for inconveniencing others.

I yanked open the heavy front door from the street. On the first landing, I would inevitably pass Frau Zwekl. I liked Frau Zwekl.

She was stunningly old, a mixture of forthright elbows, squinting eyes, and sagging belly. Her long thin hair was woven, then coiled, into a braided coronet and she wore daily the same ornate, queenly Bohemian garnets in her fleshy, quick-listening ears. Her face was as lined as crinkled yellowed paper but still she labored away, still taking laundry. She'd lived in the first-landing apartment all her life. Nothing failed to shock her. And she liked to be shocked. Her face—she had a handsome set of false teeth—would light up when she saw me coming. I suppose I was the highlight of her day. I'm sure few others found time to chat. Her big, arthritic hands would speed up over the work before her, snapping pillowcases and smoothing them into neat squares while her eyes would glisten like a monkey's, hungry for scraps of information.

Isolde, my notorious landlady, was her favorite topic. Frau Zwekl's English was even worse than my limping German and so I had no qualms about stopping and making a fool of myself while we chatted. When I'd first come to this house I'd dawdled away many an evening with her. I would bring her those little glass pots of jelly they give you in hotels and pensions. She loved them. Especially blackberry. It had all been fine at first. I learned to brave my first German sentence with Frau Zwekl. Yes, it was she who started me learning German because I hadn't really cared what she thought of me. She'd complained once how the 'Hund' on the second floor had kept her up all night.

Uncomprehending, I'd looked at her blankly. "Hund?"

"Hund," Frau Zwekl had said, turning into her apartment and picking up the small bronze Pekingese that sat with other tchotchkes on the pie-crust table. She displayed it in her wrinkled palm.

"Ah. Dog. The dog kept you up all night."

"Ja!" she'd congratulated me with a joyous smile. Her English vocabulary was about a hundred words, and so I would dig out my little German phrase book and the two of us would trade information. With a mixture of sign language and exaggerated rolling of the eyes in the appropriate places, it was amazing how much local gossip she and I managed to convey to each other. I used to save malicious little shockers for her and pass them over, like gems to a jeweler. One of these was Isolde's upcoming divorce, which she received with delight, making me go over it again and again to make sure she'd understood.

The last time I'd seen Frau Zwekl, I'd scurried past, tapping my watch and turning my face to a grimace, so she'd understand I was stuck for time. I hadn't been, but the initial glow of our relationship had worn off, and I had other things to think of now. The truth was, I didn't need her anymore and—with all the heartless hurry of youth—I'd passed her by.

"Warte nur einen Moment," she'd called out to me. Wait for just one moment!

I'd stopped on the landing and she'd clattered up after me, pressing a handkerchief into my hand. *"Ich habe es selbst bestickt!"* She'd smiled proudly. She'd embroidered it herself. It was some sort of bird.

"What is it?" I'd shifted my heavy bag from one shoulder to the other. It looked like one of those Johnny Ott hex signs they paint on the barns in Amish country.

She'd closed my hand over the fine, worn cotton. *"Distelfink,"* she'd murmured, her enigmatic eyes piercing mine. *"Für Glück."*

I'd kissed her swiftly on the cheek and run the rest of the way up the stairs. For happiness. For luck. Understanding more than I gave her credit for, she'd smiled and waved me on.

She'd catch me on a better day, she'd called out in German, and I'd laughed gaily, because I'd understood her.

She wasn't in her sentry spot today, though, and I felt both disappointment and relief.

A small boy with large gray eyes and a cat on his lap sat watching me mount the stairs. This was Rupert, Isolde's younger boy.

Well into his fourth year on the planet, Rupert was hardly known to speak at all. Not in any language. I attributed this to the fact that no one language occupied the entire space of any conversation in the flat.

"That's rubbish," Isolde would say. "Look at Dirk." Dirk was her other son, already five, who, thanks to a colorful and varied exposure to boarders like photo models and sporadic nannies, carried on in German, Italian, Slovenian, and, lately, English. The rule was that only English was spoken at table. Isolde thought it would do them good. That Rupert never spoke a word of anything didn't seem to faze her. He pounded the piano with a dramatic, almost Mediterranean flourish and this, she considered, was language enough.

"Hello, Rupert." I dropped my sack now and gave the cat a tickle.

Rupert watched me steadily with wide, unblinking eyes while I fumbled for the keys. The sound of music filtered into the stairwell. "Who's that now, Rupert? Mozart or Telemann? You know I always mix them up."

Rupert rose, casually hanging the unresisting cat by the fur of her neck, and pushed the massive door right open. He paused once for imperious effect, then locomoted through.

I flumped my sack once more onto my back and followed.

Inside, black-and-white-tiled floors gleamed under tall chalk ceilings. Couch-sized sculptures of women in bronze reclined every which way here and there. There were unframed, enormous silk paintings from Bali on the walls and zebra and fur throws all about the comfortable velvet couches. Rupert disappeared into the children's wing.

"Hallo," came a pleasant British accent through the archway. "Is that you, Rupert?"

"No, it's me," I called, dropping my sack and going in. "Rupert's in the nursery."

Daisy Dahlhaus, Isolde's English au pair whom I'd displaced, was sitting at the dining room table behind a huge pile of white asparagus.

"Well!" She sniffed. "And where have you been?"

Daisy had round, astonished blue eyes and ermine ringlets springing out all over in an unruly, Louis XIV disarray. At night, she'd take exorbitant amounts of time to manicure her well-trimmed nails and paint them up a ladylike mauve. She'd wave them at everyone on their individual way out, our sensible Daisy, while she sat before the telly learning German verb tenses in baby's-breath terry cloth, a strand of pearls, and Christmas-present talcum.

"I stopped off at the Riding School café."

"Did you now! Dressed like that? The poshest café in Munich with all the jet-setters driving their Porsches up onto the pavement . . . and you went looking like that?" Daisy regarded me with distaste.

Right. My messes of dark red hair were yanked convulsively into a knot and I could taste a smear of charcoal across my mouth. My hat was stuffed into my sack, my jeans rumpled from their long day in a heap under the makeup table. Daisy threw her beefy little arms up in exasperation. "Oblivious to all those lovely men?" she scolded. "Sitting there being Toulouse-Lautrec again, I'll wager, sketching the lot!"

"The jet-setters aren't there on weekdays, Daisy. It's just students and chess addicts and gigolos."

"Gigolos? Right. Just waiting about for the likes of you!"

"I wasn't picked up, don't worry. I was quite safe sitting with Chatreuse."

"Chartreuse!" Daisy squawked, outraged. "That pissy Frenchman? How could you? Everyone will think you're his mistress!"

"Oh, they won't. We're good friends."

"They bloody will! Everyone will think you're on drugs!"

"Well, I am, if smoking a little pot is being on drugs. Everyone smokes pot."

"I don't!"

"I know you don't."

"Claire! That hashish he peddles isn't pot! It's disgusting!"

"It is very strong," I agreed. "It's the seventies, Daisy. No one cares who sleeps with whom."

"I don't know what's the matter with you." Daisy picked up her peeler again as though her heart was no longer in it, and resumed whittling Isolde's asparagus. They're not like American asparagus, the white ones. You've really got to peel them, the way you would carrots. The end result, however, is heavenly and worth every effort. "You think you're going to catch a man when you go gadding about disguised as a soccer player, do you?" she went on badgering me. "It's no wonder no one rings you up. All the likely fellows have given up."

"Likely playboys and gigolos, you mean. No point in going out with them."

"Right. Better to hang about with a drug dealer."

"He's a musician," I said, remembering Chartreuse's guitar. "And he makes me laugh."

"Oh, he's not witty," she said with sudden insight. "You just like that he flatters you."

It's true, I realized.

"Sorry I'm so cross." She sighed. "It's a very good thing you came home. I just devoured the Havarti cheese and apricot jam on sunflower bread and was about to go back for more. God, I'll never get that bloody ironing finished. I polished the floor in there. I don't suppose you bothered to notice." Daisy's chubby jaw shut with a martyred click.

I didn't feel too sorry for Daisy. She was in fact a diplomat's daughter, born in Singapore, schooled in Dehli and Geneva, and would one day return to that life.

"I noticed everything looks exceptionally spic and span," I said admiringly, taking it all in. "What's up?"

"Oh, she's having a bunch of swells over tonight. Some big director from Berlin. He's looking the flat over to see if he'll want to use it for his film." Isolde was constantly renting out the flat to film people to make extra money.

"Oh, no," I cried. "Not again! She just got rid of that TV commercial crew."

"Film people are quite different from advertising people. Anyway, *some*one has to pay for all the fancy goings-on," she said, imitating Isolde's parsimonious voice.

"But all those cables!"

"I know. Everything underfoot. You can never shut a door properly. Still, I'm rather pleased. There's such an undercover of excitement with that lot! They take their work so seriously. You almost begin to believe in the malarky yourself! Do those gladiola look as though they've had it?"

"No. What's she cooking?"

"Lamb, I think. She's got me thawing the mint jellies from the freezer."

I was drawn to the kitchen. "Mint jellies?" I picked one up from the dish. "Looks intriguing. What is it?"

"She cuts up a bunch of fresh mint, really fine, like a paste. Then she puts them in ice cube trays with aspic. You know. That gel that forms from bone marrow."

I dropped it quickly. "Oh."

"That Tupelo Honig is coming. The film star. Isolde's fixed her up with her plastic surgeon."

"Oh?"

"Yes. I think it's sort of a trade-off. She'll bring the surgeon all her friends in the film business and he'll save her from growing old. Isolde tells her she'll get better parts if she's not desperate for them. You must admit Isolde is dead on the money nine times out of ten."

I was silent, stopping a big lemon that had rolled to the edge of the table. Its blissful smell filled the room.

"Really," Daisy continued, "Isolde's shameless! Imagine introducing your doctor to famous women in exchange for eye lifts. Yuck."

"He's the one who sounds disgusting," I called, returning from the kitchen. "And who's this Tupelo Honig the film star? I've never heard of her."

"Well, I mean, I've never heard of her, either, but the way Isolde makes astonished, disbelieving eyes at you when you say you never have, you'd think you were living on Mars if you haven't. She makes all those films with five minutes of close-up and very little dialogue. You know." She slammed the iron down hard. "Not that I ever get the chance to go to the cinema. All I ever get to go see is Pippi Langstrumpf and Paddington Bear and the like. Mind you, I'll be relieved to have some adults about."

"I don't blame you. So who else is coming?"

"She's gone and spent a bomb on these white asparagus," Daisy continued to rant. "She yells like mad at me for not shopping at the Plus, just to save a few extra crummy Pfennig, and then she goes and buys everything madly expensive at the Viktualienmarkt."

"Daisy! Who's coming?"

"Oh. Well, let's see. The hubby, Vladimir. He'll come. I know he wants to pick up some more of his records. Hell. The best ones are his, you know. How much you want to bet she'll get him drunk so he'll forget the records? And of course the one they call Blacky. The Graf. Count. Vladimir and he are both counts, you know. I suppose that's why they get on." She stopped for a moment and wiggled her head in a satisfied way. She and I both savored living with the bluebloods. "You've met him. Haven't you? No, I suppose not. You were on that bathing suit trip to the Canary Islands last time he was here, weren't you."

"I guess so."

"Now, *he* is sexy. Although," she scowled, "I don't much like him."

I looked up, interested. "Why not?"

"I suppose I'm a bit frightened of him. Don't even think of setting your cap for him, missy. Isolde's got him fixed up with that film star."

"What?"

"The one Isolde introduced him to."

"I thought she was going with the doctor!"

"He *is* the doctor!"

"Oh," I said, catching up.

"Anyway, he's no one for you. He's ten years older than you, you know," Daisy went on. "He was in the Vietnam War. Well, he was a doctor over there for a while. Detests Americans. Thinks he knows it all. Although I guess he does. His English is really quite remarkable for a Kraut. But he's a dirty sleep-around. He's even bumpsed with Isolde, if you want to know the truth. She told me."

"She did?"

"Yes. Such cheek!" And then: "He was quite good, apparently." Daisy spotted the time. "She'd better get back soon, though. Lamb takes a year and a day. We won't be eating till nine or ten. I hate that. And I hate those gladiola. They make me think of funerals. She thinks they're Art Deco." Daisy snorted. "Oh. And another thing. She wants everyone in *Trachten*."

"*Trachten?*"

"You know. Bavarian traditional dress: loden green jackets, feathered hats, dirndls for the ladies—acceptable, even preferable, in place of formal attire in Bavaria."

"I'm not going to wear one of her stupid dirndls," I muttered.

"Of course you must. If you want dinner. If I've got to wear one then so must you. She said you can have one of hers. She's got a closet full. She nicked them all from the Bogner fashion shows."

"Oh, all right," I said, imagining the splendid food.

" 'Course it's all right with you. Makes you think you're Heidi. You wouldn't much care for it if you looked like me."

The record stopped and immediately Daisy went trotting off to start another up. Isolde had a superb record collection of classical, jazz, and semi-jazz. Daisy chose her favorite part of an early Keith Jarret.

I put one foot up on the dining table chair, a position I'd hardly dare were Isolde there herself, and admired, for the ten thousandth time, the window. Or windows, really, for there were many. Lead-lined panes one after the next and up and down, some of which opened with their own little latches. The whole was as large and light as a cinema screen. I hugged my sketchpad to my chest and took a quick snapshot of the scene for later reference, found a pencil, and sketched away. The well-scrubbed antique pine table shone like honey. Isolde, with her relentless dash, had arranged the window seat with raspberry- and sage-colored silk pillows and buckets and clay pots of flowers. Isolde cried poverty all the time, but there were always opulent bunches of flowers. Flowers and candles and wine. Luxuries I'd grown up knowing only when the priest came to dinner. Now here they were, necessities, purchased routinely along with the potatoes and the laundry detergent. And fruits. Bright-colored, luscious-tasting apricots and strawberries. Where I came from, we were allotted poor-people plums, twenty-seven for a dollar, and that was it, now go do your homework. Here, blueberries cascaded casually every day from slim balsa-wood cartons on the sill.

Beside these extravagances, there were also two well-fed, muttering, surly gray parrots named Storm-Foot and Swift Wing for the Greek mythological monsters, Harpies on Phineus' island.

Each dwelt in its own jealously guarded, two-storied cage. They were known to all and sundry, though, as Stormy and Swifty.

Daisy hummed busily to herself. I stood and headed to the birds' messy cages, sticking one of my fingers in and nuzzling Stormy's head.

"Please don't go getting him all revved up stroking him, Claire. He's been squawking all day long and he's only just settled down. He so hates to be teased!"

"No, he doesn't, he loves it. Don't you, Stormy?" And it was true. Storm-Foot ruffled his feathers for me and barely put pressure at all while he nibbled away at my moonstone ring.

For me, Daisy was nothing less than gold. Who else would do my laundry, scour the bathtub, and empty out the ashtrays, quick, before Isolde saw? I smoked too much. But then, whatever I did, I did voraciously. It was gluttony. I know that now. But hedonism and excesses were the order of the day and none of us saw anything wrong with pleasing ourself. Not then. Not yet.

Daisy was invaluable to me in many ways and, best of all, was not yet fed up. Still dazed by Isolde's chic and ribald lifestyle, she'd wake each morning full of curiosity as to what would happen next.

Here I was, busy every day, feeling happy and safe with supper to come home to. It was almost like being a child, with furious, tidy Daisy barring unworthy enthusiasts from the house, the respectable agency in charge of my cash, and world-class, churning Isolde in charge of my life.

People gossiped about Isolde constantly, assuring her a steep notoriety in Munich, as far as Klosters in Switzerland, really, but they always came if she invited them. She gave, as she said, a hoot about all that. Why, this was the age of Aquarius. It said so everywhere you looked. New York had gone through it with enthusiasm and now Munich, obediently carefree, would go through it, too.

On this front both I and young Daisy were united and excited; there was lots of action going on here, enough action to get caught up in and catch tail ends of. Although we'd tell each other that we heartily disapproved, we knew, too, that it was not often in life one came in such scrutinizingly close contact with a diva. For that's what Isolde was. A drive-men-mad-and-let-them-drop authentic diva.

The whole business horrified the virginal and naive Daisy while reassuring me. No one thought to bugger me with mind-encompassing Isolde about. It was almost a replica of my life as I'd known it at home. My stunning older sister, Carmela, had always held the limelight, leaving me free from scrutiny, free to languor about, dream, and draw. I'd always felt comfortable in the background—or at least as though I belonged there, considered it my rightful place in the family. But where Carmela's beautiful, benevolent eyes had suddenly turned angry and mistrustful when I had found myself in frightening adolescence, Isolde now offered me the grace of indulgence whenever she beheld me. For Isolde really liked me. I was an immediate draw for her table, for one thing. Any foreign model was. But besides that, Isolde admired my ever-ready and loud disdain for the "glamour" of modeling, my thirsty passion for art, and the fact that I truly enjoyed being alone, something she herself never could stand to be. On the evenings Daisy would have off, out the door Isolde would spring in a flounce of spangles and perfume, saying, "Thank heavens for Claire! She's so good with the children!" And I would collapse with relief onto the sofa. I was simply lazy at heart and I didn't mind at all being left alone with the children (these I simply ignored and, sure enough, eventually they'd go to sleep.) for I would also be left alone with the refrigerator, the likes of whose innards few world-weary models got to get a whiff of. Isolde's refrigerator was small, but it was filled with cheeses, hefty, pungent cheeses. Cheeses from the countryside. From France and Switzerland and Denmark. There were bird carcasses in there, too, delicious dry things from the evening before, fragrant with herbes de Provence and rubbed tenderly with Dry Sack. Once I found that I'd eaten the miniature partridges Isolde had planned for the weekend. There'd been so little meat on the things. How was I to know? I'd taken them for leftovers. Limp, bright green beans lay in a hardened yellow coddle of butter. On the windowpane were shiny, bursting tomatoes from Israel. In the cupboard were yawning hunks of sunflower bread just waiting to be sawed into. Or Swedish wheels of crumbly flat bread. Two or three half finished bottles of magnificent Bordeaux from the night before lined the wooden counter space. And then there was the endless assortment of heartbreaking records. Duke Ellington. Ella in Berlin.

Isolde admired my ability to occupy myself, drawing or listening to music. At home, activities having to do with philosophy and art had been seen by my mother as grievous faults, fraught with laziness and self-absorption. Here, these same ways were regarded as qualities of depth. Vladimir was like that, too. Quiet and still. Watchful. Isolde would always gravitate toward that quality in others as though it were a refreshing pool. My pool, I can admit it now, was a bit put on. I'd find the record that I thought would most impress Isolde. As it turned out, I learned to appreciate those artists she held in esteem, so I guess it did me no harm. But most of all, Isolde liked that I was a bonafide American. I was somebody here, not just the little one raising my hand, insisting, "Me, too!"

Thinking of all these things I found myself in the kitchen making tea.

Vladimir, Isolde's husband, came in. "Hello, the pretty Claire," he teased me.

The kitchen was so tiny and he so big. "Oh! Hi." I ducked my head, trying to shrink but then I had the feeling that he didn't mind me. I never let myself feel what I really felt about him while Isolde was around because I was so nervous she would think I liked him *that way* or he liked me. But while she wasn't here I could be myself. He and I were actually very compatible in a friendly way. Easygoing. He slipped a pan from under the stove. "May I use your water?" he asked, bumping into the braids of garlic and drying tufts of herbs.

"Sorry?"

"Your water. In the kettle. May I have some?"

"Oh! Sure. Here, help yourself."

He poured some of it into a pan. It was already boiling and he slipped some spaghetti in after it. I thought of myself and how if I made pasta I'd fill a huge pot and have to wait forever for it to boil. He stood there stirring the spaghetti attentively. Vladimir, big and slow moving, had a particular way of looking at things—almost as though he were seeing something for the first time—and he made you feel it, too. When it was just done to the teeth he tipped the water into the sink, slipped the pasta onto a plate, poured olive oil into the pan, and cut up shards of garlic into it. He looked at me. I was dunking my teabag up and down into the teapot, watching him. "Now this is the most important moment to wait for," he warned, catching my eye. "We can't let this moment get away from us or we are lost."

"Okay," I said. Together we watched the garlic turn from alabaster to gold.

"When the perfume reaches your nose it will tell you the moment," he whispered. We waited together, watching. Just the edges of the garlic crusted brown. "Now," he shouted. I jumped and he pulled the pan from the heat. He slipped the spaghetti back into the pan, dashed white salt and black pepper over the top. There was an old crust of hard cheese on the counter I'd thought meant to be thrown away, but no. He broke off a small bit and held it before my nose. He opened his great nostrils wide and sucked in with a spectacular performance of appreciation. It smelled, I thought, stepping back, very ripe. But not bad, no, not bad, I agreed. He crumbled this small piece between his huge fingers and onto his dish, handed me a fork, poured spots of last night's wine into two jelly glasses, and there in that little kitchen, sitting on the washing machine and he standing with his great hulking self leaning across the cutting board, I enjoyed one of the simplest yet finest meals I think I've ever had. All these years gone by, so many restaurants and meals, and yet, I can still taste that nutlike and delicious afternoon.

"Upfh!" Vladimir suddenly realized the time, dumped his dish into the sink, and disappeared. When he left, the kitchen became just a kitchen again. I was rinsing the dishes when Dirk, Isolde's older son, marched in and held me up with a water pistol.

"Very funny, Dirk," I said. "Please don't get me wet, sweetie."

"Bah," Dirk maintained and squirted me in the face. The truth was that I found myself a little terrified of Dirk. I didn't know then that children love whomever loves them and he only wanted attention. I thought there was some special way to be. I thought there was a catch.

"Come in here with me now," came Daisy's arbitrary voice from the next room. "Come along, Dirk. Let Claire get on with the tea." Daisy maintained equal amounts of fair play and bullying in her tone, which is just what little boys need. The doorbell rang and Daisy went to get it. But I'd forgotten all about the tea. I went back to it, carried the tea tray to the dining table, and sat down.

Daisy came back in with a basket of clean laundry. "That was Frau Zwekl," she said, "with the children's whites. Good thing, too, because I can't keep up."

Isolde and Frau Zwekl had had words of the harshest kind some time ago. I had always supposed the confrontation had had something to do with late hours and respectable people and strangers tromping up and down the stairs.

"That wasn't it," Daisy had confided in me later. "Dirk pin-kled all over her clean washing."

Frau Zwekl held no grudge against Dirk. It was Isolde she couldn't abide. I didn't understand this at first. I thought it was stern moral disapproval. I know my mother would have been appalled at the goings-on. Frau Zwekl didn't like men in and out at all hours. Empty French wine bottles twice a week in the overflowing recycler. Twice a week! she would sputter, horrified. Later, I imagined it was jealousy. I saw it glitter like hard stones in the old woman's eyes when I helped Isolde carry fourteen potted mums up to the flat. Up and down the stairs we went, our boots tromping the tight snow loose on her clean floor, our arms laden with vibrant color. I'd gone down for the last load and sat for a moment on the step with Frau Zwekl. Snow-lit sunshine filled the stairwell from the skylight. I felt guilty for the sloppy steps. I knew I shouldn't. We had every right to go up and down. And it was her own problem if she chose to scrub the darn steps. Nobody made her. But I couldn't help sympathizing with her. We were chums, sort of, by now.

She didn't like that Isolde had access to mums in the middle of winter when everyone knew they were only to be had in the fall. "Imports!" Frau Zwekl would shake her head emphatically. It was unnatural! I explained they were from Israel. "Ach," she'd snorted. "And red tomatoes she buys in the middle of winter!" She didn't much care for that extravagance, either.

Frau Zwekl had told me other things, things I'd rather not have known. Her husband had been much older than she. He was a kind man, but she hadn't loved him. He used to make her kiss his thing. She'd shuddered. You see, there were no other men around. They'd all gone off to war. "*Schwierigkeiten.*" She would shake her head, fold the linen sharply. Hardships.

Isolde had told me that whenever she smelled oranges it made her think of Christmas. She'd never smelled them before that. I was beginning to realize that this affluence was new.

"Isolde will be home any minute," Daisy reminded me, bringing me back to the present.

"Who's that in there on the sofa?" I gave a hitchhike nudge across my shoulder.

"What? Oh, him. He's been here so long I'd almost forgotten him. That's Harry Honeycutt. Is he still asleep?"

"I guess so. I can only see his head. Harry?" I called. We looked toward the living room. There he was, just coming to. He didn't answer.

"He's always hanging about," Daisy grumbled.

Harry Honeycutt, with his plump form and excellent shoes, was becoming rather an embarrassment—respectable Englishman though he was—who would mope about the house waiting for everyone to leave, consuming great quantities of scotch in the meantime, hoping to have a quiet word with Isolde. If Isolde fancied someone, she'd simply boot Harry out. If she didn't, he'd be allowed to park his inebriated body on one sofa or another for the night. Isolde didn't bother to sleep with him. He was so useful in restoring her antiques, having redone all the picture frames and most of the better furniture. He had been very kind to me, admiring my moon-phase wristwatch when everyone else had laughingly deemed it junk. It would be years before such things would become fashionable, but Harry had the eye. He also wrote the occasional critical column in fashionable artsy magazines and had a standing vanity column in the *Times* Sunday supplements.

"Isolde says he's a big shot in his field," I reminded Daisy.

"It's very hard to think of him that way when he acts like a sheep. Don't defend him. You shouldn't defend him. He's a man. He ought to get on with his life."

"You're right. It isn't that I like Harry, because it's difficult to like someone who so obviously despises himself, but he gives me the opportunity to administer pity, an uncommon luxury at our age, don't you think? He reminds me of the hesitant ant you let live. Poor thing, you think, imagining it on its way home from an enterprising exploration. So you keep your god feet to yourself, admiring its perseverance. And you forget it. Then, before you know it, there are seven hundred of them marching obliviously across your ledge. And now there is no stopping them."

"Do you hear yourself? The way you talk? It puts people off. Please do watch your cigarette ash, Claire."

"Hello, darlings." Isolde, strong as Hercules, swept into the room with a box of groceries and two woven Spanish shoulder baskets filled with stuff. She clomped the carton of Nutella and bottles of wine and produce in the midst of our tea, rattling and almost upsetting the saucers. A paper of bright black cherries spilled across the table and we all filled our mouths as we reached to refill the horn of greengrocer's paper.

Dirk flew in and squirted the parrot with his water pistol and Rupert attached himself to Isolde's leg. Harry woke up from his nap on the couch and followed Isolde into the kitchen.

"Haven't you got any pots of water going on the stove yet?" Isolde returned almost immediately and attacked plump Daisy.

"No," Daisy said, "I thought we were having lamb and I was just waiting for you to come back and—"

"Well, then, the oven should be hot! And who," continued Isolde, "used up all my Jil Sander perfume . . . You?"

Daisy and I exchanged panic-stricken looks. Both guilty in all things concerning Isolde's sumptuous properties, we shared some unbreakable bond. It wasn't as though Isolde really cared, we told ourselves. She'd push things on us when she was in a good mood.

"Dirk!" Isolde ordered. "Dirk, come over here and give your starving mother a sloppy wet kiss. There we are. What's that on your forehead?"

"He's been tattooing himself once again with the fruit gum tattoos," Daisy calmly explained as she proceeded to unload the stuff from the carton and carry it into the kitchen. She had to do it around Isolde, whining Dirk, who was having his head wiped, and the yawning and belching Harry, whom Isolde had not yet chosen to recognize.

"Claire," Isolde said, "please write the place cards out. You do it so well with your fancy pen." She moved into the kitchen and picked up the phone.

"Okay," I said, eager to please in a way that wasn't too exerting.

"Let me think who all will be here," Daisy thought out loud, counting on her dainty fingers. "Vladimir will come. He'll be at the head. She likes him at the head. Let me think. There's you and me." She meant herself and Isolde. "Then there's you, Claire. And Dr. von Osterwald."

Isolde came out licking her fingers. "And Wolfgang, the film director. Put him down the table on my left."

So he can see your best side, I thought meanly, but didn't say. I was always a little bit afraid of Isolde. Everybody was. You measured how much you could say by the mood she was in.

"And here I am, the goose." Daisy passed us, laying down the place mats, miffed and getting used to it.

Harry padded back to the sofa in his rumpled cashmere socks, sat down, and began feeling around the floor for his shoes.

"So," Isolde stood still for a blazing moment, "let's start again. The three of us and Tupelo Honig. How many men have we? Blacky, Vladimir, Wolfgang the director . . ."

"This Wolfgang has no last name? Just 'Wolfgang the film director' on his card?"

"It's Wolfgang Scherer," Isolde replied acidly, "but no last names on the cards. It's not a wedding."

"What about Harry?" Daisy said in her persistent way. She rather liked Harry, no matter what she said. She fed him delicacies when no one was watching.

Isolde gave a dismissive swipe. "Just leave the bottle next to him," she advised, not even lowering her voice. "He'll be asleep before they get here. Claire, after this, why don't you arrange those flowers in a vase? What I need," she chewed her lip, "is another man." The doorbell rang.

Daisy trotted away and returned with Chartreuse.

"Well, that was fast," Isolde said.

"Chartreuse!" I cried.

Chartreuse held my chalk box up. "Your pastels," he said. "You left them on the table."

"I did?"

"She's always forgetting things," Daisy admonished.

Chartreuse touched his heart. "I intrude?" He bowed, his accent rich as Dijon.

"On the contrary," Isolde looked him up and down, "we were just needing an extra man for dinner."

"But I am honored." Chartreuse sniffed the air like an alert bird dog, taking everything in at once. The Biedermeier furniture. The hand-carved frames. And, I gulped, the antique sterling.

"Asparagus?" Chartreuse eyed the ragged pile upon the table.

"That's right." Isolde smiled over one shoulder, kneeling down and pulling different cheeses from the fridge. And then, worriedly, "And a still partially frozen lamb."

"Ah! You must allow me to join you in the kitchen." Chartreuse rolled back his sleeves and held both arms up in the air. "I shall prepare for you my béchamel."

Isolde, recognizing a connoisseur and ready to ooze charm equal to his, saw her chance to duck out for a shower. She led him into the tiny kitchen.

Chartreuse seemed right at home in the winsome pine kitchen. He scrubbed his dirty hands in the sink with the impressive care of a surgeon, then conspicuously scrutinized them under the light. This pleased Isolde, I could tell. Then, with a flourish of his crushed velvet magenta scarf, he rattled each pot testingly, provocatively, found what he liked, and went straight to work.

I was a little surprised. Isolde was attracted to only very rich or at least successful men. Chartreuse was so obviously neither of these. Although he was devilishly good-looking, with his long, wavy brown hair, his silky black lashes, and sparkling yellow eyes. He had a modest, close-mouthed smile. I knew he was sensitive about his teeth and often suffered with them. Still, he was dashing, in a theatrical, world-traveler way. He wore those fuzzy, loose-fitting pants from Nepal, a saffron *langee* from Ceylon, and a burgundy shirt from Rangoon. His eyes were exotically rimmed in kohl. It seemed he knew his way around a kitchen. I remembered him once telling me he'd traveled around the Mediterranean as a chef on a handsome, eighty-foot Brigsom yacht.

Isolde probably concluded he was artsy enough for the film people. If I knew her, she'd pass him off as her chef. I remembered my box of pastels on the table. Funny. I really did remember packing them away.

I left them laughing in the kitchen. Isolde was back, crouching on the floor with her head in the refrigerator. Out came vegetables and fruits from Africa. Chartreuse was hacking garlic expertly with a glinting knife, *tzack tzack tzack*, in lugubrious time with the rhythmic American music, which stopped again and again at the end of the stuck, long-playing album.

Harry staggered into a hassock in the living room.

"Bloody hell, Harry," Daisy shouted. "*You're* up! Put something new on the stereo, will you? Be useful."

I remember thinking she was enormously disrespectful to a guest. But, compliant by nature, Harry made his careful way to the corner of the room and lowered himself gently to the floor. "Who shall we have, then?" he called out, immediately awake.

"Oh, make a decision," Daisy practically screamed.

Coleman Hawkins's banana rich tones set a new, more sultry atmosphere for us all. "Taste," Isolde leaned sideways and confided to Chartreuse, "his only attribute." Chartreuse chortled with a cruel French snort. His happy knife sped on.

Poor Harry. I did feel sorry for him now. Fondly I watched him, his pigeon toes, his roomy bottom, his plump lower lip out, sorting through the albums. Before the week was over, he'd be back to his auctions and country estates, hunting for treasure. He knew all about what was valuable and what wasn't. I sighed with pleasure. How different all of this was from the ordinary. The mundane. From Queens. And then suddenly I remembered. I had placed my pastels on the top, inside my bag, before I'd stood to leave the Riding School café. Yes, I remembered it exactly. "Look," Chartreuse had said from behind me, "how extraordinaire the light at this moment." I'd felt his kindly hand on the strap of my sack. And then I'd turned around and he had grinned, his little teeth almost visibly aching with sugar and desire.

chapter five

I eased myself into a nice hot pool, oozy with capfuls of
Isolde's fine imported bath oil and snowy with bubbles.

The bath itself was very pretty: all mirrors and brass fixtures
and Japanese seagulls swooping across a pale blue ceiling. Unfortunately, above the waterline it was freezing cold. I wondered
why Germans found it utterly frivolous to heat an entire room,
however small, for any longer than the short, industrious time
one would and should be in it. Another thing I found: they
refused, en masse, to support the phenomenon of the shower curtain. You were expected to manipulate your body between the
spout and the rim of the tub so that you became a sort of bounce-
back for the stream of water.

I could hear Isolde and Daisy scuffling about and shouting
outside the door.

"Run into the attic and get that white wine out of the
Kühlschrank, Daisy!"

"Right. *Schon erledigt*. Already done it."

"Then could you get the good scotch away from Harry? He'll be asleep before anyone gets here."

"That would save you a lot of scotch in the long run."

Daisy walked in.

"At least you could shut the door," I said.

"Oh, sorry," Daisy said, paying no attention whatsoever and leaving the door ajar, then dabbing herself with a robust flounce of Isolde's dusting powder. She sat down companionably on the rim of the tub and rumbaed in place. Peaches, cream, and flapping lashes. A corpulent Betty Boop. "She's driving me mad." Daisy sighed. "And she's going to be home all week, too."

"Hmm. That's bad." Isolde, as marvelous as she was to be with, was also quite a pleasure to be without. She did have the good grace to be off on location somewhere half of the time, shooting a film or modeling fur coats on some runway or other, leaving Daisy long, lazy mornings and nights undisturbed by guests and great meals to clean up afterward. The boys, her real job, were never really that much trouble, having early on learned to fend for themselves. But Isolde was always up to something that required group participation: furiously cleaning out a winter closet at two in the morning, deciding suddenly to paint her bedroom red when the yellow wasn't dry a month. There was Daisy, then, right behind, sulking, but doing it just the same. Lost in the trap, as everyone was, of not being able to say no to Isolde.

Daisy tugged at a piece of her mop of brown hair turning into determined ringlets from the steam. "I'm going off and get a normal job," she said. "That will teach her. She'll never find another slave like me."

"She'd find someone right away. Don't be such a teenager." I blew a glob of bubbles at her.

"You should talk! You're not that much older than I!"

"It isn't that bad. What else would you do? Wait tables? You wouldn't like that too much after a while. Why don't you just go back to school?"

The truth was that Daisy was already better educated than most. She patted her hair. "Because it's more fun here. I know. I'm just sick of all her stupid men hanging about. And it's no better when she's gone. They call her nonstop, you know. I'm like a bloody secretary."

"At least your German's getting decent. I can't say half the things you can."

"Yes, I've become a regular little Bavarian, I have." She sighed. It wasn't easy cavorting with models who ran off to exotic ports while you were left holding the laundry bag.

"Has Harry gone?" I asked, to change the subject.

"Certainly not. He'll stay for supper. And long after that if she lets him. Funny about men," Daisy marveled. "They can't seem to help themselves when it comes to Isolde. Even respectable businessmen like Harry. Poor sods. They just sort of melt beneath her bossiness and get lost there, don't they? Poor, poor Vladimir."

"Oh, come on, little Miss Priss. Vladimir's been with everyone. Why do you think Isolde started fooling around in the first place? He left her long before she left him. She told me."

"Phhhh. She tells you everything she thinks will amplify your sympathy."

"She doesn't need my sympathy."

"Yes. For some reason, she does." Daisy admired me with envy.

"I'm sorry I took your lovely apartment away from you," I said. I wasn't really sorry, though.

"It was you or someone else."

"By the way, I saw Vladimir at the Riding School café with an exotic girl."

"Yeah? Was she a looker?"

"A stunner. And she was our age. Younger."

"Oh, don't let Isolde hear you say that! She's jealous."

I put an arm across my bent knees. "I'm absolutely sure Isolde has no intention of giving up Vladimir. She just figures let him have his little fling."

"Nothing she can do about it, is there? I mean, he just up and left."

"Oh, Isolde will think of something."

"She'd better get cracking, then. She's *got* to be thirty."

"Yes," I agreed. "Yes, that's true."

We sat there silently for a while, thinking about all these things, when in barged Isolde herself, noticeably filling up the bathroom. "What's this?" she said. "The clubhouse?"

"Mm-mmm," we murmured noncommittally, preoccupied.

"Where are my black mules?" she demanded. That was the thing. The flat was cool and huge until Isolde came home. She filled it with heat and business and things and perfume the moment she walked in. It was always the same.

"Oh." Daisy turned bright red. "They'll be under my bed." Then, "I was trying them on."

"By the way," Isolde said to me, "don't invite that Afghani anymore."

"Chartreuse? He's French."

"Tch. Of course he isn't. He might have been in prison there once."

"I'm sure he would have told me if he was Afghani," I said, almost to myself.

"He looks like a Moroccan," Daisy said.

"You're the one who invited him," I reminded Isolde.

"It's no good to be seen with someone of that caliber."

I looked away. I wouldn't invite him back here to Isolde's house, but no one told me with whom to be friends. No one.

"He's dangerous," she added, pointedly scrubbing behind the

faucet with a thrown-away toothbrush. She did this as a reprimand to Daisy.

He's harmless, I started to say, but then I remembered that of course he wasn't. His velvet pouch of opium-veined hashish was in his pocket, ever at the ready. His secretive, conspiratorial eyes promised crime with a nudge from the top of the head and fun and who knew what all.

"Company's coming in thirty minutes, you two," Isolde fumed, as though this were our fault. "Well, you might have come home a little earlier, then, to get things started," Daisy dared.

"I was at a cattle call. *Twen* magazine is doing a bathing suit layout in the Canary Islands, Claire. You might want to try out."

"Not me. I never want to see the Canary Islands again. I was just there. Don't you remember? That was some horrible trip. The photographer was awful. Mean."

"Who was it?" Isolde said.

"Reiner Decke." I loathed even to say his name.

"Reiner? He's brilliant. I *love* Reiner." Isolde stretched herself in isometric detachment.

"Uch." I grimaced and went rigid. "How could you like that creepy man?"

"How much money did you make on that trip, Claire?"

"A ton," I admitted.

"And every catalog house in Germany started to book you right after he used you. I think I'll give him a call. I wonder if it's too late to invite him for tonight. . . ."

"Oh, no," I moaned. But I could see she'd already made up her mind.

"Don't put him next to me," I warned, "because I won't come."

"I'll bet I could catch him before he leaves his studio." Isolde was halfway out the door. "We'll put Harry next to him. And I need you, Claire."

"You don't need me," I phiffed.

She actually looked hurt. She came back in. "Yes, I do. You're pretty. So no one can say I'm the only good-looking woman I allow at my table. You're quiet, so you don't get in my way—"

"I'm not that quiet. Oh, please don't! Isolde, I beg you. . . ."

"Why not?" Her eyes already danced at the thought of him admiring her across her wonderful dinner table. And if his presence made me suffer, all the more fun! "Maybe he'll book me for his fall catalog. I was just thinking I could use new pictures."

It occurred to me that Isolde really did want me for something besides money. She thought my newness would rub off on her. This vulnerability in her touched me.

"I wish someone would choose me to go to the Canary Islands," Daisy said thoughtfully, her eyes still round, pretending not to notice Isolde's last barb about the only other good-looking woman. Isolde was so thoughtless.

Isolde leaned up against the mirror, peering suspiciously at all her nooks and crannies. "You know," she said, "anyone might arrive any minute. You'd better not leave me alone with them out there." What she meant, of course, was that she didn't like the two of us conspiring in here without her and we'd better get the show on the road.

"Don't be long," Isolde called back to me. I knew where she was going. Off to telephone that Reiner Decke.

"And gussy yourself up a bit, will you?" she added. "Sunday's Pfingsten!"

"What the hell is Pfingsten?" I called after her.

"Why, it's Pentecost," Daisy said and skedaddled off.

Pentecost! The feast of the Ascencion. My impulse was to immediately say a Hail Mary. Pentecost was big. At home we would be gathering the family together. But I didn't believe in God anymore, did I? I remembered. So how, I reasoned, could I pray through His mother? I thought guiltily of my Queen of the

Rosary beads left dejectedly in the back of a drawer in my old life back home. I could never have thrown them away. But neither could I have brought them along. For no God would have allowed my brother to have died back there in that filthy hallway. Not like that. And no mother of God. I shivered. Michael would never be there for me now when we were older. I'd always thought we'd be out in the yard raking leaves in some faraway October. I'd seen it. And now it would never be. We would never laugh together again. Never. Nor would I have my faith to console me. Still. There were times I missed my saints. I'd had one for each occasion. It had been a handy and fulfilling system. But I was grown up now, a friend of sophisticated Isolde's. No one was going to put one over on me.

The air was cold. The idea, though, of once again sitting at table with the horrible Reiner Decke was such a shock that I plunged obliteratingly under the stolen, perfumed water and—as it always does when you try purposefully to forget about something—the entire memory played before my closed eyes like a film.

I'd hardly been in Munich a week when my agency had sent me out to Grunwald to see this "big" photographer.

I'd gone on the tram. His studio was a huge beams-and-stucco affair in a pretty courtyard behind a pocketbook factory.

Reiner Decke sat on his palomino-skin sofa, flipping through my portfolio. This was right after I'd left Milan. I hadn't done well there, but I had some great tear sheets. Reiner just raced through these but stopped at my horrible commercial stuff from New York—really ugly shots of me for *Ingénue* and *Seventeen*. I'd only kept them to fill up my empty pages and to prove I'd worked in New York. I wasn't yet aware of just how impressed with anything American the German was.

"Na?" He'd leaned back and gleamed at me. "How would you like to go on safari? To Africa! Groovy, *or*?"

"Safari?" Not a year ago I'd been a mere senior in a Catholic high school. Safari sounded just the thing. No need to convince me. There would be excitement. Experience. The eyes of tigers. "I'd love to go." I nodded excitedly.

Oh, boy. A trip like this was big. Really big. I went outside to catch the trolley back to Schwabing. There was a pay phone at the tram stop. With my resigned New York skepticism, I put in my coins and was surprised when it worked. I called the only number I knew, my agency. The girl on the other end was very excited. Reiner Decke had just booked me for two weeks' catalog in the Canary Islands! I lit an HB cigarette and sucked it in. How much was I going to make? Wow.

Only a few days later I was on a charter flight to Tenerife. I had my newly purchased, slumpy burlap bag and my extra carton of cigarettes. I sat alone on the plane, my head filled with dreams. I wondered what I would do when I saw my first tiger. Would I be up to it or go numb with fear? There was no question of charcoals. Wild animals came and went like a flash. I would photograph it and draw later. What film would I use? I checked my camera battery.

Everyone spoke German, of course. I didn't mind. Anyway, all the other models were old. If not old, too old for me. They were cool and never looked my way. Now I know that they were afraid of me. But I hadn't known that then. They could hardly speak a word of English and they probably thought I was pushing them out. Quite a few times I would overhear them saying, "*Ausländer*." They said it so often, and with such specific disdain, I was beginning to wonder what it meant.

I remembered the first night there very well because that was the first inkling I'd had things weren't going to be all hunky-dory. We'd all sat down to an elaborate dinner. I was still a little aghast at the high-rise hotel. I'd imagined native huts on stilts. What with Reiner's Ronald Coleman attire there had been nothing else *to* think. He wore his many-pocketed vest and bush hat like a daring trooper, his elbows out, his cameras at the ready. Reiner spent a great deal of time admiring, in English (and so for my benefit), one of the other models. "Just look at Helga. She's the picture of a ballerina, *or?*" he kept urging. "Yes," I must have agreed ten times. Although I must admit, I'd found her too remote and brittle for my taste. And too tall for any ballerina I had ever seen.

"Just look at the way she eats," he approved, "like a little bird."

While I, on the other hand, shoveled in like an old farmhand whatever I could get my greedy hands on. Was that what he was implying? But I wasn't one to take offense. It was for just this sort of information I had come to Europe. I tried to eat a little more slowly and delicately.

"Americans," Reiner pointed out, "have absolutely no culture. And their homes," his expression withered, "are pure kitsch!" Without waiting for a reply to this, he went back to speaking German from the head of his long banquet table. These were *his* well-done sides of beef, his attitude implied, *his* paella, and his models, assistant, and one radiant, miniature client.

Uncomfortable, I patted my mouth with my napkin. And just when was this safari about to begin? I wondered. It was more like Spain than Africa. The whole setup was suspiciously touristy. Even I gave the room a sweep, like a little low-end Atlantic City.

There were some English. A bevy of retired Liverpudlians. They sat politely at their assigned places eating shiny shrimp and drinking umbrella gins. Enjoying the flamenco dancers on the portable stage. Taking it all in. They looked nice, I thought, sunburned and convivial. I was, however, loudly discouraged from making contact with any of them. Reiner reeled me back in the minute I would strike up a conversation with anyone. "We need not associate with working-class foreigners," he advised me. "*Or?*"

"And just what class do you think I am?" I spoke up boldly.

"There has never been the slightest doubt as to which class you belong," he snorted.

So it was to be a disgruntling two weeks.

Reiner Decke was mean because he was vain. What he'd wanted was my admiration and I withheld it simply because I had none. I embraced this refusal tightly in my clenched, hurt feelings.

Day after day, the front desk rang up before dawn and we girls staggered to the Range Rover bus. Up the landscape we would climb, Styrofoam cups of delicious coffee warming our hands.

I was directed to the rear of the bus. I honestly didn't know any better than to do as I was told. It was all so much like school. Here I was, in trouble again. Only instead of aggravated nuns, I now had Reiner Decke.

He was angry at me because I turned out to be so short. I had misrepresented myself, he said, wearing my platform shoes. They would have to prop me up on three telephone books. Big deal, I thought. I didn't see why we couldn't all just adjust. My latest offense was that I had no accessories with me. Who knew? Where I'd come from there were stylists and makeup people, I harrumphed to myself.

The other models were induced to grudgingly come up with hair falls and scarves and jewelry for me. They would hand over such items with distaste. The one named Helga had an entire suitcase just for ribbons in every color. She hated to give me her precious ribbons but my hair kept blowing in front of my face and Reiner insisted I use them to hold back my unruly mane. I learned to return each item swiftly. The owner would take it back as though she were receiving something unctuous, like snails, because, I supposed, it had come into contact with me.

So there I was with Helga and Werma and Unke and Uli, six-foot-something women, while I perched on my Tenerife telephone books.

Only the model called Helga spoke some English. Unavoidably

I learned a couple of German words. Things they'd say over and over, separate from complete sentences. "*Wirklich?*" (Really?) "*Genau!*" (Exactly!) "*Scheisse!*" (Shit!) Never to me. No one ever spoke to me. But occasionally, Reiner would shout at me, "You are too short!" or "I don't understand! You presented yourself as such a professional! Where is your fingernail polish?! You are being paid for this, *or?*"

There was a clerk who sat at the greasy reception desk at the hotel. "What does the word '*Ausländer*' mean?" I asked him on my way out the door.

He looked up from his Spanish true crime soft cover. "Foreigner," he told me.

Yes, I knew Reiner Decke. I gave my hair one last long rinse and climbed from the tub.

chapter six

*I*t was eight o'clock. I had donned one of the pretty dirndls that hung like spare girls in Isolde's wardrobe. You couldn't wear a bra with the senorita blouse that went with it but it didn't matter. No one wore a bra back then. Just wait till they get a load of me in this, I thought as I shut the door to my knotty-pine apartment and tiptoed through. Someone was tromping up the stairs. An unfamiliar voice I felt I recognized. I stood very still and listened. Someone important, I thought. I stood behind the nanny's green door and watched through the new moon sliver of stained glass. Although I didn't know it then, this would be the night when everything would change and my life would launch off in another direction.

Dr. Blacky von Osterwald huffed his irritated way up, up the tedious staircase one step at a time. I caught my breath. It was the man I'd seen that time six months ago at the airport in Milan!

So this was Blacky. He was angry, I could see that. And unhappy. Blacky was a medium-sized man with an open, clear-skinned face. He was good-looking, all right. His eyes were wide-set jel-lies of green but the whole effect was nothing dramatically dev-astating until you came to the hair. Great trundles of pure black hilarity that even his brittle comb would find it difficult to tame. He would pretend to be annoyed when anyone mentioned it, as most people eventually would, but women loved it and he knew they did. You could see the women who had loved him on his face. You could see them in the way he stood, sure and aggra-vated. His mother, his lovers. Girls who watched him from afar. He was too restrained to swagger, but the impetus was there. I held my neck, admiring any woman who could keep him. Wish-ing, for the second time, it was me.

Out on the landing, Harry Honeycutt sat across at the top of the stair alongside Rupert. Together they petted Rupert's cat.

"I have yet to climb this thing without cursing Isolde," Blacky panted from below. "How can she continue to live on a mountain-top? She doesn't need it now that Vladimir's gone. It's a sculptor's loft, not a fit home for them. She certainly has the means to move."

"Yes," agreed Harry. "Although one would never find ram-bling, enormous rooms like these in a modern building with a lift. Nor a window with a view as magnificent."

Blacky paused for a breather at the second-floor landing. "I suspect I ought to give up smoking," he said. "And drinking." He frowned. "We all drink too much." He carried a bouquet of white freesia with lily of the valley and a good Würzburger-Franken wine. I'd never been in love. Oh, I'd had my share of successes on the open field. But that just had been a series of wins and near misses. Like sport. I suddenly felt that where he was was where I wanted to be. I could just be near him and the air would be enchanted. I didn't even have to be near him. Just to know that he existed. That he lived. It wasn't like they said, time stands still. It quickened. Heightened. Glistened. I didn't need to talk with him. God, I think I wouldn't have known what to say. And he was cruel, yes. You could see that right away. But there was something bountiful about him, too. Measured. Discerning. I opened the door a whisper to hear them better.

Harry was saying, "You'll make us all look bad, never arriving empty-handed. What year is that?"

Blacky held up his bottle of Franken wine. "Seventy-one."

"Oh! I'm impressed. You must be infatuated."

"We got that business over with some years ago," he protested easily with a laugh, "and have settled into a comfortable and more convenient understanding. No, I'm simply very well brought up."

Harry, very well brought up himself, said, "Yes, Isolde likes having you because you're an aristocrat, there's no denying that. A count, in fact, isn't it?" His voice betrayed real bitterness. "Although she will always pretend that has no influence on her."

Blacky stopped to catch his breath. "It's because I am single, charming, and, once you get me stewed, a lively conversationalist."

Not only that, I confirmed from my covey of secrecy, but I would bet he knew what he was doing when it came to women.

"No, really, I hate this," Blacky complained, "too many flights. But where else in Munich would one find a table as sumptuous as Isolde's? And," he added, "where one could at the same time flex one's English; where one might and often does meet one pretty boarder after the next."

Harry said, "Wait till you see the one she's got here now."

My breath stopped.

"I don't care to meet her," he went on. "What a flippant little baggage *she* is! When I telephoned, she took it upon herself to correct my pronunciation, as if an American dare correct anyone's English! American women really are distasteful. Acidic. Isolde ought to go back to renting out to the Swedish girls. No irritating, superior attitudes. Just hupla into bed and gone before you wake. Americans put so much stock into 'meaningful' relationships. Well. One knows where that leads."

"Yes." Harry feathered Puss's head.

"The men I know enough about from the year I spent as a volunteer medic in Vietnam."

"Yes." Harry stifled a yawn. "We've all heard how you went to Vietnam. Several times, I think."

"Uneducated buggers," Blacky, ignoring this, went on, "forever destroying perfectly decent scotch with horrid jolts of Coca-Cola." He'd reached the top. "Do something with these, will you?" He dropped his soft bouquet onto Harry and strolled inside.

The party was a glimmering affair, candlelit and charming, the way only Isolde could do it. All old models know how to do lighting, but some are better at it than others. She had the knack, all right. The room was warm and glowy. I waited until they were all seated, took a deep breath, and went in. I felt Blacky's eyes sweep me up and down and a thrill rushed through me. I trembled to my seat. His eyes, taken, followed me.

"Ah," said Isolde, watching, "you haven't met our Claire."

"From America," Harry just had to add.

He liked that. I could see the spot behind Blacky's eyes reach toward me.

"Hello," I said.

His eyes met mine.

I was sure his lit up.

But then—what was this?—at exactly the wrong moment, Tupelo Honig swept into the room. The actress was a voluptuous vision of flowing beige and loose chiffon.

All the men stood up at once. Tupelo Honig, however, had eyes for no one but Blacky. She moved provocatively toward him. Her cheekbones popped up like prizes and the edges of her glossy mouth went up and down in almost comical sensual allure. Her fingernails were delicate and filed into fancy sherberty ovals. She wore green pearls. I'd never seen green pearls before. Not real ones. They shone with an uncanny phosphorescence. They were dark yet light at the same time. Blacky reached across the table and took her hand. He pulled it to him and kissed it.

I was crushed.

It would have been very hard not to be captivated, I'll give her that. I'd assumed she'd be older from all the films I'd heard she'd done. If she was, it didn't show.

Everyone in the room leaned unwittingly toward her. Even as she stood there presenting herself, she moved like pudding, with no discernible bones. Her hairdresser must have sprinkled her head with glitter because as she went in in her fluid, captivating way, the candlelight seemed to shine out from her. Here was a woman who knew how to make an entrance. She was one of those dark blondes, with nutmeg eyes and dark brows, but hair that lightened into the color of corn-husk silk as it grew to its luxurious, uneven lengths. Her waist and ribs were preposterously small and her shoulders and breasts were, by contrast, big creamy things a man would love to touch. It wasn't fair. Any thoughts I'd had of actually "getting" Blacky evaporated at the moment I saw his expression change from amused for me to rapt for her.

"*Liebling*, I said *Trachten*!" Isolde chastised her. But she wasn't angry. She was thrilled just to have her famousness in the house.

"You must forgive me," Tupelo beseeched us all. "I've just come from *such* a grueling rehearsal at the theater."

She said this as one would say "such a grueling time at the supermarket," and we all obediently gazed at her with sympathy.

Blacky still looked at her with something else. I'd known jealousy before, but this was something new. He might have wanted me for that one quick moment but her, with all that sexual allure . . . he wanted her for keeps. And Blacky was impressed by other things. What chance would I have against fame and fortune?

"Don't fuss for me, now, darlings, I beseech you!" Tupelo smiled sweetly at everyone. All the men were standing, tipped forward toward her. "My needs are so simple. I only eat raw foods, you know. High-energy foods. Or carrot juice. I love my carrot juice."

From here things only got worse. Isolde asked me if I wouldn't mind scooting one seat down so we could have boy girl, boy girl. I don't turn red in an attractive, virginal blush. My nose and ears become bright dots. I felt suddenly scrawny and ridiculous in my dirndl.

Isolde introduced Tupelo to me.

"Ah." She took my hand, purring, "Named for Claire of the poor Claires!" showing off her knowledge of America.

"No, actually," I stared right back, "named for the song 'Claire de Lune.' " But she'd already turned her back.

Then Reiner Decke, that awful photographer, arrived in a loden cape. I never would have thought I would be glad to see that man. But I was. I was glad for anyone who would change the dense, oozy tone of that room to something less seductive, even if it was to Reiner's unpleasant cockiness. He had somehow assembled his trickle of hairs into a tail at the back of his head. It made him look like a degenerate rock star from Peru, I thought. And in all my life I have never seen a larger, more sparkling watch on a wrist.

Wolfgang Scherer, the filmmaker, arrived. Well, he appeared suddenly more than arrived. One moment he wasn't there and the next he was. He was a little man, soundless, with a long trunk and short legs, his eyes very blue and sharp. He had outstanding, listening ears low on his head. He wore a flimsy neck scarf like an adolescent boy would at a dress-up, looking just the way you would imagine a filmmaker should look. He had well-formed shoulders and very frail little arms, almost childlike, but quick, high-arched feet that he tended to kick in the air as he moved like a kung fu artist, or a man with a fever. He must have had a horrible childhood, I remember thinking. He wasn't pleasant to look at—and however much you tried to look at him from different angles, you couldn't find a good view. Despite this, you continued to look because there was something captivating. He had a wonderful deep, full-throttle voice when he at last spoke and eyes that—no, it wasn't that they twinkled. They didn't twinkle, they glowed. Yes, there was something wonderfully hidden and compelling about him.

I tried to appear as though I were enjoying myself and, in a way, after a while and a few glasses of white wine, I thought I was. After all, I told myself, this was just what I'd always wanted: to be hooked up with aristocratic and decadent film people. This cavalier set were perfect for my needs. Wasn't I determined to live a detached life, dedicated only to fundamental art and beauty? There was no room for such foolishness as falling in love. I told myself I felt much better. And I had my loathing of Reiner to keep me company. Reiner was in raptures to find himself dining with the famous Wolfgang Scherer and the actress Tupelo Honig. And when he was introduced to me, he acted as though we were old buddies. "Of course I know the little Breslinsky!" He dismissed me by never really looking at me. "We were together on safari!" His beady eyes twinkled from guest to well-heeled guest. The *little* Breslinsky? How demeaning. And again with the safari. There was nothing for me to do but smile.

Isolde led him to his place at her left.

Almost immediately, Reiner was fawning over Wolfgang. Anyone with half a head could see that he didn't take to Reiner at all. Reiner didn't notice this, or if he did, he figured dogged time and effort would bring him around. He went chummily on, happily intimate, even giving Wolfgang tips on new filters and revolutionary underwater camera attachments. Wolfgang, resigned, proceeded to make an origami bird from his napkin.

Tupelo and Blacky seemed delighted with each other. His seductive way with women was effortless. I helped myself to a glass of wine.

Vladimir, Isolde's husband, handsome, heavyset, red-faced, blond, burly, sweating from the strain of the staircase, arrived last. He was laughing and carrying a bottle of Châteauneuf-du-Pape. I liked Vladimir. You couldn't help liking him. He looked at you with his frank, sensual, handsome face, unimpressed with important people. *"Wo ist mein Bier?"* he shouted, filling the room. "Where's my beer?"

Walking toward us, his big hand took hold of the neck and then the arched back of the huge sculpture he'd done of a girl on her knees. He ran his hand right down her back to her rear end, all the while holding eyes with Isolde.

"Well?" she confronted him. "Did you ask her?"

"No, I did not."

Isolde threw up her arms in despair. "All I asked you to do was knock on Frau Zwekl's door and ask her to come."

Daisy choked on her olive spread. "But you hate each other."

"I know." Isolde busied herself, putting the flowers off to the side. "But she's all alone."

"I don't like old people sitting about." Vladimir grinned at the rest of us. "It's depressing."

Silently I resolved to go down and see Frau Zwekl in the morning.

Isolde, her hands on her hips, informed us, "He doesn't realize that he'll be old one day, too. Old and alone and grateful if someone invites him along."

Vladimir smiled. "I'll never be alone, though. There'll always be someone around for me."

She has no shot, I thought. He's so much stronger than she is because he doesn't care. He's not even teasing her. He could not care less. Rings of perspiration had wet his shirt. He didn't seem to mind that, either. He shook hands all around, then went back inside and saw to the music. He put on Billie Holiday, making sure the bass was very loud.

"Wow!" Isolde said, coming around, in an unlikely attempt at cool. Isolde became a different person when Vladimir was around. She came as close to obsequious as I'd ever seen her. I didn't like it. You always knew when Vladimir was coming because the whole apartment reeked of her perfume beforehand. So already she was trying too hard. And your glamour rushes to the floor like sudden rain when you become needy. It angered me to see her so trivialized.

At least, I reassured my unhappy heart, Blacky hadn't known that I'd fallen for him before he'd fallen for Tupelo Honig. At least I didn't have to tolerate anyone's pity. I couldn't have borne that. Because I was young and inexperienced, I still believed in the importance of saving face. It was painful enough for me to watch Isolde when Vladimir was around. Whatever she did, it was never enough. Or too much. One morning, when he'd just moved out and I'd just moved in, I'd overheard them arguing in the dining room. She'd held a dinner party the night before and he hadn't come after saying he would. I turned discreetly to go back into my little suite of rooms but not before I heard him say, in English—because of the children, I suppose—"Well, don't," he'd cried. "That's just it. *Don't* love me so much! You . . . you . . . want potted *geraniums* on every *windowsill*. That's not me, Isolde. I want none of that."

He'd said "potted geraniums" like "bubonic plague," like there was something so wrong with the idea of them. As if you could accuse Isolde of being conventional! And he should have known the fastest way to teach children a language was to argue in it.

I was devastated for Isolde. And embarrassed. She would have hated to know I'd heard. It was one of the most brutal things I'd ever heard anyone say. Now here he was at last, and all this, I knew, had been for him. As for Vladimir, he couldn't very well not enjoy the good meal before him, the enchanting company, but for him it was nothing more. Isolde's eyes followed him wherever he went. And he never felt at home. He paced. He kept getting up and peering out the lead-paned windows as though someone were downstairs waiting for him in the car. There might well have been.

But now that I look back, I think she would have only loved someone not crazy about her for the simple reason that most people were. So in a way it was her fate.

Tupelo Honig's flattered, ladylike laugh tinkled distractingly over everyone's conversation.

Later in the evening her joy would loosen to a slightly raucous and hearty bellow, but I say that only because I was leaden with jealousy.

Chatreuse came in with half endives, baked and topped with steaming, crumpled, runny Roquefort. There were intermittent corniches of parmaschinken, so thin they were almost translucent.

I clapped my hands with joy.

Blacky smiled at me. His eyes twinkled. "I'm famished," he confided.

"Oh, no!" Tupelo Honig suddenly threw her napkin onto her plate. "I can't eat food like this." She said it as though reprimanding and let the words sit there on the table.

Isolde moved uncomfortably. "Well," she said, "I have artichoke but they're for later. They're not cooked through yet, I think. Are they, Chartreuse?"

Chartreuse trotted accommodatingly back to the kitchen.

"I'll wait. Don't think of me." Tupelo smiled benevolently. "Eat. Eat!"

Her color was high and she wore an expression of excitement.

No one liked to start until we all were served. Eventually, however, Isolde insisted we eat before the food got cold. It sort of took the fun out of it, though, with Tupelo sitting there very pointedly doing nothing. You could almost feel Chartreuse in the kitchen willing the tough artichoke to soften. When the rest of us had finished and the artichoke finally did arrive, she sat there comfortably, taking her time, enjoying it. Her eyes took in each of us. Anyone else would have dashed through it out of consideration but Tupelo luxuriated in the attention. She picked up one of the leaves. It was oily and pearly and luscious with green edges rimmed in pink. She held it up for us all to see and slit it open along the seam with one of her pretty nails. The succulent innards were revealed. She licked this. You could see her saliva on the leaf. She took her time. You'd have thought she'd tinged her fork noisily on a wineglass, the way we all stopped and watched. Then she dragged her teeth over its top, holding the flesh on the tip of her tongue and then swallowing it with a close-mouthed, feline smirk of satisfaction. She did this with every solitary leaf, laughing with merriment once in a while, placing each one ornamentally around the choke on the plate as she finished it, the pointy end out. The completion looked like a sunflower. I remembered thinking she had a lot of nerve, keeping everyone waiting like that, but you had to give it to her—she knew how to captivate an audience. I made a note to eat each artichoke that came my way in exactly the same fashion.

Then, as if that weren't enough, she made each one of us close our eyes in silent meditation, thanking the universe for its bounty. (She made no mention of Isolde's or Chartreuse's part at this point.)

Indulgently, we all obliged. We closed our eyes. I peeked. Chartreuse watched me with his bright yellow eyes.

Daisy had at last lost interest and was trying slyly to read her horoscope upside down in the newspaper on the hassock.

Blacky tore himself from Tupelo's attentions. "Claire," he addressed me, "it must have been a marvelous trip you went on with Reiner."

"Ah," Reiner agreed before I could say a word. "So much

adventure! We had so much fun. So much fun!" I didn't know which trip *he'd* been on. It had been the worst trip of my life. His obligatory words to me said, Blacky returned his attentions to Tupelo. Tupelo was obviously besotted with Blacky and Blacky with her.

The party was progressing gaily. Chartreuse would slide into the room, shoulders hunched protectively forward over yet another delicious concoction. We all would "ooh" and "ahh" and he would distribute portions with womanly care.

"Good God," Harry would say each time a dish was placed before him.

It looked like Isolde had found herself a kindred spirit, there, despite her words of distaste. She and Chartreuse consulted each other, madly serious, at short intervals in the kitchen, then burst forth from that little galley with brilliant, relaxed smiles over platters of superbly prepared food. They played off each other, each wanting to impress, but more than that, being both truly talented, it was each other they most enjoyed impressing.

Chartreuse had solved the problem of the too great leg of lamb cooking through in time by hacking it into small raw bits and artistically modeling these into a cunning small lamb held together by a paste of garlic, olive oil, and sea salt. Any bit that wouldn't hold was anchored together with lengths of mint stems as threads. These he fastened with sailor's slipknots, easily loosened and pulled away so no one got chewy bits of it in his or her serving. It rested, well done and crispy, with raisins for eyes, on a bed of airy white rice.

I'd never seen anything like it. He'd taken a blue satin ribbon from a jam preserves jar in the cupboard and tied a bow around the neck when it was steaming and perfectly done. A latticework of rosemary and garlic framed the tray like a woven basket rim. The latticework continued into gated arbors up the handles on each side. Hothouse primroses were stuck at the last moment up the arbors like summer vines. He'd fastened two soft, furry sage leaves inside the lamb's ears.

"Charming!" Vladimir said appreciatively. "I could take you on as an apprentice!"

Chartreuse explained that he'd worked long hours as a teenager in a bakery kitchen in France.

"Wie süss!" Tupelo Honig cooed. (How sweet!) She might be a German film star but she wasn't born German. Every now and then a trace of Eastern Europe slithered from her tongue. Which was, I suppose, part of her appeal. Well, I wasn't going to let her ruin my fun.

I went briskly to get my camera. No one minded waiting. Done meat should rest for a bit before it's cut and it would be a shame not to admire it. It was a wonderful lamb. Chartreuse's stock had jumped through the roof.

I still have that picture somewhere. There is the lamb gazing benignly at the rest of us and we at it.

I snapped the picture and everyone applauded. Daisy put down her basket of steaming green beans and went to get the salad.

Vladimir carved one ear off the lamb and put it on Isolde's plate. *"Mein Schatz,"* he said, in an offhand, easy way. My treasure. It was as if he had forgotten for a moment to be caustic with her.

Wolfgang said he hadn't known I was a photographer.

"Hah." Reiner laughed. "She's not."

"Oh, no," Isolde explained, "Claire is an artist. Show them your drawings, Claire," she urged. "Go on. Where's your sketch-book, hmm?"

Daisy, clearing the table, said, "They're here." And she handed Wolfgang my precious book.

"Oh, don't!" I protested but I was thrilled at what was about to happen. Blacky would see that I was not just a model. They would all see.

Proudly, Daisy and Isolde presented my work. I enjoyed each picture more than anyone, I think, reliving the moments I'd drawn them. Cherishing the end of the grueling effort that had gone into each. Daisy turned the pages reverently while Isolde gave a running monologue.

She rattled her head at Wolfgang. "What do you think of our Claire, eh?"

"She is a most serious young lady, I think."

I'd been smiling, my expectation of his praise already evident upon my face.

"Yes?" Isolde waited. "Come on. What do you think of her work?"

Wolfgang looked down at his plate. He rolled his tongue across and around his teeth. Then he said, "What difference does it make what I say? I am a filmmaker, not a critic." Suddenly he leaned forward. "Harry here is the critic. One of the best in his own field, from what I've read. So. He's the one to ask, not me." He smiled gently and handed my precious book across the table and over to Harry. I could feel my heart beating in my chest. What was happening? What had Harry to do with anything?

But Harry was not *just* Harry. He'd studied, reviewed, published. He was a renowned critic not only for the *Süddeutsche* but the London *Times* as well. I remembered Isolde saying he was an art collector and had become quite famous in his own small, elite world. There were others who were impressed to no end by our bumbling Harry. Take a swan out of his pond and he waddles, isn't that it? We'd only ever seen the waddle.

Harry, slipping imperiously back into his own pond, adjusted his glasses and cleared his throat. "Yes." He nodded. "They are lovely pictures. Yes."

He looked at my pictures for a very long time. At last he stopped. He pursed his lips and leveled his gaze at me. "Are they good? Of course they are good, they are lovely to look at." He looked up. He looked right at me. "Good, yes. But never great."

For a moment I thought he was joking.

"I'm so sorry," Harry murmured, "but it's best to know the truth."

He must have seen my shock.

"Forgive my bluntness, my dear. But if I'm to be honest, this is"—he searched the air helplessly for just the word—"amateur. This is a young girl's memory of a European tour. Mediocre. Nothing more."

Thunk, thunk, thunk, each word took me down another step. "Oh. I see," I agreed casually, my hopes and dreams of a lifetime dashed. "Yes, of course," I whispered. "As much as it hurts, it *is* best to know the truth."

Isolde threw back her head. "*I* think they are beautiful," she said loyally.

I should have been glad. But it only made it worse. I could have wept. I would have rather anything than let the tears fall, though. I think the only thing that kept me from it was my pride in front of Tupelo Honig. She would have enjoyed that so, so much.

Daisy trembled with plump indignation on my behalf. She said fiercely, "One man's opinion means nothing, though, if one is set upon making it work. What was it your American, Ray Kroc, said? 'It is perseverance and perseverance alone that determines success.'"

"Yes, of course." Harry seemed to come to. He handed me my book. He looked kindly at me, sadly. "But life is short. Don't waste *too* much time."

I almost fell off my chair. I continued to smile, yet I was so hurt, so devastated, I almost couldn't see straight. Remembering my manners, I thanked Harry for his expertise.

Blacky gave me a crooked smile. It was made to console me.

There was something about the closeness of this man, this Blacky, that allowed me to feel things I'd pushed off. Scary things I'd been too frightened to admit to myself. Things I felt I *could* feel and still be safe. All these things go running through your mind. Although Harry had proclaimed the judgment, it was the nearness of Blacky that opened some door in me, allowing me to think what I'd dared not think, perhaps to admit at last to myself that my drawings *were* not really as good as my brother always boasted they were and it was all right, not the end of the world. After all, my brother had had his vested interest. He'd wanted me to be happy. Nothing had pleased him more. He'd pumped me up. That very sweetness had been the saddest thing to lose.

The worst part about losing someone is not what goes with the tears. That's the luxury. The most awful part is the dry, unrelieved ache, the moment when you know you'll only ever have the memories. No present. No future. No dreams of laughing together in the garden while you seed the grass, year after year. Never. And that moment comes again and again and stretches at last and long into the future. At the thought of Michael I felt the tears welling up and was horrified they would overflow. But the next moment the lights went blessedly out. Chartreuse entered with a cake ablaze with candles.

Evidently it was Vladimir's birthday. I wiped my eyes in the darkness and pasted a grin on my face. I sang along but I wasn't really there. I was numb with shock and outrage.

"Turn the lights on, please," Vladimir said when he'd blown out the candles.

Someone threw on the bright overhead light. I struggled to my feet then sat back down. We had moved on to the oddly shaped bottles of Würzburger-Franken wine and I was too drunk to go anywhere now.

"I say." Harry, his thick glasses still on, scrunched his face up.

"Excuse me, Vladimir, but who took those photographs? You?"
He indicated the pictures of the children and the Leopoldstrasse
on the Peg Board.

Isolde, still peeved, said defensively, "Claire took them all."

Harry crouched forward to get a better look. "But these are
superb." He looked at me above his spectacles. "Have you others?"

"I take photos of all the subjects I sketch," I said.

"May I see them?"

May he see them? I think for the first time in my life I let my
dessert sit. I tried not to think as I went obediently into my small
apartment. My hands were trembling when I fished the photos from
the desk. Shortly, I returned with a dossier folder. Harry followed
me into the living room. I let the photographs slip to the coffee table.

Harry perched himself on the edge of the sofa and inspected the
lot I'd taken in Milan. There was the dark and firelit composition
of the whores along the Autostrada, the road stretching toward the
lurid sunset. The early morning eeriness of Luna Park in ghostly
scarves of fog. After a minute he looked up. "You might not be an
artist at drawing, young lady, but I have rarely seen such a fine eye
for photography." He regarded me again sternly from beneath his
heavy brows. "In *this* you are an artist."

Yeah, right, I thought. Throw me a bone. But I wasn't drunk
anymore. "I am?" I said.

"Yes. Did you *really* take these, Claire? They are good. Excellent in fact."

"Yes."

Distrustful of the slender vein of hope that was beginning to
surge through me, I asked him softly, "You're certain?"

"Yes."

"My whole life," I could feel the words cracking in my throat,
"I wanted to be a painter."

"My whole life," he surprised me by glancing quickly over his shoulder and then saying, "I wanted to be a ballet dancer. To soar through the air with beautiful women in pink tutus. I have, how-ever, two left feet. In life, we work with what we've got. We work with our gifts. Our blessings. Not our unrealistic desires. In this way, we are useful to ourselves and others. Why? I'll tell you why. Doing something to which we are unsuited is tedious and frustrating. Doing something *really* well is fun."

I felt my cheeks grow warm. "I didn't think I was *that* bad," I said. "Couldn't I become better with hard work? I'm not afraid of hard work."

"My dear," this gentle, kindly man went on to ease me for-ward, to help me understand, "is that what you want for your life? To be not bad?" He held up a crooked, moonlit picture I'd taken of the Viktualienmarkt in snow. "As a photographer, you could be one of the *best*! You have the talent! The real thing! Wasn't it fun to take this photograph?"

I remembered the moment well. Yes, it had been fun. Easy. I thought of all the struggle and impatience that went along with my sketching because it never went smoothly. No. It was never *fun*, that was for sure. "You think I could be a great photographer?"

"I could guarantee it."

"Come back in here, you two!" Isolde demanded.

She acted as though she were annoyed at me, but I could tell she was pleased.

I was suddenly embarrassed to have taken so much of his time. "Your dinner will be cold."

"What sort of a hostess do I look like? Daisy!" Isolde bel-lowed. "Go get Harry's plate from the oven."

"Look, just look at this." Harry held up the photograph to Wolfgang. "And this one." He held up one I'd taken in a dressing room. Eleven beautiful women at their worst, curlers in their hair, everyone looking unhappily, even tragically, into their mirrors.

He pressed another into Wolfgang's small hand. "Take a look at this." It was the picture I'd taken of Rupert's back, his head out the window, behind him the rooftops of Munich.

Wolfgang said grudgingly, "Yes. That is good."

Even Blacky seemed impressed. But only for a moment. Tupelo, sensing mutiny, leaned opulently forward toward the package of HB cigarettes at Blacky's distant elbow. Obediently distracted, he reached into his pants pocket and provided her with a light.

"It's so easy to conjure a good layout with the camera," I said.

"Of course," Wolfgang agreed, one professional to the other. "But that's the point, darling. To follow your bliss. Not your headache. You see, you've already found what you do well, you just didn't know it."

We smiled at each other. Wolfgang was sitting directly across from me and, because I wasn't an actress interested in being discovered, he took a liking to me. I asked him a couple of questions about black-and-white photography and depth of field and he answered me in a simple, easily understandable way.

I got the distinct impression that this business was beginning to annoy Reiner Decke. He sat there, jealous and aggravated. I'd spent two weeks with the man and by now knew when he was upset. I couldn't figure out why, though. Surely he wouldn't rather be the one showing me how to use my camera? No. Then I realized it was Wolfgang Scherer's attention he wanted.

I turned my attention back to Wolfgang. "Everyone else I've ever asked has got me so confused that I was almost ready to ditch my thirty-five-millimeter camera for an automatic," I told him.

"Oh, but no," he insisted, "the less contraptions on a camera, the less can go wrong. There's less that can break on it. Just keep it up, you'll get it." I felt somehow protective toward him. There was something virile about him, though, an underlying heavy beard he took great pains to keep at bay, and a thirsty darkness to his voice. There was something, certainly not feminine, but feline

about him. I hated even to think it but there was something
dwarflike about him, too, with his short little arms and legs and
big feet and head.

Still, we hit it off right away. His English was very good. He
liked to tell a joke and I liked to laugh, almost always doing so at the
punch line, so to him and everyone else we were having a fine old
time. Despite my disappointment, there was something magical
about that evening. Maybe we had the right chemistry; the party
never seemed to want to break up.

"An opulent feast." Harry licked melted butter from the tips of
his beautiful fingers. "I adore white asparagus."

"So much left over!" Isolde cried, eyeing the expensive surplus.

Chartreuse, piously righteous, observed, "That would never
be a problem in India. In India there is always someone waiting
just outside to take the food home."

"Did I hear you mention India?" Wolfgang turned his attention abruptly from me to Chartreuse.

"Yes."

"Have you been there?"

Chartreuse gave that dramatic, negative French shrug of his.
"But of course. Many times."

"You know, if you don't mind, I'd love to pick your brain
about it sometime."

Chartreuse said, "*Bien sûr*. At your service, eh?" He looked up
from the joint he was rolling and grinned at Wolfgang in that
wicked, childishly happy way he had.

"I've always wanted to make a documentary about India,"
Wolfgang said. "You know, a train-of-thought film. Just go to all
these unusual places and film as you go. I might really have time
to go to India if I plan it well enough. I can't start filming *Brazil-
ian Love* until the fall. I wonder if I could change it to next fall."

"Is that your next film?" Blacky asked Wolfgang.

"You know," Wolfgang grew excited, "perhaps I could get up

a little band to go there. To India, I mean." He was unable to give it up.

"Ah, that would be the life." Blacky tore himself from Tupelo's gaze and sat back in his chair. His eyes shone at the thought of such a trip. He put his hand through his silky dark hair and combed his long fingers through. "You've got the right job, all right," he said to Wolfgang. When he spoke I had an excuse to gaze at Blacky outright. He was one of those rare people who was content in his skin, comfortable, even, in his envy. He stretched his legs out. I admired the circumference and length of those legs. He saw me looking. I pulled back, caught.

And then Chartreuse said, "Why not drive?"

"Drive?" Tupelo guffawed. "That's ludicrous. Can't you see it?" Her green pearls shimmered with laughter.

Everyone tittered obligingly. Chartreuse sat back in his chair. His eyes shone with the memory. "Each day," he said, "the light climbs easy, easy through the curtains into your caravan. If yesterday was bad, today begins a new landscape, new people, new country! This is a wonderful thing, I think."

We listened, transfixed.

"The blue sky," Chartreuse said, "each day, only sun and sky . . ."

"Drive to India," Vladimir went on, tasting the idea. Then he said, "It would be like flying to the moon."

"What do you mean, the moon?" Reiner Decke's head bobbed and he squinted at him in an unpleasant way.

"He means," Isolde said, "metaphorically." Because she was happy, she wasn't on her toes. Vladimir looked at her crossly. "Why do you interpret what I mean? Do you know what I am thinking?" He stood up. "Am I not even allowed my thoughts?"

"No." She touched her chest. "I didn't mean—"

It was so like Vladimir to attack her like that in front of everyone. But this time he kept on. "Then why do you say 'metaphorically' like that? As if interpreting for me! Do you want my thoughts, too?" He turned to me. "She even wants my thoughts!"

I think we all thought the same thing, that Vladimir was coming unhinged. For a moment I thought he would hit her.

"Don't worry," she said carefully, "you'll soon have them all back. Anyway," she laughed nervously, as if none of this bothered her, as if it were all nonsense and she was in on the joke all along, "you who gets carsick driving to Salzburg—"

"That's because I hate to drive there." He sat down.

"Doesn't your mum live in Salzburg?" Daisy asked stupidly.

"No," Vladimir said, "Isolde's mother does."

"Ah, so." Reiner Decke grinned maliciously.

Isolde smiled at everyone.

Wolfgang said, "No, I was just thinking, why shouldn't we all go?"

"We?" Reiner Decke shunted his knife into a lamb haunch. "As in everyone at this table?"

Conversation stopped as each of us digested the idea. We looked one another over.

"I mean," he went on, lowering his voice so we all had to lean closer, "it seems you can drive through easily enough."

I was beginning to get the idea how he got things done. His sense of drama and timing had everyone mesmerized. But it wasn't only that. It was the way he stayed on track. How he remained intent on this one thought. I wasn't surprised he made good films. For all his Puckish looks, his big hands, and his probably oversized scrotum, his voice so hypnotic and deep, he had us all mesmerized.

"Would you be interested in such a venture?" Wolfgang peered into Chartreuse's eyes and I thought for a moment, He *is* a hypnotist!

For all the hash he'd smoked you'd have thought Chartreuse would be more stoned. But he was alert as a chipmunk on a fox's hill. "Do you mean you would want a guide? Someone who would know the way as I would?"

"Exactly!"

Chartreuse pressed his elbows together. I could almost see his mind lurch into gear. He would get back to enchanting India, where he could wangle Lord knew what sort of deals, and now, on top, he'd be paid. He pretended to mull all this over, "Hmm," he said. "I know of an excellent van, totally equipped for overland travel. I might be able to get it for you for a good price."

I almost laughed out loud. Now, if it broke down, it would be someone else's problem. And he would have money. Not only that but he could do whatever it was one did under the prosperous and respectable title of "film company guide."

"The Orient," murmured Harry.

I became unreasonably jealous. The Orient was *my* idea!

Blacky said, "You know, I'm coming, too." He meant it when he said it.

Tupelo threw back her head and laughed. "Darlink! You cannot! You are a doctor!"

"Yes, I am quite sure I am. But it's not as though I can't leave when I want. I can lease out my practice. There are at least ten doctors who will jump at the chance to take my place. Munich is the most desirable place to work in Germany."

"You can't be serious," Reiner said.

We all watched him. This was beyond us all. A doctor, willing to give up his hard-earned position. I found him so idealistic and beautiful. His sooty curls.

Blacky drained his glass and looked around for the bottle. "When I come back," he said, as though he were talking to himself, "I'll take it over again."

"But what about *moi*?" Tupelo asked in a baby doll voice. She twiddled her fingertips in the candlelight. It was an action related to the scent of money.

"You're always flying off on a filming trip," Blacky reminded her. "Here. There. You probably won't even be in the country while I'm gone."

"I'm doing that play." She frowned. "In Munich. Right here."

Chartreuse stood up and circled the table, sidling ingratiatingly, on his way to refill Blacky's glass.

I watched Tupelo Honig's bright little eyes calculate her next move. She was a quick study as to which direction things were going. And although they went along well, Hollywood had not yet cabled. After all, one doctor in the hand was worth two in the cattle-calling bush.

"Wolfgang," she announced, "I want to come, too!"

"You!" Wolfgang looked at her with startled eyes. "The first time there was no regular bathroom you'd be looking for the nearest airport!"

"No, that would be me," Isolde interjected.

We all laughed.

"No, really, *Liebling*, I would return broadened," here Tupelo paused, "as an artist." Her head swung majestically atop her neck. She said it all with a queenly pout. I think I hated her completely at that moment. Not only had she taken Blacky from me. Now she was the artist. And, on top, she was taking my place as a gal on her way to the Orient.

"What about your play?" Daisy reminded her.

"Ach." She made a shrug and a gesture as though that were of little consequence. "Any actress could play that part," she said, using Blacky's tactic. "But India," she wobbled her head like a Jaipuri temple dancer, "people would see me as an actress who could play any role." She lowered her voice. "They run documentaries at Cannes, don't they?"

Isolde added, "Or even at the Berliner Film festival."

"Hey," Wolfgang leaned forward, "it would be wonderful. I could get no end of backing if you came along."

"But *I* wanted to go," I blurted tipsily.

"Oh, you! You just want to go to Afghanistan!" Daisy dismissed my credibility with a demeaning little swipe of the hand. "You're not up to the grand trip."

I was a little stunned that Daisy would demean my wishes in front of all these people.

There was a sliver of true malice in her attitude and I was surprised and a little hurt. Daisy and I had always been close.

"My dear Claire, Americans don't want to go to Afghanistan now," Harry said. "It's absolutely perilous." I think he was the only one of us who wasn't noticeably drunk. Well, he was so used to his alcohol.

"All the more reason you should come along," Vladimir said. "One of the last great frontiers."

Isolde said bluntly, "You're Afghani, Chartreuse, aren't you." She didn't say it as a question.

He flinched without flinching, if you know what I mean. "My mother." He glanced momentarily up from the joint he was rolling.

"But," she pursued, "you were born there, surely."

He returned her gaze. "Herat." He said the word fondly.

"Well, then you know better than anyone," Wolfgang said. He turned to me. "Why would you want to go to Afghanistan, anyway, Claire?"

I closed my eyes and went to see what I imagined when I thought of me in Afghanistan. I saw the silk route of the past winding its way through the yellow mountains. The marketplaces. Men sitting cross-legged in apricot shops. Fierce women. The color red. I found I had said all this out loud.

The cool silence that greeted me opened my eyes.

Then, "India, too, has red," Blacky said.

"Pink," Tupelo corrected. "India has pink." She loosened her shawl. "Hot pink."

But his green eyes held me from across the table. They were interested now. Indulgent and captivated.

The way he said the word. "Inja." With such refinement. And yet, there was passion. I heard the sounds of marketplaces and the roar of nearing elephants. The jingle of ankle bracelets on brown legs. The homespun white of Gandhi. Suddenly I wished very much that I could go. Go to India, where no one I had known at home had ever been. From where I, too, would come back changed. I asked myself why was he looking at me like that. There was something so charmed in that. I felt that I could trust him. I also felt the blood well up in my cheeks. Then I burst out into nervous, hysterical laughter and he looked away. Oh, I loathe myself, I thought.

Wolfgang turned to me. "Why *don't* you tag along? Afghanistan is on the way."

"What, me?" I touched my throat, chickening out. "I couldn't."

"Why not?"

"I haven't got that kind of money put aside," I admitted. "Anyway, anything I've got right now ought to go toward a car." I sighed. "I spend so much on taxis"

"You've got tons of money," Daisy said. "Come on. We can both go." She opened a nail polish bottle and she drew an iridescent stripe down the middle of her thumbnail.

Vladimir's mouth dropped open. "I wouldn't do that so near to the food."

"And I wouldn't admonish someone publicly who is just about to possibly shrink your shorts in the dryer," Daisy shot back. She smiled. "Those are your things left in the hamper, aren't they?"

No one said a word. This was new. What had got into Daisy, acting up like this. So cryptic. It was so out of character that nobody knew what to do. And yet Vladimir couldn't let this go unpunished. It occurred to me that Daisy might like to be fired. They'd have to pay up, wouldn't they? It was known that they were very cavalier about paying. She had no expenses. But she did keep track. Her back wages would add up to a nice sum.

"Claire doesn't have enough money to stop work for a couple of months." Isolde sounded angry. Naturally. She wanted me here with her, handing in my tidy rent each week in cash.

"I think it would be all right," Wolfgang said. "You could do the still photography."

"Oh, I'm not good enough to be professional." I laughed.

"That's true," Isolde said. "You're not."

"Yes, you are." Daisy poked me, changing sides. "Those shots you did of the children were lovely!"

"There's a bit more to it than that," Reiner tut-tutted with a patronizing smirk.

"Claire can't leave Munich now." Isolde looked around worriedly. "She's just beginning to save money."

"Yes, I could," I announced defiantly, noticing Blacky's interest in Tupelo waver and hoping it was due to my independent swagger. "I can go wherever I choose." Then, in a smaller voice, "I'd just have to save a bit more first." Everyone was looking at me. "And then I would work hard when I got back. I would work really, really hard!" I heard myself. I sounded like a child.

"The thing is," Chartreuse said, "everyone comes back from India looking like merde."

"What do you mean?" I asked.

"Everyone gets sick. Or covered with some fungus."

"And yet here you are, alive."

"A girl I was with died in Afghanistan. A Dutch girl. We foolishly shared a mere sip from a glass of unboiled water."

Isolde said, "But you didn't get sick?"

"If you reach the age of five in Afghanistan, it is pretty hard to kill you. We have enough antibodies for ten people. I should have known better than to let her drink, that's all." He looked desolate with the memory.

"I see."

"Filthy country," Harry told Daisy.

Tupelo said, "Blacky would make sure nothing happened to me, wouldn't you, darlink?"

"I would shoot you up with gamma globulin before we left." He moved his lips at her with a push.

"Anyway," Reiner said, "no one wants to photograph a girl with fungus on her face, eh?"

"I'm healthy as a horse," I announced defiantly. "I just don't have enough money."

Everyone laughed.

"Oh, you poor little thing!" Tupelo said dismissively. She would sum you up with her eyes and, finding you unable to advance her in any way, give you a swift write-off. She had a way of looking at you as though you were an invalid. It was a look full of false pity, demeaning and leaving you feeling superfluous.

To ease my embarrassment, Blacky said, "There is nothing so refreshing as a healthy woman." But then he turned bright red, as though regretting his words. He'd said it out of kindness, but there was truth in it, for him. Again he looked at me and I at him. Tupelo Honig might have captured him, but the look between us had fireworks in it. And I would have my fireworks.

"But my dear," Harry told me gently, "a model only has so much time when things are going well. Once you fall from fashion, the cash flow stops abruptly. You must make hay as the sun shines, my dear."

I was unimpressed with this argument. I would be young forever.

"Still," Blacky pointed out evenly, "a trip like that . . . difficulties would surely arise."

"Not if you have a translator with you," Chartreuse assured him.

"Well, do you speak Urdu?"

"That I do not speak but we can easily hire some—"

"I do," Daisy spoke up. "I speak a lovely Urdu."

"Don't be ridiculous," Harry said.

"What ridiculous," I interjected. "Daisy grew up all around the world, didn't you, Daisy?"

"That's right," she said. "My Punjabi's a bit rusty, but it ought to suffice in a pinch."

"And I speak all the local dialects one needs overland," Chartreuse put in.

"I see," Blacky said, "a real gadabout." He said this almost arrogantly and he said it to Chartreuse. I hadn't heard him use that tone before. Then he said, "Chartreuse . . . sounds French. Surely not an Afghani name . . ." His smile was sweet.

Chartreuse returned his sweetness. "I said my mother was Afghani. My father was from Toulouse. But when I was born, I did not want to come out. I was almost a ten-month baby. Really. I was green. Covered in green slime. *Merde alors!* my father cried out upon seeing me. *Il est chartreuse!*"

They all laughed. I was appalled and revolted. I wished he hadn't told me that. "What did you mean," I turned back to Wolfgang, changing the subject, "about the still photography? You mean I would get paid?"

"Not a lot, assuredly," he hiccupped. "You've not made a name for yourself as a photographer, have you?"

"No." I ducked my head. "We all know I'm the amateur." I'd heard Isolde say Wolfgang was mean with money—for all his success. I could feel him watching me, which pleased me. The great filmmaker captivated by little me. Still, he looked so long and hard there were moments I felt intruded upon. His eyes were not just pleasured, but scrutinizing.

Isolde put in, "It isn't as though photography were brain surgery."

Reiner sat up at this and sputtered, "And it's also not as though just anyone can pick up a camera and make a go of it."

"Oh, calm down," Daisy sassed him. "Nobody's challenging your profession."

"Surely you could muddle your way through it," Harry said, "I mean with so many exciting subjects. Even if you botched the half of it, some of it would surely turn out right." He turned to Wolfgang. "And that half might be frightfully exciting."

"Film is still expensive," I pointed out.

"Certainly that would be included in expenses," Chartreuse negotiated.

"Yes, I suppose so." Wolfgang placed his knife and fork down on the plate in a final gesture. "But why not come?" He rubbed the palms of his hands together. "It would cut costs to have an unknown."

Reiner said, "Of course, if I decided to come that would solve all your problems. Then Claire wouldn't even have to come."

"But," I was outraged, "I might *want* to come."

"Claire could still do some of the photography," Isolde said. "She could be a backup. For insurance."

"You wouldn't need insurance with me as photographer," Reiner pointed out.

"But you know," Wolfgang said, "that just might work . . ."

"Look," I protested, "I'm just a model. Maybe I'm in over my head here."

Blacky turned in his chair. "No, but being a model has its own cachet. Fashion and film mix very well, I think. The newspapers love that sort of thing, don't they? You could send back intermittent stories, Claire. They could print them. *Quick* would love a travel story like that. Didn't they use you on a cover?"

He'd said my name so gently. And he was sticking up for me.

He might be dazzled by Tupelo Honig but he was on my side. I felt it. And what an idea! Artists weren't worth their salt until they'd traveled off the beaten path. I'd be gaining experience. And an eye. I *would* become a real artist. Just a different sort. *And* one could make a living at photography.

"You'll have to write the stories." I smiled gratefully at him. "But it's a wonderful dream. One day I think I might manage the pictures." I frowned, remembering the reality. "If only you could wait a couple more months."

Blacky said, "I'm disappointed. In a couple more months, you will have met a handsome young man."

Isolde joined his mocking tone. "Who will help you spend your money."

"And," Blacky reached toward me with his eyes, "he will have filled your head with dreams . . ." He bit the rim of his wineglass, his white teeth on the edge. The wine swirled in a tantalizing circle. Was he flirting with me?

I shook my head, denying such a future. But I raised my glass to him and finished it. To add to my confusion, Blacky now turned back to Tupelo. Right away, she was basking in his refound admiration. I caught the glint of satisfaction in her eye. Gaggle on, she must have been thinking to herself as she shimmied in place, I've got the goods.

That's all right, I told myself with all my newly learned bitter, sophisticated reasoning. Let her have him. He'd be back. And how did he know I'd done a cover for *Quick* if he hadn't seen it? So he did like me. I didn't have him, but there was something in his eyes that told me one day, if I was lucky . . .

Wolfgang put his plushy hand on top of mine. "Where is it you said you were from?"

"I'm from New York," I said.

"But not New York City, surely?" Reiner said, already knowing the answer. His hair had come loose from its rubber band and

I couldn't help thinking he looked like an old transvestite done up like a nun at the end of a long, happy night.

"No," I said. "Queens. Just outside."

"Oh." He caught the eyes of all of them. "Queens! That stretch of curb that lines the Van Wyck Expressway from the airport all the way to the city. I know. I've been to New York so many times." He slipped a spoonful of peas into his mouth and chewed them thoughtfully. "Where stray dogs roam. Isn't it true?" He didn't wait for an answer. "Not a shred of culture. And graffiti everywhere. Dreadful!" He turned to Tupelo. "All the houses have bars on the windows."

"Uch," she said.

My throat closed and I could barely speak. I wanted to defend my home. But where would I start and what would I do, describe the trees, the beauty of the old Victorians, the rain-washed light? Whatever I would say, he'd turn it around and make me look foolish. He had the knack. "What's the matter, Reiner?" I said. "Do you hate Americans?"

Isolde raised a hand. "Oh, please, Claire, don't go getting defensive and patriotic. It's so gauche."

"Especially from a country involved in an illegal war," Wolfgang put in.

"Where in India," Harry kindly changed the subject, "would you be going?"

Wolfgang looked to Chartreuse, who said blithely, "To Goa, of course."

"Goa?" Harry said. "Portuguese Goa? That's where all the hippies and drug addicts go. Beach after beach of naked Europeans, isn't it?"

Chartreuse said, "Goa's wonderful."

"You'd get sick of that quickly enough," Harry said. "There is one place, though, in the Indian Himalayas . . . a Tibetan Buddhist refuge."

"Ah," Chartreuse remembered. "McLeod Ganj. Just above Dharamsala."

"Isn't that where the Dalai Lama lives?" Blacky put in. Wolfgang said, "Now that would be interesting!"

"Me, too!" I heard myself lament. "I want to meet him, too!"

Harry fondled his earlobe. "There was some talk within the trade a while ago about a missing tabernacle, a gift from Tibetans to Papist Catholics, as it happened, who'd been sent to China as missionaries then lost their way. Lavish with rare gems, that sort of thing. Was supposed to have turned up there and then didn't. Raised quite a fuss. I must have that article somewhere. Would be lovely to stumble across that, eh?"

"There it would be," Daisy said, "just waiting for you."

It was very late. Still no one seemed to wish to be the first to leave. Suddenly I felt so warm I became dizzy. I excused myself and went down the hallway to the bathroom. I was just consoling myself in the mirror, washing my hands under a stream of delicious icy water, when Tupelo slipped in and shut the door behind her.

"Oops," I smiled, feeling slightly better, "just going."

But she hadn't come to use the ladies'. "Let me see your bosom," she said, peeking over my shoulder.

I thought I must have got something on Isolde's pretty blouse. Interested, we both looked down. She took the elastic top of my blouse and, with two hands, slipped both sides over my shoulders and to my waist. I stood before the mirror, exposed, my arms imprisoned in the sleeves. From behind, she weighed me with her eyes.

"What a curvy little thing you are," she said. Then she threw back her head and laughed, one up on me.

"Keep your hands to yourself," I said, regaining my composure, pulling my blouse back in place. It had all happened so fast.

But it was too late. She'd seen the pupils of my eyes dilated with pleasure in the mirror.

"*Sei vorsichtig, Kleine,*" she warned me pleasantly, looking keenly at herself now, for she'd accomplished her task. I knew enough German to understand. Be careful, little one.

"And just what is that supposed to mean?"

"You know exactly what I mean," she hissed in her heavy English. "Europe is not like America, you know. You'd just better keep out of my way."

"Hey, don't be so shy." I returned her intimidating tone with an exaggerated swagger of the head, reenacting washing my hands, the soap slithering in and out of my fingers. "Just spit out the way you feel," I said, not feeling as brave as I sounded.

She ignored the irony. "Things happen here to young girls." The way she'd said it, it frightened me. I became aware of her size and strength. We stood there for a moment, at an impasse.

Then she said, "You're not the first little flootzie to step in my path, you know. They come and go like, like popcorn."

"Flootzie?" How dare she! She was the flootzie. I mean, floozy. I returned her scoffing tone.

"Like popcorn, eh. Really? How unusual. That's quite a threat."

But she wasn't wounded by the absence of subtleties in one of her many languages. She smiled, a nasty smile that reached one eye and left a twitch.

"It's your boyfriend you should be worrying about, not me," I came up with, scrambling for any defense.

Isolde and Vladimir were coming down the hallway to go check on the children. Vladimir was grumbling, "I've got to find a flat nearby, that's all. I can't be wasting time driving back and forth."

Isolde was laughing and hopeful. "I'll help you look," she murmured in the voice she saved for him.

Tupelo put a reassuring palm on my shoulder, as though we'd been in there confiding secrets. "Go home. Things will be safer for you in the States." She let me pass. "I promise."

I wiped my hands hastily on a towel and got away.

She made light conversation with Isolde and Vladimir.

Trembling, I went in and regained my seat.

"You must try these peppers." Chartreuse leaned over me with the frying pan when I sat down. "These are *magnifique!*" He swaggered the top of his head. "Hold your plate up. Careful! This oil is hot."

Tupelo was just returning to her seat, her face a radiant mask of changing smiles. Harry leaned back at that moment and Tupelo seemed to trip and bang into Chartreuse. The oil splashed down, splattering onto my lap.

"Ow!" I cried out. It was furiously hot. I couldn't believe how much it hurt. Everyone made confused and sympathetic noises and I wanted to make light of it, but the oil blazed into the inside of my thigh and it was all I could do to keep from crying.

"How clumsy of me!" Tupelo clapped her hands together.

Everyone rushed to assure her that of course it hadn't been her fault at all.

"Oh, the poor thing! Oh, the poor thing!" she kept saying. But she didn't say a word to me. Blacky came over to me. He pushed the folds of the green skirt up and inspected the angry map of red on my thigh. I took no joy in this. At the moment I was in so much pain I could only rock back and forth.

With a concerned look, Blacky lifted me by the hand and I followed him into the living room. He led me to the couch and Harry went to Isolde's medicine cabinet for gauze and salve. For a few minutes, I saw nothing but white pain. But after a while, the intensity subsided and I could almost see the humor in the situation. Tupelo watched with a feverishly craned neck from her spot at the table, hardly noticing Wolfgang, who had seen his chance and was gesticulating at her in vivid conversation. I imagined Tupelo was intensely frustrated at that moment. Then I heard her say, "Can you imagine? She exposed her breasts to me in the toilet!" I don't know what they all thought.

Blacky's gentleness was something I wasn't prepared for. I certainly understood why he'd become a doctor. There was something so empathetic and thoughtful about his touch. There seemed to be nothing else he could have been.

"I know it hurts," he said in a caring, intimate tone. "The pain will subside shortly." He seemed totally taken up with me and I relaxed.

I imagined him in the hospital in Vietnam, saying the same words over and over to American boys with gravely serious injuries. For that reason alone, my heart would have flown to him. When he finished applying the salve and, with a feather-light touch, wrapped the wound, with me lifting my leg at the appropriate moments so he could slip the gauze strands under and through, he looked into my eyes with concern.

"Thank you." I smiled. "I'll be fine. Really."

He, too, relaxed. "Do you always get into trouble like this?" He smiled, too. There was a hint of mischief in his sparkling eyes. Well, we were both over the limit.

Suddenly embarrassed, I drew my legs together.

He gave me a patronizing little pat on the knee and stood up, the cool, professional doctor once again, and I his little charge. He offered me his hand with deliberate politeness, steadied himself, and escorted me back to the table.

Tupelo held up one arm and rattled her noisy bracelets, as if she were calling a cat. Blacky seemed to float toward her.

Everyone made a fuss for a moment or two.

"Has anyone seen that piano player Emmanuel at the Kleine Rondelle? "Isolde changed the subject and they were all off on a different foot.

"Ach, that reminds me!" Vladimir jumped up with an uncharacteristic burst of energy and went to the stereo to gather his records.

Wolfgang was talking to me; my face was toward him but my full attention was with Blacky and Tupelo. My ears strained to hear everything they said. After our short encounter, I felt proprietary rights toward Blacky.

"You know," I overheard him tell Tupelo, "my mother telephoned this evening. She loves the theater. You can't imagine how excited she was when I told her I'd taken you out. Really. She's a fan."

"Drop me back at my hotel after this." She smiled at him. "I'll give you a photograph with a really special message for her."

"I'll bet she will," Reiner, listening, too, said to me.

I felt sick. All at once, it became obvious to me that they would sleep together. It was hopeless. I knew I'd had too much to drink. Everyone was laughing.

As I left the room I looked in the mirror. Above Tupelo's shoulder I saw Blacky's face. He watched me go. He could have had me, but he watched me go.

I went to my bed. I didn't cry. I lay there looking out the window at the navy darkness and the drowning fall of stars. I pulled myself up to the sill. I looked to the east.

chapter seven

That probably would have been the end of it. That sort of people makes all kinds of plans at parties and nothing ever comes of them. But then something happened that changed everything.

It was some days later. I was sitting on the window seat thinking what a wonderful apartment for Vladimir for his sculpting, so filled with light. I wasn't surprised Isolde felt assured he'd be back. The flat alone was compelling enough to draw him. And it was odd here, with the bronze women statues in positions this way and that. They looked longing and desolate, not sexy and brazen as I'd first thought. It was as though they missed him, too.

I'd just finished cleaning my brushes, having formally readied them for retirement. I was enjoying a pale cup of tea with no milk, which is not the way I usually like it. I was feeling a little perverse and I was still sulking about my drawings being judged no good. I couldn't just stop being who I was like that, in a flash. And yet I had. But giving up a lifetime of dreams is not an easy business. Harry had told me to go sleep on the idea and for once in my life I took someone's advice. It's not everyone who gets a chance for guidance from a master, I realized; I ought to be looking at this as a gift.

Halfhearted little snowflakes fluttered, directionless, through the sky, but they had no real chance. The afternoon sun kept bullying its way through, knowing that the winter was over. Islands of daffodils clung confidently to the light. I had no plans for the evening. I'd enjoyed my afternoon of solitude but now I'd had enough of my own company and was wishing someone would come. Then the telephone rang.

"Hello?" I said eagerly.

"Hier ist Tupelo Honig," a cold voice said.

"Oh," I said, just as coldly. "Hello. It's Claire."

"Claire?" she repeated, pretending to be puzzled.

"From the other night," I reminded her. "Here."

"Ah," she said, unimpressed. "Be so kind. My luggage is arriving within the hour. Would you see to it?"

What's this? I thought. "Are you coming to stay here?" I asked.

"Yes," she said, "I'm renting the small apartment while we're here."

The small apartment? *My* apartment? "There must be some mistake." I stood up.

"No mistake, darlink. Isolde has it all arranged. I'll be needing somewhere quiet to study my lines."

I was outraged. How dare Isolde rent my apartment? I was paying rent. I said so.

"Oh, I don't know anything about that," she said in a hurry. "Just look out for my bags, will you? And bring them up if the driver won't? You are a darlink."

I could hear Isolde coming. She was a large woman and she had her own rhythm of taking the stairs.

"Tupelo," I said decisively, "there is no such thing as the letter *k* at the end of the word 'darling.' " I hung up the phone.

I'd better look as if I'm doing something, I told myself out of habit, and then remembered it was Isolde who owed *me* an explanation.

Isolde burst into the room. She looked at me with glowing eyes. "You won't believe it," she said.

"Isolde," I began.

"Claire! Listen! Frau Zwekl is dead!"

I looked at her. "What?" I said.

"She's dead."

"No," I said. "How?"

The phone began to ring again.

Isolde shrugged and licked her lips. "Yes." She sat down excitedly and did not pick up the phone. This was rare indeed. I imagined I knew instantly what she was thinking. She could install Vladimir in Frau Zwekl's rambling apartment. He would be near the children. And, of course, her.

"Isolde," I frowned at her disapprovingly, "how did she die?"

Isolde leaned forward and said, in a conspiratorial tone, "She cracked her head and broke her hip. She fell getting out of her bathtub."

"Oh, no. No, no!" And I hadn't even gone in to check on her! I lowered myself into the chair.

"Four days ago!"

Four days! The day of the party. The very day I'd met Blacky.

"And here's the ironic part. Herr Kleiderschrank said he tried to get her to go to the doctor and she wouldn't go. He told her she'd better watch her health, he told her she was looking for trouble, they say."

"Who's 'they'?"

"Herr Kleiderschrank from the second floor. You know him?"

I shook my head vaguely, half remembering a slim, quick-footed little man dancing up and down the stairs. Frau Zwekl detested him and made a fishy face whenever he went by. "Go on," I said.

"Well. He told her she must go to renew her blood pressure medicine. She refused to go and he threatened her. Good-heartedly threatened her. You know. But then she promised she was going to see her doctor soon and what happened next? She fell and cracked her head and that was it, she just lay there!"

God rest her soul—my heart sent out its message before my atheism reinstalled itself.

"Well, everyone knows she's always out there. But Herr Kleiderschrank has nothing to do but mind everyone else's business, you know. So he was the one to notice."

I realized she must feel guilty to say such a thing. I warmed to her. Isolde acted tough but her heart was in the right place. She wore a smart dress, yellow and black, and earrings, cameos—they were Vladimir's mother's. She would never give them back. Never. They dangled now, dull ornaments on dainty chains. She went on. "Herr Kleiderschrank went in the next day with the police. There she was, dead! And the place cold as a morgue. All the heat must fly up to us because her apartment was cold. And that's the way it always must have been."

We watched each other with horrified eyes. Hers were sparkling.

"What a place she's got! He was tickled pink to get inside. No one ever gets in. Not even him. You leave your laundry at the door and that's where you pick it up. All old paraphernalia from before the war. And not the second war, the first! Oh, Kleiderschrank was carried away with the excitement. Nothing ever happens to him."

I felt so sad. I remembered how I was always flying by lately and never stopping to chat. All she'd wanted was a little confidentiality. I knew our chats had given her pleasure and I'd deprived her of them out of selfishness. I felt ashamed.

Isolde, having departed with the brunt of her news and receiving as much reaction mileage from me as she was going to get, picked up the phone to spread the word.

I remembered Tupelo Honig but my heart wasn't in making interruptions and recriminations. I just sat there and listened as Isolde telephoned around and I reheard the story again and again. After the fifth time I could have retold it in German myself. Poor Frau Zwekl.

Isolde held her hand across the mouthpiece and said, "You look tired, Claire. Why don't you go lie down for a bit."

I knew she wanted to be rid of me. She was deciding how she would tell me about Tupelo Honig. Down in the street, I heard a car door slam. That would be Tupelo's bags.

"Yes," I said, stretching the top half of my body sideways. "I think I will." I blew a kiss and left.

There was a commotion out in the apartment while I lay there. Well, I was ready for them. Just let her come in here and try to move me into the nursery with Daisy and the boys. Just let her. I was prepared to pack my bags and leave. There was a charming place near the Englischer Garten called Erna Morena. Erna Morena had been a silent screen star and her daughter had made a pension filled with her memorabilia. A lot of the models stayed there. So could I.

But then, as it so often is when you're prepared to stand firm, nothing happened. I put on the "Consolation Number Three" of Franz Liszt—a beautiful piano piece that sounds like water tripping over stones—in memory of Frau Zwekl and fell asleep and when I woke up, everything was the same as usual. Daisy was setting the table and the boys were eating soldiers of toast with cinnamon and butter.

"She's gone out," Daisy said over her shoulder.

I sat at the table with the boys. Dirk perched his fork and let fly a juicy piece of toast. It landed on my nose. This must have been the funniest thing that ever happened for the amount of time they laughed. Then, wiping her eyes with the tip of her apron of 1940s cherries, Daisy sat down across from me. "Did you hear?" she said finally.

"Frau Zwekl?"

"Yeah. Tough, isn't it?"

"Yes."

"Hope I don't go like that. All alone. No one to care. Well, what do you say, boys? Shall we go for our walk?"

"Yay!" The boys climbed over each other.

I stood up. "I think I'll go back to bed."

My room had grown chilly and I covered myself with the eiderdown. I had to take a train to a studio in the eastern part of Germany that night for a week's work and I knew I ought to rest.

I lay there. I heard them go out for their walk. But then I heard the front door open again.

Oh, I thought. They've come back. But it wasn't them. It was a quiet person. Someone crept around the hallway. I lay still, pretending I wasn't there.

I felt someone at the entrance to my room. My door swung open silently. I could see the threshold from the mirror. It was Tupelo.

She came into my room. I lay there watching her through half-closed eyes. She stood before the window looking out. Then she shut the door. Like a whisper, she climbed in under the sheets beside me.

I was still as a dead girl. I could hardly breathe.

We lay like that a long, long time. And then, just as the bells rang out in the kirk tower over the street, she slipped her silky fingers in between my legs and touched me there.

When it was over she took me by the neck. "Don't you ever tell a soul," she warned. "Promise."

I studied her, naked except for her green pearls. She was perfect. Except for one L-shaped scar on her shoulder blade, as though a tuck had been taken in her body, there wasn't a mark on her. I raised myself up on one elbow. I traced the scar down to the curve of her back and I felt her body shiver. "All right, all right. I promise." I shrugged. I watched her animosity subside. But I wasn't afraid of her anymore. If anything, it was she who should be afraid of me. For although she was the one who had boldly come to me, once the line had been crossed, something had shifted in the power department. It was I who took over, seeking her most hidden places with such appetite that she cried out not once but many times. And I knew she would be back.

One dream out the window, one in the door. Learning I was no artist. And now this. What was I, after all? What sort of person? And what had taught me to be so expert at an art of which I knew nothing? Or had thought I knew nothing. Because it seemed I knew instinctively just what to do. It is the hunger that pleases. And I had the hunger.

chapter eight

The next days were busy ones and I was out of town, a good thing, too, because I needed time to think. I was far away up at Bauer Berg Kunstadt. This was a studio near the Czechoslovakian border. They worked you hard up there, but they paid full catalog rate and fed you well, marvelously well. All the models sat together at night in the warm and cozy hotel restaurant, ate bratwurst and *Jäger Schnitzel* and drank white wine till they couldn't see straight. I was starting to enjoy those enforced convivialities. I was beginning to understand what was being said.

While I was there, I confided to the photographer that I was saving to buy a good, professional camera. When we had our break, he came over to me and told me about a little secondhand shop in the town where you could buy really excellent equipment; the town was so far from everywhere that he was sure I could get a good deal—much better than I would get in Munich.

The next day we finished early and I borrowed the photographer's bicycle to ride into town. The store was down a cobbled road and the cameras in the display window were mucky with age. The owner turned out to be a kindly old man with one arm and a limp, who came rushing out from a kitchen when I opened the door and the hanging bells tippled. Not only was he delighted to share his expertise and advise me on which camera would suit me, but he was thrilled to speak a halting English.

Although it was old, I decided upon a Nikon, an excellent camera, he said. It would never fail me. None of the newfangled attachments came with it but it was as good and professional a mechanism as I'd ever find. I didn't wrangle. I paid him in cash. He was so excited at the sight of it he threw in a zoom lens.

When I came home Friday night, I was whooped. I staggered up the stairs, not wanting to even look at Frau Zwekl's door. But as I crept past, noise and music came through and I thought, What's this, a funeral party? It sounded a little rowdy for Frau Zwekl's sort of funeral. It took me until the next landing until I realized Frau Zwekl had no one to party for her. I went back down the stairs. The door cracked open with a push. Everyone who was normally upstairs was now down here. I stood there.

Harry came down the stairs from Isolde's apartment with a bucket of ice.

"What's going on?" I asked.

"Claire? When did you get back?"

"I just walked in."

"You look awful."

"What's everybody doing here?"

"Isolde arranged with Mr. Kleiderschrank for Tupelo to stay here in Frau Zwekl's apartment."

"So you're having a shindig?"

"Isolde has to wait here with the building superintendent for Frau Zwekl's solicitor from Zurich. There was a snowstorm in the mountains and he was delayed. We're keeping her company."

He gave a sidelong glance into the apartment. "It's so depressing waiting by yourself."

I looked in. Herr Kleiderschrank was mournfully exhibiting Frau Zwekl's 1890s Japanese Hirado porcelain vase. It was a soft light blue and there were cranes flying on it. Next thing you knew, he'd be hauling out the Rosenthal.

"Coming in?" Harry went over my head with the ice bucket and gave a thrifty sidestep past me.

"I'll pass. I'm beat."

"You're missing a lovely party," he said. "Oh. A Herr Binnemann telephoned. I took the call. His number's on the table."

The apartment smelled stuffy. I opened the windows to the rain and spotted the piece of paper for me on the table. It was a number in Switzerland. More work, I thought dully. It's amazing how until you get work the very word seems like magic and then you begin to take it for granted and realize why they call it "work." It occurred to me that Tupelo would wonder why I hadn't come in. Perhaps it would even please her. She would think she'd scared me off. Suddenly I was tired of being tired. I washed my face and went back downstairs.

The first one I saw was Blacky. He was sitting on the couch. Tupelo's eyes charged with something when she saw me but she wouldn't look in mine. I didn't know if she was glad or upset. At that moment I didn't care. The most important thing, I imagined, still willing to cooperate with her dictate, was to ignore her. I supposed at that moment that I could pretend to forget all about it if she could. The room was full, they were all there, even Chartreuse, but I saw Blacky right away. He seemed strong and pink against everyone else. It was as if he gleamed with cleanliness and good health. It occurred to me he might be the reason she'd slept with me. Maybe it had been nothing more than a ploy to move me away from him, like in chess when you corner a pawn.

Chartreuse was playing the guitar, an American song, "It Never Rains in Southern California," and some of them were actually singing, in that bump-de-bump German way. Outside, the rain came down. There were cups of tea, tangerine skins, and empty champagne glasses on the mahogany coffee table.

"Guess what, I've bought a camera!"

"No!" Chartreuse cried.

I could tell he was furious. If I bought anything, he wanted to be the salesman, or at least the agent.

"Yes," I said. "I've brought it down."

Everyone except Tupelo got up and tromped to the table, where I carefully slid it out of its soft gray pouch.

"That?" Isolde sputtered.

"This old one?" Chartreuse said.

"Yes," I said.

"You must be joking," Daisy said.

"You can't go wrong with a Nikon," Reiner pitched in doubtfully. "Still, the idea was a camera, Claire, not a corpse." He guffawed at his wit.

I was a little hurt. Couldn't they see what a wonderful mechanism I had here?

"It's lovely." Harry picked it up. "Timeless."

"Thank you, Harry," I said.

"You'll get yourself dirty, Harry," Daisy said.

"Well," I said. "I haven't had time to dust it off."

Isolde suddenly threw back her head and roared with laughter. Vladimir wasn't here and so she was her normal intimidating self. Before long, they were all laughing along with her. I stood there, my lips pursed, my indignation glowing like hot coals.

Tupelo was looking smug. I hated that look. I wondered how I could have even touched her.

Blacky came up behind me. "How's that wound coming along?" he said.

"Oh. Fine," I lied. It throbbed as we spoke and I could feel myself turning red from the memory of him seated at my parted knees.

"You'll be spending all your money on film now," he said, shaking his head disapprovingly at the camera.

"Manuel, wot?" Harry rocked to and fro in a tipsy reel. "Not automatic at all."

"Yes," I admitted, not minding that. "The man who sold it to me advised against automatic. He said more could go wrong."

"Well? Shall we go get more champagne?" Harry asked. "To celebrate the beginning of your new career?"

"Sure," I said, as it was in my honor. "I'll come. Anyone else?"

But no one else wanted to come. I'd secretly hoped Blacky would step forward and I'd be able to sit beside him. He stood there with his hands in his pockets, though, and peered at me and I thought for a moment, Oh, God, she's told him. But of course she hadn't. I wished I hadn't said I'd go. It was raining. All I wanted to do was relax and now here I was off again. And I half hated Harry to take his car out of his hard-earned parking space just for me. Parking was always a problem. But then I remembered the honesty he'd shown me—telling me the truth about myself. He could just as well have tossed me off with a lie, but he hadn't. It must have cost him to hurt me like that . . . and I thought, oh, well, it would be fun. We drove to the Roland's Eck for the wine. The only cold they had was *Sekt*, which is German champagne.

"Get the Henkel Trocken," Harry said. "It's lovely when it's cold." We bought six bottles and were off again.

"You know, Harry," I told him, "if you didn't drink so much, you'd make some girl a great catch."

"Oh, I don't drink so very much, you know," he protested.

"I'm what you call a cheap date. Three or four glasses of wine and everyone can have their way with me."

"I see."

"By the way, what do you think of our filmmaker, Wolfgang Scherer?"

"I've never even seen anything he's done."

"Neither have I," he said and we laughed.

"Do you think he slept with Tupelo?" I broke in.

"Who? Wolfgang? Oh, no. She's keeping him for advancement, nothing more. He loves to film her. I suppose she's what you'd call his muse. Together they make enormous amounts of money."

"Must be tough. Daisy says they always write about him in the papers. He gets great reviews."

Harry contented himself with his earlobe. "Oh, that's because the Germans love all that wicked self-abasement." Then he added, "I rather think they pay him so much attention because she's in his films. As much as the other way around."

We were silent. "What do you think of *her*?" he said while his old Jaguar percolated in the rain at the red light in front of the Hertie department store.

"The Hungarian rhapsody?"

"Yes. Do you like her? And I think she's from Estonia. She only learned her English in a classroom in St. Petersburg."

I said nothing.

He gave me a quick, suspicious look. "You're not jealous?"

"How can I be jealous? She's old enough to be my, well, sister."

"Atta girl. Don't let her know. She'll eat you for supper."

I heard myself saying, "She actually grabbed me in the bathroom at the party. She—" I stopped. "And then she warned me."

"Did she? I'm surprised. You must frighten her. That's good, of course."

"It was kind of horrifying." Then, "She's terribly sexy, isn't she. Kind of like a sexual predator. A sadistic one." I went on, not caring.

"She can tell you like him."

"Is it that obvious?"

"My dear. You turn vermillion at the sight of him."

"Shit," I said.

"Not to everyone. But Chartreuse sees it. He doesn't like it, either. His eyes dart about like a jealous cat. It's pitiful."

"Oh, Chartreuse! He's not my boyfriend."

"I'm glad to hear it."

"Why?"

"Oh, I don't know. He seems the type one imagines cuts one's throat for the luggage."

"Tch. He's not like that at all."

"All right. I'm sure I don't know what type he is." He smacked his cheek in a drama of frustration. "And there's something I haven't told you."

"What?"

"Well, you're not to mention it."

"All right. Honor bright. What's up?"

"Someone stole Tupelo's green pearls."

A lift of something ran through me. "Who told you that?"

"She did."

Of course I thought of Chartreuse. I remembered the silver forks. "So, why shouldn't I breathe a word?"

"Maybe she just reported them stolen to get the insurance money. I don't know. But she did report it to the police. She asked me not to tell anyone. Not to be paranoid but sometimes I think it might do us all good to take a break from Munich."

"Yes, well. Look, Harry, it's easy for you to say just up and leave. You've got pots of money."

"I could always lend you some."

"No. Thank you, but no. I just never know how long I'm going to be making any. In this business you never do know."

"Such an affectation, Claire. Acting like a Goody Two-shoes when we all know you are as devious as the next."

I looked out the window at the pouring rain and the blurring lights, trying not to think of what I'd done. I cranked open the window so he wouldn't see my face. Had Tupelo confided in him? No, of course not. If a clear conscience has the strength of ten men then a guilty one certainly weakens you. I was nervous as a cat. But his news was sinking in. "So you really think there's a thief? And I'm sure you think it's Chartreuse."

"No. No, you're right. I'm sure he's nothing quite so dashing. Don't jewel thieves plan rather glamorous crimes?"

"I don't know. I wonder why they didn't interrogate me? I would make a wonderful suspect."

"No," Harry went on, "Chartreuse is more interested in his joint and his meal and his pleasure. In the here and now. See what I mean? He'd far more likely be the slash-the-purse-strings-when-no-one's-looking sort of fellow. Then over the fence with the goods, if you see my point. I'm sure he values being part of the gang at Isolde's more than acquiring a string of pearls that would bring the police straight to him the minute he tried to see how much they'd fetch. He's a damned slippery bloke but he's strictly small-time, if you ask me. He hasn't a farthing. Of course he loves to gad about with you. Makes him look the man about town, being seen with a model."

"It's not like I'm rich, Harry. I'm more like an indentured servant."

"You're young and thin and American. That's all one needs these days."

I yawned with fatigue.

"Cranky?" He looked at me from the side.

"I guess I am." I shivered. "I'm cold and damp."

"I do hope Vladimir isn't there when we get back. For someone who's left his wife, he's hanging about an awful lot."

"I like Vladimir."

"Oh, yes, I know. The great artist. Everyone likes Vladimir," he muttered sourly.

"Is it just that it makes it so damned inconvenient to flirt when he's there?"

"On the contrary. That never stops Isolde. She flirts more because she thinks it will make him jealous. It never does, though. *Malheureusement*. No, it's not his presence I despise but his absence I require. I just like the pretense of being the man of the house. You know, feet on the sofa, the *Times* strewn about. Even the kiddies grow rather accustomed to me."

"It's just Isolde who treats you so badly, then."

"Yes, actually. Well, I'm pigeon-toed," Harry said with distaste, as if that explained it.

I imagined it must be difficult for an aesthete to be so physically repugnant. "I wanted to see the world," I said, smiling at him. "Now at least I've met my first full-blown masochist."

"Claire," he touched my nose, "you're a nice sort of girl. But I'm certain that Catholic school in Queens you attended was seething with masochists."

I thought of my old Christ the King, that ugly modern building set in the midst of the cemetery with its acres of rolling hills and ornate gravestones. The Daughters of Wisdom, outfitted like Dutch cleansers in those days, gliding through the polished hallways. There was nothing masochistic about any of them. If anything, they'd egged us on to be liberated, useful women.

"Oh, and *Schatz*," he interrupted my thoughts, "don't bother too much about Blacky."

I tried not to look too attentive. "Why not?"

"Well. You might do well to consider it a schoolgirl crush. You don't even know him. I can't help feeling you have no chance. Oh, don't look like that. You know what I mean."

"No, I'm sorry, I don't."

"Well, his family, for one thing. They'd never allow him to marry someone of your . . . er . . ."

"Class?"

"Social caliber."

"Jesus, Harry. You talk as if we're living in the Victorian era."

"Things don't change much over the centuries when it comes to land acquisition, my dear. And that's what marriage within that family is about. Tupelo's money could refurbish many an exhibitable ancestral chamber for that bled-out clan."

"A plastic surgeon isn't exactly a low-income job."

Harry made a face. "Running off to Vietnam and donating a year of your life to broken soldiers isn't exactly building an empire. It holds you back. Er . . . financially, I mean. Pop in that lighter, would you! Bloody social democrats. Meanwhile others are furthering their careers. What he makes is chicken feed compared to what she pulls in."

"I never said I want to marry him, Harry. I only want him for illicit sex."

I almost laughed out loud at Harry's shocked expression. He recovered quickly enough, though. He said, "Well, that's good, then, because he's asked her to marry him."

I'd just turned to reach for the plaid horse blanket from the backseat and that jealous place inside me shrieked with protest. I bit my lip and wrapped the blanket around me like a shawl. Back and forth went the windshield wipers, back and forth.

"I wanted to break it to you gently."

"Gee. Thanks."

"Well, I didn't want you to hear upstairs . . . in front of that lot."

"Oh. I see. Thanks for that, Harry." I tried to smile.

The lighter popped out. He put a cigarette into an ivory carved holder and lit it.

"Harry!" I recovered enough to say. "*Such* an affectation." I couldn't resist.

Unharmed, he said, "Not at all. Affectation is when someone of a lower class *pretends* to be upper."

"Ah," I said, "like me."

"Darling. If the shoe fits . . ."

I was taken aback. Then I assured him meanly, "By the way, engaged is not married. So don't worry your pretty little head. I've got just as much chance with him as you have of getting Isolde."

"Ah, but that's where you're wrong. Once they divorce, Isolde will no longer be the countess, will she?"

"What do you mean?"

"It's Vladimir who's the count. She's only noble by marriage."

"I thought Isolde was an aristocrat."

"Isolde? Isolde's people were hops brewers."

"No!"

"Yes."

"But she went to boarding school in England and all that."

Harry laughed. "Oh, she was *there* all right. When the hops crop failed several years in a row, her mother worked as a cook at a posh girls' boarding school. She took Isolde with her."

"She did say the other girls gave her hell. No wonder."

"Yes."

"Gee." I remembered the other side of her, the schlepper. "That explains a lot. But don't let on that I know, okay?" I said. "She'd hate that."

"Oh, yes." Harry continued. "And," he grimaced fiercely, "your precious Vladimir has made it so if they divorce, she loses not only her title, but the children as well."

"No!"

"Yes."

"But he's the one who wants the divorce."

"I know," he said pleasantly. "It's so unfair. So don't go think-ing your horrible artist friend Vladimir is so wonderful. Because he's not." He studied me in the dark. "Artists are not always good people, as you seem to think. Remarkable, yes. Good? Not always. So," he raised one eyebrow in the fogged-up mirror, "I do have a chance, you see. I might not look it, but in my part of the world I'm actually considered quite a catch."

"I don't know what to think anymore," I said.

He said, "You realize, of course, there's a sadist on every street corner. It's the good masochist who's hard to find."

On that note we ferried home.

Luckily, no one had parked in his spot. We slid into the teem-ing lamplight. Harry put his hat on—Harry always wore a noticeable hat—and we ran through the rain to the house. With a little less bounce than before, we climbed the first flight and returned to Frau Zwekl's apartment. I'm often mildly flippant in my retorts, but the truth is, everything Harry had said about Blacky had hurt me and my words were only meant to cover it up. One thing, I was determined not to blush in Blacky's presence anymore. I wouldn't even sit near him, I decided. The hell with both of them.

When we went in, they stopped talking when they saw me and I thought, Oh, they've been discussing me. "What's up?" I said, shifting the cumbersome bottles and handing them over.

"Have a seat," Chartreuse said, his eyes feverish.

"Let me just go change," I began, for I was sopping wet, but, "No," they all said at once. "No!"

Isolde pushed me into a chair. She was wearing her aubergine linen dress. There was something frenzied in her voice. Herr Kleiderschrank was there, hunched over. I got the feeling there was something wrong. Suddenly I went icy cold. It was like when my brother was killed and no one would tell me. They looked at me and still no one said a word. "My parents!" I cried and stood up, grabbing hold of Wolfgang's little arms. They felt like a child's broken arms, dangling and clammy.

"No, no, nothing like that."

Over Wolfgang's shoulder I saw that someone else was here. A man in a suit. He stood speaking confidentially to Blacky in the corner near the kitchen. They held on to their teacups.

"She was like a mother to me," Herr Kleiderschrank was sobbing at the kitchen table, trying to make a scene. I realized this was about Frau Zwekl. Of course Herr Kleiderschrank was lying. Frau Zwekl despised him and had told me so, vehemently, every chance she got. Daisy, unable to be still a moment longer, cried out, "Guess who Frau Zwekl left all her money to?"

"Herr Kleiderschrank," I finished for her, for why else would the lawyer be here.

"You," said Isolde.

"Me?" I touched my chest.

"You!" cried Herr Kleiderschrank from the kitchen. There was narrow-eyed accusation in that "you."

"There must be some mistake," I said.

"Oh, there's no mistake." The man in the suit came hurrying forward. "She's left the lot to you." His accent was Swiss. He opened a book and was about to show me the columns of figures and sums that would change my life.

"It can't be," I said, somehow inexplicably crushed, disappointed, for here was my camera and my new career as a photographer to be discussed and instead . . . but I ought to be delighted. I said, "I still think it can't be. Are you sure? I mean, the name's right and all?"

"*Jawohl,*" said the suit. "If you are Claire Breslinsky."

"I am," I said. "Did she leave me a note?"

"No. I'm afraid there was none. Just the will. To whom and how much."

"But I hardly knew Frau Zwekl. Oh, I feel so bad."

"I don't think that's the way she had hoped you would feel," Blacky said, his kind eyes searching for some joy in mine.

"No," I smiled at him, "of course not. I just mean I feel bad that I never did something nice for her." My eyes filled with tears.

"Still," Chartreuse leered, "she must have liked you, eh?"

"Yes," I said. "She did give me something once," I remembered. "A cloth." I could hardly speak.

"Not quite the same but never mind," Harry said.

"Well, it was a hand-embroidered handkerchief," I said, "with a bird on it. A bird, a heart, and a tulip. A special bird. She'd embroidered it herself when she was young. The heart stands for love and the tulips for faith, hope, and charity. I have it upstairs," I went rattling on. "I wash it in the sink so it won't come unraveled in the machine."

"A lucky bird, that was." Daisy elbowed Chartreuse in the ribs.

"That's it," I said. I had kissed Frau Zwekl on the cheek. She'd felt brittle as parchment. But her eyes had shone with memory and were still wet and beady with life. "The *Distelfink* it was called! That's what she said. The bird of luck."

"Thistle finch." Isolde translated the name of the bird, for she was our linguist.

"Ah, the goldfinch." Harry put his finger in the air. They quarreled over the more correct translation.

We were, all of us, stunned. Upstairs, I could hear the parrots squawking their outrage. Light at night was unacceptable to them unless they, too, were in on the party. Even in my confusion I noticed Tupelo looking bitter, as though something had been taken rather than given.

"Put up the heat, Isolde," Chartreuse, Frau Zwekl's chenille bedspread cloaked about him, complained. "It's freezing in this place!"

"Yes, I thought it was supposed to be spring," Wolfgang said.

"It's the cold from the Alps," the lawyer explained, "it followed me here from Zurich."

But I had stopped listening.

"Get her a drink," Chartreuse suggested. "She might pass out."

Daisy moved to get the *Sekt* we'd brought in and more glasses, for there was no alcohol left and no one had wanted to go upstairs and fetch more. They'd all wanted to see my face when they told me. Terrified of missing even a beat, Daisy returned in a minute. Isolde popped open the bottle. Blacky, concerned, poured a water glass half full with it and gave it to me. His lovely hand grazed mine and I felt it there as I drank. I felt it like the golden liquid, glorious, and a moment too sweet.

Wolfgang had picked up his camera and was filming me. They all were watching me.

"What am I going to do?" I said. But I already knew. I could send money home, it occurred to me with a thrill. Pay off the rest of Michael's funeral. Buy them a new boiler. And—I took hold of the arm of the chair—I could go on this trip they had planned!

I looked to Isolde, posed there on the green velvet fainting couch. She sat with Reiner and Chartreuse. They'd been playing Ciao Sepp but the cards lay abandoned now before them. She rubbed her thumb with her forefinger as she watched me, waiting to see what I would do. There was something new in her expression; some unearned respect I didn't know what to do with.

"Hang it all." Harry laughed. He sat on the hassock and held on to his knees. His penny mouth spread wide and his roomy bottom squashed. He was glad for me. But I thought then and I remembered often afterward that he seemed to be in the throes of despair. When great good fortune falls into your lap, the expressions of everyone else remain with you, like separate packages, to be opened and reopened later, explaining the past.

Tupelo, silent with annoyance, pulled Blacky down onto the faded loveseat. She held one of his clean hands in hers. Yes, the emerald on her finger twinkled. While she had him in her grasp she was almost complacent, her normally vigilant eyes in a glaze. There was that old song on the radio, "Deep Purple."

His eyes met mine. He took his hand away from her and put it into his own, unwrinkled lap. Out the window, past the blossoming pear trees, the raindrops falling so heavily lightened like parachutes opening, and they turned into whispery snowflakes—my snowflakes now—amast in the wind.

chapter nine

*W*e left at the height of summer. Out of Bavaria, over the picturesque hills, our caravan wound its way.

Watching Munich disappear before my eyes, I loved it so much. Art galleries. Farms in the middle of town. Flowers, so abundant they traipsed across each path. Cozy bakeries and streamlined autobahns. Window boxes. Railroad stations linking everywhere with history. The soft pastel colors of stone houses. Clock towers with clocks that actually worked. For a minute I couldn't for the life of me think why I was leaving.

But leave we did.

"Harry," I said, for Harry and I rode those first days together, "here I am with my dream, off to the Orient, and I've got to tell you, I'm sad."

"What about?" He fiddled with the radio and found us a waltz.

"I'm not exactly sure. I just feel my life so profoundly, I could cry."

"You're not sad, my dear, you're happy." He lifted himself

and adjusted so the seams of his white duck pants would align, the change he always kept in there jingling. "You just don't recognize it as you've never felt it before."

"Really?" I looked into the rearview mirror to see who I was. Yes. There I was. Young. Happy. Although Tupelo, to my great disappointment and confusion, had managed to come. It wasn't I who'd held everything up in the end, but she, whose busy schedule had had to be reshuffled. She'd moved heaven and earth to get out of a contract.

Grudgingly, I'd conceded defeat. Blacky, busy tying up loose ends at his practice, was nowhere to be found. So I'd worked through the summer. The money I would have coming from the will would take time and red tape, and the apartment and its contents would have to be disposed of. As an American it was simply less complicated for me to let the estate lawyer handle everything from Zurich. But the money would be mine to come home to. Unrequited love leaves actually quite less of a broken heart when there's a consoling chunk of money in the picture, take it from me.

I wore Frau Zwekl's Bohemian garnets in my ears. They glittered and swung with my every movement and each time I saw their reflection I thanked my lucky stars. Unfortunately, they'd come to me in a what-nots cardboard luxury soap box along with Frau Zwekl's blue crystal rosary beads and her complete set of grinning false teeth. That was a shock. Still, I couldn't throw the teeth away and kept them just as they were in the black box with roses on it she must have always kept near her on her nightstand. I felt I owed her that. I put my I Ching coins in there and the *Distelfink* handkerchief. I tried to give the rosary beads to the children but at the last minute, I couldn't. I wrapped them back up in the handkerchief and returned them to their box.

I'd known already in July that my hopes for Blacky had been dashed. I knew it the moment I'd heard that his mother, the Countess von Osterwald—in my mind a sort of queen of the Black

Forest—had invited Tupelo home for an early summer weekend. I could fight but I had no power against a purse-strings-toting countess mother who was in fact a besotted fan. I imagined she cared more about Tupelo than Blacky did. I told myself he was accommodating the countess.

At first I refused to look at Tupelo's ring. Then, heartbroken, I forced myself to, as if that would get me over it. It did not. Though unrequited, I was still in love with him—so much so that I considered *her* affections for him nothing more than greedy self-preservation. I thought I could see right through her. After all, she'd been the instigator in our liaison. If she loved him, how could she have? Then again, I loved him and I'd participated, too. So I was just as bad as she.

I consoled myself with wondering if Blacky didn't occasionally feel as though he'd moved too quickly. Would I have been a satisfactory lure to him with my newfound money? Or was I fantasizing, deluding myself? And what the hell was I thinking, wishing for a man whose prerequisite for love might be money!

Even I was wise—or greedy—enough to see that any feeling of love was preferable to me to no feeling at all. And I'd been hiding for so long inside a state of numbness. This feeling of "in-love-ness" enhanced my very essence of life; went along with it, like a river beside it, refreshing and, sometimes, flooding. In a way, it had nothing to do with Blacky. It was all about me. I could *feel* the passion, as anyone who has been in love will remember. It sentimentalized the going to bed, delighted the closing of eyes, the looking up, even—on fair blue midnights—to the canticle of stars.

That evening, just before the border, I sat checking and rechecking my purse, thick with passport, visas, and camera equipment.

At that time in my life I always seemed to be grappling with the contents of one bag or another. At least that's what Isolde said. She was quick to point out one's faults in her charm-school-mistress way. I think I was afraid to lose what I hadn't already received. Holding on to everything, sort of.

Everyone was a little nervous and anxious before we'd got under way. We'd gathered in a huddle like before a big game, Isolde restlessly moving from van to van, checking our inventory, hoping to remember in the nick of time some vital forgotten item. It was the early days of Clinique and we thought that without that particular soap and moisturizer, we'd be lost. We had stacks.

Isolde's van looked very chic, all red and paisley, with voluptuous pillows and huge mirrors in frames along the walls so it actually looked really roomy. She was very proud of that van. The *Abendzeitung* had run a story on us and shot the interior. They had, however, shot Tupelo inside it—looking like a harem goddess in a cacophony of scarves—and run that picture on the Sunday supplement cover.

Isolde's nose was out of joint. But Tupelo hadn't actually *said* Isolde's van had been hers. She'd simply happened to be there when the photographer arrived and, as Isolde was off somewhere, planted herself inside and let them assume what they would.

I knew it was bad-spirited of me, but I was delighted to see a crack in the veneer of Isolde's adoration for Tupelo. Childishly, I wished for Isolde's fondness again. I was always second now.

In Blacky's and Tupelo's van, sparse by comparison, sleeping bags were rolled up neatly, a refrigerator was stocked with antibiotics and Chardonna for diarrhea and so forth. Tupelo rode, head held high, beside him. I know she thought she looked like a "real" person. She'd even put orange madras plaid curtains on the windows. She probably saw herself as Nurse Nancy to his Dr. Dan. My upper lip curled into a sneer the moment I thought of her. Still, it pleased me to see there would soon be roots growing out of her "real" blond hair. And as if that all wasn't enough, Chartreuse had found Tupelo's green pearls in a hock shop—at least that was his story—and then presented them to her, like she was the queen.

Wolfgang, our filmmaker, had the most official-looking van. His was new and stocked with film canisters and camera equipment. He was used to taking off on trips to far-off places. He carried a clipboard and checked things off. There was, I thought, an excess of extra batteries and spare tires in every vehicle but there would come a time when I would delight in the existence of these things, too.

Harry's van was the best. He'd hired Chartreuse to outfit it much like a yacht, and along the walls were cabinets and shelves chock-full of books and leather straps with snaps to keep them in line in case of jolting roads. He'd done it in pine and then polyurethaned it. We were all enthralled with Chartreuse's masterpieces of deception: false-bottom drawers and cubbies. Sort of a drug dealer's delight, I thought. But really, it was wonderful. I loved sitting in it. Harry kept a bowl of bananas on the shelf at all times, believing that this was the only food you could eat and not get sick from while traveling. He'd fastened a brass bell up in front outside the driver's seat. The open cabinets displayed all sorts of things to stave off boredom: game boards, a chess set, even two plastic suitcases of badminton, the only sport he allowed himself. The closed cabinets were housed with items Harry assumed Far Eastern people would be interested in and would want to barter for with their small treasures. On Chartreuse's advice, he had one section filled with nothing but short-legged jeans. Believe it or not, there was a time when jeans only came from the West.

Reiner, once again outfitted in dry-cleaned Hemingway African safari gear, his vehicle heavy with good German Überkinger bottled water and Spaten Bier, had papered and shellacked his walls artistically with a collage of German photographers' black and white art.

Vladimir wasn't traveling with us. He had a show of his bronze women in Zurich on the sixteenth, which might prove too lucrative to forego, and would fly out later to meet us in Istanbul along with Daisy, who would stay on with the children until they were assimilated at their grandparents' home in the country. Daisy was enormously put out by this. She hadn't wanted to miss anything. But it was settled. Her translating capabilities wouldn't be needed until farther down the road.

Evidently, Isolde and Vladimir had postponed their divorce. I think neither really wanted to go on the trip at first but neither could they figure a way to afford the trip separately, nor could they bear the thought of one having so much fun without the other. Their van, secondhand, commandeered by Isolde, beautifully lit and inviting, was, in a way, a second chance. I know Isolde practically glistened with hope.

When we'd pulled away from Isolde's earlier that evening the cobbled street was yellow with light. The plan was to race through Austria and Yugoslavia and Greece. I was disappointed not to linger awhile longer in what was then Yugoslavia. So many houses were straw-thatched, with quaint little bridges and donkeys on low green rolling hills everywhere. But I was outnumbered by my friends, who'd grown up avoiding Middle European quaintness as hopelessly behind the times.

Six colorful vans fashioned the chain of our eastbound caravan. Isolde's van started off first. Well, you know Isolde, she always had to be first. Vladimir would ride with her, of course, after Istanbul. Reiner's van ran second. He too, drove alone. Later, Daisy—poor thing—would be stuck riding with him. At that point we weren't all that flexible. We had our chartered spots and for some reason felt we had to stick to them. Later, Wolfgang would insist his van take the lead because coming onto any scene would be preferable photographically as a surprise.

Harry and I drove along next. Then came Blacky and Tupelo behind; I was happy not to have to watch them before me. As it was, I often lay in the back of the van with the curtains split just a crack, watching them sitting there driving along. I waited for them to do something lewd—something that would hurt me so much I would get over my terrible affliction—but they never did.

Chartreuse's van took up the rear.

Just before we pulled away, Reiner came over grumbling about American politics. Without waiting for a reply, he walked away shaking his head, outraged. I would never be anything but American for Reiner.

The weather, however, was perfect. Westerners with knapsacks were churned into dust for Wolfgang and his film camera perched out the window. Still, they'd wave us pleasantly on. We motored through northern Greece without a hitch—everyone in our group had been to the Greek islands on vacation many times. We wouldn't venture south. I didn't mind. We were all excited to get to Asia. Istanbul, intoxicating and intense, was our gateway to the East.

It takes such a while to get used to driving great distances. You don't realize how far it is when you look at a map. You can't understand. But days and days go by and nothing at all happens. If it is not your turn to drive, you read. And then you can't read anymore. You spend a lot of time with Chopin. Then Pink Floyd. Elton's "Bennie and the Jets." The landscape rides away and comes toward you and then away again. You can almost feel them at first, the arduous miles; long and dusty and weary—so long you think you won't be able to bear it much longer. Only after a while they raise you up like a plateau of movement and they become life itself.

Harry kept me entertained with stories of his youth. One story was about his mother keeping his hair very long, like a girl's. "I was a regular Shirley Temple," he confessed.

"Kind of hard to believe when all the curls you've got to show for it is your little cowlick there."

"Oh, that's a story in itself. One day I took it upon myself to cut my own hair. I remember it as though it were yesterday." He pulled his cowlick up. "I must have been six or seven. I took this piece of hair right here and cut it off. My mother came in before I got any farther. Oh, she screamed! I was so frozen with fear by her scream and by what I had done that this piece of hair never grew after that. Never."

"That can't be true!"

"It is. It might look like a cowlick but it's really a child caught in rebellion. Oh, I was punished. I thought she'd kill me! Ah, yes."

We looked at each other and laughed. That was the good part about riding with Harry. He revealed so much.

"Claire!" he cried. "Look! We're going to stop up ahead. You see? It's Istanbul!"

We peered out the window. He looked at his watch. Istanbul had arrived in a sudden flurry of activity. Neither of us was prepared for such noise after four days on the road.

Already we looked very different. Appropriately bedraggled, we fell into our roles as film people with gusto. But really we knew nothing yet. We still considered it a hardship to have to wash up in public bathrooms. We didn't realize that on the path we had chosen there would be no such things as sanitary bathrooms.

We parked at the Hippodrome across from the Pudding Shop on Divan Yolu. The Pudding Shop was an indoor/outdoor café filled with Western travelers, hippies, drug dealers, and trilingual Turks. Chartreuse had informed us that this was the only place to go. Everyone traveling to and from India met up there and we would find out all the news of the road. The Pudding Shop was a pretty place in those days, the smells of hashish and peppermint tea reaching the tables and chairs out along the curb.

Things caught you off guard. There was the peculiar smell of coal dust and the calls to prayer that flew across the minarets and Byzantine rooftops. There were entire lanes of cobblers, pairs of grown men walking together hand in hand—so many of them fair and blue-eyed. ("Ah, the Crusades," Harry reminded me.) It was all so new, so different, we followed Chartreuse's instructions with docile, wide-eyed cooperation. After all, he seemed to know what he was doing and we were all suddenly like children, eager to be shown what we should do. We were none of us sure of ourselves but we imagined we carried with us a certain glamour. We thought people would vie to get close to us and our theatrical aura but we were wrong. The stars here were those travelers returning from India. Their eyes were rimmed in kohl and, yes, it must be said, there was an aura about them. A few wore earrings in their noses. They looked glamorous in their soft clothing and outstretched, unwashed hair. There was something detached about them. They weren't like the few tourists who never left the grand hotels or even like us, our crew, excited and disheveled. These weary, slender creatures gave you the feeling they'd seen it all and were at last blasé. Little did we know that most of them were holding it in for fear of some quick-conquering venomous parasite. Well, I thought, if it's all going to be like this, it won't be bad at all!

I was still too shy to hold my camera in front of me and I would place it on the table and take pictures without anyone aware that he or she was being shot.

On Thursday afternoon, Chartreuse and Isolde went to pick up Vladimir and Daisy at the airport. Isolde drove. She always drove. "I drive like a man," she would boast. More like a teenage boy, I would think.

The first thing I noticed as they wheeled Daisy's sensible Samsonite through the thick haze of cigarette smoke into the Pudding Shop was that Daisy had circles under her eyes and had lost some weight. I knew she must have had a very hard time with the children, because we would be gone for months. I didn't dare ask about them for fear of upsetting Isolde. I needn't have worried, though. It wouldn't have bothered her. Isolde was free for the first time in years. She looked like a great big thundering hippie goddess, all hooked up in her chains and belts and stomping around in her Wizard of Baghdad curled-toe men's wedding shoes (there were no women's to fit her), ready to do anything: anything at all! She ordered lunch for us all as though she were about to pay—which certainly she would not do.

"Well," we all wanted to know, "how was the show?" Vladimir rubbed his palms together. "Excellent," he beamed, looking around the ceiling, not meeting our eyes. We all knew then it had been a catastrophic failure. I thought of his latest presentation. I remembered his one upside-down woman and another unfortunate sort of stuck-in-a-can woman. I supposed it wasn't a popular time to be berating women, placing them in demeaning positions. It had occurred to me, why then not to the critics? I noticed Harry said nothing. I wondered what Vladimir would do. It was a shame, too, because the figures he'd left behind as too mundane for the show were beautiful ones, graceful and noble. I was sure they would have impressed and delighted everyone but he'd pooh-poohed this as naive. Beauty, it seemed, was not enough in this art world of his. He thought he needed shock to get the American and Japanese buyers' attention. I couldn't imagine why. But he'd been so knowledgeable and convincing in his scorn for the conventional.

Vladimir brushed his handsome new traveling trousers. He kept seeming to want to wipe his hands on something.

"Just wait till you get a dose of the road." Isolde touched him lovingly on the shoulder and handed him a napkin.

"Well, sit down, for heaven's sake," Wolfgang said.

There was a rumpus in the small park across the street. Some American boy had staggered out of his van half asleep and peed on the statue of Atatürk. The townspeople were outraged. He was being arrested.

I stood up and tried to push my way through to see. There was a bustle of travelers at the bulletin board, searching for messages. But Wolfgang came out and motored me back to the table. He put his hand on the curve of my back in an unnervingly familiar way. "Please don't get involved, Claire," he warned. "The next thing we know you'll be arguing for his rights and getting us all arrested."

"I just want to see what they're going to do to—" I began, but I didn't like his closeness and I let myself be persuaded back.

Vladimir, quickly recovering and in his all-encompassing, hulking way, held up his hands and announced, "All right. *Ruhe!* Silence, please. I have news."

Through the lattice I watched the police taking away the scruffy, confused American boy.

"Claire." Reiner rapped on his clipboard. "Are you paying attention?"

"No."

"Well, please do. And if you're going to get upset about every American catastrophe we pass on the road you might want to turn around and fly home. Lord knows there will be enough of them. Now, that fellow made his own choice to do what he did. We all must be responsible for our decisions. Into each life some rain must fall. *Ja? Or?*"

Reluctantly, I sat back down. "Sure," I muttered. "Like some days you're the windshield and some days you're the bug."

"What did she say?" Reiner said.

"Doesn't matter," Blacky said. "Go on, Vladimir."

Vladimir cleared his throat. Enjoying the bunch of us hanging on his every word, he flagged the fat waiter leaning against the wall. "Could I trouble you for a cup of that delicious-looking coffee? *Danke. Danke.*"

Daisy gave him a hefty push. "Well, go on, then! Show them!"

"All right, all right," he said, unrolling a newspaper. It was the *Münchner Abendzeitung* and there, on the bottom part of the front page, was a story about us! STAR JOINS FILM CARAVAN TO HIMALAYAS, it read. There was Tupelo in a publicity photo. There was another, smaller picture of our vehicles being readied for the journey, Wolfgang and his camera at the helm.

Our audible intakes of breath capsized the room.

"I'm dashed," said Harry.

"No!" we all cried out. "Wow!" This was the sort of news we all relished.

The waiter placed a thick white cup of foamed coffee before Vladimir, and Isolde automatically nudged a paper napkin toward him. He moved it an inch back in the other direction in a dismissive, corrective motion and I thought, Christ, he's a pill. I was getting a little sick of his finicky arrogance toward her.

Harry, always moved by food, put in, "You *must* try this *tziziki*!"

"Look, Tupelo," Blacky patted her shoulder, "on the next page, too. It's you!"

"Oh! How thrilling!" Tupelo snatched the paper. We all stood around her scanning the column, each of us hoping to catch sight of his or her own name.

"But they only mention Tupelo, Wolfgang, and Vladimir," Isolde said at last, disappointed.

"Well," Vladimir explained, "that's understandable. They're only really interested in the newsworthy members. The eye-catchers. They do mention models aboard."

"Yes, but——" Harry started to say something, then, remembering he'd long ago chosen the behind-the-scenes world, gave up.

The waiter arrived with our lunches of spicy lentils and yogurt kabobs. After days of moussaka, this was a happy change. We all sat down and settled in, passing the paper around the Pudding Shop, delighted at our own notoriety. No one seemed as impressed as we were, though, and each of us thought longingly of people we knew in Munich and what they must have thought when they saw us in print.

Then Vladimir said, in a drawling way that told me he'd been saving it up, "They tell me at the paper the readers absolutely devour anything to do with Tupelo."

Tupelo did not move. She was hunched over her plate and now her eyes—only her eyes—followed him with catlike intent.

Vladimir leaned back in his chair. "You see, you're the only recognizable name to the everyday reader and—well, I thought we might keep them in touch with your experiences."

"You mean like a travelogue for the stay at home?" Blacky said in his trying to get a grip on the situation but reasonable voice.

Vladimir's amused eyes returned to Tupelo's. "Yes."

"Tell-tell-tell you what," Harry stuttered with excitement, "let's find Tupelo some native paraphernalia and wire the shots directly to the paper."

"Claire could shoot you," Daisy said.

"I certainly could," I maintained glibly.

"No," Reiner said, "this is too important. I'll handle this."

I looked at Tupelo. She was looking at me. The cat had the cream.

"Well," Isolde drawled unenthusiastically, "they've already *done* the story." It was hot. The air was close and she leaned her head back to catch the draft from the overhead fan.

"Nonsense," Wolfgang said. "People love to feel as though they're along for the ride, but without the danger."

"Not only that," Reiner put in, "it's automatic publicity for the film."

"If they're not sick to death of it by then," Isolde said. There was a stillness to her voice.

Daisy said, "Oh, I think it's more of a tease. Get them interested. You know. And involved."

"It's a good idea," Harry admitted. "Think of the reflected glory once we get back to Munich."

That made good sense to us all. I picked up Chartreuse's guitar and strummed. I was useless, though. They all told me to please stop. Wolfgang leaned across and took it from me. I didn't know what was with him. He kept looking at me with this goofy smile.

"Look, Tupelo." Vladimir snatched the rest of Harry's baklava and wolfed it down. "What do you say let's trot over to the bazaar and find you some agate and funny baubles, shall we? Dress you up."

"Oh, agate!" Tupelo jumped up. "Agate brings good luck!"

Chartreuse had been very quiet. Always one to see which way the wind blew before he staked his direction, at this proposal he stood right up. "Excellent." He carefully wiped his mouth. "I have a cousin with one of the best shops in the old bazaar. Amber. Agate."

"Don't go buying all sorts of rubbish so early on in the trip," Blacky warned Tupelo darkly. "Remember we have limited space and we'll be wanting to utilize it later." It was well known that Tupelo, wild for sweets, would find these confection things in the latest bazaar, then return to her van and huddle in her cushions, grinding the sugary pinks and white halvah to a brick in her body, shuddering with disgust and delight, making herself sick.

"Oh, you silly old stick in the mud! How much room will some pretty baubles take?" Tupelo made a disdaining purse of her lips and lifted one shoulder to her ear. Her loosely knitted sweater fell over the other shoulder. The fabric teetered at the beginning of one creamy and opulent breast. She put her pink tongue to the top of her teeth and mischievously peeked around the room. When she had everyone's attention—and she certainly did—she shrugged. "Anyway, darlink, it's for publicity." She leaned over and took my hand in hers and put it on her breast. "Feel my heart," she breathed. "It can't catch up!"

An unnatural stirring slithered through me. I pulled my hand away and drained my coffee cup.

"You think everything is always about you." Daisy narrowed her eyes.

"Everything *is* always about me," Tupelo said.

"How quickly the voyage to enlightenment reverts to shallow commercialism the minute there's a mark to be made," Isolde remarked, sliding her elbow out on the table and fitting her chin in her hand.

"That's a funny thing for you to say." Vladimir signaled to the waiter. "Now if the shoe were on the other foot . . ."

"Hooph." Harry laughed. "Insult to injury."

I didn't like that, either. I thought Vladimir had gone too far. I'd almost forgotten how nasty he could be.

"You don't think I came along to seek enlightenment," Vladimir admitted. "I *am* hoping to take in those erotic sculptures in India, though. You know, in Khajuraho. I mean, just because I'm not interested in trading all my worldly goods for a song—"

"What worldly goods?" Reiner was setting up his portable backgammon game. "I seem to remember you've more or less chiseled them away, too, eh?"

I was glad. I was actually happy to see Vladimir thrown a loop.

Avoiding Isolde's dejected eyes, Vladimir took a long last draught of his coffee. He was startled by the dregs at the bottom, however, and had to spit them inelegantly into his napkin.

"Yes, indeed." Harry stood, scraping his chair against the play of mosaics. "Public relations. All tax deductible. I'll come along, if you don't mind. They have something called the Sahaflar Carsisi, if you can believe it. It must be a marvelous antique books area. Do you know it, Chartreuse?"

Chartreuse tossed an inadequate coin onto the table. His eyes gleamed. "*Mais bien sur*. It's just outside the Western Gate." He turned to me. "Claire. Here's your key. I borrowed it to put my guitar case in there."

I hadn't even felt it missing. I pocketed it.

He extended a benevolent arm in the air and ushered them away. "*Venez, venez*. I'll take you there."

Daisy and Reiner were already hard at a game of backgammon. I had to give it to her. She hadn't once complained about being saddled with Reiner. She really was a good sport.

Isolde sat there pretending not to be fuming. I knew just what she was thinking. How could Vladimir come all this way and not want to spend time alone with her first thing?

"They'll be right back," I said cheerfully. "And Chartreuse is with them."

She gave me a black look. "I know Vladimir," she said. "He'll want her to model for him."

"Well," I reasoned, "he'd be a fool not to. What with business not going so well." I saw her quick look. "I mean," I revised, "artists always have to be aware of the whim of the public, don't they?" You had to be so careful. Isolde wanted solidarity but she also didn't want you to notice that Vladimir might be floundering. I went on. "At least you'll be able to keep an eye on them. Well. They can't exactly wander off. Really. How far could they go?"

"To hell and back," Daisy, who'd seemed so oblivious, piped up. She took a bite of a hard peach and made a disgusted face. "Tupelo makes me sick. Thinks she's a goddess! Did you catch that shimmy-shimmy business? What a tease! She just loves to be looked at, doesn't she!"

Actually, in my heart of hearts, I enjoyed looking at Tupelo. I liked it especially when she was being exhibitionistic and often replayed such moments at night when I was in my sleeping bag. I understood that many inexperienced women fell in love with the bad guy, were attracted to the bad guy—but here I was finding myself attracted to the bad girl! "At least they remain predictable." Isolde fluffed her long dark hair up as though she could care less. She pulled a beaded headband down over her forehead. It didn't suit her. As a matter of fact she looked ridiculous. I hated to see her look foolish. She was my friend. And it burned me up that Vladimir treated her so offhandedly. I leaned across the table and adjusted the band, moving it closer to her hairline.

"You are a funny little thing," she told me. But I knew she felt better.

Blacky took me aside. "I'm off to the mosque Sofia," he said. "The Blue Mosque. Want to come?"

I looked back at Isolde. She'd recovered enough to fall into conversation with a suspicious-looking group of travelers from Australia. One of them was letting her sample his dish of *sutlac*, the famous milky pudding. Boldly, he'd moved to our table.

I didn't have to think long. "Of course!"

Our van was parked just across the road. I ran a brush through my hair and locked the van.

I flew toward him.

"You'll need something to cover your head. They won't let you in like that."

"Oh." I went back and got my bridesmaid's hat and jeans jacket. The minaret over Sofia sounded the wailing pledge to Allah. The sun captured the galaxies of wood-smoke dust and I breathed it all in. Here. Now.

I saw my camera bag on the floor of the backseat. It was as though it saw me. I hesitated. I didn't want to be encumbered. I wanted to fly like the wind with Blacky. On the other hand, this would be a great photo opportunity. Luckily, I am a Capricorn and duty prevails. I took the camera.

And then we were off, jostling down the cobblestoned hill to the mosque. The very walls were mosaic masterpieces of blue, glimmering with time and light. I took out my camera but was promptly ordered to put it away by the harried temple guard, pure central casting from the Kasbah.

A shock of street boys flew into us, knocking my hat off, then running away, laughing down the street.

We were told to remove our shoes before entering and I sat on the step undoing my complicated ribbons of ankle ties. My espadrilles were a good six inches high and when I took them off and stood beside Blacky, he jumped.

"Good God!" He grabbed hold of his chest. "Look how short you are!"

I scratched my neck and looked up at him. "Sorry," I muttered and turned away.

He grabbed hold of my arm. "Claire. You're just a bit of a thing!"

I straightened up.

He threw back his head and roared with laughter.

I felt, as usual, diminished.

"No," he said, "don't look like that! You're lovely. It's just . . . well, for a model . . ." He couldn't help it, he laughed again. "I thought you were small before but, really, you're very small."

"All right, all right." I pushed him off. "Let's go in and have a look. They don't like you laughing like that."

It was true that the local men were eyeing us with hostile disapproval.

Soberly, we filed into the magnificent place and tried to be reverent but every time he looked toward me and then had to readjust his line of vision he would start to laugh. A reverent Turk looked up from his position of prayer and clicked his tongue reprovingly at us. We moved to a darker corner of the mosque.

One of the caretakers was chasing the same little gang of street urchins away from the trundle of Japanese tourists coming in.

"When I was a child," Blacky said, catching sight and looking longingly after them, "I used to pretend I lived on the street." He wrung his hat in his hands. "I so hated the captivity of bourgeois life."

"Did you?"

"Oh, yes. I felt suffocated by it."

"How do you mean?"

"Well. I just hated the hypocrisy of it. Smiling and being pleasant to people you simply couldn't bear."

I was thrilled to imagine him young, a small boy all alone at a party in a Black Forest castle. I'd never really had him to myself. I was so glad he was confiding in me. "Is that why you went away to Vietnam? To do something genuine with your life?"

He smiled sadly at me. "I didn't go to save the world, if that's what you mean. I went to have a good time."

Feeling oddly offended, I said, "I trust you enjoyed yourself?"

"I did. It was the best time of my life."

"Isolde told me you came home devastated."

"I wasn't. I was brown as a berry."

I turned away.

"All right," he admitted. "I was drinking half a bottle of scotch a day." He peered through the splinter of glass in the wall. "I just wanted to be free. You've no idea how impossible that is with family."

I harrumphed. "I have a family, you know."

"Not like mine, I assure you."

"Maybe they are. My mother would rather have me secretary-ing from nine to five in any midtown, fluorescent-lit security. What does she care if I drive to India? I'll never get to Mass in India. How can I put it? My mom. It's like she loves me too much, likes me not enough, you know? She wanted a daughter like Daisy: tidy, discerning, a girl who makes her bed. I wanted a mother like

Isolde: sacrilegious, fast driver, out of town. We always feel like we fail each other, see?"

He said nothing. It pierced me that he wasn't interested in the least about my background. Or worse, that he thought it beneath consideration. Still, wasn't I running away from the very same thing? And hadn't we enough time spread before us when all these things could be talked about at length?

He studied me with interest but at last I did not care. I had my own pain to contend with. I began, wholeheartedly, to weep.

"What is it, Claire?" He put a tender arm around my shoulder.

"Oh, I don't know," I sobbed. "It's just, well, it's so boring driving all day that I've had the chance to think of things I never wanted to face before. Do you know what I mean? To remember what it was that kept me moving farther and farther away. And— at times—to burn with regret . . ."

"Regret?" He gave a sob of incredulousness. "At your age?"

"Yes. Once," I said, "just before I came to Europe, my American friends and I had chipped in and rented a cottage in Montauk. That's like a little town on the beach. I was in my first throes of independence—I was passing myself off as a model but I hardly worked at all. I'd had a couple of jobs with *Ingénue* and *Seventeen* and so people knew who I was but there was no money in that." My voice had calmed down as I told my tale. I wasn't crying any- more. "Actually, I think I was working as a Jim Buck's dog walker in Manhattan and didn't care to be associated with anything I actually was. Anyway, my new friends and I had this house out there in the end of Long Island, in Montauk, and my twin brother, Michael, who'd just graduated from the police academy, showed up. He hadn't paid a share and so was not officially entitled to come. Yet other boys were milling about and welcomed just because they had surfboards and wore madras plaid. Till my dying day I will see my brother's happy face coming toward the door. He was loaded down with his chess set and sleeping bag. I barred the door with fury. 'Michael,' I hissed, 'you can't just expect to come out here and stay! This is my deal, not yours.'

"I was prepared to do battle. I reared up on my indignation. He was *such* a cheapskate. He thought he could just waltz in on my coattails.

"But I hadn't had to say another word. I saw his face. Realization tapped in. He stood still for a second, uncomprehending, and then he realized I just didn't want him there. He was stung. You could hear the big waves pounding the shore on the beach across the street, behind the East Deck Motel. He just turned and walked down the pebbled driveway to his car. Aggravated, I ran after him. He didn't stop. He just carefully put his stuff in the trunk of his blue Duster.

" 'Listen, Michael,' I explained, still annoyed but realizing he was leaving. 'You just don't get it.'

" 'So tell me,' he said, rearranging his seven extra oil canisters he kept in there to keep the car going. 'Get it all out.'

" 'You can't just show up out of nowhere and expect to join in! Michael, listen to me.'

" 'I heard you, Claire.' He removed my hand from his arm. 'Don't worry. You're clear as a bell. I get it. I'm leaving.'

"Ashamed that I'd gone too far, I grumbled, 'You don't have to leave right away, for God's sake. You just got here.'

"He turned and looked me square in the eye. 'There isn't a thing on this earth that could get me to stay,' he said.

" 'Michael,' I said.

"He got in the car and he drove off, after five hours there, now five hours back. That's how he was. He wouldn't try to horn in on my territory ever again, you see. He died four days later. Killed in a filthy hallway. He was trying to get the knife away from a junkie. He just walked up to him, you know? He thought the guy was just a little kid. See, he was just a rookie. And he was so used to little kids. He thought—" I stopped, unable to go on.

Beneath the gold-crusted dome, a guide loudly commenced the history of the mosque in French to a bevy of Arabs, returning me to the here and now. I turned away, pretending dutifully to understand every word.

Blacky could have said anything and I would have stood there. We stood there for a long time. And then, unexpectedly, a robe of eroticism swept over me. I could feel the short hairs on my neck nearest him stand up. Like a plume of smoke my scent mushroomed into the air. My skin felt lewd and exposed. I guess it was everything all coming together at once. Tupelo's teasing, his gentle closeness, the emotion of my confession, the life force asserting itself after glimpsing death.

The tour guide kept on speaking. We stood there close enough to touch but not touching. It was so dark. Just being near to him, I found I was breathing heavily. It never occurred to me that he might be aroused as well. I only thought that he must feel my desire, so loud the throbbing of my heart and intense the heat seemed to me. And something else. I'd been so afraid my feelings for Tupelo would confine me to that side of eroticism forever. It wasn't that I regretted but I wondered if it eliminated me from enjoying the opposite sex. Now I knew it did not. There was my happy libido, intact as ever. Gratefulness welled up inside me and I thought I was going to cry again from the sheer relief of it. But then I remembered Tupelo and Vladimir taking off like that back at the Pudding Shop and it occurred to me Blacky might be simply using me to pay her back. Of course. What an idiot I was! Standing here telling him about my private miseries. I grew cool right away. I adjusted my spine. But when I lowered my gaze to step away from him, the light touched him and I saw from the straining outline of his jeans that he, too, was aroused.

He jerked backward, though. He'd sensed my dismissal. "I've had enough," he said and turned and walked away. Eagerly I followed him out. We sat together on the step and put on our shoes. "You have excellent feet," he observed appreciatively. "High instep. You're lucky, you know. A lot of people can't keep up."

I thrilled to these words. Tupelo had stubby little feet for her size, and flat. She wasn't a walker. I was more suited to him that way. He got up, brushed himself off, and started to walk away. "Do you know what I'd love to do?"

"What?" I tripped along after him, holding my hat.

"I'd like to take a Turkish bath." Then he seemed unsure. He said, "We'll only be here for a day or two. We'll never have the chance again."

"You don't have to convince me," I said.

He seemed to know where he was going and I followed, up the cobblers' hill and through backyards of grapevines to Sultan Ahmed. The wailing voice of Om Kalsoum penetrated the air. We walked for a long time. We went down hidden alleys and came to an Arcadian series of ledges. Blacky knocked at one of the ancient doors. "Is your heart beating the way mine is?" he asked, searching my eyes.

This can't be happening, I thought. "Yes," I admitted.

"Good God, that coffee was strong! We'll be up all night!"

"Oh." I saw what he meant. Actually, now that he mentioned it, I realized my heart was indeed hammering away from the caffeine. "I thought it was you," I said.

That got me a hearty laugh. But I'd meant it. Wait a minute. Had I only imagined his arousal? Now I was unsure.

There was a towering wooden door, studded with brass and turquoise. I took its picture, then one of Blacky before it. The door was creaked open by two old men, twins, one with a milk eye. Because I held my camera already cocked, I was able to take their picture before they realized it. What a shot! I congratulated myself. Blacky cleared his throat and proceeded to address them politely in first English, then German, then French, then Italian. None of these was understood. However, money was the key. They had a swift discussion without words: he held some out, they took it all. We entered a sort of tiled bank where our belongings were put in a locker. Then, together, they led the way down a dark and hollow-sounding corridor. I was placed in the hands of an old woman and carted off behind a lattice, through a door, and down a tunnel. I assumed this was the women's division. She handed me over to another hobbling old woman, this one as good as naked and with no more than four or five teeth in her mouth. Now I was not only disappointed, but frightened. She was carrying what looked like a mild cat-and-iron scourging broom. She scurried me down another long, dank corridor; we seemed to be going underground. A door opened and suddenly we stood beneath a huge dome. Tiny stained glass windows here and there let in rays of light that pierced the thick steam.

Alabaster sewers emitted drizzles of water from copper spigots, like Greek aqueducts. The water tripped and danced along, then poured into the center of the room. I caught my breath in wonder. The women waiting to grab hold of me nodded in jabbering approval. There seemed to be no other customers so I got their full attention. I removed my clothing. *"Naa naa,"* the one wagged at me, implying that I must give her my underpants, too. Awful feeling. "No, no," I said. There was a moment where I thought I could still run. But I thought of Blacky, going through the same procedure down the hall somewhere. I almost laughed. Still, I tried to stop them but they persisted, a little bit angry now at my ignorance. I was reassured by this outrage and finally surrendered. What the heck, I decided. This will never happen to me again. So off went the underpants and I lowered them over to her—she was all of three feet tall—gingerly. She snatched them up and I wondered if I would ever again see those tanga Triumph briefs that had cost a good eighteen marks. And if I did, what Asian strain of virus would they carry? They transported every strip of my clothing away. That startled me. I thought of stories of girls dropped down false-bottom rugs and kept as harem slaves. Steam weakened and softened me, though, and all the while these women with their broomy things swept away at my skin. It went on and on. Waxy balls of sugar were applied to my legs to remove any hair, their old sacks dangling and penduluming past my horrified nose. They didn't care. They chattered and hummed—these were their working clothes. At one point they tried to do away with my rusty thatch of pubic hair and were surprised that I should want to retain it. When I was finally drunk with dampness and heat, they laid me down on a loose mat and began to rub me. Shyly I tried to smile. "Aaahhh." They liked that, rubbed harder with their loofah sponges. Embarrassingly, gray gobs of skin were coming off my body; layers, like from a filthy snake. I couldn't believe it. Was that me? But another one of the women was at my top, cranking away at my head, loosening my neck. I remember lying there half asleep, half euphoric, a line of dribble falling out the side of my mouth and me not minding, my feet being wheedled and prodded and massaged on and on. In the distance I could hear the calls to Allah.

When it was over, I was given my belongings. My clothes had been cleaned and pressed. I remember being let out the great studded door and my wonder as I emerged from that place into the Turkish evening. It had felt like we'd been far away for a long, long time. Blacky and I beheld each other. Distractedly, he patted his cigarettes down into his shirt pocket. He had this way of smiling. I don't know. It made you feel like you were part of something.

There was an alley that sloped to a cellar. It was all tiled like the inside of the baths but it was abandoned, probably for years. I leaned against the yellowed, grimy tiles.

"Look at you," he said and came toward me.

We stood like that for a long while, then suddenly he seemed to come to himself. He sort of shook himself off and turned away. I followed. We began to walk up the crooked path and with every step I felt as though I were lifting, physically lifting, above myself. I said so to Blacky and he said, yes, he was experiencing the same sensation. I can only liken it to when as a child you'd stand in a doorway and press outward with your hands then step away and your hands raise themselves up into the air.

With wonder he said, "I can't imagine ever forgetting this feeling, can you?"

"No."

Our eyes locked in a bond of souvenir. That would have to be enough for me, I told myself. This wasn't a man who slept around. Once he was committed, he would honorably restrain himself from frivolous dalliances. And, I realized now, that's what I would have been. He didn't belong to me.

It was warm outside, the evening upon us. We took our sweaters off and tied them around our waists. We came upon the port. Little boats bobbed in the sea. "Want to take one out?" he said.

"What, now?"

"Yeah."

"What if something happens?"

"What could happen?"

"I don't know."

So we rented a rowboat and took turns pulling all the way out into the harbor. Huge fishing boats came and went around us, rolling us in their wake. The sun had grown huge in the west. We stopped rowing and lay there under and over the uncomfortable benches, bobbing lazily up and down, the green water sloshing against us as we basked in the sun's last warmth. That was one thing Blacky and I had in common: we both loved that sun.

"So," I said finally. "You're engaged."

He turned from me, pretending to admire the delicate minarets of Topkapi. "Claire," he said finally, "there are things you don't understand."

"It's okay," I said. "I get it. You have responsibilities to your family."

He sat up. "It's not that."

"Oh. Well, if it's not that then you're right." I threw my arms up. "I *don't* understand. Oh. Look. Please don't go lighting up another cigarette. Every time something is about to be said, you light up a darn cigarette and everything gets put off. And then nothing ever happens."

He must have heard the real unhappiness in my voice because suddenly he leaned over with terrible clumsiness—as though despite himself—and covered my mouth with his. I remember that kiss. I can close my eyes and taste the salt on his full lips. Jesus, there are moments in life that are good.

It took us a long while to get back to shore. We sang as we rode: "Danny Boy," the only song we both knew the words to— me from home and he from lonely boys in Vietnam. I sang out loud and clear. I felt the air turn cold, the tautness of the rope, the peeling green paint on the oars.

When we got to shore we strode along, peering in windows where ladies in kerchiefs prepared meals. We smelled the turmeric and cumin and the sauciness of lamb. I grew excited thinking of the scrumptious food and rich coffee that awaited us at the Pud-ding Shop. We walked more quickly through the dust and com-motion of tooting vehicles.

"I'm hungry," we both said at the same moment then laughed happily.

"Come on, then," he said, taking my elbow. Looking over his shoulder, he said, "I wish I knew the state of my liver. So I could go on drinking or end it."

By tens and then hundreds, the sky filled with stars. I couldn't wait to get back and have them all see us together.

"It's too dark to shoot," I said, "just let me put my camera in the van," and I headed across the street while he stood there and waited. I always told people I only shot in natural light because I liked the result but the truth was I hadn't got the hang of the flash contraption yet. I was whistling as I crossed the street. The van had a tricky lock and it took me a while to get in. There was Chartreuse's guitar case on the bed. I looked around. I knew immediately he'd gone through our things because even Harry's neatly folded trousers were sticking out of the false-bottom back-seat, caught by the hurry he must have been in when he'd snapped it shut. I remembered Chartreuse's enthusiasm when he'd told me about that drawer. Unable to resist, I lifted it just a crack and peered in.

Why, the little monkey! A sheaf of *kimdunkari*, inlaid gems— special ones—lay there in a saddle of soft metal. The encrusted stones glimmered through years of filth. But though they were filmy with age and grime, they were very valuable; you could see that right away. He must have stuck it there when he came back from the bazaar, knowing no one would come across it.

I lay my camera under the bed. Then, uncomfortable, I picked it up. I'd keep it with me. I didn't like the way it all felt. Where had he stolen that? I wondered. And why was I spending my young life with thieves? I didn't have long to think about it, though, because once I crossed over the street I saw that Blacky'd gone in without me. I hurried in. He was already sitting at the table. And Tupelo, eyes glimmering with fun, sat rocking on his lap.

Why was it that in stories, when you found the one of your dreams, he was always one way or another, when in life, the hero might be all the things you'd ever want, but he's also judgmental, parsimonious, jealous, and, most painful of all, flirtatious.

"Hullo, Claire!" Wolfgang waved to me from behind the camera. "Come! Join us!"

I must have stood there in the doorway, my feelings written all over my face. But Wolfgang had the camera pointed toward me. He was always looking at me with it. Chartreuse played me in, strumming some dramatic opening. If I hesitated it was only for a moment. I pretended to smile. If Blacky was going to act like nothing had happened then so could I. I was getting used to it. Still, it seemed a little ironic to me that after all that had happened, once again I was alone in the world with my jeans jacket and my camera, my six-inch espadrilles, and my floppy, here-I-am-again-the-bridesmaid hat.

chapter ten

The next morning, well before dawn, I spotted Chartreuse going into the van while we sat having our coffee in the Pudding Shop. I waited. A few moments later I saw him taking his guitar case back to his van. The side door was wide open and I saw the guitar there on the bed.

I'd taken to keeping away from Chartreuse while I puzzled out what exactly it was he'd done. Certainly I knew what he was capable of. Hadn't I even excused his behavior from the start, judged his crimes purely mischief and misdemeanor?

I'll fix him, I thought. When he was busy in the front looking over his map, I reached in and snatched his guitar in the case and brought it into Harry's van. It was going to be a long ride. He would be driving and wouldn't even realize it was missing.

When I got to Harry's van I checked for the sheaf of gems. Sure enough, he'd moved them. The dickens! No doubt he'd stashed them in the case to carry them back.

A few hours later when we were well under way and had moved from coffee to tea and Harry was peeling himself a second banana, I was sitting in the copilot spot in his van, deliberating what to do. I even thought whether or not I should leave the caravan altogether. It occurred to me I might stick with them until the next big town and then take a flight to . . . where? Well. I could plan that out as I went. I'd been treated shabbily by both Blacky and Tupelo, that was clear. What reason was there to stay on, really? I'd thought Blacky's kiss was an answer, a beginning. Apparently I'd only been a diversion. I couldn't help thinking I'd asked for it.

"What's with you?" Harry confronted my silence.

"I hate washing teacups in cold water. You never really get the grit out and the tea tastes funny."

He glanced at me knowingly.

"I was just thinking of bailing out," I admitted, sipping the last of my tea.

He was silent. Then he said, "If you go, Claire, remember this. The microcosm we're just now living in is a reflection of the whole world. There will always be another disappointment to run away from."

I looked at him. He kept his eyes on the road. I wondered just how much he knew. I wondered if I ought to confide in him.

"Would you mind keeping that guitar out of my line of vision, Claire? It really is annoying!"

"Would you mind putting your banana skin out the window?" I said. But I put the guitar to the other side.

"Didn't Chartreuse ask you not to take his guitar?"

"He doesn't know. He's driving. Oh, all right. I knew I should have left it in his van but I wanted to practice."

"He specifically asked you not to, though."

"I know. It's just, I thought I'd crack with boredom."

"Claire. Do practice somewhere else. You're really dreadful. I can't take it anymore!"

"Oh, all right." I crab-walked to the back. "I'll put it on the bed." I knew very well I ought to tell Harry about the gems. Of course he'd be outraged. He was so ethical. I was, I realized, forever protecting Chartreuse.

"You know, of course," he called over his shoulder, "you know who's quite mad for you?"

"Who?"

"Wolfgang."

"Oh." My heart sank.

"Yes. And it wouldn't be such a bad idea to give him a try. He'd be a sublime catch. He's a professional. On a world scale, mind you. Any girl would give her eyeteeth to date such an important filmmaker. Can you imagine all the potential events?" He shifted gears. I could just imagine his eyes gleaming. "The mind boggles," he said.

"I know, I know. He's very sweet. It's just every time I look at him I think of a gnome."

"You could close your eyes and think of England, you know."

"No. Sorry. I couldn't. I'm a Yank, remember?"

"I wouldn't go around spouting the news. They don't much care for Yanks abroad anymore." Harry sighed. "But you would have such an absolutely first-rate *life*, Claire. Even if you went with him for a couple of years. Imagine. He could teach you the ropes of the business."

I gazed out the window at the monotonous landscape. "We've been having such a good time together. Well, that's all ruined. In my experience when someone falls for you it always ruins the relationship. They lose their sense of humor altogether and you always have to bend over backward to be understanding and kind no matter what sort of fools they made of themselves."

He started to say something but suddenly we screeched to a halt. Chartreuse's guitar toppled onto me and I braced myself.

"Claire! Claire!" Harry sobbed. Before us on the road, the cabin of a truck was stopped and facing us. The front of it had been sheered off and two men with absolutely nothing before them, both dead, stared back at us.

A herd of cattle must have run into them as they'd turned the blind curve. All the cows had been decapitated and were strewn up and down the hill. The dawn was just lifting through a mist. A smattering of country people sat on the hill waiting for what would happen next. There was a sound, a humming. It was flies, I realized, come for the blood.

Harry left the van and was sick. I took the wheel and maneuvered us through the mayhem. It was terrible. Terrible. I thought I'd better get us quickly through before some ambulance or the police arrived. I might not be much use in ordinary life but in an emergency I spring to action. All the vans followed ours and then we pulled over to the side of the road to regroup.

Harry came running and jumping over the carcasses. He'd thought we were going to leave him behind, I guess, and he was hollering and waving for all his salt.

We waited while Blacky went back and made sure the men were dead. I went back, too. We all knew they were but he couldn't go on unless he was sure. When I mentioned getting the vans out of the way for the ambulances Blacky gave a snort and said, "There are no ambulances here, only vultures." I looked to the wreck. Already people picked around the edges of the mayhem looking for scraps of value. I hurried back to the van. I hesitated. Often in my life I remember that moment and I still don't know if I was right or wrong to do it, but I took out my camera. I got the shot.

chapter eleven

We spent the next days traveling east. All the Turks we met at gas stations and roadside *chi* shops were friendly and seemed to want to take us home with them. The men, solemn and hard, broke easily into tooth-scanty grins. The women, jabbering and mostly in packs, in scarves and ankle-length robes, shyly came forward to touch my red hair and Tupelo's blond locks.

Then one day there was some trouble because of our hair. Some village women were angry. Chartreuse told us we'd better cover our heads.

"I'm an American," I snorted.

"Really, darling," Isolde said, "it's awfully gauche to be patriotic in this day and age."

"I don't cover my head."

"You will if you don't want to get us all in trouble," Chartreuse said. I'd never heard him use that tone before. He who'd been a little slippery in Munich had become assertive—more of a leader—as we traveled. I was just about to ask him where he'd put his fancy new acquisition and put him in his place but then Wolfgang came over with his soppy face and said gently, "Look, Claire, we're in their country now. What right have you to enter it and aggravate the women?"

I supposed that made sense. I did as I was told. I covered my hair with a scarf. Reiner even put away his gold watch. I washed the dishes in the stream without complaint. I actually donned a voluminous skirt. Better to be hot than be hassled. It was funny, because how kind the peasant women were to us when I followed their code! So poor and yet they'd slip us extra grains of coffee and tomatoes from their green fields.

At the *chi* shop in Enzurum, some French travelers pulled up like pirates: dirty, smelly. They warned us not to take "ze sheet ovair ze border."

"Yeah," Wolfgang said, catching my eye. "We figured that. We'll throw it all out before."

"And don't take ze short cut," they warned. "It's dangerous. These people, they're not people! They're savages. Not the same as these peasants. A different tribe. Very bad."

"Ho ho." Blacky laughed. *"je n'ai pas peur."*

I stirred my tea, certain now that we would take the shortcut. There was something about Blacky. Always daring the gods. Tell him he couldn't and he would.

As we traveled east, children began to appear along the sides of the road. They were brown-toothed and pinheaded, sprouting overgrown crew cuts. Many of the children were cross-eyed and most of them barefoot. They had their arms outstretched on the road for us to throw them filter cigarettes in passing. If we didn't throw anything there were rocks in their other hands for our rear windshields. We'd heard it was a sort of unwritten law of the road—our fault if we didn't comply.

We bathed with Blacky's antiseptic German soap and as far away from villages as possible. My fingers were toughening up, what with water so seldom available. We were in abject horror of all things communicable, from athlete's foot to herpes. ("Don't even touch the faucet!") We stayed away from grungy camping places and waited for fresh water. And then, we reached the point where there were no faucets anywhere. Outhouses were our best bet and some of them were so filthy we chose to go behind trees and rocks.

Outside Arzinshan, we found a stream dragging with willows. I waited for my chance. When everyone was busy I went to bathe in it. Blacky came upon me as I floated in what I'd imagined was privacy. I jumped, not sure how long he'd been standing there. "You startled me!" I yelled.

He pursed his lips, narrowed his eyes, and smacked a French newspaper against his thigh. "You wouldn't believe all the devastation in south Vietnam."

I wasn't going there. I put my head underwater. When I came up he was still there.

"I see you've graduated from Agatha Christie in German to Satsang with Baba," he remarked, looking at my little pile of stuff.

I kept my body well under the water. "It's not bad," I lied. I turned my face and watched a grasshopper, small as a fingernail and pale as milky jade. I wouldn't look at Blacky. He'd done to me exactly what Tupelo had. No doubt they laughed about me behind my back. My heart pumped with fury and wounded pride.

He crouched beside the stream.

I said, "Aren't you afraid someone will see you with me?"

"What do you mean?" He kicked at the mucky bank. "I have nothing to be afraid of."

"I mean, I'm beginning to understand that fearing something will draw it closer."

"I hope that doesn't mean that you're fearing me." He lowered his chin and pulled me with his green eyes.

"Is that in the hopes that we stay apart or that you don't want to be feared?"

"Hmm. Does it have to be one or the other? Can't it be both?"

A flagrant warmth had slid between my legs despite the cool, deep water. I thought I mustn't let him notice this and paddled to the other side of the stream. "I'll have to think about that," I called across.

"You do that," he said, giving up, turning away.

I'd irritated him and I was glad. And why did he think everything I thought would be about him? Even if it was true. The truth was, I didn't know what I'd meant. What I'd really wanted was for him to come looking for me. So when he'd done just that, why hadn't I responded with acceptance? Because Tupelo stood between us. My jealousy stood between us.

Wolfgang appeared at the end of the path. "Afraid you'd get into trouble," he explained. I didn't know why he thought he had to look after me. We dispersed.

At night, I kept the bunch of them entertained with stories of my family in Queens. They loved to hear about my loads of cousins and relatives. I didn't have to embroider at all to make them laugh.

"Really, Claire," Harry would say, "there's no end to the lot of you."

"It's true," I would agree. But I was tired of the same green hills. We all were. We pulled up stakes and continued on. There was that shortcut over northeastern Turkey that the Frenchmen had told us about. Wolfgang was very keen to use it because the people who lived in that region—if you got to see them—were enormously photographable. Chartreuse was wary. He'd heard stories, he said.

"We'll save two days," Wolfgang pointed out.

"Oh, come on," Blacky urged us on. "What fun is it without a little adventure, eh?"

"All right," we finally agreed. There were so many of us. What could happen?

And so we ventured toward the shortcut. The landscape changed quickly from lush to rocky and barren.

On the second day the sun beat down with no mercy, even early on. I wiped my lip, beaded with sweat, with my wrist and smelled myself—that salty familiarity. It was something I hadn't done since grammar school. "Hello," I whispered.

"Do you know," Harry read from one of his obscure guidebooks, "that this Valley of Araxes is supposed to be the site of the Garden of Eden?"

"Really?" I tried to find some trace of the Armenian River. But all was parched, sucked out and left to dry. I'd taken to writing down things as they happened into a small blue notebook. I had a feeling Wolfgang lost track of the sequence of things.

We were saving lots of time by detouring this way, Reiner kept assuring us. He gave a toot on his whistle. There was only one catch. The road wasn't a road but varying heights by now of a foot or two of dust.

Everyone seemed edgy, nervous. We stopped for Chartreuse to refill the gas tanks with a canister and funnel. He looked over his shoulder at the sunburnt hills.

There were no children on the road, which was odd.

"Get back in the van!" Vladimir shouted at Isolde when she squatted quickly behind a boulder. *"Mach' schnell!"*

"All right, all right," she said and climbed back in the van.

I took some water from the thermos. Even that was hot.

Russia was far off to the north on our left. The Iranian border ten hours in front of us to the east. Off in the distance, Ararat, honored mountain where the ark of Noah, legend has it, still lies unfound, petrified beneath the ice and snow.

It was weird, this terrifying bleakness. The dust on the road got so deep that our vans became like boats, swaying as they went.

Harry, beside me, was perspiring, his clothes soaked through. He squinted his eyes to concentrate. The road was hardly navigable. A figure loomed up in the distance.

"What is it, Harry? A man?"

"If it's a man we've hit a time warp. Look at his clothes!"

He carried a staff, wore sackcloth britches and a turban of violent colors on his head. A biblical vision. Sheep darted up, then ran off into caves along the road. Road? It wasn't a road, it was a dust channel, endless. I waved at the vision and smiled. The vision stared then turned away.

"Jesus, Claire," Harry cried out, "the van won't steer. We're actually floating along."

It was like being on the moon, this pitted surface. No this or that in either direction, just the dust, behind us an unfathomable cloud our spunky wheels kept churning up.

"If we ever get through this," Harry sputtered, "I'll never buy anything but a Volkswagen. I can't believe we're still moving!"

The dust had coated our bodies, our faces, our teeth. We tried with the windows closed. The dust seeped in the vents. Hurriedly, I wrapped my camera in two scarves to protect it.

A blind curve in the road led past a precipice of boulders. Until now we'd moved in a sort of straight if undulating line. We were moving at two kilometers an hour. Harry shifted down to one. It was horrifying. You couldn't get the feeling you were in control. Up ahead there was no clearing of gravel. We kept going. I think all of us were clinging to the sides of the vans or the steering wheels. The tires couldn't grip the road at all.

"Will you look at that," Harry said, "a village!"

"It's just another mess of boulders."

"No," he shouted. "Look there!"

"I'm looking, I'm looking." And then I focused. Colors moved. We swooped closer and the colors turned into clothing, like the shepherd's we'd passed. People, living like ants, bedecked in vibrant colors, scarlets, indigos, and purples against the powdery gray. They scattered and ran into what seemed to be the sides of hills. A spray of rubble came down on our roof, sounding like rain. A dog, not far away, barked furiously. I shot again. Whatever we shot we shot twice and, whenever possible, with two different cameras. You never knew when the film was faulty or the depth of field off.

Just then we hit some sort of solid terrain. "Claire!" Harry called out with relief in his voice. "Land ahoy!" Gravel at last. It felt as though the danger was past. All the people we'd seen fleetingly had disappeared. Unfortunately, the stones here were so jagged that Blacky's van immediately got a flat tire. We all stopped and disembarked.

It took no time at all for the men to remove the tire. Reiner lived for just that sort of moment. Out he trotted with his tools, his energy, his rolled-up sleeves. Grudgingly, I was beginning to admire his capabilities. Isolde, Tupelo, Daisy, and I sat on boulders, watching them change the tire. We looked pretty funny, covered in soot. Nothing moved. I slipped out my camera and took everyone's picture.

"Tupelo," Isolde said. "Look at your hair. What you'll be needing soon is a root job."

She looked levelly back at her. "I don't bleach my hair, Isolde."

"Are you sure?"

"Yes, I'm sure." She laughed, still coughing from the dust. "I'm from Estonia, not America."

A man appeared from behind one of the boulders. Isolde jumped. He'd come from nowhere.

At that moment other men began appearing. They were the same biblical-looking men in robes the color of the landscape and with vibrant headgear. I wasn't frightened at all. I was charmed and poised my camera.

"Don't." Chartreuse stood between me and the men I'd wanted to shoot. "They'll kill us."

"*Kill* us?" Daisy shrieked.

"Shut up," Vladimir said in a low voice, stilled by the growing number of men.

"Get back in the vans, will you?" Blacky said. "Hurry up."

The men—there must have been eighteen of them—stepped closer. They moved with long, sideways steps, stopped, then moved again. Their shoes were puffy, like muffins. They carried glinting sickles.

We scrambled into whatever van was nearest just as Vladimir and Reiner finished bolting the tire. Chartreuse stood guard, his arms crossed, while the last of us moved to our vans. "Drive!" he called out between grinning teeth. "Go!"

One of them picked up a rock and threw it. It hit one of the windshields and made a nasty crash. That was Reiner's van. Another crash alerted us that Chartreuse's rear window was now history, too. Reiner, hit by a stone and terrified, jumped into Wolfgang's van. Vladimir and Daisy clambered into Isolde's. We all of us turned on our engines. I'd climbed into Isolde's van because she was already at the wheel.

Chartreuse stayed exactly where he was. He remained in that one place, still grinning and not moving.

Before any of us knew what was happening, one of the men— he was younger, smaller than the rest, his brown teeth bared, his long robes tripping him—came rushing from behind with a raised, glinting sickle.

Chartreuse stood there knowing they were coming for him. He waited until we were all in some van or other. Then he took off at a run. I saw his eyes. He was measuring the distance. He wasn't going to make it.

I watched a stinging rock fly past, just missing his head. As it was he got one on the hip and I heard him cry out with a yelp. Isolde, her mouth in a square and her teeth gritted, swirled the van around, making a shield of it between Chartreuse and the oncoming man. I struggled to open the side door. The centrifugal force was holding me back. Finally it slid open with a merciful groan of rolling metal and he flopped in. Daisy and I dragged him across the floor and we floated away in a pelting of stones.

Reiner's and Chartreuse's vans remained aground where they'd left them. The men kept coming toward us, their sickles raised in throat-slashing gestures. Daisy and I groped to our seats. The dust behind us rose up thick as a curtain. We could make out just one of the men now, still following us at our own miserable pace, his brilliant colors and the glint of his sickle, unbidden, a blurry star in the muck of our rearview mirror.

Daisy kept crying out, "But the vans! They've got our vans!"

Nobody answered. Nobody cared about the vans.

It was then, for the first time, that I realized our caravan might be catapulting into terrible danger. Trembling, I reached into my purse and grabbed hold of my Queen of the Holy Rosary beads. "Mother of God," I prayed to the one I'd so long ago deserted, "protect us on this journey to the unknown." There are no atheists in foxholes, at thirty thousand feet, or hightailing it out of the Garden of Eden.

It was four hours until we reached the main road once again, six until we sighted the wasteland comfort of the seedy shack and desolation that was the Turkish border. The border was nothing more than a shack, a ramshackle patrol outpost in the middle of nowhere. It didn't look very official at all. It actually looked more like a den of thieves. Some sort of crap game was taking place. Out trudged an entity in army clothes. He was hiking up his suspenders, tromping in unlaced, mud-caked boots and the filth of unwashed weeks-old stench. He took one look at us and waved us through with his rifle and we, relieved, rode the mysterious distance of no-man's-land for some minutes before we caught sight of the Iranian border.

This border bore at least a resemblance to someplace official. A couple of broken-down vans were parked along the side and we jumped out. Chickens scratched in the dust by ugly little buildings with real glass windows, barred; announcements and a picture of the stern and handsome shah and his family watched us from the wall. The realization that we would be safe left us trembling with fatigue. It was by now late in the day.

We tried to report what had happened but we were all speaking at once and in so many different languages, the official slammed his window shut and the guards at the door refused to let us pass.

Daisy raised up her formidable little self and told us all to be quiet. She'd come up with a plan. She covered her head with what I recognized as my pillowcase and approached them. She spoke to them in her polite Farsi. At last the guards parted their rifles and they let her in. She was in there so long we were beginning to wonder if she would ever come out again. At last she emerged. She sat down on the wooden step, disheveled and exhausted. We gathered around.

"Why were you in there so long?" Wolfgang cried. He lugged his camera with him but he didn't point it at anyone. He didn't dare put it down. He was terrified of something happening to it.

"He gave me tea." She loosened her head scarf. "Somebody give me a smoke, will you?"

"Daisy," I said, "you don't smoke."

"I do now," she said.

"Just give her one," Reiner said.

Chartreuse lit a cigarette and passed it to her.

She kept shaking her head. "Well," she said, "it seems we weren't the first Europeans to pass this way this week. Three days ago two truck drivers—a Swede and a Frenchman—made their way through the area as well. They were shortcutting, too, but from the opposite direction. From Van Gölü. That place is a village, if you can believe it. Those people actually live in those caves. Anyway, the truckers were stopped in their tracks by fallen boulders blocking the road. The men—the very men we saw, no doubt—came out to give them a hand. The truck drivers let the villagers clear the boulders. They stood there leaning on their trucks, smoking, watching them work. Their mistake, as it happened. The villagers finished the job, cleared away every last boulder, then, when the way was cleared, they chopped the truckers' heads off with their sickles."

"No!" we all cried out at once.

"Yes. And that's not all. They put the Frenchman's and the Swede's heads on sticks, or poles or something, and put them out on the road. The Australian van—remember the Australians we ran into in the Pudding Shop?—well, they came through yesterday and saw the heads like that up on poles. You can imagine. They practically flew here! The officer's men just returned from retrieving the heads." She took another drag of her cigarette. She didn't even cough.

I looked over at Chartreuse. His poor old van was gone. He sat in the road on his haunches shrugging and muttering "I told them so"s to himself in a mixture of French and Afghani.

"What about their trucks?" Blacky said.

"All gone. That was the last anyone will ever see of them. As with our vans. They took them apart in no time flat. He says we're lucky we got out alive."

"Where are the dead men?" Tupelo cried.

"Well, the heads are in there." She pointed toward the office. "Right next to the typewriter. In two lunch Styrofoams. He was pleased to lift the lid and show me! Oh. I thought I'd—" But she couldn't go on.

Reiner sank to his knees. "There, there." He patted her hand gently. "They won't get you. I'll see to that."

"But I don't care about me! Your lovely cameras!" She touched the side of his cheek. The remains of her bright Munich manicure stood out in still partly pink shreds.

"As long as you're safe." He gazed into her eyes.

Isolde and I looked at each other at once. Reiner and Daisy? It couldn't be.

"Reiner, you can use my camera," Blacky volunteered.

"Oh, I couldn't." Reiner sank to the ground in exhaustion and dismay.

"Yes, don't give it a second thought," Blacky pushed generously forward, "I'm a dreadful photographer anyway. You'll be doing the world a favor!"

Reiner dropped his head. "Well. For the good of the cause, I accept. Thank you, Blacky."

There was a long, crowded moment while I, too, thought about offering him my camera. But if I did, who would I be then? A girl along for the ride, that's who. He would always be a photographer, camera or not. He'd made his bones. And Blacky would always be a doctor. I shifted my weight from one leg to the other, trying not to let them read my mind.

Wolfgang said, "Pity we weren't prepared to shoot."

"Yes," Vladimir said, "shame you didn't have any film in."

"I was just changing film," Wolfgang lied. "The dust would have ruined the quality at any rate. Film's in now, though." He flashed a look at me, walking in a circle with his camera, demonstrating his preparedness.

None of us brought it up that Wolfgang had been too frightened to film. Nobody dared. We weren't as backbiting as normal because we realized at last we were all in this together—and each of us had been just as terrified. Not one of us had thought to aim a camera.

Wolfgang said, "Do you think they'd let us in there to film the heads?"

"Good God!" Blacky threw down his cigarette. "What sort of film are you intending?"

"I was just thinking out loud," he said, frightened by Blacky's innate moral rectitude. Blacky was the only one who did frighten Wolfgang, I'd no idea why.

"Actually, I think it would be foolish not to try," Vladimir said.

"If you do," Harry stood, "you can count me out for good."

"Oh, all right." Wolfgang caved in. "Forget it. I'm just grateful it wasn't my van they got. All the equipment! That would be the end of any film at all. The end of the whole trip."

Tupelo looked off into the distance. "This trip isn't about just the film anymore."

"We're looking for enlightenment now, are we?" Wolfgang said sarcastically.

"I just mean that there is an intensity to life when it's not taken for granted." She blushed with a shyness not typical of her.

I sort of loved her at that moment. And I liked Wolfgang less. I said, "It isn't right just because you think you knew someone so well that they dare not move ahead of who you think they once were."

"Aren't we the philosopher," Vladimir retorted snidely.

I remained stubbornly thoughtful. "Philosophy is love of wisdom, so, yes, I hope I am."

"Pfhh," Isolde pretended to stifle a laugh, "the American philosopher. An oxymoron."

I was speechless. As much as they loved the States, they hated the U.S.A.

"Look," Blacky said, "we're all overwrought! Don't listen to Isolde, Claire. She's great in the pinch and then falls apart when things calm down."

Vladimir raised Isolde's chin with a finger. "Na, little mouse, it's all been too much for you, eh?"

They threw back their heads and laughed.

"I can't believe you wanted to photograph people's cut-off heads!" Isolde charged convivially as they walked away together toward the trees.

"Ach," Vladimir looped his arm through hers in an easy, married familiarity, "these people have no sense of the absurd."

"Come over here." Isolde turned and instructed us with a wave. "There's a little shade. We might as well eat. Bring those crates. We can use them for chairs." Fully recovered, she kicked away the smattering of chickens and arranged the larger bunch of crates into a picnic table. "Come on, Claire," she called. "Don't be hurt." She stamped her foot. "Vladimir, we hurt Claire's feelings!"

"You started it," I accused her.

Vladimir said, "Oh, rubbish. We all consider you more European than American, Claire. Come on. Let's have some food."

Some germ of my father's indignation should have irked me but, to be honest, I was flattered. I let them get away with demeaning me because they let me share their incredulity.

"How could you eat?" Tupelo exploded.

"Don't be silly." Isolde hoisted open a madras blanket for a tablecloth. "I could eat a horse. I'm not going to waste my lovely goat cheese."

"And we've got pickles." Harry moved closer.

"How *can* you think of food?" Tupelo held her head and her stomach and reeled in a dramatic swoon.

"Now, now," Blacky said calmly. "Isolde's right. We must fortify ourselves. Come on. I brought along that flat bread."

Harry peeled himself a banana. "Do you know they bake it in ovens fueled by camel dung?"

Tupelo pretended to faint.

Reiner wrung his hands. "Those savages! They won't have a clue how to use my beautiful equipment. Gone." He shook his head wearily. "All gone."

"How are we going to divide up now?" I asked. I noticed I was still trembling but I pretended to have moved on, thinking of the future.

Blacky said, "Wolfgang can take Reiner and Chartreuse. Daisy can come along with us."

Tupelo sat up, livid. "Oh, no, she can't!"

Reiner was attaching Swiss knives and flashlights and things to his bullet belt. "Daisy comes with me." He thrust out his already pronounced chin. "And I think it's time we bought a gun."

"No guns," Blacky said.

Reiner turned on him fiercely. "It was your idea I put away my watch. If you hadn't butted in, I'd still have it!"

A tear slid down Daisy's cheek. "Your lovely watch!" she sniffled. "Not to mention your van."

Reiner threw back his shoulders. "The van has gone the way of all good, noble steeds. To van heaven."

"Well done," Harry remarked to everyone, flopping onto the ground. "He's taken the obvious and carted it off to the ridiculous."

Wolfgang said, "Why, they can drive with me."

Isolde whispered to me, "I didn't see that coming. Daisy and Reiner. Did you?"

I was setting the red plastic plates around the makeshift table. "God, no!" I whispered in return, relieved to be back in her good graces. "What does she see in him?"

"Excuse me, darling, but she seems to have made a better choice than you."

"What are you talking about? He's so condescending toward women!"

"He's only condescending toward you!"

We looked over at the two of them. Daisy was indeed newly pretty. And you couldn't say he wasn't kind to her.

"Yes, but—"

"No buts. If it works out she'll be rich."

"Tch. He'll work her to death."

"Na? And? Isn't it better to work for your own? Better than working for someone like me!"

"That's true," I said and we both laughed. She went on." Daisy's clever. She could watch his books. Go on all those exotic trips with him. Book the models." She brushed herself off. Clouds of dust rose around her. "And love suits her. You can't say she doesn't look well. It wouldn't be a bad life."

Chartreuse raised himself and struggled over. "Where can I go?"

"You can come with us, old chap," Harry said. He looked at me. "You don't mind, do you, Claire?"

"Mind? None of us would be here talking like this if it weren't for your bravery, Chartreuse! Why, if you hadn't stood up to them! Mind? You can have my sleeping bag if you want."

"No, no, *chérie*," he tut-tutted. "I need one blanket. This is all I need."

But everyone realized that what I'd said was true.

Wolfgang chewed his lip, considering. "Perhaps we ought really to have a gun."

"Look," Blacky said. "Weapons beget violence. We've come so far with no mishaps."

"No mishaps! Oh, brilliant!" Daisy cried. "And what would you call all Reiner's expensive equipment lost forever!"

I could hardly believe this, Daisy sticking up for Reiner. He was horrible. And she was actually falling for him. She was completely not his type.

Blacky was earnestly pursuing his point. "No, I mean human mishaps," he was saying. "We're all here in one piece. I'm only saying that weapons, any weapons of destruction, carry with them a vibration which might attract that same vibration—like a magnet."

"You mean like carrying your white light around you?" I asked. "Imagining it there so that it is? And it protects you?"

"Yes," he said simply.

"That's rot!" Wolfgang threw up his arms. "Hippie drivel. I'm surprised at you, Blacky."

Blacky gave a short laugh. "I'm surprised at me, too."

Isolde said, "Well, it is true that we stand here all alive. If someone had pulled out a gun, who knows how it would have turned out."

"I'm so sorry about your van, Chartreuse," Blacky said with sincerity, putting a hand on Chartreuse's shoulder. "You saved our lives."

Chartreuse looked away. "I don't even mind so much the van," he admitted, "but my guitar . . ." He looked out to the distance, bereft.

"Chartreuse!" I cried and ran to Harry's van. I came back carrying his guitar. I must have been grinning ear to ear.

"Oh!" he cried. "My beloved!" He took the instrument and kissed it ardently. "Claire! How good of you to steal it away!"

We gathered together with gratefulness. Isolde, God love her, crammed some weeds into a jar and made a pretty table. Wolfgang brought out some of his clandestine and precious bottles of lukewarm beer and Harry even came clean with his last Italian salami. Daisy went and got the guards and the official to come out and join us. They skulked over but they loosened up quickly enough. The one in charge brought some delicious plump figs and a basket of eggs. Not only that but the roof of the outpost was covered with vines. One of the guards, a poor fellow with one ruined eye and a beautiful smile, climbed up and brought down some melons. They were warm from the sun and sweet as sugar. Isolde made some omelets in her wok. Chartreuse strummed his guitar. We sat in the shade of that straggle of trees, the sky very blue, and we sang out long-forgotten passages of a song Daisy and I, between us, had taught them: everyone's latest favorite, "Molly Malone." The guards hummed nasally along. Blacky and Tupelo sat close together, leaning against each other. Blacky couldn't sing, but that didn't stop him. I was singing so hard, I didn't have to think. I suppose the moment to declare I'd be leaving the group had passed, but I didn't want to leave anymore. I might be odd man out, but I wasn't the only one in this motley crew. And we *were* a crew; my heart warmed to the thought.

Harry cut the melon open, blotted some of the seeds with a handkerchief, and put some of them into an envelope, for the future. What I liked about Harry was that he went for the broad scope. "I was just thinking," he said, gazing dramatically into the distance, "one day sooner . . . it could have been us with our heads on the poles."

"That's true." Vladimir shivered.

"No," Chartreuse objected, "we would have helped them clear the boulders from the road. Those lazy fellows won't be going home now."

We all sat there looking at him.

Isolde sucked the juice of her melon with greedy lust. "Dead is dead," she pointed out.

I saw Daisy signal Reiner with her eyes. They stood up and walked away to a spot in the trees. He was much taller than she. They had their arms around each other, hers only reaching his waist, and they were walking in step. Chartreuse shuffled cheekily behind them on one knee. He shimmied his shoulders in an affectation of innuendo. They didn't seem to care. My heart, for some reason so full a moment ago, felt alone as could be.

chapter twelve

*I*ran was as different from northeastern Turkey as was possible. Immediately there were superhighways and modern buildings. Even small towns we passed through teemed with men dressed in snazzy gray modern suits. Handsome, thin, dark men who might have just stepped out of Milan. The women, however, were covered from head to foot in chador, robes that let the eyes peer through only a screen of lighter fabric. And throughout the entire country there were only five patterns on these chador, each assorted variations of black. I found Iran drab and insulting. Small but modern cars drove down clear-sailing roads and highways. Buildings had sprung up wherever you looked; but they were modern buildings that looked like the ones on the periphery of the Belt Parkway landfill into Brooklyn; modern, but in an East Berlin sort of way. Whenever I meet Iranians and tell them I visited their country in 1973, they go all glowy and murmur, "Ah! The good old days when the shah was in power!" But I didn't like the country one bit and couldn't wait to get through it. I would have enjoyed the primitiveness of eastern Turkey more had I known we'd be back in civilization the moment we crossed the border. I hadn't understood that throughout our journey there would be pockets of the past and then bursts of modernity. I'd thought we were spiraling downward into a continual past. I did not know then that the influence of the West was intermittent.

Then one night I found myself in the back of Harry's van. Reiner was driving. I'd thought things through and felt better. I was glad to have the bed to myself and I stretched out comfortably. When we stopped to tank up, Tupelo threw open the side door. Reiner was in the front seat. She said, "They're playing poker in the back of our van. They are drivink me crazy. Can I sleep here?"

He was thrilled to have her aboard and told stories and jokes one after the other to impress her. He wanted to be chummy with a famous girl. You could tell. We'd entered Teheran. Between the berserk and rattling cars and carts, he had to keep a sharp look-out. I turned my back and froze Tupelo out. But she covered the both of us with another opened sleeping bag and lay herself side-ways in front of me, her rump to my front. I certainly didn't want her. What did she think, she could find me whenever she felt like it? No. The last time was just that: the last time. But before I could even turn, she flounced her skirt up to the middle of her back and pushed her naked rear end into me. I went to wrench her from me but she wriggled so seductively that I took hold of her fiercely. She went limp in my arms.

If Reiner had any idea what preoccupied intent was going on behind him that night, I doubt he'd have bothered to waste his best stories. As it was, his outlandish boasts flew around us like butterflies, weightless and dancing on silently quivering air.

chapter thirteen

Afghanistan came on like a magic carpet ride into another century. We caught sight of our first camels in the distance, grazing near black tents stretched across the horizon like sails. Goats were tethered to their stakes. Bright moving specks of color became women, serious women with black luxurious hair flowing into the wind, women without chador: beautiful, strong-faced women in voluminous dresses of red and navy who strode boldly toward and past us. "Chartreuse," I took hold of his arm, "who are those women not in chador? I thought all the women—"

"Ah! Those! They are Kuchi!"

"Kuchi?" I tasted the word.

"That is their tribe. Kuchi tribe. No man will harness them." He slapped his thigh. "They walk the silk route. This is the silk route now, Claire. You are on it. Did you see the black tents on the desert? That is Kuchi."

"They live there? On the desert?"

"They live nowhere and everywhere. They walk from Dun-huang in China all across Mongolia to Persia. They walk, some of them, to Rome."

Rome? I thought of my gypsies in Milan and wondered if they sprang from the same source. Was it possible? I was fascinated with the very idea of the Kuchis. "Chartreuse, tell me more about—"

"Look," he grabbed Harry excitedly, "Herat! My home! Herat!"

It was the first town we'd come to. It appeared in the distance, golden and oblivious. Herat. It looked like a fairy tale, soft and precious, built from the golden soil of the landscape.

I still could not believe the beauty, the out-and-out beauty of Afghanistan. It was not the way you are thinking, the dusty, color-less scenes of mayhem we now half regard on TV. Afghanistan was swollen with fruit, copper with earth, and green with clover. Apricot trees toppled with fruit from behind walled gardens.

But for a smattering of jeeps and decrepit Land Rovers, there were no cars. Men rode horses. Fierce men with strong noses and broad mouths. So beautiful they were, they carried rifles across their chests and wore turbans and had furs and tassels that hung down. They looked right at you, right in your eyes. There was the slap of leather and horse harness. Bells jingling, horse carts sped through the picturesque marketplace. There were women in chador but the Afghani chador, or burka, came in soft pastel colors. The women in them seemed to move differently than any I'd seen before. They were lithe and spring-footed. Children, bold and laughing and free, ran, shouting at the sight of us. Mud-baked houses with turquoise doors ran down intricate alleys. Blacksmith shops with the sounds and smells of iron and oil opened onto broad roads and there were trees, rows of them, clusters of them. There was lush shade over ancient, crumbling, rose-covered buildings.

We drove into town carefully. Children tugged at our doors and flew along beside the vans. We approached a broad lane of shops. They were on stilts and without fronts, wide open to the air. Men in pajamas were coiled on cushions, smoking water pipes, their turbans purple and green and paler green and navy and silver. Rolls of Oriental fabric, silks and tapestries, were lined in bolts behind them, fruits piled in fragrant pyramids: apricots, mulberries, melons enormous and small. Burlap sacks of walnuts, dangling braids of dates and figs. There was the warm smell of coal. And everywhere the fine golden dust kicked up by the languid, trotting horses. It wasn't like the suffocating bone dust of the Valley of Araxes. It was soft as a vapor.

"An oasis!" Harry breathed.

Chartreuse bolted from the van the moment we reached the marketplace. For a moment I thought I would never see him again, never know exactly what had happened, and Harry said, "That's all he bloody well wanted, was it, a lift home? I told you I never trusted that bloke!" but then out of the humming yellow light Chartreuse emerged, teeth bared, riding toward us on a small, fierce horse. He'd covered his head and shoulders in a yellow and green shawl with little dots along the rim. His hair was black and he came at us with his yellow eyes. Whatever the men had grumbled about at first, we were all thrilled and reassured to see him like that. Wolfgang turned the camera on him. No matter what else would happen, we would all keep that image, I think, of Chartreuse swashbuckling toward us with a leather strap between his teeth, smacking his gray, galloping horse, the men in their stalls in the marketplace watching, peacefully sucking on their water pipes.

We all climbed out of our vans and petted his horse. I was suddenly a little shy around this new Chartreuse. He seemed more important, more powerful, in his own world.

He led us outside the town to a walled garden. This, Chartreuse announced, was his mother's home. A wild little figure in a plum burka came running from the kitchen house and threw herself on Chartreuse. He hugged her and I could see tears spring to his eyes.

She, clinging to him ecstatically, addressed him as Mohammed, which should not have been a shock because every man has Mohammed for a first name in those parts.

There were several buildings inside a seven-foot wall. The four vans fit snugly in the yard. We climbed out, all of us excited. It was good just to get out and walk around.

At last—we all felt it—at last we'd landed somewhere different, totally uninfluenced by the modern West. Blacky stood in the middle of the courtyard rubbing his hands. You could tell he was happy. When everything was different, there was no discontent coming from him. Not like Reiner, who suspiciously patrolled the peripheries with his club drawn, his bullet belt and no gun.

Inside one of the buildings was a tiny glass-blowing factory. A windmill turned on the roof. We peeked in. They were making liqueur bottles and bowls, all in a blue color particular to Herat. There was a dirt floor and a chicken pecked. The couple of women covered themselves self-consciously and we stepped courteously away, back into the golden evening light.

We were invited to sleep in the house and were glad to take advantage of a night outside the vans. We all dragged our sleeping bags into the two fragrant rooms provided for us. They smelled of spices and the mint tea that Chartreuse insisted on pouring endlessly. Hookahs of hashish and washing bowls of hand-painted porcelain awaited us. It was all so exotic and delicious. Wolfgang was in his glory, filming in every direction. "Look, why don't we stay here for a while?" he kept suggesting. Tupelo and Isolde put on two of the pastel chador and ran through the rooms for him.

We ate that night in those blue-painted rooms, sitting cross-legged on the floor on top of our sleeping bags and cushions and carpets. Food was carried out from the kitchen house by doubtful-looking menservants, small, slender people with long black beards and ski jump–toed slippers. They were poor but they were eager to be with us, happy to bring us great flat bowls of yogurt, sallied goat and vegetables, and crusty bread you used as a fork, everyone dipping into the same vast flat bowls.

Chartreuse paraded one after the other of his male relatives—cousins, uncles—and childhood friends. There seemed to be no end to them. I have a vague memory of a lavender-veiled woman being slithered in and then just as swiftly out. Some entity kept hidden, a flash of toothless gums and beautiful green eyes. A feeling of happy privilege as she was sped through to greet the Europeans and one American. I don't know if she was Chartreuse's sister or his wife. I don't think he'd have answered me directly so I didn't ask him.

Through all this Vladimir had finally loosened up and was telling us about his catastrophic show in Zurich. He was far enough away from it now to see it in perspective. It seemed his idiotic publicist had booked the opening at the same time a Japanese artist from America was having his show in a rival gallery. Privately I wondered if this was the true reason for the show failing. I could imagine critics taking a nice bite out of him. I remembered he hadn't brought all the papers with him. Just the one about us.

Delicious smoke-flavored beans and peas arrived, then more vegetables and goat simmered in exotic herbs.

Isolde stood up and rolled back her sleeves. "Do you know what I'm going to do?" she announced. "I'm going to go to the kitchen and get those women to give me their recipes."

Determinedly she pushed her way into the kitchen but the women fled at the sight of her. Ruffled, she came back out.

I got up to try my luck and Blacky pulled me aside. He seemed to want to tell me something very important. "What?" I brought my face down close to his.

"But you are not like Isolde," he whispered. "Please stop trying to be. You will wear yourself out. She is a Viking. You are—"

"What? What am I?"

"You are a sweet and innocent child," he said and kissed my hand. I was so relieved. I thought he was going to say I was just a girl from Queens.

I turned in time to see Tupelo laughing derisively. She wasn't afraid of me or what Blacky might feel for me. She held on like a fox to the glamour of wickedness. If there was a moment which changed me, that was it. That condescending look in her eyes. She thought I was beneath her contempt. She believed that her seductive spirit was so superior to mine, that there need be no concern for my power. I spread my hands out before me. I turned them over and looked into my palms. Then I looked into her crooked eyes.

"What are you looking at?" she said blandly, unworried.

"The cat can well look at the queen," I said.

After dinner we were invited to partake of the terrifying, waist-high water pipes, which we did. It was horrifying and wonderful, the smells and tastes so different from anything I'd ever imagined, and we, lying around on filthy cushions, breathing the exotic incense of adventure, were sheltered from the road and any fears for at least one happy night. Harry had the runs, Tupelo a terrible cough, and Isolde an ear infection. But Blacky treated everyone with the latest German antibiotics and we all felt well taken care of. He made you feel safe, did Blacky. We lay there listening for the hundredth time to the comforting if by now distorted sounds of my Pink Floyd tape and to the hilarious snores of the disgruntled camels out the door. We fell asleep to Harry and Vladimir's stoned-beyond-belief hysterical laughter.

I awoke the next morning and climbed over the sleeping bodies of my friends to get outside. There was Chartreuse, sitting cross-legged in the entryway. He didn't see me. He'd returned to his origins, wrapped his head in a turban. I saw it in his eyes. He was himself, completely himself. Now was his time to remember and just be. I went around to the back of the house and across the yard to use the outhouse. A glamorous rooster strutted before me. There was a refreshing stream outside the wall. I left the compound and washed myself briskly in the early cold. It felt wonderful. Chartreuse's eyes crinkled with delight when he saw me and he signaled me to follow him. He handed me a sweet *shaplam*. It was delicious, and still warm! We walked together through the orchard. He presented everything with his arms, showing me this tree, heavy with apricots, that vine, pulsing with melons. We walked past the grain windmills, their sails catching the wind in the sunshine.

I pointed to another group of heavily laden trees. "What sort is that?"

"Pistachio."

"Pistachio?"

"Yes. Very good for the heart."

"Oh, Chartreuse! I've never seen one before! They're delightful!"

"Yes."

I remembered the gypsy woman saying if I were a tree it would be pistachio. So this was my tree! I was thrilled. "Tell me about them."

"Well, uh, what can I say, they are the family Anacardiaceae."

"The who?"

"Sure. You know. The cashew family."

"No, I didn't know."

"Also mango, poison oak, sumac, poison ivy."

"Yikes. But why are they like that, like two trunks stuck together?"

"Both are needed for pollination. That's why we graft them together."

"Why is that?" I tripped happily along through the grass.

"One is male, the other female."

I stopped. "What?"

"They bind together a male and female at the beginning. You know. So they produce fruit."

"But, but . . ."

"Sometimes the farmer relies on wind to pollinate. For fruit to set, you understand? But mostly, to be sure, we bind the male and the female trunks together when they are young to make one. See?"

Oh, sure, I understood, all right. I wasn't a woman. I was a man and a woman. My gypsy lady in Milan had seen me for who I truly was. As in most momentous moments in my life, I did not let it show. I kept walking, pretending to be interested for interest's sake.

Here." Chartreuse shook one of the trees lightly. "Try one!"

"No."

"Yes, come. Try it."

"All right." I had to admit it was delicious, very different from what I'd known. More sumptuous. I looked back at the crumbling, opulent house where inside slept the objects of my passion. Blacky, the open truth, the impossible dream. Tupelo, the secret, the clandestine and available fulfillment of forbidden desire. I swallowed. Crisp, sweet. If this was me, then this was me. I was, I reminded myself obliquely, "protected." By what, by whom, I did not—nor might I ever—know. And then, while Chartreuse stood there, high priest of the moment, while wild Afghani birdsong filled the clear morning air, I took hold of that melding of trees and wrapped my arms around both sides of it, holding it dearly in communion with myself. It was an end and a beginning. An acceptance. Yes, then, this was me, the both of me, the pistachio girl.

The next days were spent in enjoyment. We rode horses and ate and smoked the gurgling hookahs of hashish. On a bright afternoon one of Chartreuse's cousins took the group to the marketplace and then to visit the tomb of Jami, a famous Persian poet. There wasn't enough room for everyone. I volunteered to stay behind. So, at the last moment, did Blacky. He jumped off the Land Rover. I'll never forget Tupelo's face as they pulled away. She was fit to be tied.

"That was a fast one you pulled," I said as we stood there waving. The Land Rover sped into the distance.

"Well, I wasn't going to let you stay here with no one but Chartreuse. Lord knows what he would have done with you."

"Chartreuse would never hurt me," I said with confidence, disappointed that it was chivalry that kept him rather than yearning to be alone with me. "And anyway," I stomped after him back to the enclave, "why do you say that? We hung out together in Munich. Did you know that he helped out Frau Zwekl when she needed it?"

He gave a disbelieving snort. "If he says so."

That was the one thing I noticed about Blacky. He was convinced of his own good intentions but skeptical of everyone else's.

Chartreuse was in the little courtyard. He was saddling a horse. I was a little mad at Blacky for not trusting Chartreuse and a little mad at Chartreuse for not being trustworthy. I ran up to him. "Where are you going?"

"Bamiyan."

"Where's that? May I come?"

"No. I'm riding."

"I can ride," I lied.

He looked to Blacky standing there smoking a cigarette. "He will be angry."

"Blacky? He certainly doesn't tell me what to do." I looked to the ground. "He doesn't care."

Chartreuse spat in the dust. "Go and get him then. We'll take the truck. You can both come." I felt him watching me as I ran off to tell Blacky.

It took us most of the morning to reach Bamiyan. There was no road. We just headed north over the desert, guided by landmarks of which only Chartreuse had any inkling. My original excitement wore thin after three grueling hours in the open-air back of what must have been some sort of a manure truck from the smell of it. Blacky had the infuriating capacity—learned, no doubt, in medical school—of burrowing in and going to sleep under the worst of conditions. Because I was loathe to cuddle with the stinking tarp, every time I'd get comfortable we'd go over a bump and I'd be thrown into the air, sending Chartreuse into peals of laughter.

I saw in the distance a sea of red. Chartreuse was driving so fast I was afraid we'd fall into it.

"Red!" I cried out, remembering, for this was surely the red of my imagination, the dream I'd unknowingly been sure I'd find. Well, drive into it we did. We seemed to be sailing through the brilliant red.

"Poppies!" Chartreuse called over his shoulder.

I stood up in the back of the truck, holding on, the wind thrashing my hair. Miles and miles of poppies in full bloom surrounded us like a vast crinoline. Blossoms moved in waves, a scarlet sea. My heart, catapulted back to its innate first visions, ached with the beauty.

As suddenly as they had begun, the poppy fields disappeared and we were returned to the golden desert landscape. Rapid mountain streams cascaded through gnarled and ancient apple orchards. Fields of graceful young birches swayed toward one sunlit ravine.

There were gorges of monumental rocks perched dramatically after landslides, and snow framed distant crests. Spectacular, unsuspecting butterflies tripped through the bright air and smashed against the windshield. As we neared Bamiyan there were cracked, mud-walled castles, fortresses where colorfully overclothed tribesmen crouched. Slant-eyed, round-faced boys swung slingshot rings in the air.

Then, at last, when I was too weary and saddle sore to care where we were, off in the distance, three towering statues of Buddha appeared standing upright and balanced, carved and elite, within the sides of a mustard-colored plateau. Even then I knew that I beheld something mystical and reverent. They were more impressive to me out there in the wild land, those still figures, than any ornate cathedral I'd ever beheld. Even at this distance, though, we could see that there were no faces. "But where are they?" I asked.

Chartreuse said, "The hands and faces were cut off long ago by different armies on their way to India—probably the Muslim armies that brought Islam to the area in the ninth century."

"God. How old are they?"

"Fifth century," he said, driving even faster. I clung to my tarp.

Blacky, wide awake now and avidly reading from his guidebook, added, "The thinking was that by carving out the head and hands, it would take away the soul of the image."

As we neared the Buddhas it became evident that there was no town, just a crumble of ruins, some tents and caves. Men were gathered at the feet of the Buddhas, though. They'd been waiting for Chartreuse and were delighted with the unexpected gifts he had packed under the tarp. I thought they must be drugs, the way they secreted them away, but in their hurry they ripped open a scar of burlap, revealing the butt of a rifle. I looked away and smiled politely, pretending I hadn't seen.

Stiffly we disembarked and shook hands all around. The men were shy and sweet, offering us figs. They took us to a kettle of dark water where we refreshed ourselves, then brought us into a huge tent that was so dark at first after the daylight that we had to stand for a moment to adjust our eyes. I remember the tent. There were chests of drawers and carpets everywhere, even pictures on the walls. A fire was in the middle with stones in a circle and an elegant kettle. We had some greasy, delicious tea and bowls of lentils while Chartreuse was brought up to date by one of his cousins. The children sat with us. They were so different from American or European children. More ignorant, but wiser. I gave them my bangles. It didn't matter, they were cheap bangles I'd bought on the Leopoldstrasse. I wished I had more to give them. They were barefoot, with soles crusty and thick, used to the desert. Then we went back out into the daylight and, blinking and blinded by the sun, into the mysterious dark caves that led right to the feet of the Buddhas. There was certainly nothing else to do. But for the Buddhas, we were literally in the middle of nowhere. Carefully we negotiated the worn, centuries-old sedimentary earth steps, the dirt caking between our fingers as we pulled ourselves upward through the honeycomb of caves. Light streamed in at different intervals.

"Here we go," Blacky called back to me, his eyes lit up with adventure and high spirits. "These used to be the cells where more than a thousand monks would contemplate."

The height was dizzying when we reached the top and climbed out onto one of the heads, a space the size of a small balcony. I climbed to my feet but kept both arms to the wall. The drop was straight down and the wind blew fiercely. We were a good ten stories high.

"For centuries Bamiyan was the center, the heart of the Silk Route," Chartreuse shouted. "Can you imagine? This very spot was pulsing with people! Look down! We're standing where the face used to be."

The crisp wind died suddenly and I was so relieved. "Was this really the face? What a shame," I said. "Why would anyone want to destroy such mysterious treasures?"

"The Muslims," Blacky said. "They were image breakers."

"There can be no image resembling Allah," Chartreuse explained.

"It's really interesting when you think of it." Blacky wiped his glasses clean with the edge of his shirt. "The whole idea of Buddhism is nonattachment. That means to ideas, to things, to people, and even to existence itself. You really have to wonder if we are dishonoring the very intention of the creators of these statues by placing undue attachment to them. I mean, *can* the doctrine of nonattachment coexist with the need to preserve antiquities?"

We looked out over the seemingly endless valley, pondering this. And, I thought uneasily, that was no doubt why a man like Blacky would never be attached to someone as worldly as me. He thought great thoughts, did Blacky. Although I could not help remarking to myself how similar the doctrines of Buddhist thought seemed to be to my old grammar school nuns' doctrines of basic Christianity. Wasn't perfect contrition supposed to be selfless? Sorrow for one's sins supposed to stem at best from the wish for the greater good? And how staunchly the nuns had taught us never to pray *to* a statue but through it.

Blacky stood taking the newly revived wind, enjoying letting it throttle him. I admired his slim hips and fierce beard. No matter how often he shaved there was always that underlying blue threatening to come forth. Chartreuse sat on his haunches to make a shield from the wind. He lit a joint and the two of them passed it back and forth. They stood untethered. I thought if I smoked I would fall off. I felt as far away from safety as possible. For who were these men? Did I really know either of them? I had the sudden feeling that my only weapon against them was that I was not alone with either of them. As cool as it was, my forehead suddenly beaded with sweat. I stepped back and clung to the—what?—sort of nasal passages of the great Buddha.

Blacky said, "It wasn't always like this. This was an important city, one of the major Buddhist centers from the second century up to the ninth century, when Islam entered the area. Can you believe it? Look how desolate now, and how peaceful!" He pointed out across the valley. "Think of it! This is the very spot where Buddhism was transferred to China, Korea, Japan, along this very old Silk Route."

I could tell he was moved. These were the sorts of things that he was passionate about, that really riled him up, and I berated myself for imagining—even for a moment—that he, of all people, could ever be violent.

Below us stretched the valley of Bamiyan. If you squinted you could imagine the past, busy and thriving. Now a family of white dogs, huge as polar bears, romped freely. You could just make out the persistent *ting* of some worker's hammer.

Chartreuse, his pajamas snapping in the wind, his animal skin vest still smelling of animal, said in a dreamy voice, "In India, the great king Aśoka's edict was, 'All sects deserve reverence for one reason or another. By thus acting, a man exults his own sect and at the same time does service to the sects of other people."

"Yes," Blacky said. They grabbed hold of each other, clasping arms and grinning. I got a lump in my throat. I thought, I'll never forget this moment. This crux in my life. Never.

But below, some children had climbed onto the roof of the truck. They began to dance on it.

"Hey!" Chartreuse shouted. "Hey!" Frantically, he clattered

down the steps threatening retribution and leaving us alone on the magical summit.

We stood listening to the wind-furled echoes from Chartreuse's shouts.

"Do you know where we are?" Blacky asked.

"Where?"

"In the third eye of the Buddha."

How poetic he was. And how crass my perceptions had been. I would change, I resolved. Then out of the blue a huge hawk appeared in the sky. Something flaccid was between its beak. It landed near us on one of the ledges, but just out of sight. We could hear how close by the flap of its wings. We could hear hungry squeaks, and something else, a trial of agony, and then resigned silence.

Fascinated, horrified, we stood together.

"Claire," he said and he sort of laughed at himself. Then he came at me, his face pitted with grime, his eyes wet and intent with desire.

I am his moment of weakness, I thought. I was right. He fell upon my red hair like a thirsty man to water. His head was tipped and when I turned I saw his eyes, anguished and filled with heat.

"It's Bamiyon," I said, excusing his behavior. "It's this place." But then I remembered that demeaning look in Tupelo's eyes and the last veneer of my defenses was garroted and kicked away. I opened my vest and let him taste me. He held on to me like a viper. I became feather light. We stood there and the wind came up again. He wrangled his hands into the waistband of my jeans and groaned at the touch of my flesh. I kissed the salty neck that had been to Vietnam, that had studied night and day and become a doctor, that had slept with women left and right and made them cry, that had a mind that soared and pierced and—what was this?—oh, my God, was it blue?—and now . . . he dragged me back into the darkened tunnel, strange as a lighthouse made of mud, the wind whistling around us in a back-and-forth as old as time itself, and no . . . Yes. Oh, yes. Now it was my turn. He was my captive. And I was his.

chapter fourteen

We arrived back in Herat very late. I expected Tupelo to be waiting with, at the very least, a loaded gun. She had been to the silk merchants' stalls, though, and was guiltily folding away her packets of glory. She had her back to us but I could see the ribbon of vermillion being stuffed silkily under the table. Yet I was too thirsty to worry about her vain acquisitions. She turned with a big false smile on her face, the tea pitcher in her hand, and cups for us all. She had poise, I'll give her that.

If I hadn't known she'd been up to something already, I would have then, because she was nice to me in front of everyone.

"You look all in," she said, handing me the first cup. We all sat down. Greedily, I finished mine and turned back for more but she was just reaching across to give Blacky his and we got in each other's way. It seemed we were always getting in each other's way. Clumsily, she stumbled and dropped the pitcher. It fell to the ground and crashed apart. Everyone gave a cry of vexation. It would take a while for the next pot to boil. Boiled water was precious and there was no drinking anything not boiled.

We were both sorry, the others—dying of thirst—more than me. We sat about the fire waiting for the pot to boil.

"We've been to Bamiyon," Blacky announced.

"Ah, Bamiyon," Vladimir said, munching on walnuts, his legs up on a hassock. "The faceless Buddhas of time. I would have liked to come." Isolde crouched at his feet, massaging them. He didn't seem to mind. His head was thrown back in ecstasy. He lowered his chin with effort. "No chance of us going back?"

"No!" both Blacky and I shouted, our muscles sore from the hours of tedious throttling. But Blacky was happy. I could see it all around him. And I was happy, too. We kept bursting into laughter at odd moments. We arranged ourselves on cushions on the rug and ate mutton strips and hunks of bread soaked in chicken broth. There was yogurt—there was always yogurt—and grapes and pomegranates. Wolfgang walked around us in a circle, filming. It was our last night in Herat and he wanted to make sure he got it all. Daisy and Reiner played badminton. They got more use out of that set! Reiner would give a short blast with his whistle every time he scored.

"What's with you, Claire?" Reiner poked me. "Don't you think you ought to be shooting?"

"I know I should," I murmured, "but the thought of getting up and changing film seems like an enormous job." I just lay there. Blacky smiled at me from across the room. I noticed Chartreuse watching me. He seemed glad. Everyone was getting along so well. I stupidly believed it was all the good karma Blacky and I had produced. I should have taken better note of Tupelo's glittering emerald, telling and alive in the firelight.

Harry couldn't resist showing off all the treasures he'd finagled from the locals. Pots old as the hills. Kuchi dresses. He flung them over us; wonderful, many-colored, vast-skirted dresses with beading and sleeves in still different colors. "Claire!" He slung one across my lap. "I bought this one for you!"

"For me?" I held it to my face. It was cotton, very soft, made of jewel colors: lapis and ruby and on the bib rows of vibrant, hand-worked beading. The skirt had so much material that if you twirled, it would stand straight out. I'd never had anything so gorgeous, so detailed. "I don't know what to say!"

Harry, pleased with himself, brought out his little gifts for everyone. Then he stood there rocking back and forth, watching us, jingling the change in his pocket.

"But, but . . ." everyone protested.

"Tut, tut." He brushed away our protests. "We all needed a little treat, what? Time for a bauble or two!"

We ate ravenously that night. Although we tried our best to refrain from openly showing affection, Blacky and I kept smiling at each other. And we all got stoned. Except Harry, who seemed content to reap the emotional rewards of his own generosity. "Don't forget to lock up your things," he would say, like a parent. I didn't think he'd got on well with his. When he spoke of them he spoke of punishments. It was his own private mantra.

Vladimir said, "I really wanted to go see those statues." He turned to Isolde. "You know, if you hadn't had to go to the marketplace—"

"Oh, stop glowering!" Tupelo defended Isolde. "Look at all the wonderful souvenirs she bought!"

"Go on," Daisy urged her, "show us what you've bought." She stood in the hard glow of a dangling lightbulb with a fingernail scissors. She was trimming Reiner's straggly ponytail. "And so cheap!" Isolde marveled. As if to prove it, she opened her basket of hand-knit, leather-soled socks. We all agreed they were practical, beautiful, and would make excellent gifts when we returned to Europe.

"Yes, but did she have to buy so many?" Vladimir cried.

"How many?" Wolfgang asked.

Isolde looked at us with innocence. "Just eighty pair," she said. I think we laughed for half an hour.

The next morning I slept longer than anyone. I awoke with a raging headache.

Wolfgang came in. "I can't believe you're not up yet! Come on, Claire! We're going to Kabul! Don't you want to shoot it?"

"Yes," I said and tried to get up. I felt my brain move. I squinted and looked at him. "I think I need a cup of tea. That hashish must have been too strong for me."

I wrapped myself in one of the blankets and went out to the others, who were already set to leave. Isolde handed me a cup of tea. She looked at me strangely. "It's warm in here," she said.

"No, it isn't," I argued. "It's freezing."

I was feeling low. I sat down. "You know, I don't think I will go."

"She's depressed," Daisy told the others. It was beginning to annoy me that she always felt she had to interpret my motives. I said so.

"Claire, there's no staying behind. We're leaving," Harry said.

I stood there in my blanket. "I'm dizzy," I said in an aggravated tone. "I need some time, all right?"

"Tch." Tupelo snorted malevolently. "She's showing off. Looking for sympathy."

Isolde screwed up her face. "Sympathy for what?"

Reiner said, "It's not like you to be cranky, Claire."

Blacky put his hand on my face. "She's burning up," he said.

"Oh, great. Just great," Vladimir said.

Chartreuse dashed in the door. "Let's go! Off we go!"

"Claire's sick," Isolde said.

"Merde," Chartreuse said.

I ran at breakneck speed for the outhouse. When I returned they were all standing there, waiting. That's all I remember. I must have passed out. There was no possible way I could travel. I was ill. Really ill. Too ill to be frightened if I would live or die. I was simply, all-consumedly ill.

For many days and nights I remained sick. It was holding everybody up. "Well, she must be getting better now," they would say. But I did not. Blacky came up with all his superior German medicines. "She must be taking a turn soon," he would reassure them.

Still, there was no turn for the better. It went on for so long, it became at last a possibility that I might die. Through a haze of fever I heard them discussing me. Daisy was concerned that my family be alerted so they could come for the body. It was Blacky's anger that jolted me to consciousness. "Just wait until she's dead before you start referring to her as a body!" he yelled at them. He realized what he'd said and that I'd heard him. From my ravaged body on the cot my eyes met his. He sank down to the chair and put his head into his hands. The fever washed over me and I was gone again, but I remember his despair.

There was not one moment in all that time as he cared for me that I saw any sign of disgust or aggravation. He wasn't just caring, I realized even in my delirium, he lived a vocation. If you were sick he was yours. I shall never forget that. And another thing I remembered, in and out of my nightmares: Tupelo's face as she'd handed me that cup of tea. It hadn't been hot, that tea I'd so ravenously drunk. It hadn't—I realized now as I lay writhing on my cot—even been boiled. And Tupelo, it occurred to me in my moments of clarity, was many things but never, to my knowledge, clumsy.

One time I awoke with a jolt and saw her sitting on my bed. She held a silk scarf over her nose and mouth to cover a cough. But she wasn't looking at me. She didn't seek me out within my eyes. She was scrutinizing me, weighing, I thought, just how sick

I was. It was like I wasn't a person. I was past being a person. Like I was already dead because I had no more sexuality. And she'd only seen me as sexually useful.

I remember quite clearly that I turned my back on her.

The rest of them decided to carry on. They were terrified. I could see it in their eyes when they peeked in, not coming close. Although Blacky insisted what I had was probably not contagious, there was no way he could be sure. They didn't want to die. I couldn't blame them. They couldn't afford to wait for me to die and so Blacky would stay on with me until I did.

I dreamed. Nightmares. I saw my brother. He was in that hallway where he met his death. How had he felt? How long had it hurt? I struggled to run. "Claire!" he called out to me. "Claire, come back!" I woke up to Blacky sitting there on the edge of my cot, his sleeves rolled up, his glasses on. He puzzled over what to do next, for although he still had me on his strongest antibiotics, nothing seemed to work. He rocked with exhaustion. Then came the cooling gauze on my hot forehead. Cool water dripping down my cheek. I clung to that.

Once, Chartreuse came in and placed a small red velvet cushion under my head. He looked at me and shed a tear, then walked away, anguished.

However, fooling everyone, I lived. One morning—the very morning the others were packing up to leave—I awakened to see the vans pulling away. Helplessly I watched them go. I was so weak I could barely lift my head. What will become of me? I thought. But I noticed Blacky's Roy Orbison eyeglasses left behind on my nightstand. And then, I was astonished to see Blacky sleeping on the cot beside me. He was exhausted. One arm was flung across his face. His foot, lumpy with mosquito bites, hung over the side.

A bird sang shyly in the courtyard. I lifted myself to a sitting position. Putrid gauze was stuck to my arm, my neck. I peeled it from me and reached for the fresh cloth. I dipped it into the fresh water and caressed myself with it. It felt so good. Then, exhausted, I lay myself back on the pillow and gazed out the window with hollowed eyes. I had been near death, I knew, because I was now so far from it.

He opened his eyes and looked at me. The air must have been unpleasant. But sun shone weakly through the vapid windows. "I'd kill for a cup of tea," I said.

He rolled over to me and touched my cheek. "Fever's broke," he said and folded himself onto the chair, falling asleep almost instantly. I watched him sleep while the sun rose in the sky.

A man came in. He jabbered in Afghani. I'd no idea what he said. He poured the night's water on top of Blacky and I thought, That's it, it's all over now, he'll die of the germs. But he stood up, shaking himself like a dog, and came over to me. He sank down onto a stool. "I was so afraid," he confided. "I thought I'd have to go to America and tell your parents you were dead and I hadn't been able to save you."

"It would have been terrible for them," I found the strength to say. I realized he was weeping in relief.

The man had gone outside. Suddenly Blacky stood up. He sort of sniffed the air.

"What?" I said.

He hardly heard me. He went outside to the van, picking up a shovel as he went.

There was a terrible commotion. Blacky was shouting. Other men shouted in Afghani. I was terrified. Then he came back in holding his shovel over his head. I must have still been delusional because for a moment I thought he'd come in to bury me.

"They dug a hole and positioned us over it," he hissed. "Remember when they guided the vans into the enclave? I remember thinking they'd put us right over a hole and I'd better watch it when I backed up. Well, now I know why! One of them laid himself nicely into the hole and wedged a huge brick of hashish under our van! Can you believe it? They expected us to carry it over the borders, I suppose. Then they would have come and fetched it."

I gaped at him from hooded eyes. "What did you do to them?"

He swung the shovel and stopped it midway. "I just threatened them with this. I threw their hashish at them. They won't come after us for that. But we'd better get out of here. The honeymoon's over in this place. Without Chartreuse here I don't know what they'll do. We can go on through the Khyber Pass and drive until Rishikesh. We'll catch up with the gang in the Himalayas. Okay?"

I was still so weak I merely nodded.

He rushed around the room. "I'll help you collect your things," he said.

What things? I thought. "My camera," I managed to say. My throat closed. My mouth was dry. I wanted to tell him he couldn't possibly drive in his condition; if he took sick I wouldn't know what to do. We could die in the desert. I wanted to thank him, to tell him I loved him. I wanted, even then, to sleep one whole night in his arms.

chapter fifteen

"Don't get up," Blacky called dismissively. "This Khyber Pass is a bit of a letdown when you see it." He drove steadfastly through. He was still protecting me, afraid I might relapse. But I loved it. I loved the very words: Khyber Pass, the dull red earth and crouching men in their baggy *kortahs*. I wrote about it in my blue cloth-bound notebook. I raised myself up to look out the window. One saw me there and threw himself along the side of the van. *"Baksheesh! Baksheesh!"* he cried, cupping his hands in the universal alms-for-the-poor plea.

"Bugger!" Blacky swerved to avoid him.

I lay back on my worn red velvet pillow. I'd brought it with me from Chartreuse's house. Certainly nobody there would have wanted it. They'd have burned it. But it was my resting place. While I'd lain there supposedly dying, flashes of pictures I'd taken had passed before me. In a way, those pictures had refreshed me like lozenges. And now, as we drove out of Pakistan, I was beginning to have what I thought might be a really good plan. Something had bothered me since the beginning of the trip. No one had given me a contract for my job as junior crew photographer and all the work I was doing was on spec. Ever since Frau Zwekl had left me her lot, no one bothered to worry if I was all right financially, they just assumed I was. But really, I wouldn't see that money for a good long while. What, I'd worried, if they let me go? It rankled because everyone else had got a cut of the layout money up front. I'd been so grateful that they had me along that I'd never mentioned it. But as we made our way through the Khyber Pass a new thought occurred to me, and it occurred to me like an epiphany. In the same way that they were not bound to me, I, after all, could not be held bound to them. And perhaps this wasn't such a bad thing—might even one day become an advantage. They didn't own my film if they hadn't paid for it. If I could make a book of all my pictures, I bet I could find a buyer for it. I knew some of them were good just by the thrill I felt at the moment I shot them. Yes, I felt myself glow with the realization.

Especially the women. Heck, I had a way with the women. I shot them from inside out. There was a certainty there you couldn't manufacture with any hype or praise. No, they were good. So good that I kept the finished rolls of film in a tapestry sack, along with my camera, that I wouldn't part with. Even while I'd been ill and was past recognizing anyone, I'd known my bag of film was in its spot. Neurotically, once I'd been well enough to think, I'd grope in the dark to make sure it was still with me. The first thing I did in the morning was look for it. Yes. The bumpy tapestry sack was still there. My future was still there. A camera could be replaced, but never the film. Whether or not the film crew kept me on, my future might be assured just with those precious moments frozen by my choosing. And whatever I looked like when I got back to Munich, I would have a skill. I unlaced my towering espadrilles and took them off. I was done with discomfort. I put on a pair of Isolde's famous socks with the leather soles sewn on. I could wear them out and simply move on to the next, she'd given us so many. There. And if Blacky didn't like me as I was, I told myself, he could find someone else. I wriggled my toes. Wow. The moment of true self-possession. I would no longer go through life trying to impress. I'd walk this world allowing myself to be impressed.

I bought a ceramic yogurt pot through the van window from a poor man. I gave him so much money for it he started to choke and Blacky reprimanded me for a long time. I took a little umbrage at him telling me what to do with my own money. That's the thing about men. The minute you sleep with them they think they have rights. As we drove along the air seemed to hum with both our indignation.

After a while, though, he climbed into the back of the van.

"Are we moving?" I asked.

"No, of course not." He put his head on my stomach. We lay there like that.

"It feels like we're moving," I said and we started to laugh. I touched the lush black curls. An arrow of fine hair slid in a marking down from his neck to the tail of his spine. It sent a shiver of lust through me. "Where are we?" I asked him when I caught my breath. "It feels so noisy. What town is this?"

"Rishikesh. Just southeast of Dehra Dun." He stood. "It's ten at night. You've been sleeping for days."

"Yes." I stretched, gloriously rested and replenished. Just being well was enough.

"We're in India, finally." He returned to the wheel. Off we went.

India. I remembered the first time I'd heard him say the word so seductively, long ago in Isolde's flat. I pulled myself up, spread the curtains, and looked out the window, feasting upon the scene.

Droves of Indians milled around the van. Rishikesh! Through the dark streets hummed a seedy, noisy little town. It was a holy city, traditionally a stopover for Hindu pilgrims. The streets clattered with horse carts shuttling ladies in saris from ashram to hotel. Curious truck drivers stood gaping in doorways cut through with harsh white light from dangerously low-hanging, flickering lightbulbs, and barefoot, orange-robed sadhus paraded about with waist-length hair and glazed-over eyes. There was a tremendous jingle-jangle going on, prayer bead hawkers and street vendors clanging in a hubbub. It was all so hectic after my silent stretch of healing, I instantly longed to get away. "My God!" I groaned. "So many people! Like ants. Where do they all come from?"

Blacky said, returning to the wheel and starting up the engine, "I'm having a tough time not hitting any of them. They act oblivious. It's like they don't care if they get hit or not!"

The van inched its way through the crowds. The town cringed and jangled with activity. Lepers bounded up and shoved each other in the way of the van. *"Baksheesh! Baksheesh!"* they shouted.

"What do they want?" I cried and climbed into the passenger seat.

Blacky gently took my hand as he continued to drive. "Every city in India has its lepers, Claire. The holy cities attract more simply because business is better there. Indians on retreat are noticeably more generous than those at home. Because we are situated here within one of the most backward regions of India, where leprosy is believed to be the punishment of a crime committed in a previous life, the city carries the burden of these blighted inhabitants blindly."

"But why? Why does no one help?"

"Because to approach or associate with them socially would mean to interfere with the leper's karma, thereby contaminating one's self not only physically but spiritually."

"Oh, God, they're horrible!"

Blacky's jaw set. "Not as horrible as those Westerners who ignore them. You'll see. It rubs off. You'll find you can simply avert your eyes and walk on by."

"I could never ignore them," I protested.

Sitar music yelped tinnily from cheap radios skeletal women had traded for now-forever-gone fertility. (Have your tubes tied, here's your radio. Next!) Their noses were pierced with silver hoops, and the stuffy odor of sandalwood and curry incense lingered over the stink of worse and rotten smells. Teams of beggars outside air-conditioned restaurants spat horrid gobs of "oyster" where the swarthy Sikhs in turbans hustled by in rubber-banded beards and arrogant disdain.

"Don't worry, Claire." Blacky twirled the wheel happily. "Chartreuse told me about a magical guru who runs a quiet and reasonably priced inn. It's called the Alpine Cottage."

"Really?" I drew back, horrified, from the window. "I can't imagine anything peaceful around here. This is worse than Penn Station at rush hour! And the dust!"

"Chartreuse said he's the real deal," Blacky forecast enthusiastically.

I knew he'd been looking forward to this. I just wished we would get there soon. The arid ground, the throngs of people— it was like being caught in a wind tunnel. The Ganges, fortunately, moistened the dust with whale-sized puddles and rivulets. We followed it out of town to find that peaceful inn.

We got lost several times and by the time we drove into the hovel of trees behind the pale sign announcing ALPINE COTTAGE— ALL WELCOME, it was the wee hours. A dog barked. I saw a rainbow parrot stomping out on a tin roof to see what was up. A white-haired swami, maybe sixty, his face coffee white, his body hard as a nut and like a boy's, came out to greet us. He seemed pleased to see us and folded his hands into a steeple. The kitchen was just a table and a bubbling cauldron in the yard, but the library was lined with books and in the welcoming room doilies graced the ragged cashmere easy chairs.

Blacky had been expecting an impressive ashram, I think, and I could tell he was disappointed by the paltriness of the place, but

I reminded him that by the standards we were by now used to, the place seemed almost elegant.

There were no other guests in residence and the swami had only one apostle. His name was Narayan and he was no more than a slip of a boy. He was incredibly beautiful. He didn't seem very holy. What most impressed him was my dazzling collection of beads, which he walked right up to and took hold of. Narayan had a way of standing too close to you. He had no sense of discretion. The swami collected our passports himself and sent his apostle off to make us some *chi*.

I didn't want to stay in the cloister-like room allotted us. It was light green and had the fluorescence of a Chinese restaurant. I thought Blacky wouldn't want sex in a room like that with two cots and the thin walls. "Why don't we stay in the van?" I persuaded, leaning against him. He gave in and we climbed back into our cozy womb of bliss protected from invaders by the Alpine Cottage's strong walls and gates.

That night he climbed in the van and on top of me. I protested, "But I'm so not ready!"

"I'll take care," he breathed, aroused, in my ear.

"Okay, then. Sure." I gave in, easy.

He pulled my hips up onto him and straddled me, entering me with his dark penis, eliciting from me those moans of acquiescence you can't help making, you can't help the rapture. It just goes on and on until you know you've found it, there. Yes, there, your teeth little cushions around his shoulder's flesh, your inner parasol opening, opening, pouring with rapture's own rain.

When I woke up in the morning, Blacky and Swamiji were already drinking *chi* out in the garden. They'd hit it off very well. They were discussing philosophy, a subject they both seemed well up on. There were German newspapers and a copy of *Der Spiegel* on the small table before them so I knew Blacky had already been up and out to the embassy. My heart sank. One copy of *Der Spiegel* and I'd lose him for days. But life is not about controlling someone else, it's about bringing the best out of him. I put on my biggest smile and went over.

Blacky gave a wave when he saw me. I sat down and joined them on a rickety stool. Someone had gone for sweet buns. I could have eaten them all. I hadn't had an appetite in so long, now I was prepared to eat the plate.

The Alpine Cottage might not have been an established, touristy holy place, but it was authentic, I thought, very peaceful and well kept, however poor. Narayan seemed to spend most of his time sweeping the place out.

When I was in the middle of my second bun I realized they were looking at me in a funny way. "What's wrong?" I said.

Blacky held out an old copy of the German paper. It was crumpled, having been read many times. It was dated two weeks ago.

"What is it?"

"It says here," Blacky read excitedly, "members of the Democratic and Republican leadership of the House of Representatives began talking publicly and seriously about impeaching President Nixon."

"Wow. Let me see that."

"Oh! Almost forgot!" Blacky patted his shirt pocket. "Claire! Here." He passed me two letters, one an official-looking beige envelope on hefty ivory stock from Zurich and the other a flimsy blue airmail letter from America.

I opened the official-looking one first. It was from Herr Binnemann.

"What's it say?" He hovered at my elbow.

I blinked. I took my time, rereading the letter twice. "It seems," my voice was thick as the words came out, "that Frau Zwekl had some debts. I won't be seeing as much money as I'd thought from her estate."

"Oh." He raked his hair back with his fingers. "How much *will* you be getting?"

I handed him the letter.

"Hmm," he said finally. Then, "Well, cheer up. It will pay for this trip, won't it?"

I felt sick. "Just." I sat down on a pile of straw mats. This was a blow. From heiress to adventuress.

He was disappointed for me, I could tell. But I couldn't help feeling I'd toppled in his estimation. He assessed my misery. "Look," he said, "you'll make tons of money modeling when we get back to Munich. You know you will!" He flicked the bottom of my chin.

I'd thought we both knew I was going to try my luck as a photographer when I got back to Munich. "But, Blacky—"

"Hey. Come on! You have another letter. Maybe it's good news! One bad, one good. That's how it goes."

Doubtfully, I opened it quickly. This was from Carmela, my sister, the older one, the beauty. You know. Looks like Snow White but mean as the stepmother. I felt myself trembling already. "Dear Claire," it began, "What the hell do you think you're doing traveling around the goddamn world when I'm stuck here like this, divorced, with mommy and daddy? What are you thinking? And Zinnie says when she graduates she's going into the police academy! That's your fault, too!"

I folded up the letter and stuck it in my bag without finishing it. I pushed it out of sight, out of mind. But I could just see my little sister, Zinnie, short and blond and fierce, making claims to go clean up the world. "A clear conscience has the strength of ten men," Michael used to tell us. She'd fallen for it, all right.

Blacky, acting as though all of this were nothing more than one more thing to deal with, went off to the swami's welcome room to see what he could dig up in the way of more knowledge to go. I proceeded to chew off my fingernails, something to go with the buns. After a while I washed myself at the pump and then cleaned my assortment of lenses. Blacky had come across volumes of books on the shelves about the Dalai Lama and announced that he planned to look through them. This would take hours. I was beginning to realize he was a bookaholic, it didn't much matter in which language. Maybe he really didn't care if I had money. I was very unsure. Not knowing what to do with myself, I swung back and forth on the macramé hammock there behind the courtyard. When Narayan saw me sitting in the garden, he decided to show me the town.

He was a wonderful guide and I wound up spending almost the entire day with him. He took me all sorts of places, the most memorable of them the Monkey Temple. It was exotic and marvelous and thoroughly overrun with darling, precocious monkeys. I asked him to remove his shirt while the monkeys climbed all over him. He had a way of looking at the camera with this pleading happiness. There was so much life and excitement to him. He practically exploded with it. He reminded me of me when I first came to Europe, which led me to think of my bad news. Never mind, I told myself. I could make money with my pictures. I *would* make money with them! Then I let Narayan shoot my picture while the monkeys traveled over my head, jumped lightheartedly into my arms, scrupulously checked for fleas on my scalp. I started to feel a little overwhelmed. They were becoming a swarm. They must have heard the fear in my voice as I called frantically to Narayan but, enthused as he was with his new job, he just kept taking pictures. At last I got through to him and he plundered through the rush of smelly creatures, who'd by now enveloped my entire body.

There was one saucy one who wouldn't be put down. It turned vicious and latched on to the flesh behind my knee with its demonic teeth. I cried out and Narayan threw me to the ground, clearing it and the others off in a scatter. He yanked me away before they could climb back up and we ran, terrified, Narayan's shirt gone for good. One monkey slithered through the branches overhead with it draped around its shoulders like a lucky shawl.

When we got back to the inn we were laughing but it hadn't been funny at the time. I shuddered as we told our tale to Blacky and Swamiji, who listened with his bright eyes. There was a wonderful ambience at the Alpine Cottage, like there was something genuine going on. I couldn't put my finger on it, but there was something holy there. You wanted to be good. It was that little swami. Even if you weren't talking with him—and Blacky was doing a good job of monopolizing him—he made you want to please him.

Narayan was quite taken with my makeup bag. I'd never thought of it as valuable, but suddenly, here, it became his focus. His eyes would follow it when I would carry it past him on the way to the outhouse. Suddenly he would come up to me and caress it from beneath, his raisin eyes glittering, his perfect white teeth gleaming. The next afternoon I sat in the window in a shaft of light and there he was suddenly, ogling my stupid, old-as-the-hills JCPenney bag. "Tch," I said, losing patience, aggravated at being caught clandestinely tweezing my chin hairs. "Take the darn thing."

He stood up, offended. He looked as though I'd slapped him. "Oh, no," he wiggled his head in that funny, wobbly way they have, "not like that." He went away.

And I'd thought he was shallow. I felt really ashamed. I looked around. Really. These people had nothing. I went out and sat on a canvas chair in the garden. My fault, too, the letter had said. Well, that was just it. At home I was always just "Me, too! Me, too!" And I hated it.

Narayan reappeared. He climbed up and stood on the garden wall. He put one slender brown foot in front of the other, balancing himself like a tightrope walker. Behind him palm tree fronds moved, thick and green and yellow.

"Where is Dr. Blacky?" I asked him, hoping to start fresh.

"Dr. Blacky is in the meditation room," he said, "trying to meditate."

For some reason this aggravated me. "How's he doing?" I inquired.

"Trying too hard." He shrugged.

I laughed, pleased. I didn't really mind if Blacky beat me in the holier-than-thou game, but I'd heard that part of the requirement for enlightenment was relinquishing sex. That I absolutely could not have. We were just getting started.

But then Blacky and Swamiji, deep in conversation, strolled into the garden and sat beside us.

Imagining I'd gain points with Swamiji, I presented Narayan with the makeup bag. I'd thought the things inside were what had appealed to him but he just tumbled the entrails onto the ground and attached the bag to his holy beads.

"What a rubble!" Swamiji remarked about the pile of stuff.

"That's the one thing about Claire," Blacky sold me out without out a thought, "she's a clutter bug."

I was a little stung by that remark because although it was true, I tried my best to be tidy in front of him.

Narayan said, "Goodness, Claire, your leg is festering!"

I twisted my body to see. "Yeah. I thought it wasn't much, but it seems—"

"Let me see that!" Blacky took hold of my leg. He changed his glasses and looked more closely. "Looks mean," he murmured, pressing the swollen flesh.

"Pity," Narayan said, combing his coconut-oiled hair with my clean brush.

"Those monkeys have rabies." Swamiji wrinkled his brow.

"Oh, no. It couldn't be." I shook my head. "Those animals were healthy. They—"

"Oh, we have four or five deaths a year from rabies," Swamiji interrupted, pursing his lips. "Not pleasant."

Blacky and I looked at each other.

"Is there a health clinic nearby?" Blacky asked.

"Oh, I'll be fine," I said.

"You're going to have to have rabies shots," he said sternly.

"Oh, no, I'm not," I said, remembering hearing tales of agony from childhood. Something about needles directly into the stomach and excruciating pain.

"I'm afraid we can't take that chance," Blacky said.

"No," I shook my head vehemently, "not after all I've just been through."

"Especially because of it."

"I can't."

"You must."

"I won't."

"You can't not."

Swamiji went into the house. We sat on the swept ground and waited. No one said a thing. I remember there was a snake, a little one, taking the sun. It was very still. We were all very still.

Swamiji returned a short time later with an address. "Here we go. It's across the border in Nepal. But it's not far at all. Their clinic is quite good. Better than ours. It's just—" He stopped. "Well. If you can bring your own needles . . ." He moved his Adam's apple up and down carefully. "Their needles are awfully thick. Quite painful, I'm told."

"Oh, I have my own needles," Blacky assured him and looked at me with those sea green, don't-worry-about-a-thing eyes.

I began to tremble.

Swamiji walked over to me and put a hand on the top of my head. Immediately I stopped trembling. It wasn't anything eerie, it felt more loving: like a favorite uncle's touch. "Claire," he spoke softly, "no one will make you do anything you don't want. All right?"

"All right." I nodded, immediately feeling better.

"That's right," Blacky reassured me, "we won't even leave until you're ready."

Swamiji padded over to the banyan tree, unwound his cloth, and folded himself into the lotus position. We all watched him. It was as though he'd left us, gone far away. We sat there for a long time watching him.

Blacky and Narayan discussed astrology, which Blacky knew nothing about. He had only scorn for astrology when I talked about it. I thought of what it would be like when we rejoined the others. Every time before this Blacky had reverted to being Tupelo's fiancé. But he was my sweetheart now. He couldn't deny it. I took his picture sitting there. And I wasn't going to let the past ruin everything. I thought of the film and how it would be when we hooked up with them all again. "I miss our friends," I said, a tear slipping out.

"But, darling, we can leave today." He took my hands in his. He'd never called me darling before. He pushed his glasses up with his pointer finger in that endearing way he had. "A week or so more and we'll be with the others."

My heart leapt with joy. Then I realized that his did, too.

He said, "It's all been too much for you. Once it's over and we get you your rabies shots we can head for the village of the Dalai Lama. Just think of it, Claire! We're *that* close. In all our lives we will never meet another living god. It's so exciting. Come. We'll get your rabies shots taken care of in Nepal. I'll be with you the whole time. Every minute. All right? And then we'll drive up to Dharamsala and rejoin the gang. I've cabled ahead." He wrinkled his forehead. "I mean, I can't be sure they got it but they most probably did. I know Wolfgang will be thrilled to see you looking so well." He narrowed his eyes in a pretense of jealousy. "I'm not sure I like the thought of that."

"As if you had to give him a second thought," I sneered, heartened by any insecurity on his part, even if it was feigned to make me feel better.

"I wouldn't mind one of Isolde's omelets right now," he confided.

"Me, too. The way she whips it up with her finger! Or a song
from Chartreuse's guitar."

"Even Reiner's complaining I could take." He smiled.

"I'm dying to see if Daisy's still smitten or if he's driving her
mad with his endless quotations."

We both laughed.

"And I miss Harry's observations," I said. "I think I miss him
most of all. I can't wait to see them." I was just about to say something about Tupelo when I realized so was he and at that moment,
fearing saying the wrong thing, we both stopped ourselves and—
not wanting to break the spell of closeness—said nothing.

As much as I looked forward to it, I was troubled with the
prospect of leaving. The truth was, I was frightened. I felt as though
the closer we got to the others the sooner we would be jimmied
apart. I wanted to tell Blacky this but I was afraid it would break the
trust between us. "Fine," I said at last, "that would be fine."

Out of nowhere came the voice of Swamiji. "When there is
fear, Claire, you must run like the wind through the rain. But you
must run," he shook his head in that rubbery, Indian head-
shaking way, "toward the fear." I was sure he'd been eavesdrop-
ping. Then I remembered I'd been talking to myself.

"Swamiji?" I turned to the little man cross-legged under his
banyan tree. "Is that right, Swamiji?" It's impossible, I thought.
Had he read my mind?

But Swamiji had gone into heavy meditation. Or light meditation, depending how you looked at it, I guess; his eyes were, if
you can believe it, turned back in his head and the whites gave
him the look of the blind. The wind continued to rise and objects
flew over the wall into the garden. A pair of shredded bloomers
dropped in and then flew out. Then a sheet of copper flapped in

with a dark rattle. Narayan picked it up, puzzling how to make use of it. "Do you think I could become a film star in your country?" he asked me.

Startled, I looked at him, his shoulder-length hair and slender waist. "If that's what you want," I said. "I mean, you could always take a shot."

"Will you give me your address in America?"

"Oh, Narayan. I don't live near Hollywood at all. I live near New York."

"That's good. New York is veddy good!" he said excitedly.

My heart sank with weary premonition. There would be my mother at the front door and this Indian would stand there with his cardboard suitcase. They would call the police. "I will give you a letter from me, okay?" I said finally.

"Yippee!" Narayan cried and jumped down to the ground. He ran to the house, presumably to look for paper and pen. The palm trees above me rattled, living oars against themselves. I sat there beneath this umbrella of shade. The grassless dirt was raked in harmonious, undulating lines, Narayan's creation. It stayed powdery and still with perfect dust, untouched by the stirring wind. The cloying smell of incense reached us even out here. It rose in snaky fumes that widened into clouds of jasmine and sandalwood.

Swamiji said, "Claire. Come and sit close to me."

"I'm afraid to go over there. There was a snake there."

"Ah. That would be a good thing. A sign. Come. I'll tell you a secret."

I walked shyly over to where he was.

"This is from the Bhagavad Gita."

"Okay." I strained to listen well.

"The mind has to be concentrated on God, and not on any other deity or nature." He looked past me at Blacky then back at me, his eyes prickling with good humor. "See?"

"Yes." I smiled back at him. But I didn't. I didn't understand until much later. When I would run like the wind through the rain.

We left the Alpine Cottage the next day. Although it was Blacky who'd spent most of the time with Swamiji, it was me to whom the old man presented a gift. It was a large book made of burlaplike material. It was the Bhagavad Gita, what you would call the Hindu Bible.

"But, no," I said, "I have nothing for you."

"Don't let the last word be no." He bowed in a presentational way.

"Okay," I said, "yes," and took the book. He started to walk away and then he stopped and turned back to me. He smiled his sweet smile. "May I give you some advice?"

"Please, yes." I thought he was going to give shortcut directions.

He folded his hands. I had to lean toward him to catch the words. "Just remember this: Water is fluid and yielding, but water will wear away rock, which is rigid and cannot yield. As a rule, whatever is fluid, soft, and yielding will overcome whatever is rigid and hard. This is another paradox. What is soft is strong."

I stood there looking at him. "Thank you. I guess I'll never forget you. Are those words from this Bhagavad Gita?"

"No. That's Lao-tzu." He shrugged, enjoying himself. "Truth," his glittery eyes shone with humor, "is international." Those eyes continued to hold mine as Blacky marched toward us.

"Thank you, Swamiji."

He padded silently away and disappeared into the lush garden trees. "Did you pay them?" I asked Blacky.

"Of course I paid them." He shined his glasses with a wet handkerchief. "Well. Sort of a donation. He just wanted a donation."

"It wasn't what I expected."

"No."

"It was kind of weird. I mean in a beautiful sort of way." I looked back toward the trees and briskly rubbed my arms. "So many different smells! It's all so exotic and Garden of Edeny."

"Yes," Blacky said. Then, "There was bird shit on the out-house seat."

"And mice in the cupboard," I added.

"Still . . ."

"Yes," I agreed. "We both loved him, though, didn't we?" I trotted back into the house for a final good-bye but Swamiji was nowhere to be found. I stood in the room, saying good-bye to it. A fine old Victorian clock ticked loudly.

I went out to the van.

Blacky emerged from the outhouse, swinging his arms. He sat down at the water jug and fastidiously washed his hands. Then he climbed into the van. He was always in a good mood when we were about to be off.

I said, "I've decided I want to change."

He said, "There's that lovely blue dress you bought in Afghanistan for a special occasion."

I sat up. "That isn't the way I want to change," I said, wondering fleetingly, though, at the same time where *had* I put that nice blue dress? I couldn't find it anywhere.

Blacky pulled out his great bundle of road maps. Another minute and he'd be unreachable.

All right, I said to myself, this is it. With much deliberate aplomb, I said, "Blacky, I have to ask you a question before we drive anywhere, before I go one step further."

He was all ready to put the van in gear and resignedly sank back. Yet another delay! His posture sent its aggravated message.

"I know this isn't the right moment. God, I can feel that. But this is—well—it's plaguing me. Look. It's just this. I know that everything in life is how you perceive it, I know that. And I just don't quite know how to see myself with you. (I didn't have the nerve to ask him if he *loved* me. Love had to be given freely or it didn't mean anything.) But," I went on in the softest voice I could muster, remembering the advice of Swamiji, "you have to give me some assurance that you're not going to throw me over the moment we reach the others." By "others" I meant Tupelo. Well, he knew that.

Then he said, "As long as we're clearing the slate, I have something I'd like to say, too."

The sky in the distance had turned an ominous purple. I thought, Oh what have I started? For some reason my heart began to trip.

He turned and looked deeply into my eyes. He said, "Look, Claire, I know you think that—I mean, well, I haven't been fair to you, really. I mean about Tupelo."

"That's right," I whispered, hardly able to speak, "you haven't." He hadn't been fair to Tupelo, either. But this was my moment.

He combed his fingers through his hair and made a tortured face.

Here it comes, I thought. At last. I realized he was going to tell me he loved her and he just hadn't been able to resist my throwing myself at him.

"It was damned awkward the way it all happened, you see," he began. "Well, awkward is certainly not the word." He snorted at the inappropriateness of it. He sounded bitter. He was talking to me but he was somewhere else. "I'd better start at the beginning." His hands clenched the steering wheel and as he talked he loosened them enough to travel his palms in a distracted up-and-down. "Tupelo came to me one day in April. It was a beautiful day. The trees were all full and—Well. She came to my practice. She'd got my name from Isolde." He looked past the tall stone wall and Rishikesh down the road. He was remembering.

I knew something terrible was coming. Oh, Lord, I thought, he's going to tell me he'd got her pregnant! But that wasn't it at all. He went on. "She was so beautiful. I thought, I must send her to someone else so I might date her. Really, that was my first thought."

"Gee, thanks for telling me that."

He ignored this. "She had this mole on her shoulder blade she wanted removed."

Yes, I acknowledged silently. I knew the scar. I'd kissed that scar and she had writhed in a gossamer way.

"Very tiny, but angry," he went on. "She wanted it removed. You only had to look at her to know she was healthy. I sent her over to Frank Mullermai in Dermatology. I knew he'd take care of her. He's a good man. But then her tests came back. I couldn't believe it. She—" He stopped talking and looked at me. "She had—she has cancer."

I shook my head. Tupelo? No. Tupelo would eat you for supper. She wouldn't have cancer. No. What was he talking about? The sky had become thick and still. Blacky lit his Wills's Flake cigarette.

"What kind of cancer?"

"Melanoma."

"What do you mean? Will she die?"

"I can't believe she's still alive," he said through closed teeth.

"But she's not sick!"

"She will be soon. I don't like that cough she's got. That's why I'd like to get—"

"Yes, of course," I said. Then, unable to stop myself, I added, "And so you asked her to marry you."

He set his jaw. I thought he was going to say he most certainly would marry her. But he said, "I'll stick by her until," he looked away, "until she—"

I blurted, "But why did she come on this trip if she's going to die?"

"And what should she do? Stay in Munich and wait for it? You don't have any idea what it's like. It's not as though it were early on and something could be done. All Mullermai could say was, 'If she'd only come in a few months earlier!' And to think she'd put it off because of some idiotic publicity photo session she wanted to look perfect for!" he flared at me. I'd never seen him so angry. "That's why I could never say a word," he went on, spitting his words through clenched teeth. "She doesn't want anyone to know! She doesn't want horror and pity in people's eyes. You can't blame her. I told her I would help her through it. I promised her I wouldn't let her suffer. I won't." He scrubbed his knee with his fist. "I won't."

"But, your mother's ring . . ." I said stupidly.

"Tch. It's not my mother's. It's hers. She bought it for herself when she found out. She said it was the color of my eyes and when she looked at it she'd remember I wouldn't let her suffer. 'It cost a fortune!' I reprimanded her when I found out what she'd paid. Can you imagine what a fool I am? Do you know what she said? She was very calm. She said, 'But it's beautiful. And who else will buy me such a ring in my lifetime? So what difference does it make?'" He leaned his head back and breathed out, relieved at last to share the burden of this terrible knowledge. "What difference does it make," he said again, rocking his head.

We sat looking at the road to Rishikesh.

I thought of the glitter of that emerald stone. How I'd envied her!

"It's very still again," he said finally.

"Yes," I said, "the wind's died."

Just as we said it, thunder rumbled. A rickshaw took off toward the Ganges. I remember that moment as though it were etched into my consciousness. I tried to think of all the times I'd misinterpreted her words, her actions. And after Bamiyan when

I'd fallen ill and Blacky had chosen to stay with me because he'd thought I was going to die first. For a split second I relived Tupelo coming into my sickroom, where I lay presumably dying. I remembered how I'd thought she was checking to see if I was almost dead. Perhaps, I realized now, she'd been coming to see what it looked like, this dying. How she must have felt! Oh, it couldn't be! She was too beautiful to die so young! Everyone is going to die, but *knowing* someone is close to death—oh, it changes everything!

He'd put us in gear and the van had begun to roll. "No!" I cried out mindlessly.

At that moment Narayan came running out to wave good-bye. He climbed the wall and stood on it, waving. Swamiji plucked his way from the dark inside and stood in his doorway. It occurred to me just then that Blacky hadn't answered my question. I thought, Oh, what's the difference? All the wasted time on jealousy! What good was it? Life was too precious, every solid moment of it. The best thing to do would be to forget all about it. We waved to Narayan and Swamiji and drove away.

The rain came down. It was just minutes later we drove into a flock of vultures, huge vultures. They smacked the van with such force we thought they were *in* the van.

We rushed out to see the damage but, oddly enough, we were pretty much intact and so were the vultures—though one of them hobbled in the rainy distance behind us, then took off and we lost him. We'd rammed into them with such force, I was sure at least one of them would be dead. The throngs of people passing by on foot and bicycle hardly reacted to what had just happened. I found it hard to believe, but all was well. We climbed back into the van and as we joggled along through the ruckus, I returned to telling myself over and over that I would never be jealous again. And not only that, but the worst of it was the tiny, desperate seed of relief, yes, relief, that it was not me who was going to die. Not yet. Oh, thank you, God, not yet!

I got my rabies shots in a humming little suburb of Katmandu. The officials seemed to think I would need a series of only six days, not ten. We were both glad for this; the sooner we would catch up to the others—for now there was an urgency we both shared.

Ten o'clock each morning we would all line up at the health clinic—there were always at least seventeen possible rabies victims. I had to show them my American passport.

The thing was, the others—almost all children—had to have those fat needles. It was embarrassing to have such special privileges in front of them. The little boy before me—he must have been about eight—made not a whimper as they placed the fat needle into his stomach and plunged the stiff fluid in. I couldn't very well cry out after that.

Blacky kept a forbidden bottle of apricot brandy for medicinal purposes. I made good use of it that week. And we spent a lot of time in each other's arms. At first I thought he was consoling me. Then I thought we were consoling each other, both putting off facing Tupelo and her inevitable illness waiting for us up in the Himalayas. There was a little of that I guess. But the van those mornings was filled with love. "Shut the window, quickly," he would say. I loved his voice, the unusual, churning timbre of it. I wanted to own him, really, his lovely feet and hairless toes. There was a pulse in his throat I wanted, too.

The Nepal sun through the orange plaid curtains would fill the bed and he would fill me with insistence. We could hear people passing by. We'd parked our van very close to the clinic. We lay on our souvenirs and embroidery, rolled over them, creasing our naked backs with their imprints, and he would climb between my legs and I would moan with the pain and rapture of our now very constant lovemaking. The van would lurch and bobble.

Blacky had a normalcy about him, a clean and plain lust without deviance. It was a time to reap. He must have been crazy about me, my young American body with its ardent center, and yet when I look back on our lovemaking it is my lovemaking I remember most; my greedy thirst for him, with my tender body wanting more and more, and the fear and hope of what would happen next, and what would take him forever away from me. Even then I knew to be here now, aware that bliss lasted not at all forever. I held each moment like a jewel in the palm of my hand, like a pulsing dove lulling only on furlough until its own intended flight.

chapter sixteen

The Kuloo Valley was like a ride into a Chinese teacup. The landscape rose up Himalayan heights and down rice paddy chasms. Tension bridges spanned outlandish drops. Cherubic Buddha faces on the narrow roads. Backs bent over with small-car–sized packets of straw. There were no more Hindu or troubled Muslim faces. The inhabitants mellowed in their pace, their mood, their manner, the moment the altitude rose. The Dauladhar Range was pebbled with sweet beings, complying, moving right off the road in the wake of the van. Not like those below, who would bob their heads belligerently as you shaved them by an inch. Even the faces on the water buffalo turned pretty.

I peered at the women through the window in their costumes of reds, blues, and yellows; gold in their noses; turquoise headdresses; clusters of necklaces jangling. Pad pad paddy, they scurried aside with their moonfaces and cranberry mukluks; innocent children old and young: refugees from Tibet.

"What if we can't find the others?" I worried, unpacking layers of clothes and putting on everything I owned to ward off the chill.

"They know we're coming," Blacky reassured me. "They picked up the cablegram at the American Express when they passed through Delhi. I'm quite sure they know you're alive." He smiled cheerfully. "They just expected us some days ago. They couldn't know about the rabies shots, though, could they?"

"No."

"You know," he said excitedly, "Swamiji told me about a wonderful leper colony hereabouts."

"Wonderful?" I replied skeptically, plunging my arms into a sweater.

"No, I mean in the sense that would be a wonderful experience. Worth the entire trip. You know, Claire, there aren't that many lepers left in the world."

"That's good news." For a moment I thought he was going to turn off and take us there. But of course there was Tupelo to think of now, and so we continued on our way.

The frosty air was thin as a willow, cracking and whirling the night about, winding through the first town, Dharamsala, its stores on stilts and crumbly buildings and tea shops forming a tiny boulevard. Bicycles and wagons were everywhere. We passed through there and continued farther upward into thick and furry trees, past running streams to what was once an English officer's retreat, huddled snuggly in McLeod Ganj.

Blacky wove the van around the last right-angle turn and pulled to a stop between the blue night and the kerosene-lit street. A waterfall dropped enchantingly from an evergreen peak. Tea shops clustered up and down the rowlike, wide way, humming with voices and warm yellow flickers. Wooden buildings, some on rickety slender poles, stuck upright like splintered boxes right and left of the Buddhist Stupa. There was open-air all day and night devotion in the backyard of the Dalai Lama's temporary palace. Tiny, strangely garbed Tibetans with rosy skin and gentle expressions circled the prayer wheel even at night. They touched the walls and turned the wheel while it clanged, each sound a prayer. Children bundled up like panda bears reached up and rang the bells along the side. It was such an eerie, yet a friendly sight.

Blacky parked the van and slammed his door shut. We were both keen to find the others after weeks of separation but a thrill of joy ran through me just to be in this magical place. I am well, I congratulated myself, taking great gulps of the delicious air. And we would meet the Dalai Lama, perhaps even photograph him! Blacky had been talking about it for so long I'd begun to think of it as his destination, his goal. But now, suddenly being in this place where all night devotion turned the prayer wheel, I recognized something: I felt as though this was it, this was the place you dug toward as a child with your shovel when you aimed for the other side of the world. It was the most exotic place I would ever experience, the other side of everywhere. I knew it then. I know it now. How far we'd come! I could hardly believe it was happening. As I stepped from the stuffy warmth of the van there were more stars than darkness and I thought I'd arrived in Shangri-la.

We headed for the Kailesh hotel, where groups of other Western travelers sat over miniature tables gobbling noodly soups. CHAPADEE AND TEA said the sign on the wall, TWO RUPEE. A feeling of dread overtook me then. I didn't know what I'd feel seeing Tupelo. She would by now be physically changed. Was I to feel guilty having kept Blacky from her when she needed him most?

Blacky found a table with two mended chairs in the corner and we shuttled them over to the warmth from the potbellied stove. There was a proprietor at a massive wooden desk directly in the middle of the room. He wrote exotic-looking numbers into a cloth-bound blue book while his daughter sat owlishly on his comfortable lap. His wife, dressed in the traditional Tibetan apron, bustled about the tables carrying away empty plates and scolding customers who hadn't finished. I diverted to the restroom—not much more than a rattletrap enclosed chamber with a hole in it, and then I hurried back, not wanting to miss a thing. I loved the smells of McLeod Ganj, coal and kerosene and wood fires, delicate incense and vegetables cooking. We ordered noodle soup, which was delicious, and buttered tea, which took some getting used to.

Children with round faces and snotty noses leaned without fear across my knees. They touched my red hair, braceleted my wrists with colored paper.

The Westerners spoke openly from one table to the next, trading travel information and discussing meditation courses to be taken at the ashram or the library outside of town. On the side tables there were more than a few well-worn copies of the ever-popular *Tibetan Book of the Dead*.

We were just about to inquire of the next table if they knew of a film company hereabouts when, at that very moment, in floated Reiner. But it wasn't the Reiner we knew, it was some sort of high priest of a Reiner, done over in burgundy robes.

He was pleased to see us, if not outwardly very expressive. He glided over to us, pressed his palms together in welcome, and lowered himself, spine rigid, into a chair. All this in three short weeks. I felt like saying, "Snap out of it!" but I didn't. Everyone's entitled to their day in the impersonation world. I reminded myself of the heavy French accent I'd affected around New York before I'd ever left Queens.

He took my cheeks in his thumb and forefinger and studied my eyes. "Well," he said, "you look like the devil but you're alive."

"Where are the others? Where's Isolde?" I charged.

"They're most of them down at the ashram taking a class."

"What about the movie?" I said.

"All in due time." He smoothed the air with a patting-down hand. "There's no rush."

"I can't believe we just ran into you like this," I said. "I imagined we'd be going from hotel to hotel."

"Oh, everyone haunts the same spots. They'll all wander in here in a little while. I'm delighted to get to see your first impressions. You don't get a second chance at a first impression."

Blacky said, "I parked near the waterfall. Is that all right? I didn't see any signs."

Reiner raised a benedictory hand. "Everything is all right, man."

I squirmed in my seat, impatient to see the rest of them.

"What a wonderful place!" Blacky marveled.

Reiner said, "The palace of the Dalai Lama is just down at the end of the street. The whole village of two thousand is in reality a refugee camp Mrs. Gandhi has given them. They're homeless, actually, waiting to be let back into Tibet. I don't think they will be, though." He surprised me by spitting out the window. "The Red Chinese are already using their photos on their travelogues to get the Westerners to come to fun-filled China, see?" He looked at me. "Much like the buffalo and feathered Indians you destroyed and use to attract German tourists at the travel bureaus on the Bahnhofstrasse."

"*I* destroyed?" I sputtered.

Blacky stood up and tucked his shirt into his blue jeans. "When do you think I can get in to see him?"

"Who?"

"The Dalai Lama."

"Oh, you won't be seeing him. He's off to Sweden."

"*Wie bitte?!!*"

"Yeah. Collecting money for his people. Pity. After all that."

"But he'll return shortly . . ."

"Oh, I don't think so."

We looked at one another.

"This can't be," Blacky said.

Reiner said, "It certainly has taken away the feeling of urgency with the film."

Blacky sat down, personally betrayed. Angrily, he slurped his buttered tea.

It had never occurred to any of us—after all we'd gone through to get here—that the Dalai Lama might have gone away somewhere. I didn't even dare look at Blacky. I knew he was furious and somehow this would be translated to me. Suddenly he stood up in an aggravated fluster. He said, "I've got to see Tupelo. Where is she?"

Reiner made a face. "Oh, I wouldn't go trouble her now. She's meditating."

"She'll want to see me straight away."

"They won't let you in." He yawned raucously. "Blacky, there are other interesting people here, you know. You might be interested in the doctor of the Dalai Lama, for example. Or the hermits living in the caves. There are dozens of those. Veritable Saint Francises. I've already got them on film."

But Blacky would not be consoled with substitutes. Already his thoughts had moved on. He'd taken out his little record book and was recording the outrageous cost of gasoline. "I wonder if it would be simply cheaper to fly at this point," he said. He consulted his map. "We could hop over to Kashmir."

"We won't be going anywhere soon," Reiner put in. "The lines at the fuel pumps are six hours long."

We all looked out the window. Yes, there they were, the last threads of local men with their empty canisters.

A Tibetan family sat in a corner trying to sell their last pieces of turquoise to Westerners who must be rich to have come such a long way on a whimsy. They were shy and polite. One of them held out two stones to anyone who would look. Travelers walked past and kept on going. From across the room, one dark red stone glimmered. I went over and admired them.

"They're uncut, Claire," Blacky said from across the room.

"And they're only semiprecious," Reiner added.

Suddenly I wanted those stones very much. I didn't care what the two of them said. I thought the little family sitting there offering them were so pure and lovely. I wanted something of theirs, not because I wanted to help them, but because I wanted a part of them. "How much do they want?" I asked the proprietor. He answered in rupees. Something ridiculously low, I thought. I was well into the habit of bargaining, had become a regular little rug merchant. I knew it was expected. But I kept looking back to the innocent faces of those little people. It was like they knew God would take care of them and they weren't going to worry. I opened my velvet film pouch and counted out the rupees. The woman pressed the stones into my care. The red one had a vein of green down one side. It was the size of a walnut. I don't know what it is about those Tibetans. They break your heart. My eyes filled up with tears at my generous gesture. The family stood and filed out the door, who knew to where?

"You shouldn't have done that," Blacky reprimanded me.

"Why not?" I sniffled.

"Ach! And tears on top!"

"Oh, shut up." I sat down.

Reiner came down from his cloud just long enough to point out, "They're only garnet and turquoise. Not worth much like that."

"But I'll keep them forever," I swore, meaning the family, folding the stones away into my sack.

Wolfgang stood in the doorway. He screeched and charged across the restaurant. You'd have thought I was back from the dead for the fuss he made. He began touching me as if to make sure I was real.

Then they all came in. "Darling!" Isolde threw herself across the room and actually picked me up and twirled me around while Wolfgang filmed our reunion from every angle.

They all stared at me as though I were make-believe. Blacky stood beside me proudly, exhibiting my good health.

"Give me a squeeze!" Daisy clucked.

"Blacky saved my life," I told them.

Isolde observed, *"Wenn es dir dreckig geht, der Blacky ist ja immer da."*

I perked up, alert, always looking for the clue to who Blacky was.

Reiner translated, "That means when things are down and dirty, Blacky's the one who's always there for you."

"She knows what it means." Daisy nudged him playfully, lovingly, and I was captivated by their affection for each other. Even Isolde and Vladimir seemed changed, second honeymooners at the ashram.

"It's true," I said, "he is." I stood there letting them gape at me, feeling suddenly like the little corpse who could.

Blacky, by now bored with their astonishment, said, "Didn't you get my cables?"

"We did," Harry assured him. "We got one. But you know it was all so iffy when we left, remember? Anything could have happened."

"But I sent two."

"That's India," Chartreuse explained.

"And all you said was she was on the mend." Harry petted my shoulder with one hand. "But then you didn't arrive and we thought Claire might have had a setback—and we haven't been back to Dehli because there's no benzene. None."

"There is," Chartreuse put in, "but you've got to wait for hours on lines." Harry threw his chubby arms around me. "There, now. There, now," he crooned. "You're alive then, aren't you." The whole world loses weight in India. Harry, on the other hand, thriving on endless bananas and peanut butter sandwiches, looked like he'd gained seventeen pounds.

"I think we should have a party!" Isolde said to the whole room, "like we used to have at home!"

"Don't be stupid," Vladimir fell into his old habit of eradicating her joy, "there's no booze."

Chartreuse whispered, "No hash. Nothing." His eyes were feverish with the very idea of such scandal. "I haven't had a joint for over two weeks! None of us have."

"You all look like part of a religious order," I said, trying not be judgmental but knowing that Blacky, too, must find them sort of ridiculous gussied up the way they were, looking like part of a sect. I don't know how it happened but an uncalled-for, childish rivalry seemed to have developed between everyone over who would wind up more holy. This was true except for Harry, and of course the now slender Daisy, who'd gone along with it but whose miniskirt peeked through from a slit in the flowing guru garb. She made a show of her worry beads, dangling them before me like a lure in a magic show. "What's different?" She kept looking me up and down. "You're awfully short," she observed.

"I've given up my facade," I announced proudly.

"What, you've taken off your brilliant shoes?"

I held up my short legs and wiggled my happy toes. "Yup."

"Do you still have them? Might I have them, then, do you think?"

"Of course you may have them. They're in the bus. You're welcome to every pair. But wait till you hear what else," I said, now enjoying my newsworthy saga for the first of many times, "I was attacked by rabid monkeys and had to have rabies shots."

This achieved the hoped-for response.

"Well, that's why we took so long!" we explained.

"Ach!" Wolfgang smacked his head. "If only I'd been there! What a visual that would have been!"

"There's a nice thing to say!" Daisy reprimanded him.

"Of course you're right. Forgive me."

I waited for Blacky to inform them of my sorry news from Herr Binnemann. He didn't say anything, though, and then neither did I because, I guess, I enjoyed my status as a lady of means, whether it were true or not.

Harry said, "Here's something you didn't know."

"What's that?" Blacky asked.

"We've got a telegram from Wolfgang's agents. Listen to this! The Americans are interested in buying the film."

"No!"

"Yes. Can you bear it? We're practically a hit already!" Reiner threw back his head and bellowed a laugh.

Isolde threw her arms wide. "*Now* what do you say to a party?"

"A party," Harry repeated. "With what, noodles?"

"I knew it. Didn't I tell you we would be successful?" Reiner rubbed his hands together. "Didn't I say so?"

"Don't forget to lock up your valuables, Claire!" Harry warned me, eyeing my turquoise and garnet. "It's not the Tibetans you have to watch out for. Golly, they're honest to a fault. But I've noticed a band of unlikely travelers around the edge of town."

"Where's Tupelo?" Blacky and I said at almost the same time. And then there she was, timing perfect as ever, standing in the doorway with the light behind her, not emaciated at all but slender and compelling. She looked like an angel because she was wearing that pale blue dress I'd bought in Afghanistan and could never find and now I knew why.

"Tupelo!" Blacky rushed over to her and sheltered her in his arms.

Next patient! I remember thinking.

That night when I returned to our van—now I thought of it as our van—I was a little cranky. I'd been getting used to being the number-one girl, chauffeured through the Orient by my stunning private doctor. It was unnerving to watch Blacky switch concern from the now healthy me to the authentically, seriously in need of attention Tupelo—not that she looked it. Blacky was still locked in a huddle alone with her near the waterfall. An unnecessarily *long* huddle, I thought. Was it possible, I interrogated myself, that I was jealous of a dying girl? The thing was, she *looked* so darn well. I even wondered if all this was a hoax. But of course I was just stuck in another unworthy, malicious thought. Everyone else had been behaving so magnificently, I knew my sour tone was going to reveal me for who I realized now I really was, a green-eyed monster. I even was loathsome enough to worry that before she died, Tupelo might confess to all and sundry that we'd slept together. I punched my worn-out pillow. I wasn't used to being the worst in the bunch. Even Vladimir had pulled in his horns and given Isolde a heartfelt massage in the tea shop. How out of character was that?

The prayer wheel's music seeped across the square and into the van. Someone was out there praying for the world even now. I remembered reading something about Hermann Hesse. There was an order of silent nuns in the inner-most part of Switzerland. All they did, day and night, presumably besides eat and drink and sleep, was pray. He believed, did Hesse, that the very world remained on its axis because of the vibration these holy nuns' prayers maintained. I lay there quietly, listening to the steady tinkle and gong of the prayer wheel. Then I thought, Suppose I'm wrong and everything will work out after all? Good things did happen. Look at the way these poor Tibetans, chased from their homeland, had humbly settled in. This place did seem to be working its magic. I took a deep breath and pretended to be happy. As so often when you pretend something, it occurs, and I slipped into a long and delicious sleep.

The morning arrived with the bright incessant droning of the prayer wheel. These were the last warm days of October. A red dawn waited on the horizon and we brushed our teeth in the stream. Yesterday's moon hung still, lanternlike and see-through, in the china sky. I reloaded my film, waiting for the light. Wherever I pointed my camera was new and unusual. Although my starlit Shangri-la looked somewhat ramshackle in the almost daylight, it was in no way less captivating. You could see just past the stupa and outside the little village to the palace of the Dalai Lama. It was painted in beautiful bright colors but it remained remote, standing behind iron gates and an impenetrable growth of forest. We walked past the stupa to Hula's Tea Shop. The shop glittered white from the shackled-down tin on the roof. I was so excited. It was like going up into a tree house.

They were all there, our motley crew, dressed as prophets, behaving virtuously as novitiates, actually praying over their bowls of honey and oatmeal! I could hardly believe it. My appetite had returned in full force and I dug in with gusto.

Chartreuse came in with eyes shining. Isolde scrunched over, making room for him on the bench. "What is it, Chartreuse, you look like you're about to bust?"

He cocked his head, leaned forward, and whispered, "We have benzene."

We regarded him skeptically.

Reiner said, "Do you mean our tanks are full?"

"*Exactement.*"

"Just how did you manage that?" Wolfgang asked.

"You might not want to know. Okay?"

We all looked at one another.

"What do you say we drive over to that leper colony?" Blacky suggested. "Claire?" he looked at me beseechingly. How could I deny him this pleasure, I thought—if going to explore a leper colony could be considered pleasurable—for nothing else pleased him since learning there was to be no Dalai Lama. I was glad to see him happy about something. I'd been happy to see him at all, especially when he'd come quietly into the van late at night, smelling of nothing but himself.

"I'm staying here," Isolde announced. She was playing Pickup Stix with Harry.

I didn't really want to go to any leper colony, either. I said so.

But, "You must come, Claire," Wolfgang insisted. "Think of the pictures!"

"That's just it. I am thinking of the pictures."

Wolfgang seemed to hesitate. He picked up the incense holder on the table and rolled it around in his little hands; then he said, "We've had to be very patient with you, Claire, because you were ill. But now I think you ought really to pull yourself together and do the job we're paying you for."

"As of yet nobody's paid me a nickel," I had the wherewithal to say. But even as I said it, I knew I'd made a mistake.

He seemed to look into the newly vast beyond. He cleared his throat. With elaborate patience he said, "We've all of us laid out time and money, Claire. Your job is an apprenticeship, and there are hundreds of established photographer's assistants in Munich who would have paid *us* to let them come along."

"Yes, of course." I scratched my head, embarrassed. "I'm sorry."

"And I might add," he gave a laugh, "that if your pictures are not up to snuff, you never will be paid."

"Well, that's not fair," Daisy whispered, but she didn't say it out loud. Nobody did.

I felt like I was standing before the principal, in trouble again. But I couldn't just leave it alone. I said, "So, what? Like, I'm just along for the ride?"

"You are an independent. Yes. If your pictures turn out, we'll probably buy them."

"Why would you want to go to a leper colony anyway?" Isolde grumbled, just to change the subject.

"Because Blacky needs to feel like a savior," Daisy chided.

I defended him with, "I suppose I could think of a lot of things worse than that to want to be."

I got no grateful side glance. Instead, Blacky spoke to Isolde. "I think we should all stick together. Except Tupelo. I've given her a sleeping pill so she won't be joining us."

"Why?" Isolde said, instantly alert. "What's wrong with her?"

"Nothing's wrong with her," Blacky busied himself rolling up the map and putting away his book, "she just has that persistent cough and she hasn't been able to sleep, what with the prayer wheel going day and night. She's in my van."

Reiner rubbed his large palms together and strode about. "I think it's a good idea to attend meditations first, though. For one thing, Claire has never been and I think it's an important experience."

"Why, Reiner!" Isolde chided him. "I didn't know you were so thoughtful."

"He rightly is providing me with the opportunity to get more footage," Wolfgang said. "They wouldn't let the camera in before so now he knows enough to sneak it in."

There was sense to his reasoning, so we went, all of us tromping piously over to the meditation center. I wasn't very talkative along the way. I was still stinging from Wolfgang's reprimand. I knew he was right but I also knew he'd never have crossed me had he not noticed Blacky and I were now an item. Men were, it occurred to me, just as silly as women.

Anyway, the sky was bright blue and colorful prayer flags snapped in the wind. Although the temples here weren't what you'd call impressive—there was no loud gold or towering spire—the buildings and flavor and people were so transcendental you couldn't help being inspired. But for all they thought they were turning me on to a brand-new experience, I couldn't help feeling it was exactly like when my brother would altar-boy the six thirty Mass when we were kids and I, always the tagalong, prayed in the pews. It was the same wonderful fervor, the same rays of honeyed light through stained glass, the same connection to the true source. A strange pain came over me then, because although I despised all the hypocrisy in my own church, there was a beauty there, back there in my past, in my home, that I was still proud and glad to be a part of. I prayed for my brother's soul that beautiful morning, prayed without guilt, prayed at last with a joyous heart that I had known such a good and gentle spirit in my lifetime. It wasn't that I began again to believe in God. It was more like picking up a thread that had always been there, but just let down.

When it was over and we walked along Sangee Road toward the vans, I hesitated. I said, "Why can't we just stay right here, in McLeod Ganj? It's so charming and special!"

"Come on, Claire." Harry prodded me with his cane. He didn't need a cane but he very much liked the look. "This will be fun!"

Fun! I was afraid of lepers. I was afraid of catching it. But we fit ourselves into the one van and off we went.

"So why didn't Tupelo come?" Chartreuse asked no one in particular.

I overheard Isolde say to Vladimir, "I have to tell you, Tupelo isn't half what she used to be. She was always so filled with mischief. She never wants to do anything anymore."

"Yes," he agreed, "she's turned into a lemon."

"Dehli Belly," Reiner scoffed and they all laughed.

I held my tongue. We were all squashed together and there was hardly any room but I managed to sleep the whole way there. "Where are we?" I rubbed my eyes and turned over hours later.

"Claire!" Blacky almost exploded with joy. "We're almost there! The *leper* colony!" He smiled at me from the wheel with boyish anticipation. Chartreuse laid down his guitar and pushed the curtain open a crack. The weather had changed and the light was pure aluminum.

"Get up, you lazy thing!" Daisy sang from the front. She was brushing her hair. "It's half the morning gone already. We've been on the road for hours. You missed the gorgeous landscape, Claire." Isolde poured steely tea from the thermos and passed it back. I sipped the ghastly liquid, grateful for it. My alternative Kuchi dress hung crumpled on a hook.

"That's it!" Chartreuse hollered. "There's the tea planter's cottage. That must be it! Go on! Turn left!"

We pulled into a dusty, ugly drive that led past a clump of tin-roofed huts and ramshackle, whitewashed buildings. A garbage pile was festooned by eagles. Magnificent, enormous eagles swooped and dove and gathered about the rotting mess of litter. Just then, the main house door opened and out stepped a formidable-looking woman. She was of uncertain age but she moved with vivacious energy and her fine long hair, still red, hung down her ramrod back in a loosely held tail. There was the lilt of an elf about her dignified person. A rawboned, brawny Hepburn.

"Now who is this?" she called testily and peered into the van at the lot of us.

I supposed we looked ridiculous, more like a religious sect than who we really were.

"Good day!" Blacky stepped out and yelled to her.

"Good day, my foot!" she shouted back at him. "Have you come about the water or not?"

"Oh, dear," said Daisy.

"I'm afraid not," Blacky admitted. "Just visitors."

"Well, you can turn yourselves right around the same way that you came, in that case," she scolded with just a trace of a German accent. "I don't have all day to sit around here and entertain hungry tourist hippies. Visitors indeed! Go on!" She poked Blacky and directed him point-blank to the van.

"See here," Blacky stood his ground, "I am a doctor. *Ich bin Arzt.*"

"My English is very good, thank you. Excellent, in fact." She rubbed the galaxy of freckles on her arm. "We have no use for German here. Or a weekend doctor, for that matter." She squinted at Blacky. "I've seen your type before. Come in here and expect a grand tour and a hearty dinner. Go home and write an article— yes," she turned to Wolfgang, who was trying to step from the van, "I see you with your big camera! Turn right around!" She turned back to Blacky. "—make a fine lot of cash and all your colleagues think you're quite a guy! I've been through all this before."

"It's not that way at all," Blacky sputtered, deciding at once— I could tell—that an article would be just the thing. "I don't even have batteries for my tape recorder," he swore, eyeing me combatively, for I was the one who was supposed to worry about such details and hadn't.

The woman continued to rage. "What we need is a plumber. Our pump hasn't run for three days. So unless one of you ridiculous-looking people happens to be a plumber, you can turn right around and get the hightail out of here! Go on."

Blacky continued to try to reason with the woman. Reiner slipped off to have himself a look at the lepers around the back. I just knew he was going to photograph them, beating me to the punch.

"For God's sake," Blacky finally gave up, "we've been on the road for hours. Just tell us where the camping place is and we'll come back at a more convenient time."

"There hasn't been a camping place around here for three years! Now you listen to me, young man," she raged, "I've got three hundred men and women here who need facilities and if they don't get some water I'm going to have another *Ruhr* outbreak. For *that* we might need you. Now round up your band of gypsies and get, please, back where you came from."

She went on tirading for quite a while. I imagined Blacky thought he'd let her wear herself down, but she didn't show any signs of slowing. He continued to reason with her and she just kept refusing us entry.

Finally, "Come along, Blacky," Daisy sniffed, "we'll find some other lepers somewhere else."

But just then from behind one of the ugly buildings came a grinding, metal scraping sound, and then a gurgling slush.

The tyrant lady perked up her ears and dropped the box of wires she was holding. "My water!" she exclaimed and ran behind the house. Blacky was right behind her and I took up the rear. Sure enough, water streamed. Filthy water, but water nonetheless. It rose from an ancient rattletrap pump. And there stood Reiner, surrounded by some dozen lepers, very dirty with grease all over his guru shirt. He was holding a wrench.

"You did that?" the woman called in disbelief.

Reiner puffed up his chest and cocked one leg up on a pail. "Nothing to it." He did a little sidestep of modesty.

"Reiner!" Daisy tripped toward him in her new fancy espadrilles. "You've saved the lepers!"

The forbidding Agnes, finally subdued, sat tall and stooping but smiling in her creaking rocker over a mug of Nescafé on the makeshift front porch. Now that she had her water she'd become hospitable and even friendly. An aged leper who still had the use of his hands poured boiling water into chipped mugs from a kettle. The damp coarse grains of Nescafé he doled out as though they were gold; everybody got half a teaspoonful. Still, it was the first trace of coffee any of us had had in quite some time and so we savored every wily sip. I did refuse the pitcher of warm milk that was passed around—though I longed for the taste of it—as I imagined it would be seething with leprosy germs.

Not one to let go of a good thing, Agnes had sent Reiner and Chartreuse off to see if they could repair a faulty loom. Blacky sat cross-legged on a mat beside her. He stirred his watery-brown liquid enthusiastically. "Whatever got you started in this line of work?" he asked her.

She peered at him under orange brows. "I was a social worker back in Germany." She smoothed her lilac skirt. "That was my background. Years and years of taking in the most hopeless cases I could find in the postwar years. As time went on, so did the desperation of my charges. Then I heard an Indian bishop who was attending a nearby conference describe the appalling conditions of the lepers."

The old leper stood directly behind her chair and nodded his head. He held the burning teapot in the palms of his hands. Agnes lit a cigar and continued. "I impulsively asked him if I could come and help. Well, the bishop hemmed and hawed, then finally gave his consent—on the condition that I pay my own fare," she suddenly snorted, shocking Daisy so she jumped out of her seat. "One sunny day, much to the bishop's surprise, I arrived with a little money, a packet of books about leprosy and the Hindu language, and *dauntless* bundles of energy. If I had known then what hurdles lay in front of me, I don't think I would have felt so optimistic." She swept a very weathered, sturdy hand in a broad gesture and smiled. "But as you see, in a way, it *can* be done!" She turned without looking at the man behind her and removed the scalding pot from his unfeeling hands and put it down on the floor beside her long feet. The man just stood where he was and continued to smile.

"The bishop did not know what to do with me, but he sent me out to a recently donated plot of land in the outskirts of Dehra Dun. I persuaded thirty lepers who made their livings naturally, by begging, to join me. They thought I was a rich philanthropist and their days of work were over. Ha! What a shock they were in for!"

There was a funny smell around the place, chlorine and formaldehyde. While Agnes spoke I peeked into her room. It was cheerful, lined with books and rows and rows of classical music albums. Agnes pursed her disapproving lips at me. "Nice," I said.

"Yes, they are. Only I have to get up before dawn to hear them. After about six A.M. the electricity just goes kerplunk."

A blind, partially limbless leper shuttled past the porch supported by a stick. "That's Jagjivan, our favorite citizen." Agnes chuckled. "He's too far gone to work but he sits all day with the women who do, telling them all sorts of stories and fables. He's got a wonderful wit. Everybody works nowadays, only his job is keeping the citizens' minds off their troubles."

Blacky shook his head in wonderment. "How do you ever get them to sustain themselves?"

"Well, the German Relief Organization agreed to finance the maintenance of the inmates for a while. I was busy learning by trial and error how to dress their wounds when Jürgen, a trained mechanic on vacation, dropped by to see what was going on. We desperately needed a latrine and he just pitched right in. With the help of the patients, he built one. It was the first time any of the lepers had known the experience of work that wasn't begging. They grumbled a lot about the effort, but I think they really enjoyed it. When it was finished everyone sat around the thing for days admiring their work. And Jürgen. He wound up staying for two years."

I glanced furtively at Blacky, praying he wasn't coming up with any noble ideas.

"You must understand," Agnes sighed, "what life means to a leper in India. There are more than a million cases and it is by no means confined to the lower classes. Many are educated, cast out from good families. Because of its terrible connotations, anyone contracting the disease hides it as long as possible so he may go on living in society. Because of that it's usually in the advanced stages by the time treatment is sought.

"A leper must leave his home and family once his secret is learned. His wife breaks her bangles in the tradition of all widows, shaves her head, and wears the traditional white sari of mourning. There is nowhere for him to go, only begging from the distance of a curb and watching the years rot away his miserable body. Even if he is successfully treated and cured, he is barred from everything, even religious services. Come along," she said suddenly, jumping up, "I'll take you on a tour." She turned and glared at Wolfgang. "But no pictures. These people have their dignity. I insist you respect that."

"Yes, of course," Wolfgang said.

"Of course." Blacky hurried to walk beside her.

"I got the idea to start the patients with hand weaving one unbearably hot August or September, I forget which," Agnes was saying. "We all got together and built ourselves a loom. We were determined to become self-sufficient."

We followed close by. Daisy was having a bit more trouble keeping up in my shoes. We entered a white building filled with snapping, whirring looms. It made a cheerful picture, all those yards of colorful woolen thread, and might have been a factory anywhere but for the fingerless, feelingless hands pushing and pulling at them. Layers of multihued carpets, wall hangings, and bedcovers littered the tables.

Limbless lepers smiled to greet us but kept on working. Agnes rambled about gossiping, hollering, making special note to compliment the finer, more intricate pieces she examined. "Oh, Lord!" she cried out. "I've forgotten to send someone for lotto cards! I'll be right back."

With that she marched out the door, leaving us alone in a room of curious, half-eaten-away faces. With the boss gone, the women felt a little bolder, made jokes about Daisy's sexy miniskirt and laughed happily. Jagjivan sat on the floor of the threshold and noisily sucked his pipe.

Chartreuse enthusiastically demonstrated to the men outside how to take their normal game of checkers and turn it into "strip" checkers. They watched him with intense concentration. We all stood laughing at Chartreuse's attempt to make them laugh with his striptease.

Agnes returned with her hair askew. She walked right up to me. "It is surprising," she smiled cheerfully, "how fast you find yourself *not* trying to avert your eyes from the gruesome mutilations and stumps, eh? You see, when you are surrounded by a clean and healthy atmosphere you can look at it as though it *is* a treatable disease rather than a hopeless, frightening plague. The inflicted become fellow human beings that are within your comprehension. When a man grovels in the gutter like an animal— pah, you can't help reacting to him as though he were one, no?"

"Oh, yes!" I agreed.

"The beggars in the city call for pity and the coins are thrown with pity. But pity leaves the receiver still begging. And why shouldn't human beings like you and I not give a higher side of the coin: compassion?"

I took a step back, knocking over a bolt of purple fabric. Three women raced to pick it up, not one of them sporting a full set of fingers.

Agnes, engrossed in her speech, went on. "These workers not long ago lay on the street like all the other animals. I can't say now that their faces shine with the light of holy redemption but once again they are part of the human race.

"But where," Agnes went on, "are the rupees, the millions of dollars that people in the West give every week on Sunday for those who really need help? Where is it? Where does it go, all this money we never see, eh?"

I stood there staring back at her, dimly regretting the glittering bangles I'd splurged on in Nepal.

"We will leave our workers to their work," she said, steering me into the fresh air. Her sneakers, I noticed, were battered with holes and laced up with red string. "You're headed back to Dharamsala, are you?"

"Yes, we are."

"The home of the Dalai Lama." Agnes made a sign of respect. "He might be a king. But he is also a refugee, like the rest of his people. The Chinese have chased all the Tibetans of power away. They've murdered many and, naturally, stolen much treasure. Ah. Even the holy ones are driven out."

"Not many holy people left in the world anymore." I nodded.

Agnes looked at me with shock. "Don't say that. Even where you're going, up in those hills, there are many hermits in the caves. Great hermits. Of course there are charlatans and tricksters, too. Their powers are quite strong and very real." She let go a caustic snort. "They achieve these powers by sacrilegious means, such as consumption of their own feces when the moon is full, reciting ancient and diabolical chants. Of these you must beware. And another thing: the monkeys. They live there in tribes. The most enlightened monkeys of their race. Unfortunately, they are quite frisky and they are also pranksters. You must be careful because they are dangerous."

I was just about to tell her my own sad monkey tale, when Daisy and Reiner—the man of the hour—waved to us as we walked down the path. They were surrounded by stubby-nosed leper children who wanted cookies, a story, a smile.

"I wonder where Blacky is?" I said.

"I asked him if he would give me some aspirin for my arthritis, and he went back to your van. I suppose he's found the clinic by now." Agnes chortled. "I'll take you there." We strolled along a winding path toward a building set in the shade of some nice old trees.

"I have to say it's very pretty here sometimes," I said. The clouds had cleared away and I noticed someone had planted flowers. I looked sideways at Agnes and thought, She must have been a picture once. "Did you," I ventured, "ever marry?"

"Marry?" Her face took on the strains of a cello. "No, I never did. I guess because at the time when I was a girl, all the marriageable men were at war. And when they came back I went off to India. I can't say that I feel as though I've missed anything, though." She laughed outright and rivets of wrinkles filled up her face. Nice wrinkles. Not like those ugly, overpowdered ones you see at charity luncheons and afternoon movies. She relit her cigar. "I've got a family big enough to keep me busy. Right now we're counting our pennies to buy more land between here and Rishikesh. We've almost got it, too. When that happens we can build a new colony and produce more work. And," she hastened her step, "I'm not really alone, am I? I have my music and my books. The hardness of my life comes when I have to turn away lepers who ask for entrance. Every day they come. Every day I condemn them to a life of begging by saying no."

We reached the clinic and I caught sight of Blacky before he became aware of me. He was stroking the head of a small child. Sometimes, seeing his goodness, I had the feeling I would never be able to hold on to him, that he would need to be kind to everyone and that I would never find within myself what it would take to live with a sort of a saint. I walked up to him and touched his shoulder. "Would you prefer to stay here? Is that it?"

"The thought did cross my mind," he admitted.

"But?"

"But, with my specialty, I think I can do more good where I am."

"Yes, of course." I sighed. "I, I, I" was always his tune, it came to me. What about "us, us, us"? I grumbled to myself. If this guy didn't have some sick girl between us, it was an important illness itself. He was just too good for me. If I wasn't going to be first now, I supposed I'd never be. I might as well try to get used to it. It was a good lesson for me to learn. Why did I think I was supposed to be number one, anyway? I ought to be grateful to be the sidekick to such a wonderful person. One of the lepers, a girl about my own age, was managing to get to her feet with a stick. She hobbled past. I caught a whiff of her decaying smell and I thought, Why *do* I spend so much of my time preoccupied with dread? Compared with this girl's, or Tupelo's, my complaints were nothing but vanity!

At the gate, as we were about to leave, Agnes took my hand warmly and smiled. "I'm not alone here, you see." She picked one of the children, a scabby, grubby little boy, up into her arms. "Three years ago they planted a *piepa* tree up the hill there." She pointed to an attractive spot in the distance overlooking the camp. "And when the tree is big enough, and I am old enough, they will build a little house for me under it."

"May I photograph that tree?" I asked her.

She thought for a moment and then she said, "Oh, all right, but do it quickly. You won't want to give the others ideas."

She waved us away.

On the road back to Dharamsala I was full of my own thoughts and only half aware of what was going on, but then I was distracted by Wolfgang unloading the film from his camera. I kind of looked at him because of the way he slipped it into a can. Then I realized why. He was trying to do it in a sneaky way.

"What did you do?" I confronted him, my hand on his wrist. "You filmed the lepers?"

"Wait until you see the footage I got," he snorted. "This here is award-winning stuff."

"Wolfgang, you have no scruples! She specifically asked you not to!"

He gave a short growl of disgust. "And how will she ever know?"

"I wouldn't have done that if I were you," I said. Gone were the days, anyway, when I was his pet, that was clear.

He made a cockeyed, know-it-all face. "That's why I'll get a first at the Berlin Film Festival and you, missy, will still be shooting bathing suits and wedding gowns in Tenerife."

"No, I won't," I shot back but I saw that he was embarrassed. I said gently, "Wolfgang, we used to be such good friends. And now . . . how did this happen?"

"I know exactly what happened." He spit the words out savagely. "Chartreuse had the bright idea to fix you up with Blacky."

That's ridiculous," I said. "You're nuts."

"You're right," he said, "I was."

"Claire won't be in Tenerife," Daisy said for me, "she'll be a doctor's wife in Munich, raising little kiddies."

"I'm hungry," Blacky announced. I noticed he didn't say something to back me up. Then he laughed uproariously and said, "I can't get that picture out of my mind of those fellows playing strip checkers!"

Chartreuse grinned with him.

Blacky continued. "And when some poor chap is down to his undershorts he can snap off a finger. You know, if it comes down to it. Can't you see the table in the middle of the night? A shoe, some shirts and pants, and—ho ho—a nose or two!"

They laughed and laughed and I, feeling both worse and better, realized I might actually have a good shot at this relationship because Blacky, good as he was, was no saint after all—and worse, because it seemed that I, bad as I was, would never be good enough.

chapter seventeen

*I*t was very early the next morning, before, even, the sun. We were headed for Hula's, looking forward to warming ourselves with cups of *chi*.

Refreshed, Tupelo was standing alone at the top of the tall narrow stairs. She was still wearing my dress. Blacky was thrilled to see her looking so well. I aimed the camera at her but it was still too dark. "How *did* you get my dress?" I called out.

She leaned across the wooden railing and stretched. "I took it because I thought you were going to die and I wanted something to remember you."

"And for that you need a dress?"

She smiled and moved toward me, kissing me plunk on the lips. Right in front of Blacky. He came over and put his arms around both our shoulders. "That's what I like to see," he praised us happily, "camaraderie."

We watched him march briskly on ahead into the tea shop.

"That's funny," she wiggled her nose in my ear, "what I feel doesn't feel like camaraderie."

I knew exactly what she meant but I didn't like her to think she was running the show. And I couldn't stop myself from thinking that this time it was I who thought *she* was going to die.

As though she'd read my thoughts, she said, "You just want to be the one who decides when and how. You think you have that power. You're wrong, you know. We none of us have power."

Of course she would realize that now that she was ill. I felt immediately sorry for her. At that moment I wanted to reach out to her. I wanted to comfort her in some way but I didn't know how without revealing what I knew and betraying Blacky's confidence. She glanced over her shoulder to see if anyone was watching and then she yanked my hair, pulling me toward her, saying, "You think you are so clever, so good."

Exasperated, I moaned, "Oh, Tupelo, what is it you want?"

"I'd like to beat you up. That's what I'd really like to do."

I tried to laugh. "You are ruthless," I said.

She put her hand on the small of my back and her mouth against my ear and narrowed her eyes. In a croaky voice she answered, "Yes. I am. I am ruthless."

You know how they say it's not what you say but how you say it? Well, I swooned with the intimacy of her voice. She knew how to recognize my stream of sexual preparedness and dive into it. Yet how could it be? What lack of character persuaded me to be affected like this when I had all the love I needed with the man of my dreams? Was no betrayal beneath me? My head hung loose with vanished self-esteem and illicit desire.

She wrapped her body closer still. Her breath was on my cheek. "What's the matter, Claire, you're afraid to be alone with me?"

"Of course not." But I was. I was fine as long as we weren't in close contact. But I knew what would happen if she started up again. I might wind up sleeping with her just to prove I wasn't turned off to her because she had cancer.

"Look," I pulled away, intending to be firm, "all I want is to be here now."

She gave me an alluring side profile. "Are you sure that's all you want?"

"Oh, Tupelo," I laughed, giving in, taking her hand and walking with her that way, girlfriends, "what's to become of us?"

"Nothing, I hope. I just want to stay here forever." She laughed. Then, decisively, turning away from me, "I *am* going to stay here forever."

The air was filled with mist. The waterfall roared with melted snow and you could smell it, you could smell the snow. It was cold and would be until the sun peeked through. I looked at her carefully, her face lit green by the flickering kerosene lanterns. It was true, she seemed blissful. But Blacky would never allow her to stay behind without us. I knew that for certain.

"Tupelo, you can't be serious."

"Oh, I am. I've prayed about this over and over."

"Maybe too much," I suggested.

"No, Claire, because I knew one thing; prayer is talking to God, meditation is listening to Him." She smiled to herself with that irritating holier-than-thou expression they'd all perfected since they'd come here. "I've been listening."

"All this meditation stuff has got you hoodwinked!" I told her.

"And what do *you* know?" She resumed her true personality without missing a beat.

"Well," I said, angry at last, "I know I'm not reaching for the unobtainable."

She turned and looked at me, raising an eyebrow. "Ah! You say that in such an assertive, I-got-the-guy way."

"No," I protested, "I didn't mean that."

"You love him, don't you think I can tell?"

"Is it that obvious?" I admitted sheepishly.

"Of course it is. You love him and you think that's enough. You believe that will sustain you," she rocked back and forth, "but there are other things. You and I both know there are other things. . . ." Her voice trailed off.

I looked, to see if anyone was coming. "Yes, it's true. There are 'other things,' as you say. But in the end, it's they that are always not enough."

She laughed. "That's not what you said in Iran!"

"No," I admitted, laughing with her. For although there had been something unfulfilling in our dalliances, something that could never be combined and completed, for me the negative had always been in the betrayal afterward and not in the act itself. There'd been a closeness reached and shared like nothing else. And now she was seriously ill and I was going to lose her. "Tupelo," I said, becoming frightened, "we're going to have to have a talk."

"Ah." She stopped in her tracks and glared at me. "So he's told you."

I held my breath. "You had to know he would."

"I was so afraid of it I probably made it happen," she admitted, perching herself on the edge of a woodpile.

"Tupelo, you've lost touch. When we get back to Germany—"

"Germany! What? What then?"

"Well, there's something to be said for Western science and conveniences."

"You can believe what you want. I don't fall for any of it, anymore."

"You can't think that staying here will change everything!"

"I don't care anymore. It's funny but I don't." She plucked at the lacy, ragged strands of wood. "Death isn't so bad. It's love that's the killer."

She held my eyes and I hers. I took her hand. Her fingers were like ice. I sat down beside her.

She said, "You're going to laugh at me when you hear this. . . ."

"I won't."

"Cancer is the best thing that ever happened to me. It straightened me right out. Oh, it's hard to explain. It's not that I wouldn't rather not have it. But I do, you see. I do have it."

I didn't laugh. I wanted to cry. Of course she felt that way now, when every moment was so intense. What about when the pain began? What then? I told her so.

"Oh, Claire," she shook her head, sorry for me, "you think that going into hospital will somehow make everything all right. But nothing will. All because the rooms are white and the nurses are there—it doesn't change what's happening. It doesn't stop the process. Because the truth is they know not a thing about how to stop it. Not a thing. And Blacky will see to it that I won't suffer. He's promised. He'll take care of me."

I was silent. I almost said, "Me, too." But I was done with being the "me, too" girl.

She coughed a laugh. "I'm going no matter where I do it from." She crossed her eyes in horrified jest. "And fast. Fast, Claire, that's the beauty of it. I'm not going to linger like a bother." She gnawed her thumbnail cuticle and spat it out. "I'll just," she snapped her fingers, "go! One day I won't be here anymore. Nobody can change that. But at least I can choose the point from which I leave the earth." She held her arms up toward the sky, great actress that she was, and she beamed. "What finer place than this mystical village of goodwill, eh?"

We looked together at the quaint and eerie loveliness. Chimneys smoldered and puffed. A tinker's hammer pinged. One Tibetan woman in her striped apron and bent with an enormous pack of straw—as big as she was—padded politely by us up the little path. "All this before the sun is even up," Tupelo pointed out. "They'll write about me in the papers, Claire," she went on, "they'll say, 'Tupelo Honig, Film Star, Dies in Himalayas!' "

"You don't care about that!"

"Oh, but I do! I really do. And while we're on the subject, I have a favor to ask you. But don't think badly of me now, that I am egoist. You won't?"

"No. What is it?"

"And you won't laugh?"

"No. I said I won't."

"For my funeral I want Debussy."

"Oh, please." I held my head in a dramatic woe-is-me pose.

"No. Come on, humor me. That nice one. You know. You're named for that song."

" 'Claire de Lune,' " I whispered. "You remember that?"

"You told us the night we met."

I hadn't even known she'd been listening. I'd only thought of Blacky at that time. She went on to tell me hurriedly—as though there was little time left and she'd been saving all this up—"And I want to be cremated." She looked down and shuddered. "I don't want to be put in a box in the ground where there's no air, no sunshine."

I tried not to pay attention but she pressed me, locking her pinkie with mine. "Promise."

"All right, all right."

"I mean, I really *do* have regrets, though, you know?" She turned and looked into her lap. "Now that I know I'm leaving the planet. Not things you would think, like not 'making it' in America, you know? I really don't care at all about that. Funny." We watched our legs dangle over the side of the woodpile, the brilliant jewel colors of our Afghani slippers sharp in the subtle half-light. "One thing is, I would have liked to speak to you in my own tongue. What? What are you thinking?"

I heard myself begin to cry. "Only that I'm honored that you find me that important in your life." I sniffled.

"Ach! Don't be so stupid. You make me sick!" She shoved me and sputtered at me with loathing, spitting the words. "Stop crying immediately or they will all see from the window. I mean it, Claire. Just stop crying and listen. That you know is one thing. But I won't have Harry coming at me with get-well flowers he picked in some sentimental field. Or Isolde checking me out, trying to figure how long it's going to take, kneeling at my shrine with, with sacrificial lamb shanks." We both laughed and she went on. "You have this *thing* about your lack of importance. I think it's very Catholic."

I remembered her crossing herself at Isolde's. "You're Catholic, too."

"Not so very much as you."

"Tupelo. You never talk about your family. You must want them to—"

She put up her hand, stopping me. "You think everyone has family because you have family. But I have no one. They're both dead, my parents, can you believe it? All gone." She shuddered. "My mother from the breast and my father from the colon. It was terrible when they were dying. I had to go to the hospital and sit there and look at them and look at them, each one in turn, and you know, they took their time. It was awful. It went on and on and on. There was something so disgusting about them wanting me to always be there and witness their pain. I hated it. It was like their pain gave them some privilege, some license to all my time. And I was young. All I wanted was to be out of there. Oh, it was horrible." She lit a cigarette but the coughing stopped her and she couldn't smoke it. "That was how I met Wolfgang. He found me in hospital where he was filming a scene. I was sitting in the cafeteria, passing time so I wouldn't have to keep looking at my father suffering. He took some film of me and came back looking for me two days later after he saw the rushes. I was still there. He told me my skin was cream. He said he would make me an actress. 'Good,' I told him. 'Anything is better than this.' "

"You should have told me all this sooner."

"Why, so you would sleep with me because you felt sorry for me? Pfhh. Who wants that?"

"Tupelo. I never realized—"

Her eyes were shining. They were deeper than they'd ever looked. "Why, I remember the very moment I met you. When I saw you for the first time at Isolde's. You were wearing that ridiculous dirndl."

"You were the most beautiful woman I'd ever seen," I blurted.

"I fell in love with you right then," she smiled ruefully, "right that moment," and she stood abruptly, as if to close the discussion, as if she'd said more than she'd intended.

"But then why—" I began but gave it up. What was the difference? I walked her to the tea shop. The sun had sprung up over the mountain. It blazed and I couldn't see her. It was like when you're driving a car at sundown on the Belt and you're scalded by the light but you don't pull over. We walked along, blind, lit up, following the path with only our slippered footsteps.

That afternoon while Tupelo slept I wandered around the town taking pictures of all the lovely gentle Tibetan faces. They were so healthy-looking. Finally, I came back to Hula's and sat at the top of the steps. I was tired. I guess I wasn't as recovered as I'd thought. I put my head on the railing and watched Isolde and Vladimir walk past the prayer wheel and the Tibetan Moon toward Hula's. He was animated, discussing something relevant with her, his hands moving in dramatic expression. Isolde walked elegantly beside him, her one ear cocked and listening, her arms folded behind herself in an easy, contented pose. This trip had brought them back together, returned them to each other. I sighed, surprised at how well everything had turned out for them.

"What are you doing?" Harry was suddenly behind me. He reached for my arm and pulled me up. "I'm the cat. Let me drag you in."

"Oh, Harry," I said, slumping into his arms, "I've missed having you around to talk to!"

"That's right," he smoothed his tie, "you'll never find another me." Of all of them Harry was the only one to have maintained his identity. Even Blacky wore an uncharacteristic leather bracelet and his blue jean ensemble carried traces of dilapidation. Harry still wore his same old university-don clothes, his tweed jacket and balderdash trousers. He was the only one who appeared out of place.

It was dark when we walked inside against the bright wall of outside. Hula's was like an old-fashioned schoolhouse complete with wooden benches. Hula herself, a fine broth of a Tibetan, a survivor, gold teeth still in place, sat on the floor near the potbelly stove and strained tea into a bucket of milk. The sign on the wall said, MUST BRING OWN PEANUT BUTTER. The others were already there, all but Tupelo. They were bathed in steamy sunlight at a table rocking with one leg shorter than its other three.

I took everyone's portrait. They sat patiently, each one of them wearing the same benevolent expression. However, once they were photographed—as though for proof they'd been here—they did become a little more relaxed. I perched myself on a stool off to the side. Hula's father, a wizened old fellow without a tooth in his mouth, sat down comfortably beside me. I wondered if I was in his spot. He took out his worry beads and hummed his prayers. I picked up a jar from the table and rudely licked some honey with my finger.

"Here, Isolde, take my biscuit," Vladimir said with his new show of generosity.

Hula's husband, a roll to his step, was just coming up the plank over the mud road. He was returning from a short drive to Delhi. She dropped her spoon and ran to him. He was covered in coal dust and sweaty but she took him in her arms as though she hadn't seen him in years. They were both plump and middle-aged but there was a glamour and a privacy to their love, you could just tell.

"Claire," Chartreuse came in, brushing the fir trees from his jacket, "try this peanut butter. You won't believe it."

Daisy pushed him gently away. "Chartreuse, your breath!"

Chartreuse opened a packet of sen-sen he had in his pocket and popped a few in his mouth. He picked up his guitar and began to play, but it was a different sort of music. He played each note as though it were a mantra, low and resounding. It was interesting enough, sort of Oriental, but after a while I thought, Jiminy, they're all in such a hurry to get devout. They reminded me of the gossipy rosary society in my hometown during Lent when everyone became charitable.

Isolde was on her hands and knees jimmying an Indian matchbox under the one short leg of the table.

Daisy pulled an extra shawl around herself. "It's awfully cold."

"I told you it would be cold here," Chartreuse said acidly. "No one took my advice. I told you we should have gone to Goa. It's not my fault."

Harry said, "No one's blaming you for the weather, Chartreuse. Calm down."

"I say," came a voice from the next table, "wouldn't you rather fancy some pineapple jam with your *chapedah*?"

"Why not?" Wolfgang accepted.

The man who offered the mighty-sized jar of jam was a tall, shaven-headed Englishman wearing a burgundy lama robe. More brisk than brawny, he was still very tall. "I see you have a valuable camera," the Englishman said to Wolfgang. "Unusual sight here-abouts." A sardonic demeanor ruled his fleshy, firmly held lips. There was an air of triumph about him and a nervy solicitousness. He seemed quite taken with Wolfgang, who nervously clung to his expensive camera, even moving it possessively to his other side. Beside the man sat his very pregnant wife, a rather attractive girl with hennaed permanent waves. Also at their table sat two fellows robed like the first, their heads shaved as well. Their names, the first announced, in order, were Charles, Betty, Mr. Auto, and Park. Charles, the spiritual leader of the group, was a self-proclaimed unorthodox Buddhist monk. All Londoners—but only in this incarnation, Charles specified—they'd met Park and Mr. Auto while traveling through Goa.

Introductions went around.

"Not *the* Harry Honeycutt?" Charles said when they came to Harry.

"I'm afraid so," Harry muttered, pleased.

"I read your column every week!" Charles said. "Well, I used to! What a column! Refreshing, informative. You spoke about everything I was interested in!

"Betty! Betty, don't you remember the chap I used to read out loud to you, from the *Times?*"

Betty, too swollen with edema to be flustered, simply shook her head no.

He rubbed his huge hands together. "What a pleasure. What brings you all the way up here?"

Harry stood there letting everyone get a good look at him, all the while rattling the change in his pocket.

Wolfgang, miffed that he was no longer the cheese, informed everyone unnecessarily that a film was being made.

Charles had cradled in his voluminous sleeve an unfortunate-looking sort of Yorkshire terrier named Fancy. She was well groomed and wore a bright blue hand-carved Tibetan barrette, but she trembled almost constantly. I thought she looked like a rat. Charles caressed her simpering body continuously while tending to avoid physical contact with his wife. She, nervously hovering, watched the dog with greedy eyes. Park and Mr. Auto spoke only when spoken to. Charles, it seemed, had convinced them to shave their shoulder-length hairdos and follow him north to the Himalayas. Their names, Charles explained, were derived from the car they'd driven from Rome to Calangute and had eventually been forced to sell in order to support their holy man, him.

Wolfgang's creative juices were wetted now. He was back in the mood to film and he went and readied his camera.

"When's your baby due?" I asked Betty.

"Any day," Charles answered for her.

"But where do you live?" the practical Blacky inquired.

"In a room behind the grain store, but it's not very clean so the Tibetan Moon restaurant is letting us stay in a room upstairs," Charles said.

"How nice for you." Harry raised a disapproving eyebrow.

"Actually, it's not nice at all. The wind pokes through the boards and there are rats."

"How awful," I said.

Charles said, "Betty used to be a stewardess. She's tough, our Betty." He smiled at her.

Isolde said, "Supposing something goes wrong with the birth. Don't you think she ought to be in a hospital?"

"I happen to know nothing will go wrong."

"Ah. Let us just suppose," pressed Blacky, "that it did?"

"Then a doctor," Charles lay out his upturned hand to demonstrate how simple it all was, "would appear."

We all looked at one another.

"You're very sure of yourself with someone else's life," Blacky ascertained.

"Her life is mine in privilege as well as responsibility," Charles stated smugly.

Betty, nodding doubtfully, shifted her uncomfortable belly and lit a beedie.

"Uh!" I exclaimed in outrage.

"Make a nice piece of the film." Wolfgang chewed his lip. "Baby born in Himalayas. When did you say she was due?"

"Any time now," Isolde said.

"Om Mani Padme hum," Mr. Auto addressed our table.

"Yes?" Vladimir looked up. But no, he didn't want anything, he was simply announcing his chant. Park chimed in and the two of them kept time in a low-volume series of 'mani's, 'om's, and 'padme's. "Hummmmmmmmm," they chimed together in an Everly Brothers and often practiced harmony.

"We are on the path of Sri Aurobindo . . . to find the truth," stated Charles.

"If you don't mind," Harry blustered suddenly, "I'd like to enjoy my breakfast without hearing the words 'truth,' 'path,' or 'find.'"

"You're right, Harry," I agreed with him. "That's all anyone talks about around here."

But the men's muttering chants had hypnotized the room with a monotone that droned together with the *shshsho* of the waterfall. They sat curled in the lotus position on each end of their little bench. The cookstove glowed with a cozy orange warmth. Suddenly Charles hoisted his pointer finger into the air, saying, "Harry, I remember reading about a Christian tabernacle in your column. You remember the piece?"

"No, sorry," Harry said and turned away.

"But of course you do, Harry," I piped up, happy to be of service, "You were the one who told us about it. Remember? You were so interested to come across it. That's why you wanted to come!" I was pleased with my perfect recall and thought he would be, too. But when I looked into his eyes I saw nothing but savage rebuke.

I think I literally shrank in my seat. It wasn't the kind of look that would allow you to say, "What's wrong?" It held a warning, his look—a nasty warning, I remember thinking, that I'd better shut up, which I did. I said nothing more. Harry adored me. What had I said?

He stood up and did a delicate little tour of the room. He came back to where we were sitting and said, "I seem to be caught with my pants down."

We all looked at him, puzzled. The others had even stopped their chanting and were all ears.

He swayed, hunched in a position that neither moved nor stood still. Finally, defeated, he pulled out a chair and sat back down. "I suppose you are all disappointed in me," he murmured.

"Harry," Reiner put down his spoon and wiped his chin, "we haven't a clue what you're talking about."

He looked up, surprised. "What? Really? Oh, well, I might as well tell you, then. You'll figure it out sooner or later." He took a deep breath. His vest button popped at that moment but he went on. "When I organized this trip, I was feeling a bit low. You'll remember I had a staggering crush on Isolde—" He looked at Isolde. "Yes, well, you all knew this. Even you, Vlady, admit it. The sad thing, for me, anyway, was that you didn't even consider me a threat, did you?"

Poor Harry, I thought. We all looked accusingly at the bewildered Vladimir.

"But the point is," he went on, "I wanted to get you all on this trip so that I might find some sort of treasure and come back home the hero. You know." He cleared his throat. "They were making noises at the paper about letting me go. . . ."

"But, what's he talking about?" Reiner asked Daisy. "It wasn't *his* idea!"

"Oh, shut up," Daisy said.

"And I thought, if I could stir up some publicity about something exotic and romantic . . . Well, so, I came up with that story. You see, all that about a Christian tabernacle being a gift from Tibetans to Papist Catholics sent to China as missionaries . . . it was just nonsense. I pretended I'd read it in an article when the truth is I *wrote* it in an article. I just made it up, actually. No one ever *gives* you anything real."

"Oh, I see," Charles interjected from the next table. "And my reading about it in *your* article and then saying so gummed up the works."

"Exactly." Harry sighed.

"Harry," I touched him, "you don't have to tell us this."

"But I already have done," he said.

"What *are* you talking about?" Reiner said.

"I never would have pieced it together," Blacky said.

The kettle screamed and we all jumped at once.

Tupelo stuck her head in the door. She motioned for me to come.

I put up my hand. "Come in," I said. "Come sit down."

"Come for a walk with me," she said.

"Just a minute," I told her, waiting to hear what else Harry was going to say.

"No, now," she insisted.

"I can't," I mouthed across the room.

"Honestly, Harry," Blacky admitted, "I never would have given it a second thought, either! It was all so long ago!"

Daisy said, "What do you mean, you carried the tabernacle here from Germany?"

Tupelo gave me one last look and then turned and went out the door.

"Yes, yes." Harry was by now totally irritated. He searched through his pockets and fingered the smooth felt of his lapel. "I thought I'd come across it very soon, really. I was going to pre-tend some refugee family sold it to me."

After a long silence, Wolfgang said, "Actually, we might just want to leave it in. It makes a great story when you think of it."

"You mean like a hoax?" Isolde said, her eyes shining.

Blacky kept shaking his head. "Well, I can't get over it. You would have had me fooled."

"I thought this trip was my idea." Wolfgang held his chin. "It *was* my idea." He paused, thinking. "Wasn't it?"

"I let you think so." Harry stood up and put some unnecessary rupees on the table. He hadn't had a thing. "As I said, you would have figured it out eventually. Anyway, it doesn't matter anymore. It was a stupid plan. Unorthodox, I'll grant you. But beneath me." He turned on his heel and walked out. "Don't forget to lock up your peanut butter, Charles," he remarked on his way.

"Poor chap," Charles said.

Wolfgang turned his camera on Betty. "Mind if I shoot your picture, Schatzi?

"Good God!" Charles cried out. "We really must be off. It's almost too late for our meditation class. Do you mind paying for our breakfast? We have no money, you know."

Reiner said, "Surely you don't live like that?"

"Certainly." He rose to his full six foot five. "I am a teacher and a beggar. Man must first give up all possessions to be free himself."

"But, but . . ." Blacky sputtered. "How would you have paid had we not passed along?"

"Ah, but you did." Charles handed Betty the pineapple jam to take with and plunked the little dog into the pouch around his neck. Betty, Park, and Mr. Auto all rose together at the signal. Betty looked haggard. I didn't think she'd been raised to be a beg-gar's wife.

"Blacky is a doctor," I whispered firmly but softly, so only she should hear. Her eyebrows went up in surprise and relief.

Daisy leaned over and tapped her shoulder. "Want to stay and sit for a while, dear?"

Betty, shocked by the very idea, lugged herself into step without answering.

"Betty must have her exercise," Charles announced to the room. "I see to it she covers four to five miles a day. It wouldn't do if my son were born unhealthy!"

I saw Betty's eyes glint in Charles's direction.

"This is what I mean about male chauvinist pigs!" Isolde complained loudly enough to be heard.

"Most people would be subtle enough not to get involved," Daisy reprimanded her.

"That's good, coming from you," Isolde shot back.

"What's that supposed to mean?" Daisy placed her fists on her hips.

Isolde spread her *chapadee* lushly first with peanut butter, then apricot jam. "I don't know what I mean. I just think a girl who used to fly around as a stewardess deserves better than a life as someone's servant."

"He didn't like her being photographed," Wolfgang said. "Did you notice? The minute I aimed my camera at her he stood to leave."

"Maybe she's a wanted criminal. What do you think?" Vladimir suggested.

"More likely he didn't want the spotlight on anyone but him," Isolde shrewdly observed.

"What about the tabernacle thing?" Wolfgang plunged on, thinking aloud. "Should we put it in the film or what?"

"Well, we can't very well if we're calling it a documentary!" Daisy threw back her head in righteous indignation.

"Nonsense." Wolfgang defended his point. "Documentaries the world over are constructed. One has to give them form. Doesn't make them less real."

"Well, that's a matter of opinion," I said doubtfully.

He gave me a scathing look. "It is, after all, my film."

"Yes, but we're all in on it," Blacky said.

"Everything's how you look at it." Wolfgang shrugged.

"We're not turning the whole thing into a farce." Blacky gave a dark laugh. "What would be the point of that?"

"But people do like a bit of adventure," Vladimir argued.

Wolfgang shook himself like a wet dog. "My point is, there's no mystery. I mean, a reason to get to the end. The audience will lose interest."

I found myself becoming agitated. "Don't you see, if you do that you'll be eradicating the very purpose of our coming here. I mean, everything this place stands for is the opposite of what you just suggested! This whole wonderful journey to this place is enough on its own."

"You are sweet, Claire." Wolfgang petted the top of my head, making the word "sweet" sound like something stupid and naive. I was furious. It was all right for them to be righteous!

Chartreuse sat glowering in the corner. I started to go over to him but then I thought why, after all, must I always feel I had to look after his emotional state? I didn't want to sit there and listen to him complain about the lack of drugs. I was actually glad there were none around. But he stood up and threw down his velvet scarf in an angry gesture. "Not one of you is worried about Harry," he fired. "Don't you understand? He could do himself harm over something like this!"

Isolde stood up and shook her finger at him, like you would to a child. "Stop being so melodramatic! Anyway," she turned to us, "I don't think so. Harry's always looking for ways to get attention."

"I wouldn't say that at all," I disagreed. "In fact, I'd say the opposite."

Reiner, his eyes round with wonder, said, "So what do you mean, he carried his make-believe tabernacle here from Munich?"

At last I got it. Those old but glimmering gems in the van. Those were *his*, not Chartreuse's! He'd carried them in panels. "That's exactly what he did!" I confirmed. "Oh, Chartreuse," I confessed, moving toward him, "I'm an absolute nincompoop! I thought the gems I saw in the van were yours. I thought you'd stolen them in Istanbul."

"That's it! Now you call me a thief!" Chartreuse fumbled with his jacket and snatched his scarf. "I'm getting out of here!"

Blacky sipped his *chi* and grinned mischievously. "That's the best job a girl can have, really, stewardess. I mean, if you're a fellow. Four days home and then four days off to who knows where. Gives a fellow a break. Plus, you get flying benefits if you marry her. Almost makes up for the loss of freedom."

"Ha ha ha," said I. I didn't mind. I was a sophisticated traveler. And after all, he was only kidding. I hoped. I was sorry to have thought Chartreuse a thief. I mean, even if he was. We were all stuck with one another. And there were worse things than theft. It didn't help to go accusing people, though. For all I knew he'd turned over a new leaf. Anyway, I was sort of glad to see things settling down into the everyday backbiting lifestyle of moviemaking in the free world. It was a little bit too much bliss for my money, the way things had been; all that mushy good nature and angelic good works. It just wasn't us. There's nothing more vicious than one outdoing the other to see who's nicer.

Wolfgang filmed the group clandestinely from the window. Out the hobnail vestibule they went, then down the road past the prayer wheel, single file: first Charles with Fancy yapping at his heels, Betty, then Mr. Auto, then Park, a family of ducks and one to come.

chapter eighteen

We finished our breakfasts and meandered out into the sunlight. I looked for Tupelo but she'd gone off. Everyone smoked beedies in McLeod Ganj because you were so cut off you couldn't get anything else but Wills's Flake, sort of an Indian Marlboro, but those scraped your throat, they were even worse. The weather was crisp but because the sun shone we lingered, reveling in its warmth. Isolde even took off her blouse, the way she always did the minute the sun shone, which by the way every German does, but Vladimir made her put it back on because it was too cool for that. He really was very gentle and concerned with her lately.

Wolfgang sat chewing the inside of his mouth, never happy unless he was filming something. He cleaned his expensive lenses with a cotton rag. I felt sorry because he really had been good to me and I supposed I'd been ungrateful—pursuing the Goody Two-shoes route. "What's the matter, Wolfgang?" I asked him.

"Oh, I don't know. The people here are so tepid. Nothing ever happens. I'm just wanting some action, something like the lepers. You know."

I was glad to see Harry come trotting back with his travel Scrabble board. He came right over to me and sat beside me on the railing. "I'm such a fool," he said. "Shall we start fresh?"

I leaned over and kissed him on the cheek. That's what I loved about Harry. Of course I would forgive him. Why wouldn't I? There was nothing to forgive. We set up the board and had a game in the bright sunshine. I was glad Tupelo wasn't there because even though English wasn't her first language, she always beat me. Blacky was in the water closet and would be for quite a while longer. He had a touch of the runs. Everyone went through it. Tupelo came trudging back up the stone path. She still had my blue dress, I noticed irritably. Tupelo? I did a double take. She'd chopped off all her hair! It was waiflike and it stuck out in thick little blond tufts.

I stood up and knocked over the Scrabble board.

"Christ!" Harry said, going down on all fours.

Blacky—forever washing his hands—came out of the water closet at last and onto the porch, his hands dripping water. "What is it? What's happened?"

Delighted, just what the doctor ordered, Wolfgang stood up and aimed his camera. "*Ja, spitze!* But why didn't you let me film you doing it?"

She came purposefully up to me. "Trade," she said, handing me some tissue paper wrapped around something. She was out of breath now and leaned, exhausted, on a chair. The paper was wrinkled, recycled purple Indian gift paper. When I took it in my hand I thought it was something alive wrapped up, like an animal. For a moment I thought she'd handed me a ferret in a package. I wouldn't have put it past her. "For the dress." She grinned, twirling in a circle. I opened it cautiously. It was her thick, rich honey hair braided into a rope and folded over. I drew back. The hair, bound carefully into its braid, was beautiful. It was rich and still so very full of life. But somehow it felt malevolent because even though that rash and dramatic act was so obviously against herself, I couldn't help feeling it was some sort of reprimand against me, for not paying attention at the moment she'd demanded it.

Wolfgang zoomed in on what I was holding and then zoomed away. "Got it!" He grinned, satisfied.

She coolly took her hand from mine. "I'm going to go investigate the caves," she said. "Do you know there are hermits living in them? Some of them are saints. There's a woman up there, a German woman. She's been living there for years, meditating. Barren Indian women go lay gifts outside her cave and suddenly become pregnant."

"Yeah, right."

"No, Claire, it's true. Such wonders do exist."

I watched her turn and walk, lithe and swaying, down the path and away from the tea shop.

"Be careful!" I called after her. I sighed. You never knew what she was going to do. She was danger personified, that girl.

That afternoon, two policemen came from Lower Dharamsala, officious, tidy little men in crisp uniforms, very different from the soft, small bundles of people they passed. They came quickly, briskly. A man in a lavender felt topee scooted along beside them, evidently trying to keep up. They marched up past the stupa and the prayer wheel toward our little camp. Wolfgang, in charge, stood up right away and broke out in a sweat. The last thing he wanted was the police. I felt, rather than saw, Chartreuse flinch and draw back. Instinctively he knew that they'd come for him.

"Oh, no," I cried out. I put my arm into the air as though to shield him. He smacked my arm away. Perhaps, after I'd accused him he thought I was going to take hold of him for them. He pushed himself away, backward, and disappeared into the bushes. I saw him go up toward the path. I saw the bright color of his scarf through the trees climbing upward. I remember thinking, I hope they don't catch him, but catch him they did and right away, too. He didn't struggle, but came back with them, insulted, indignantly protesting his innocence. He looked very small and guilty. The man in the lavender felt topee accused him of stealing his bicycle. "That's preposterous," Harry said, but the man was adamant. A small crowd was gathering. Then Chartreuse admitted to taking it, but he maintained that he'd only quickly borrowed it to run down to Dharamsala and he would have brought it back eventually. He'd had to carry the heavy canister of benzene, he explained, and so had left it there, but then that jarred one of the local people's memory, I guess, because then *he* accused Chartreuse of siphoning benzene from his truck in the night when everyone else was asleep. This was very serious, now.

While the second policeman took Chartreuse aside, the first policeman asked if anyone knew about this. There was silence. Then, "Well, it is true," Wolfgang, falling apart, admitted, "that Chartreuse goes out in the night."

I remember thinking then that that was the absolute wrong thing to say. I mean, even if he had, Wolfgang shouldn't be a snitch. A rat, really. I have to tell you that I was astonished at that. They searched Chartreuse's things and of course it didn't help that he had a big plastic straw and a funnel, both still redolent of benzene. To our horror, he was carted off to the jail in Lower Dharamsala. We stood there, shocked and worried. Even Wolfgang hadn't thought to use his camera. I picked up Chartreuse's guitar and ran it after him. "Ah!" the policeman said, allowing him to take it. "Rock and roll!"

"Hey!" Isolde grabbed hold of me. "Let's go look through his stuff," she said, her eyes sparkling.

"What, now? What about the police?"

"Fuck them."

"All right." We snuck into the van and went through his private stuff. But there was nothing there.

The next day I announced that I thought I would go down into Lower Dharamsala and see what I could do to help Chartreuse. I imagined him in some little jail with rats or worse and I thought it must be too horrible to bear.

Reiner said, "I, for one, am glad he's off the streets."

"Yes," agreed Vladimir.

Blacky said, "You might want to give a thought to the hardworking people he's stolen from, Claire."

"I know. But all I can imagine is poor, weak Chartreuse, his disastrous life."

"He certainly doesn't give a thought to others," Wolfgang sniffed. "He might have cost us the whole film. They might have kicked us out of here!"

But I'd seen him feel for others. "I've seen him care for me."

"That's not compassion, darling," Blacky said. "It's sex."

I clenched my fists. "We none of us would be here, maybe, if he hadn't bravely stood his ground that time near Mount Ararat."

Nobody said anything to that. They shifted uncomfortably, knowing it was true.

"But there's no more benzene to be had!" Harry cried. "This is a world crisis!"

"Yeah, well, you were all fine with the idea of driving to the leper colony, even though you knew the benzene came from shady dealings. Why, Chartreuse practically admitted it." I let that sink in. "I can't help pitying him," I went on, "in that jail with nothing but his thoughts and his nightmares."

"How can you feel sorry for him when he stole from these poor people?" Isolde said.

"I don't know how I can. I just do. And he doesn't think they're poor. He told me he doesn't."

"Really, Claire." Isolde shied away from me. "Have you no compassion for the victims?"

"Of course I do! I feel so empty!" I turned away. "I don't know what I feel anymore."

"Well, then, go," Blacky said. "I suppose we can't just leave him there. Find out how much they'll take for bail."

Happily, I wrapped myself in a brown woolen Kashmiri cloak. I passed beneath the open window on my way and overheard Daisy sniff, "It's because she's American. Americans have no real feelings but for themselves. It's obvious. Oh, don't look at me like that, Isolde. It's not her fault. She grew up that way. We wouldn't be in this oil crisis if it weren't for the Americans, would we?"

I set off. It had rained the night before but now the weather was just misty and soft. It took a long time to get down there and find the jail and then they wouldn't even let me see him. There was an American girl they kept there. She must have been a drug burnout, or schizophrenic, because she swept and swept and babbled to herself. When I inquired about her they told me she was better off here because no one would rape her, she was at least safe. Frustrated, with nothing left to do, I bought some Assam tea from a street vendor and set off back to McLeod Ganj. There were only bicycles, yaks, and donkeys on the road and it was all uphill. The sun came out as I marched along and I was glad because the local people spoke forebodingly of the time when the rains would begin in earnest.

There was a commotion out in the street in McLeod Ganj. Everyone was pointing to the roof of Hula's Tea shop. "Look at

this!" Betty, the pregnant English girl, ran down the road pointing. "The roof's moving!"

I looked quickly, fearing I'd miss it, but it was in fact the sun
reflecting a swarm of undulating, phosphorescent butterflies.
Yellow and red, they were, and the size of baseballs.

They wriggled and hovered along the roof, lighting it up like
the insides of abalone, all purple and pink and blue. The roof
seemed to move and shimmer in waves, a magical sight. Then, as
I neared the camp, I heard Tupelo singing. She was singing that
old Etta James song, "At Last." I was delighted that she was up
and about and feeling her old self and I went to go see. Our vans
were set off to the side of the wagon-maker's house—this being
held up entirely by poles and stilts. She was all alone underneath
that house, washing her short hair over an enamel Chinese pail,
the kind you'd use to wash your feet.

"I can't believe how easy life is with short hair," she marveled
when she saw me.

"You *Dummkopf*! It's much too cold for that."

"No. It's lovely out." Her eyes were shining and I thought she
really did, now, look as though she had cancer. It was something
about her eyes, deep and glowing. I don't know how to describe it.

I went over to her. She had a fever. "Where's Blacky?" I asked.

"He's interviewing both the doctor and the sister of the Dalai
Lama. All in one day. So he's happy. Happy when busy, you
know him. Did you know that the sister runs an orphanage here?
I didn't even know there was one, did you?"

"No."

"Must be very quiet children." She started to cough.

"Here. Let me help you rinse the soap off." I steered her over
to the pump. She let me. That was when I began to get really worried. Tupelo never let you help her do anything. I toweled her
hair dry and let her sit against the house, out of the wind. The
sun was no use—it wasn't strong anymore. I put one of Harry's

fox fur hats on her. We sat together. I kept trying to make her laugh. I usually could, but I couldn't that day. "Do me a favor," she said, trying not to cough. "Give this emerald to Isolde. And give the rest of my stuff to Daisy." She reached up behind her neck and unhooked her green pearls. She put them in my hand. They were warm and slithery from her skin. "No," I protested.

"What the heck." She smiled. "Now you'll never forget me."

"As if I ever could."

She looked out over the snowcapped Himalayas and said, "It's like we're waiting for a taxi." After that I mostly stayed with her.

One morning I left her sleeping and was sitting outside reading. It was one of Tupelo's favorites: *Great English and American Poems*.

Isolde came dashing up the path. "What's the matter?" I said. "You look like you're fuming."

"You know, Claire," she roughly pushed up her sleeves, "I know Tupelo's sick, and I suppose it reminds you of when you were sick and we all took off, so you want to help out, but Reiner's doing *all* the work up at the orphanage. And you could at least hold the lights or the reflector for Wolfgang. You *know* Chartreuse is in jail."

I led her away from the van so we wouldn't wake Tupelo. "I have to just . . . help her through this."

Isolde gave an impatient wave. "Look. Wolfgang's right. He did me the favor of taking you on. He only did that because you're my friend. I never thought you'd be slouching off like this! What do you think it makes me look like?"

"Ouch. Has he said something else?"

She didn't answer that. She just said, "I mean, Tupelo will be fine. Blacky's a thoroughly competent doctor. Why are you wearing her pearls?"

I realized the time had come. "The thing is," there was no way to break it to her gently, "Tupelo has cancer. She really is dying."

She stopped, impacted. "What do you mean, dying? Now?"

The wind was blowing. I wiped my hair off my face. "Soon."

She looked at me as though I were crazy. "Who said so?" she asked suspiciously. She held her ears from the wind, like I'd been screeching.

"She's known all along," I added.

Just then Daisy came up behind her. "What's up?" she said.

I told her what I'd just told Isolde.

"I knew it!" Daisy said, turning pale. "I just knew she was really ill. I was fed up trotting back and forth with this and that for her and I was thinking, 'Who does she think she is?' and I went to tell her so, once and for all, and there was Blacky, shooting her up with a great bloody needle. I said to myself, 'Hello! What's going on here?'"

Isolde was stunned. "I had no idea," she whispered.

Harry came over. He had a tin plate full of muffins. I sighed and told him, too.

We all sat down in the middle of the road and ate the muffins. Reiner and Wolfgang came and sat with us and Daisy told them the news.

"They'll never buy our film now," Reiner said, devouring the last of them.

"Are you kidding? They'll be falling over each other to get at it, the buzzards," Harry said. He took out his cylinder of Pickup Stix and dumped them onto the road, out of the wind. We all stayed where we were. There was no danger of traffic since the oil crisis. Nobody went anywhere.

"What can we do?" Isolde offered.

"Wait," I said. "We just, you know, make her as comfortable as we can. Give her anything she wants, I guess."

Isolde was lost in thought. Finally she said, "You mean Blacky knew this all along and he never told me?"

I tried to soothe her. "I didn't know, either, until Rishikesh."

"Well, this really stinks," said Harry.

I left them playing and went back to the van and opened the side door. Van doors open with that enormous metal sound but Tupelo didn't jump up. I couldn't see her and I put my hand down on the bedclothes and realized she wasn't there. I thought, Oh, she went to the outhouse, and so I started down the trail to see if she needed newspaper—sometimes, when you had to run, you forgot to bring it and there was no such thing as toilet paper. But she wasn't there and I went, puzzled, back to the others.

A little brown Tibetan man, his face a mass of wrinkles, came tumbling down the road. He was terribly agitated about something but the wind was going the other way and nobody could make out what he was saying. "Probably the road to Delhi's out again," Reiner surmised and went back to his game. The man came running and slipping down the mountain toward us, unloosing a small avalanche of stones and pebbles. He was pale. He looked shocked. He held his heart. For a moment I thought he'd been shot. Of course he hadn't. I relaxed. He couldn't catch his breath. His eyes were wild and still he couldn't speak. At last he said, "Pretty lady, pretty lady!" He closed his eyes and pointed up past the waterfall.

No one knew what he meant, except Isolde. "He means Tupelo!"

We ran up the steep path, all of us, clattering to the top above the slender slope to a precipice, a ledge where people liked to go and look out over the snow peaks. It wasn't far but I wondered how she'd managed it, weak as she was. The ground was spongy.

A bevy of monks came running from the meditation center. They held their long skirts in their hands and, excited, ran up the steep path in a chain of burgundy worry.

When we got to the ledge, we crammed into the one spot. We held one another back, every one of us afraid to be pushed off the side. And it was muddy on the ledge. You could go over by just standing too close. There was a crow hovering right there in front of us, out in the sky not twenty feet away: a raven, huge looming wings black as licorice, and he looked me right in the eye. As long as I live I will still see that bird. It was as if he'd found his prey and knew I'd come to take it from him. When I craned over Daisy's shoulder to look, I saw her blue dress first. My blue dress. She lay in a bush on a ledge with her eyes wide open. We were so far up but you could see her eyes were open. She was looking up at us like she couldn't believe it, and then I realized she really *was* looking at us and she wasn't dead at all.

"Tupelo!" I cried.

She was turning over, feeling herself for anything broken, but she was actually all right—in a sense—no bones broken, just a wallapalooza of an egg on her head.

Wolfgang leaned over the precipice. He hadn't turned his camera off.

We all raced down the side of the mountain, taking different trails to reach her. When I got there she was holding her head, rocking to and fro.

Harry picked her up. "She fell." He said it over and over to anyone they passed, informing them more clearly than if he'd spelled it out that she had jumped. He lugged her together with Reiner, and then Reiner, hugely strong, and more encumbered by Harry than helped, just took her himself and carried her easily— she was so thin—back to the van.

chapter nineteen

It was Sunday. We were all eating lunch outdoors. Reiner had found a blue-painted door and we'd put it on some crates and sat around on cushions like at a table. Isolde had set herself to work, cooked a chicken rubbed with cumin at a campfire, and then made soup besides.

Somebody had to go to Lower Dharamsala to visit Chartreuse. They wanted me to go but I hadn't had any luck before and anyway, I wouldn't leave Tupelo. I thought it would happen without me there and I didn't want to miss the death. It had become the biggest thing. The truth was, we were all waiting for it. "Let Blacky go," I persuaded them, "he'll be the most impressive." Everyone agreed that this was so. Blacky showed me how to put the morphine into the syringe, looked once or twice doubtfully over his shoulder, and he went off, walking.

For a long while I was fine. But when she started to get uncomfortable, I prayed that Blacky would make it back. I wanted him to be there. It had seemed so important to me that I be there when she died and now all I wanted was Blacky. I couldn't bear to see her suffer and I was afraid to give her the needle. What if I did it wrong? She would be joking around and then, like a fish caught on a hook, she would lurch upward from the shock of the pain. There was no comforting her in those moments. I was just there, helpless. Also, she'd had a terrible night. Terrible. There'd been no helping her. She was pretty stoic, I'll give her that. But once in the early morning hours she'd lashed out, "I thought he wasn't going to let me suffer!"

I went and found an extra one of the pills Blacky had saved. He'd told me not to give her more than one and she'd had her dose a short while ago. "It could kill her," he'd warned. Without hesitation, I cut it up and ground up three-quarters of it and put it into yak butter, if you can believe it. I eased it into her mouth from a spoon. After that she slept like a baby.

There were some good moments that week—an hour or two after she'd had her morphine and before she finally went into a coma—where we talked together as right as rain.

"Claire?"

"What?"

"Give me a ciggy."

She was coughing all the time and I thought she would drown in her phlegm, but she said it like we were out in a nightclub downtown. I found a cigarette and put it between her lips. She looked so happy while I lit the match for her. She looked, one last time, like herself. She smoked the whole thing.

We told each other secrets. I told her all about my brother. I asked her to please look him up in paradise. She said she most certainly would and that she'd sleep with him, too. She noticed that I didn't like that and so to make it up to me she told me her secret: she hadn't been going to throw herself off the great mountain at all. She pushed herself up on her pillow and motioned for a glass of water. When I'd tipped the water into her dry lips she whispered, "I heard of this woman who lives in a cave up in the hills above McLeod Ganj. A miraculous woman, with healing powers. I was always too frightened to go on my own. Blacky said there was no such thing as miracles and she was probably a trickster." She tried hard to swallow. "He said it was too dangerous up there. The hills are full of vagabonds and cheaters. But now I figured I was dying anyway so I might as well go. What could it hurt? But—" She stopped, holding herself from the pain, then when it was manageable again she continued. "I went just as fast as I could so nobody would stop me. I knew you would stop me. I ran and I guess I was just too weak because I got so dizzy and passed out and fell right off the cliff. Phh. So stupid. I know." She looked up at me, and if she'd have had any tears left they'd have been in her eyes. "Don't tell anyone, all right, Claire? I don't want them to know I was afraid to die."

"No," I promised fiercely. "No, I won't tell."

She squashed the cigarette out in a saucer and sank back down into the pillows. "Let them think I was brave enough to kill myself."

"Sure," I said. "Sure."

That was the last long conversation we had.

She wanted to die outside, so Reiner, Isolde, and I carried her out onto a makeshift bed and we took turns keeping vigil. Once I fell asleep and suddenly woke up. She was awake and looking at me. The streetlamp was behind her and she looked really pretty, soft, with her little tufts of hair lit up gold like a halo. Her face held a kind of a rapture. "Hi," she whispered.

"Hi," I said.

We women had been changing her but it had been so long now since she'd eaten anything, we didn't have to worry about that. There was no terrible smell. I'd been frightened of that, but there wasn't.

Blacky had arranged for Chartreuse to be released. He was escorted back from Lower Dharamsala to McLeod Ganj in an official car, serenading the band of police people who'd come along for the fun of it. Chartreuse, they thought, was Derek and the Dominos rolled into one. He jumped out of the car when he saw us all gathered around and he tiptoed over to where we were. When he saw Tupelo, propped up on pillows and turning yellow, he began to weep. Then he set himself up right beside her and played every song he knew. Vladimir got hold of a huge parasol from one of the monks and he put it up over her, in case it rained, so we wouldn't have to put her in the van.

Finally she fell into a coma. Her hands and feet had turned all mottled and blue and yellow, even her toenails, and Blacky said that that was a sign. It wouldn't be long now. She was taking breaths in gasping puffs. Then suddenly there would be no sound and we would all look up expectantly. And then it would start up again. But the intervals of silence were becoming more frequent.

I was right there next to her when it happened. I wasn't holding her hand and later I wondered how come? But it was because of this feeling of respect and reserve. There is something so profound about death. It isn't weird at all. It seems so natural when it's almost there. You start praying for it to come. You're waiting. You don't want to leave in case you should miss it. And then, like a period at the end of a sentence, the last puff goes out and the body just stops. It's over. You're waiting for this big event and all it is, is over.

chapter twenty

 $\mathcal{S}$ he was the most elusive, the most appealing, the most precious creature. And now she was gone.

We all looked at one another with a thrill of realization. This was it. And then everyone started shouting and hugging.

Daisy held Tupelo's jaw up so it wouldn't go slack and she put coins, Swiss franc coins from Vladimir, down on her eyes so they'd stay shut.

Some of the townspeople came over. They wanted to see her. Old women—excited with the magnitude of death, prayer beads clacking, bleak with their own travails—circled the bed chanting and mumbling ancient incantations.

"They'll have to send for someone from the consulate," Blacky said.

"If they come," Harry said, "they'll take away the body. We'll never get her back."

Reiner just stood there. Here was this big ruddy fellow, bursting with good health and sportsmanship, tears running down his face, beefy hands balled into fists he ground like a four-year-old into his eyes, sobbing uncontrollably.

We kept her there for two hours. Anyone could come who wanted to see her.

We wrapped her up in muslin. The monks helped Blacky, Vladimir, and Reiner carry her up on a stretcher to the mountain. I was holding on to the package of hair she'd given me only two weeks ago. She'll need this, I told myself crazily as I followed the procession up, up. We were all gasping and out of breath. Love is the killer, she'd said. But it wasn't. Cancer was the wicked one.

We took the body out on the mountain and cremated her in the Far Eastern way. That's what she would have wanted. Everyone came, even the children from the orphanage. The Tibetans had a sort of ceremony at the site of her death. They said prayers, the same way our priests do, with incense and piety. I saw Wolfgang pass them an envelope I assumed was a donation.

"Do you know Debussy?" I asked Chartreuse, remembering her wishes.

"No." He shrugged.

"Well, will you play something she would have liked?"

"*Mais bien sûr,*" he said and picked up his guitar. He played "Imagine" by John Lennon.

"She would hate 'Imagine,'" Blacky whispered in my ear. "She loved every last possession she could get her hands on."

I laughed and all the others scowled at me.

I remembered those huge vultures from outside Rishikesh, and that terrible crow. I kept thinking I didn't want any horrible beast to touch her. I picked up some stones ready to cast them away, just in case.

You think you know it all and then something like this happens. I longed to talk to Tupelo, to tell her what had happened. But she was gone. Just like that. Then, because I couldn't disappoint her, I kept my promise and hummed "Claire de Lune." I usually have no trouble humming that or anything else, but my voice was all reedy and thin and weak. I couldn't get it strong. It was horrible. I can still hear me humming in that wobbly voice.

It was an eerie but moving and, I must say, after all the physicality of death, clean ceremony. Fire cleans. The cremation took longer than I thought and I was a little offended when people started opening up packed lunches. It was like that time outside Istanbul when the truck drivers ran into the herd of cattle and all the people from the area came out to watch, sitting on the hills, chewing betel nuts as though they were at an outdoor concert. But then the lunches were done and the body continued to burn, the skull a dour red, and we sat there hour after hour until I, too, started wishing I'd thought to bring food. In the end we all went back to Hula's and she made us special food for which we were not allowed to pay.

That night I had this dream. I was in a car, a small convertible—like a cartoon car. There was a man with me but I can't remember who. We were driving up, up the mountainside and then he said, "Watch this, we're going so fast we're actually flying!" And then we did, he drove the car right up into the air. I could feel my stomach lurch. I tried to hold on to the upholstery. "Put it down!" I cried out but he wouldn't. We were up in the air, weightless. The road was below us. I woke up perspiring, panting with fear. Blacky patted me absently and told me to go back to sleep.

The next day we gathered on the road by the main stupa. We were going back to gather the cooled ashes. Harry was always one for dream books and the *I Ching* and things like that. I asked him what he thought it meant. "Means you're out on a limb," he said right away. "Trying something you never have before." He grunted down onto the ground beside me, resting on his haunches, his well-sewn seams straining.

"That for the ashes?" I tried to smile, touching the pretend tabernacle.

"Yes." He wiped his forehead. Sheepishly, he muttered, "Might as well get some good use out of it, *wot*?"

"Come on." I took Chartreuse's guitar and carried it for him.

We climbed to the highest ridge, where her ashes lay in a gray heap. There were big hunks of bone and some of them still glowed orange with heat. It's not like you think it's going to be, all powdery and fine. Reiner, ever prepared, had come with a little hammer. I didn't think she would have wanted him to smash her remains to pieces so I asked if I might do it.

"Why should you be the one?" Daisy said.

My wrist with the hammer went limp. "Be my guest," I said.

But then Isolde said, "Come on. It's not right she does it on her own." So she and I picked up some rocks and crouched down in the ashes and smashed the pieces into smaller ones while Daisy hammered away. We were at it a long time. You'll never tell now, I thought silently, talking to her in my heart.

"Why don't you play something happy, Chartreuse?" Wolfgang asked him, filming from the sidelines. "To show life is a circle, you know? Sort of reincarnation stuff."

I have to say at that point we were all so used to the camera that it didn't even strike any of us as odd. But Chartreuse spun around in a rage. I thought he was going to hit him. Then he changed his mind and ran away down the hill.

"Barbarian!" Wolfgang shouted after him.

"I loved her!" I heard myself blurt out in front of everyone. I was pounding my chest. I sank to the ground but my eyes were dry. I couldn't cry. Harry came over, his little eyes bright with tears. "We all loved her!" he said. He helped me up. Vladimir picked up Chartreuse's guitar. He arranged himself into a photogenic pretzel and played exactly what Wolfgang had requested. We were all wretched and cold but we stayed up there with all that was left of Tupelo. Isolde wept while she hammered her friend's bones into powder. I'd never seen her cry before.

I remember thinking of all of us, Isolde had gained the most from this trip. Not just Vladimir's affections, which were to her the world, but she had grown into an amazing quietness; she'd reached from the surface down into her depth, and the desperate war she'd been in with herself was over. All she seemed to want now was peace. She'd fought for what she wanted. Really fought. And I admired her because I thought if someone treated me the way Vladimir had treated her, my pride would have interfered. I would have given up and lost. I looked at Vladimir, the ultimate artist, creativity his natural bent, unable to help his destructive outbursts. She understood. She was strong enough to weather the storms of the negative in order to be there and share in the positive. Lucky, I thought. She's the lucky one. And then I thought of what my father always said, which had never made any sense to me: that we loved someone for his faults, not in spite of them, and I thought that must be it. That must be how she could manage to stay.

At about two o'clock another one of the sadhus from the hills came up and said some prayers. You know, one of those fellows all covered in ash with the Rastafarian hair who goes around with nothing more than a loincloth and a bowl. We hadn't asked him to come, none of us had even thought of it. He burned incense and walked around in a circle and chanted for a good long while. It was very comforting, I have to say. Reiner tried to give him some rupees but he wouldn't take them.

Blacky said, "Come. Let's go back to town. You're cold. We're all cold."

There was the sound of someone coming toward us.

"What is it? What's happened?" we all said and I thought, Oh, no, what now?

Piratanzy, the local tailor, was bounding through the trees. "It's tender Betty! She having baby!"

Reiner remarked, "*Wie sagt man?* How do you say it? When it rains it pours!"

Isolde flew off down the path.

"I suppose I'd better go have a look." Blacky sighed.

"Oh, boy." Wolfgang balled up his fists like a bunny, then went about reloading his camera.

I hate to say it but Daisy and I scooped up the rest of the ashes hurriedly and poured them into the box. We all wanted to get out of there. There was so much of Tupelo left over, though. I didn't feel I could just leave her there. I blew some over the cliff into the wind, saying a last Hail Mary. It couldn't hurt. The rest I funneled into my pockets.

Harry jiggled up and down, shivering. "Hurry, will you?"

Blacky coolly went about the cremation site, kicking dirt onto where Tupelo had been. "The last thing one has to do is hurry for a firstborn. And do stop yelling. Now. I'm going to walk over to the meditation center, where I've left some things."

"What, now?"

"Yes, they won't be open later and I'll need them tonight. So. We're all going to have to settle down or we'll be no use to anyone. Now. Claire, you're quick. Run ahead and tell them I'm coming. Go down to Hula's and ask them if they'll boil some water. Reiner, come with me. Where's Isolde?"

"She's gone to find the local doctor," Harry puffed.

"Right." Blacky was already mentally putting things carefully and slowly into his doctor's bag.

"Please hurry," Harry whispered urgently.

I took off. Things were happening so fast. It was such a shift for me. I flew down Sangee Road and past the Dalai Lama's palace. It's odd but when someone dies he's closer than ever to you. It had been like that with my brother and now it was the same with Tupelo. I could feel her with me, her essence, accompanying me as I ran. It was easy to go down. You pulled back your shoulders and threw out your chest. It was like flying. The air was sparkling. There was one moment when you had to level off or you'd somersault straight down but I slowed enough to maneuver myself along to the Tibetan Moon. Isolde was hurrying up the road. "Did you find the doctor?" I panted.

"Yes, I found him," her eyes were blazing, "and do you know what he told me?"

"What?" I said, my heart already sinking.

"He said doctors weren't needed in natural things like childbirth. I said, 'What if something goes wrong?' Do you know what his answer was? He said then it was the natural way of things! That would be her karma."

"He didn't!"

"He did, too! Then I said suppose the woman was dying and they had to make a decision! What would your answer be then? He didn't bat an eye. He said, 'Abortion is always murder.'"

"I can't believe it," I said, horrified. "What if they let Betty die? Can they do that? Two deaths? No! I thought these people were enlightened. You know, that's just the kind of thing my church would say." I ground my teeth. "It's funny but this place is sounding more like home every day. Well, come on. Blacky's on his way there."

Hula leaned out a window of the tea shop. "What that? Betty giving baby now?"

"Yes, yes," we both said.

"Boy baby she go have!" Hula shook her fist in the air.

This was big news indeed. There was hardly a tea shop dweller in town who hadn't laid at least a small sum on the sex of Betty's baby.

The stairs around the back of the Tibetan Moon, steep and haphazard rickety wood on poles, led us up to the one-room dwelling, where an old biddy crouched. "Babby. Babby!" The woman grinned, gesturing toward a shredded burlap curtain someone had set up to indicate another room. I pushed it aside, almost knocking it down, and poked my head in.

There was Betty, on all fours in doggy style, on an army cot covered with sleeping bags in front of an open window. She panted up and down with quick, breathless gasps. Charles, perched atop an old sea trunk (the loftiest position in the room), legs crossed in lotus, was leading his disciples in a Buddhist chant.

Alarmed, we crept cautiously in.

"Good thing we've come," Isolde whispered. She went up to Betty and knelt beside her. Betty was huge and fully clothed in her burgundy robe. The sun made her look like an apple.

"How are you?" Isolde asked

"Great," she said, smiling, chugging, her cheeks wet with tears.

Charles stopped chanting. "Darling," he said, pressing his temples with long, patient fingers, "that last bout you had left me totally weak. Try not to feel so much pain, will you?"

"All right, dear," she murmured.

Charles had some spinach crisps, the french fries of Tibet. He said, "Would anyone like tea to go with these? Yes? Oh, good. Fine. I'd love some tea myself. It would do us all a world of good. Claire? Uh, would you run and get us some tea?"

"No."

"Oh. Well, then, who feels like going?"

But nobody wanted to go.

"I'm so sorry about your beautiful friend," Betty said.

"Yes," I said. "Thank you."

Charles held both hands up in a parody of balance. "One goes, one comes," he said with what I thought was unforgivable indiscretion.

Then Betty seemed to be overcome with pain and we all took a step back.

"I say," Charles thought of something new, "how about a little Have Agile, dear? Just the thing, don't you think?"

"Yes, please." Betty writhed and sweated, trying hard.

The sun had lowered itself in the sky, turning the Himalayan peaks outside and Betty inside almost psychedelic. The three men concentrated on their intricate harmonies. "Haa vaaaa nageeela." They started slowly then livened it up until they were singing at a breakneck frenzy. Betty moved to and fro. Even the rest of us couldn't help undulating a bit. But then, in came Blacky with Reiner and Chartreuse behind him, lugging a great cauldron of hot water. "Stop this nonsense," he ordered and everyone was instantly quiet. "Fill something up. I want cold water, too." He unraveled sterile gauzes and a pack of foreboding-looking instruments. The old woman, bent as a boomerang, came in with a kettle and two pails. We women, I must say, remained frozen and good for nothing. "Claire. Isolde," Blacky ordered without raising his voice. "Come over here now. You can both help."

He knew what he was doing, all right. Everyone calmed down. We edged closer.

"Betty," Blacky's tone was official and cool, "I want you to turn over, come on."

"No," Betty ground her teeth, "I'm better this way."

"Find me something cleaner than that rag!" Blacky threw the thing at me.

Isolde found a relatively clean towel aside the rusty basin and together we slipped it under Betty's taut body so as to cover the filthy sleeping bags.

"Turn over!" Blacky charged.

"No way!" Betty cried.

"Oh, let her be if she wants," I suggested.

"Shut up," he said and flipped the swollen girl right on her tail before she even realized what he was up to. She groaned and bit her lip.

"When I say go," instructed Blacky, "I want you to press down on her legs when she presses, like this, see? C'mon, Claire, don't stand there like an onion. Come round the other side so she's got both of you at the same level."

Charles and the others had stopped their chanting. Things were progressing swiftly, suddenly, and all of us became a unit following Blacky's every word.

"Now *push!*" he barked.

The whole room pushed. Even Charles and the boys grunted heartily in the background. Blacky sweated with the pressure. Betty kept her eyes on his. He held an impressive-sized needle up in the air and a squirt of liquid sprang out. The prayer wheel down below clanged and whirred. A group of curious Westerners had gathered downstairs.

Harry came in with a kerosene lamp but nobody moved. Everyone breathed with Betty. Blacky pierced her with a needle and she cried out, leaving nail marks like little new moons in four spots over my hand.

Then, before she saw what he was doing, he made a small, clean slice aside the canal, giving the baby's head room.

Birth gathers such profound momentum: one minute all the attention lies on the mother, then suddenly a gunky, wet top of a miniature head makes its way and in the ensuing, mysteriously elusive moments that follow, the wonder of life comes forth and every eye and heart in the room cling to it.

The room became narrow. You could hear the clock tick.

Betty gave her last mighty shove.

Pflopp, and out the baby came, soft and sloppy as a rubber seashell. All hearts leapt. The room was still. The suffocating silence waited. No sound came out to break it off. Something was wrong.

The old woman began to weep.

With deft and rapid movements, Blacky untangled the umbilical chord that was strangling the infant. The rest of us stood riveted and refrained from breathing. Betty's neck was craned to see and the sinews stood out like severed tendons.

Blacky thrust the tiny body from hot to cold water and then back again. Nothing.

"Oh, my God," Isolde said.

The prayer wheel rattled like a carousel throughout the room. I wanted to scream. The prayers from outside became louder and louder in an almost insane procession of sound.

"God, oh, God!" Betty shrieked. "Don't do it!"

Blacky held the newborn up by its feet. He slammed the infant with such force that if it wasn't dead yet, it surely was now.

Then, small and wonderful, a voice that never was before rose slowly from a pale, wet gurgle to a lusty howl.

The frozen room let go its breath and breathed again, and I cried out loud like a little kid. At last. All the tears I'd jammed up out of worry and frustration came tumbling out.

"A daughter, Betty," announced a victorious Blacky, "a beautiful daughter!"

The suck of everyone's astonished breath accentuated the fact that no one had, in those endless first moments, even pondered the until now all important sex.

Charles scurried over, every inch the beaming dad, and counted fingers and toes. Park stood up and announced the exact moment of birth and Mr. Auto fastidiously wrote it down.

Out came the violet-colored afterbirth. We all gaped at this astonishing sphere and Blacky nodded his head in approval. "All in one piece," he said. "Nothing to worry about."

Betty, two bright patches of red on her cheeks, apologized for having been so noisy. A chorus of voices shushed her down and she continued to explore the baby.

"*C'est une fille!*" Chartreuse shouted out the window. "It's a girl!"

Blacky's hair hung damp and disheveled down over his eyes. He caught my glance and laughed happily. Isolde, no doubt recalling similar moments in her own life, sobbed, "I want to go home. Now I really want to go home!"

I turned in time to see Wolfgang capping his lens, then protecting the camera with his arm as he made his way down the makeshift ladder he'd leaned on the window frame.

We all went outside to give the family some privacy. The moon was up in the day sky while the sun still shone. I loved that. It felt important and meaningful. I wiped my eyes and took the sky's picture. And it's funny how you can laugh and cry like that in the same day. For a short while we'd really forgotten our own pain. Everyone smoked a beedie in celebration. I'd pretty much given up smoking by now but the occasion seemed to warrant it. I fished around for a match. Tupelo's hair lay like a mouse in my pocket. It made me shiver. I thought I wouldn't smoke after all.

When Blacky and I at last climbed, aching and cold, into the van, I imagined we would find comfort in each other's arms. I should have known we were both too exhausted to behave decently. A part of me did know it, but I went ahead anyway, caressing his shoulders, attempting to arouse him with my touch.

He said coolly, "Do you know, Claire, you have absolutely no sense of propriety."

"You're right," I agreed.

He turned away and presented me with his handsome back.

chapter twenty-one

The very next day Betty was at Hula's with her perfect little baby. Hula came and laid a bowl of fragrant noodles on the table. Isolde passed around the bowls. Her emerald ring glittered in the lamplight. Suddenly Charles turned to me and said, "And what do you do in your real life, Claire?"

I was taken aback. "I, uh, I'm a model. Or I was."

"A model?" He looked me up and down. "Really! Aren't you especially short?"

"Well, yes."

There seemed no going on from there.

But Charles pressed on. "And why did you leave America?"

I thought this over. "I think I left because I couldn't face staying."

"Ah," he said. "That's why you condescend to be with the likes of us. Because you cannot hold your own with your own kind. That's why. You want to be looked up to. Admired! Adored!"

Blacky looked up from his book but it didn't seem to bother him that Charles was picking on me.

"No, I don't," I said, insulted. But then I thought maybe that was true. "At least I'll never be the pot calling the kettle black."

"It's interesting," Charles said, shifting his attention to Blacky. "One seems to come across two types of traveler. There's the philosopher, the searcher of truth. And then there's the runaway. Those who've gone and left an inconsequential life behind. The addictive personality, the follower, the . . ."

"Model?" I inquired.

"Well." He let the word stand there alone.

I looked to Blacky.

"Oh, Claire," Blacky gave me a sanctimonious little pat on the head, "nobody means you. There are subtleties you'll never understand. Just don't try."

I was outraged. "Ah, yes," I said, "being American and all that. I know you're all so well brought up. Still. With all my family's and my education's shortcomings, I'm the only one of all of you who really believes in loyalty and truth. And dreams. I am——" I cringe now to think I had my hands on my hips at that point. "Maybe I left home because I couldn't face the reality of my being less than I should. Maybe the people around me were so worthwhile, I felt inferior beside them. And the place I come from—which would certainly be beneath the likes of you," I could hear my voice growing louder, and I glared at Reiner, "what with our graffiti and our Van Wyck Expressway, it still holds the most sincere people in the world. The salt of the earth. People with dreams. Those dreams may not be to score a . . . a . . . a first in the Berlin Film Festival, but to get a home and education for their kids." I stood up. "But that's too corny for you all. Why, you're all a bunch of cynics. That's all your fancy educations taught you." I looked at Charles. "And if I've worn my spirituality as an ornament, at least I don't try to sell it."

"Oh, but you would have." Wolfgang sneered.

"Oh, but I didn't," I replied.

"Hear, hear!" said Harry.

"No sense taking it out on poor Charles here," Blacky reprimanded me.

I was furious that he wouldn't take my side. He just never did. I totally lost it. "And I'm surprised at you, Blacky. You know, everyone says about you that you're always there for them when the going gets tough. What was it? *'Wenn es dir dreckig geht, der Blacky ist ja immer da', gell?* Isn't that it? But when things are fine, it's like you turn your back! What are you, bored?"

He placed one foot lazily up on the rung of the chair beside him. "You mean like, 'Vanilla, vanilla, vanilla'?"

I grabbed my side. The pain of what he said shot through me. "All right, Blacky! At last the truth," I panted, deaf to who could hear us. "Come out and say, 'I don't love you.' You loved me more when I was the patient. Admit it! When I was nondescript and anonymous!"

"I loved you more when you were quiet," he said softly.

That's it, I thought. I'll never recover from this.

"Oh, calm down, Claire," Isolde said. "Sit down." She took her sweater off then put it right back on.

Harry said, "The more upset she becomes the more calm you become, Blacky. Do you notice that?"

"She's obviously getting her menses," Blacky said. "What is it, full moon? Aren't you always on the full moon?"

Isolde sighed. "I can't wait to leave here. I really want nothing more than a good *Leberwurst* and a Spaten Bier."

"Me, too," said Vladimir.

"Yes," Blacky stood and stretched, "our luck seems to have run out here."

"Where would you want to go now?" Vladimir asked Blacky.

He lit up. "You know, I did think of stopping over in Vietnam while I'm already in this part of the world. One could leave the van and fly the rest of the way. It would certainly be cheaper than buying benzene at this point."

"What do you mean?" I said. "I thought we were driving back!"

"We can't afford to, Claire. Haven't you been listening?"

"We're not all heiresses like you, you know," Daisy sniffed.

"If only we could find somebody stupid enough to buy the vans," Harry said. "Then we could all fly home."

"And what about me?" I said like a dope, flaunting my pain in front of just about everyone.

"I think you want to be on your own." Blacky looked at me sadly and waited. "Don't you, Claire?"

"Is that an invitation?" I said.

"I don't know. Is it the truth? You seem to so much want the truth."

I was too stunned to answer. I'd thought we were in the midst of a regular boyfriend-girlfriend fight. I'd thought we were going to patch it up and everything would bump itself back into order. It occurred to me that our argument and his cold shoulder suited his needs very well. He'd thought it all out. When had this happened?

I couldn't seem to pull myself together. I didn't feel anything, just numb. I pushed open the door and ran down the road. I didn't know where I was going. Then, I remembered what Tupelo had said, about where she'd been headed that day when she'd fallen from the cliff. Off to a holy hermit-lady's cave. You know what, I told myself, I'm not even afraid to go there. I'm not anything.

With a dreary gray sky overhead, I set out. I passed a caravan of shady European junkies by the river. The Tibetans were such good and worthy people, there was nothing for the junkies here and so they were pulling up camp. They looked at me and I at them. Scoundrels. It half occurred to me I should have mentioned to the others where I was off to but I didn't. I wanted them to worry. I think part of me didn't care anymore. I guess I wanted to get into trouble. I thought to myself, What could happen that hasn't already? I was in such a cacophony of rage that I thought if I did die, that would show him! The worst part was that I really was getting my period in a few days and to have my injured feelings so trivialized by this concession was too much to bear!

I began the steep climb. The path was a seasonally dry mountain stream of flint boulders. I clattered up through the hedges and over the town. The stones gave way the minute you put two feet on them. I was forced to stop and catch my breath every ten minutes. I'd imagined an unusual experience but I was ill prepared for the mystical atmosphere that surrounded me, the giant bodhi trees, the foliage alive with wild peacocks.

Alone, I was as lithe and simple as the animals who watched me. I thought of Tupelo and how she'd tried to come this very way. I let my body drop and slither to the edge and through the high wet grass as excellently as a snake.

McLeod Ganj was a jewel from above. The waterfall and stream were like a zipper through its middle. I watched the solemn parade of monks' shaved heads leaving temple and on their way to quarters. The dear ragged flags in the wind. Farmers on the lower hill bent down in rice paddies that checkered the distance in varying shades of jade and moss and all the greens of India. I felt so close to Tupelo up here. It was almost as though she were with me.

I sat there for a long time, thinking of everything. I pulled out my letter from home that I hadn't finished reading. It was all of the things I feared. Heartache. Responsibility. Familiarity. Nothing sophisticated at all. And blame. Every time I looked at it I felt like a child. I opened the flimsy blue pages and at last read it through.

Dear Claire,

What the hell do you think you're doing traveling around the goddamn world when I'm stuck here like this, divorced, with mommy and daddy? What are you thinking? And Zinnie says when she graduates she's going into the police academy! That's your fault, too! Mommy's turned Michael's room into her knitting room. But his stuff is still stuffed in the closet. Really she just goes in there and smells his clothes. It's horrible. Zinnie put your and her stuff in the back room, looking over the trestle. She went to the mall and bought snazzy quilts for the beds with her own money. Blue. Dark blue with bright red poppies all over. She says when you come back you'll want the window view so she sleeps up against the wall. Like she really believes you'll come home. I always thought it would be me on a trip around the world. I'm impulsive, you're the nerd, remember? Hope you're having a ball. It stinks here.

Carmela

I put the letter down with a heavy heart. And yet, she'd brought me right back home with her reprimanding words. It was almost as though I'd gone there. Imagine little Zinnie going out and buying quilts! And all with the hope that—I was touched, and I was also oddly soothed. I folded the letter carefully and returned it to my backpack.

I stood up and brushed myself off and continued to climb. I had the eerie sense of being watched. And then I saw why. In the clearing to my east, there were furry, beige apes as tall as small men. They were slender, beautiful—the glamorous blond color of Afghan dogs. There seemed to be a community of them. Their fur looked well cared for, as though it had been brushed. They blinked and scratched and gathered their children but never ventured toward me. If they had, I would have headed downstream immediately. But they kept their distance. These weren't like the monkeys in the temple. These were well-behaved villagers. I'd stumbled across a village! The village elder—standing there with his staff—looked at me and I at him. I made the decision not to take a picture. Some decision was made on his part, too, because he did nothing. Flocks of green parrots shot from treetop to treetop and high overhead, wondrous eagles—the most magnificent birds imaginable in flight—swooped in broad sovereign arcs. Misty clouds floated beneath me and covered the path I'd already consumed. I began to wish I'd brought a canteen—and to fear I was lost—but having come so far already, trekked on.

Suddenly a nearby growl reached my ears. Not knowing which way to turn, I climbed to the top of a huge granite boulder and stood face-to-face with the owner of the voice. A half-dog, half-wolf creature with a collar of iron spikes stood chained and guarding a grotto-like cave, the entrance of which was stopped by a gate of prison-thick bars.

Four Indian pilgrims knelt at a safe distance from the entrance. I was happy to see them. Happy? I practically sobbed in relief. I walked cautiously forward. In the dark of the cave's interior shadow, I could just make out a vague, seemingly ash-covered body in yoga position.

The animal growled but no response came from the cave. The entrance wall was dominated by a massive cement sculpture of the dancing, tooth-protruding Heirab, the awful, ludicrous god of the ghosts. I thought instantly of Vladimir. He would love this. It wasn't only awe-inspiring in its ferocity but good, really good in line and perspective. There was a primitive spinning wheel beside me. A voice came from within the cave. It asked in a soft natural voice who was there.

"It's me," I said, "Claire Breslinsky."

I don't know what she thought about that.

"I was wondering," I knocked on the cave wall politely, "if you would be so kind as to speak with me."

In German, she asked how many of us were there.

In English I answered, "Just me."

She asked if I would please wait until the other people went away.

Feeling a little foolish, my legs still quivering with the trauma of the climb, I went and hid behind a nearby boulder to wait out the exit of the Indians. Twenty minutes later, I peeked out from my hiding place and there was the hermit passing out orange slices to the pilgrims. She was swathed in a deer-skin pelt draped modestly over a sculpted silver metal brassiere. Her pants could only have been riding breeches. She was barefoot and completely dusted in ash. Her hair must have been knee-length. It was matted, tied up in a wooly brown bun and held securely by a string of dried bodhi tree seeds.

Her eyes were all-encompassing, alert, the whites very blue, the brown had more depth than color. Not a ravishing beauty, she was nonetheless ravishingly beautiful. She was obviously European by birth, but she was so otherworldly now, it was hard to tell where from. I tiptoed over and sat down, cross-legged, beside the four Indians, with whom she continued to speak Hindi. Her attention was carefully held by her hands spinning wool.

Presently she smiled at me. Her manner was pleasant and down-to-earth. She spoke to me in English, introducing herself as Lumar Racknesh and her "dog" as Bobby, who was actually half wolf. He came docilely forward for a pat on the head. The garish collar, she explained, was his protection as the hills were populated by panthers. One had jumped on Bobby the year before, nearly killing him with lacerations to the throat.

I thought uneasily of my still-to-come journey down the mountain.

The pilgrims, one by one, came forward and prostrated themselves at her feet. One of them tried to kiss them, at which point she became upset and threatened him with a scythe blade if he didn't stop. The man bowed away. As the pilgrims wove their way down the path, leaving different offerings of sugar and pennies behind, Lumar explained that they thought the cave had miraculous powers.

She seemed eager to talk and so I sat down and listened. She spoke of swamis and gurus, how necessary a guru was and how glad she was she didn't need one anymore. "Now," she said, "it's just myself and God. My guru has been dead for twelve years. He was a true master." Lumar smiled. "I don't know any other alive today. The great masters nowadays go abroad, and if they are here, they don't have time for you."

A baby goat stumbled up to her and began sucking happily away on her earlobe. "He thinks I'm his mother," she explained. "He's one of twins and his mother didn't have enough milk."

I was anxious to get a look at the inside of the cave and kept peeking over her shoulder toward the inside. Finally, she invited me in to explore the interior. At first I was blinded by darkness. My first impression was of cool deep stone surrounding me. Lumar lit three candles and gradually my eyes adjusted to the shadow. It was magnificent! About eight by five meters, the floor was solid stone covered by mats she'd woven herself, she said. The walls were not so much walls as time-molded black globs, frozen in place by the seasons. From stone and cement, Lumar had sculpted giant images of Hindu gods and goddesses. Even poor statues would have been interesting in such an atmosphere. These were breathtaking. Her scrupulous attention to hands and feet made me think that these bizarre figures actually had lived. Her goddess Fortuna had so much pride. I thought right away of Tupelo. Oh, Tupelo. I held myself up against the wall.

"Not that way," she said and led me from the spot to a form of Ganesh, the elephant god, god against obstacles, god of wealth. All her animals were spine-tingling in their realism. One life-sized panther stalked a corner of the cave, his eyes of ancient greenstone. They sparkled and flashed in the eerie light. Shiva Linga, the formless form, was an egg-shaped mass that was kind to the touch. Each of them invited caressing. Shiva, one of the three main Hindu gods, rode atop a mighty bull, his six graceful arms poised and ready to perform the dance of destruction. A god to be appeased and catered to, he dominated the cave with his presence. "I never understood the appeal of a god of destruction," I admitted.

"Why that? You can pray to Shiva when you want to destroy pain, destroy jealousy, desire. Things you've had enough of. Makes sense now?"

"Yes." I looked around. "Say. What do you eat up here?"

"Anything I can get my hands on." Her eyes glittered and we both had a good laugh.

Then, more serious, she said, "I eat rice, mostly. My goat provides me with milk and cheese."

"So you don't eat meat."

She gave me a startled look. "There's nothing wrong with a good wurst. If I had one I'd gobble it up. I eat what is offered to me. People come. They leave their offerings."

A circle of stones and ash provided warmth for Lumar's evenings. She had a vina, the slender, female-looking instrument similar to the sitar. It lay aside a fur cushion. I asked her to play for me but she refused. Still, she showed me around the cave with a candle, leading my eyes to the most delightful spots. Her eyes blazed when she stopped before an especially vivid part. She seemed to want me to enjoy her work as much as she did. She looked at it as if she were discovering it for the first time.

"I don't suppose you'd let me take your picture?" I said.

"Why not?" she said, and let me photograph the whole she-bang. After that we spoke for a while until the insistent braying of the baby goat brought us again into the sunshine.

I'd noticed that every piece was signed. It was so sad, though, that they'd never leave the cave. They were cemented to it or were part of the unusual natural formations. I must alert Vladimir, I thought excitedly, bring him here. He could see to it that someone brought them to light. Then I looked at Lumar laughing happily with her four-legged white kid and I changed my mind. Here they *should* stay, I decided, the way she'd dreamed them, in the home that would best suit them. Let them stay a kind reward for searching pilgrims and Lumar's waking moments, not chiseled out and transported to some chic studio. This was their destiny. Destiny. Was there such a thing? And if there was, what, then, was mine? Why did I always attach myself to someone else's?

I sat on a patch of grass. Tupelo was dead. How could this be so? How could all these things have happened? I let my head fall back and looked up at the sky. Here I was in Tupelo's dream, in her intent. She'd never experienced this before she died. She'd tried. She'd never made it. I'd done it for her, though. I stood to go.

At that moment a little Indian lady approached Lumar. She bent down and plucked one of the many wildflowers that bloomed along the path, then laid it at Lumar's feet as an offering but Lumar started shouting at her angrily, "Stop! You had no right to kill that flower! No right! You can never put it back, never!"

The dainty woman ran away in fear.

"I'd better go," I said. But Lumar held me back. She put something cold into my hand. It was a miniature figure of Ganesha, the elephant god. "It's very old," she said. "It will bring you luck." Then she turned and retreated into her cave. That was the end of her. I remembered what she'd said about people leaving offerings. I took out Tupelo's book of poems from my knapsack and left it carefully by the entrance to the cave. I made my way down the steep, darkening path. My knees, like vivid electrical hinges, seemed to move along without me. Down, down the mountainside I went, holding on with my hands at times, almost running at others when the path became level. It was dusk and now I knew there were panthers. But I had done something courageous—at least to me—something I would never have done before. And if the only thing I could change in this life would be me, then at least I had that.

I veered into the wind. To the west I could see as far as the Punjab. Purple stars glittered in the green twilight. I heard the evening sounds of the forest and wished again I'd stalked off with something more than my knapsack and the clothes on my back.

After what seemed like a very long time the clouds beneath me dispersed and I could see the faraway lights of the Dalai Lama's palace. That was a pretty sight, let me tell you. The path forked into three at one point and I could finally see through to where I was headed. I hastened my downward trot. The darkness hurried, too, and I was grateful for the flickering kerosene lights below that guided me.

I staggered into Hula's. They were playing Parcheesi, all of them, and the steam from the noodle pots made the room look misty and dreamlike. They all looked up, startled. I grabbed a cup of hot tea and drank it down in one draught.

"Well, *there* you are!" Blacky said. "Done sulking?"

"We were just getting worried," Isolde said.

Exhausted, I sat down on a chair. They looked at one another and I saw they'd been discussing me. What good would it do to tell them? They would minimize it somehow. I reached instead for one of their trusty peanut butter sandwiches. Fragments of ore on the wood-burning stove struggled loose and a cascade of cinders went up.

chapter twenty-two

The rains were on their way. Weeping egrets turned the ridge and circled overhead. You never heard anything like it. We filed outside to watch. After a while we stood around kicking the grass, watching the prayer sayers, the wheel turners. We found ourselves at loose ends, having sold all the vans to a cortege of wealthy but exhausted French trekkers who were delighted to get them. Chartreuse had come across one of them in prison. They hadn't committed any serious crimes, he'd explained, just a little hashish, but their vans had been confiscated. (I'd seen those trekkers, though. They looked like junkies to me.) Chartreuse lay on the grass now, smoking. All he wanted to do was to lie outdoors and look at the sky. You couldn't blame him. He pulled himself up when he saw me. He was wearing a backpack.

"Where are you going?" I asked.

He shrugged and took a death-defying pull on his cigarette. "I thought I'd join the trekkers. They need a cook. I don't know.

I'm fed up." His yellow eyes looked through me. "I'm sure Wolfgang can manage on his own, eh?"

I tried to hide my disappointment. "Yes. Yes, I guess he can."

He chewed his lip with savage intent. "It was Wolfgang who put the police on to me, you know."

"Chartreuse, it could have been anyone."

"No, but it wasn't. They told me at the station."

"Chartreuse, let's be fair. Everyone suspected you." I hung my head. "Even me."

His eyes narrowed. "He will get his. What goes around comes around, *n'est-ce pas?*"

"Yes," I agreed. "If there's one thing we've learned . . ."

We looked together, up the hill and past the waterfall, at our profound memories. I'd been so fond of Wolfgang at the beginning. But now, when things had gotten to the crunch, well, it just seemed to me that he'd shown himself a really small and bitter person. And Reiner, who I'd found despicable, had turned out to be a decent human being, with values.

Harry came bounding up the path. "Want to take a walk over to the little orphanage?" He looked at us over his armload of short-legged jeans. "I thought I'd give these to the children in the orphanage."

"Good idea." I loved Harry. I just did.

"I'll help you carry them." Chartreuse lifted them from him.

"Want to come, Claire?"

"No. No, thanks," I said. I wanted to get a couple of things straight with Blacky, this time without an audience. "Later."

"Later." Chartreuse winked and he gave me a special look, filled with charm and meaning. He feels good about himself, I remember thinking.

Blacky, however, thought the orphanage might need him to do some checkups. "I'll just run over there with Harry and

Chartreuse," he told me happily. But he said it like he was asking my permission. I held my nuggets of turquoise and garnet and rolled them around in my hands. I was sorry that he felt that way. But I had always wanted to own him. That was my dynamic with him. I smiled. I could wait. He continued to stand there. Perhaps he felt he'd gone too far. Isolde came up. She regarded the wedge of silence between Blacky and me. "Look, you two," she swung her long black hair around and pulled it into a knot, giving an exasperated sigh, "we're stuck here for a week, probably, anyway. You might as well make up."

Reiner marched up the road with his clipboard and a bounce to his step. "Plenty of rooms at the Kailesh Hotel. Daisy, I reserved first pick for you."

"Lovely!" Her abundance of Tupelo's jewelry dangled, Cleopatra-like, between her breasts. She *would* have to wear all of it at once.

"Looks like we'll be here for a while." Reiner leered at her, thinking of later. "Once the rains start, the roads turn to fudge," he reminded us. He looked skeptically up at the dirty sky. "Pity about the light."

"Doesn't matter now." Wolfgang sucked a tooth. "It will be a superb ending with Tupelo's death. We couldn't have made up a better one. I can hardly wait to get back and start cutting the film. Isn't there any other way out?"

Reiner lifted his new Tibetan bonnet and wiped away some pearls of sweat. "No chance. There's just Hula's husband and his coal truck. We'd all hardly fit. They're letting it make its delivery and once it heads back to Delhi, they'll be shutting the road."

"So how do we get—"

Not to be interrupted, he gave a small authoritative toot on his whistle. "There's a state bus that comes through next Sunday. By then the weather should relent. That will take us as far as Delhi. From there we can all fly home to Munich. Make sure you've taken all your gear from the vans as I'm giving the keys to that Pierre fellow in an hour. As we are all determined to leave as soon as possible, when the pass becomes clear I shall purchase tickets for everyone." He took hold of Daisy's hand. She snuggled up to him. "All right," she agreed.

I walked over to the half circle that was now our diminished caravan. For a moment I stood outside it, not liking to go in. I opened the door. It reeked of Harry's spoiled bananas. I had to get the rest of my things. Very quickly, I piled my meager wardrobe and my toothbrush in my largest lightweight bag. I took my best Kuchi dress off the hook, my dwindled box of personal toiletries from the shelf. I went to Blacky's van. I took Tupelo's last unopened bar of soap.

I looked around for the last time. There was a refrigerator that had broken down in Greece, a sink that had broken down in Turkey, a bookcase over the bed, and a table, if you wanted it, to raise up and peg on the floor. I touched the knife grooves in the worn red plastic plates, put my cheek against the orange plaid curtains that had let in so much light. I kept my money underneath the false bottom of a crock. It was that harmless-looking yogurt pot I'd picked up in the Khyber Pass. I put it in Frau Zwekl's soap box with the rosary beads and the false teeth, shut the lid, and took it with me. Several bottles of scotch snuggled comfortably in a pile of Pakistani scarves. The trekkers would be happy to find them, all right. You couldn't take them past the border. Under a cushion I saw what I was looking for. I'd left my blue notebook in here. I took it. Who knew. Someday when I was old, maybe people would wonder what it was like when I was young; the things that had happened here and on the way, our journey into what would be the evening of Aquarius. I picked the bananas up gingerly. I went outside and felt the beginning of the soft rain on my face. It was just a mist. I walked the bananas to the dump. The eagles swooped down instantly and tore them apart with gusto.

I had an idea. I took out Frau Zwekl's false teeth and brought them over to Hula's father. It was a long shot, but . . . I placed them on the table in front of him. You'd have thought I laid out the crown jewels. Conversation stopped throughout the place. "You'll have to wash them," I began but it was too late. He'd picked them up and already stuck them in his mouth. I waited. I thought, Surely they won't fit. The old man continued to sit there but he refused to open his mouth again. That was it, the joint was shut. I got up. "Well," I said, "good luck." I walked away.

Blacky was coming in the door.

"Claire," he said. "Sit down."

"What?" At that moment I knew he was going to ask me to marry him. He looked so earnest.

I turned on him my most bewitching smile.

He seemed a little short of breath. "They. Wolfgang. Someone stole the film canisters."

I was still smiling. "What?"

"The film," he choked. "They've stolen it! Every can."

"Who! Who's stolen it?"

"If we knew that!" he snapped.

I turned and looked out the open window. The waterfall tumbled down. Whatever had happened there'd always been that one thing that had given justification to it all: the film. Whatever had happened. I shook my head. A series of pictures, months, scenes from our journey like a shuffle of cards floated past me. All we'd been through! I looked up at Blacky. He looked away. Someone was shouting out in the street. It was Wolfgang. He seemed to be throwing a fit.

chapter twenty-three

We walked around in circles all day long. Nobody talked. It was as though another one of us had died.

Then Reiner was blowing his whistle in a rage by the waterfall. They'd found the film but it was ruined. Ruined! The canisters were gone. Whoever it was had simply thrown the film into the stream. Parts of it came rushing, useless, into town.

There was no consoling Wolfgang. I went to look for Chartreuse but he was nowhere to be found. He'd gone for good, deeper and deeper into his own borderless journey. That special look he'd given me had been good-bye.

I went to look for Blacky. He was standing just beneath the Tibetan Moon. Two new girls had come to town. Peace Corps girls. Fresh in from Sweden and Jordan. Very pretty. They were climbing the stairs and their new Kuchi skirts fluttered like flags in the rippling wet wind. They were laughing and telling him what a time they were having getting into Kashmir. He gave them no end of advice. I was happy to see Blacky wasn't sorrow-stricken.

I gathered up all my bags, hitched up my rucksack, and walked to the prayer wheel, making sure I had my camera, my tapestry sack. Blacky came up and stopped me. We faced each other, then sat on the stoop of the path that led around it.

"You didn't take much stuff," he said.

"Oh, me. You know me. 'Have little and gain; have much and be confused.' "

"Lao-tzu." His eyes twinkled.

"Right."

He glanced over at the Tibetan Moon. Those new girls were coming down the stairs underneath shellacked parasols from Kuala Lumpur. They were laughing, stumbling in the growing dark. I could feel his eyes—though he forced them to attend to mine—I could feel his full attention waver.

I unwrapped my package and settled down with a pack of brick-hard, industrial Chinese chocolate. I thought of the view from my and Zinnie's window, out past the maple tree branches in winter. Silver white icicles drop down like jewels from the ramshackle freight train tracks. I wondered who slept in that bed. Or if it still would be empty. It might very well be empty. My mother cooking crispy pork chops and my cousin dropping in. How long had it been since I'd had a good pork chop? I sighed. It might be nice to have a telephone again. To sit upstairs and talk on the phone and watch my dad come through the trellis with the mayor on his leash. It was Carmela who'd found him one day at the Regent's Row pub. He would stand at the bar in his stubborn way, not begging, just waiting, speculating patiently until some sucker would relinquish his leftovers. Carmela had carried him, that enormous vagabond dog, right through the doorway and into the harrowing protests of visiting uncles and aunts. The mayor loved his leash. Having spent the first half of his life scuttling footloose from bar to bar in hopes of grill-fried hamburger, it was no wonder that he refused to budge without it. My mother cooked in different cultures and hefty portions found their way to the mayor's dish.

"Claire!" Blacky bellowed at me.

"Oh, sorry. What?"

"Pay attention!"

"Well, what?"

"We're all taking rooms at the Kailesh Hotel. Come on." He waited, sure of me now. "It won't be so bad." He gave my shoulder a jolly push. "Not too many bedbugs. If there are two of us, they'll have to divide their attention."

He had it all figured out. I looked down the road. The coal truck was parked right outside the hotel. It was just starting up, the engine sluggish and trying.

"And we've got the whole week. Anything can happen in a week." He gave me his charming, most disarming smile.

I shivered with cold and, let's face it, fear. It started to rain harder. Night had come.

"What is it?" he pressed. He looked down Sangee Road to where I looked. He got it then. He blinked away the rain and put his foot down. "You can't ride in a coal truck all the way to Delhi!"

"Funny thing is, actually, I can."

"This is absurd!"

"Blacky, all I know is that the farther I went, the more the things stayed the same. Like, the answers were inside all along. I just had to step far enough back in order to see them."

"Oh, come on." He laughed brusquely, trying to get me in a scoffing way. "You just feel bad, as we all do. You're exhausted. Why, look at you. What you need is a warm bath and—"

Yes, I knew what he thought I needed. But it would only put things off. So it wouldn't be now, but soon. And in his way.

I stood my ground.

Blacky threw his head back. Thoroughbred, he. He became quite stiff. *Höflich.* Polite. Sometimes you recognize moments as important. If you listen, you can hear them. I knew this was it from the roaring in my ears.

He took my hand up into his and he kissed it, gently and carefully. He was saying good-bye.

I tried to smile. The burden, thick as hardened paint, fell with a gush from my heart to the ground. Just like that. He was a teacher whose words I would hear in my heart my life long. Nothing would change that.

The truck engine gave its meaty rumble. I grabbed his sleeve. "I'll take a charter back to New York by the end of the week. Blacky. Look, I'll be fine."

And as I said it, I knew it. I thought to myself I might be scared, and I might not have love, but I have this incredible whole lot of faith. Bewildered, maybe, but genuine. That was the thing about me. I'd lost Tupelo but I felt her all around me now. She lived on in me, if nowhere else. And in the end, I'd got what I had come for. I shifted my camera and bag of film underneath my itchy anorak. The wind blew a gale and we held on to each other, Blacky and me, until it passed.

He kissed me on the neck.

I kissed him sweetly on the lips. After all, you should always be a gentleman; certainly a pistachio girl knew how to be a gentleman. We held each other's gaze another time, one last lingering time, the membrane slain and feather light.

I walked away. Betty was walking by and I placed my bridesmaid's hat upon her head. She liked that. "Say good-bye to everyone for me," I told her. "Wait." I fished around in my pocket for the antique Ganesha. "Give this to Harry," I said. Then I ran— how was it? Just the way Swamiji had told me—I ran like the wind through the rain. I banged on the door of the truck. Hula's husband didn't speak much English but he'd heard enough of it to make out what I wanted. I offered him a fair pile of rupees. He was happy to have me, I think. I climbed up into the passenger seat next to another traveler, an avatar of Vishnu. His face was blue in the dark and his feet didn't touch the floor. He was saying his beads and he let me have the window. Lucky, I thought, I could just squeeze in. There was the powerful smell of the coal. The mighty engine lurched and groaned and rumbled and we were off, bouncing through the night.

We tooled along the road that hugged the mountain, making time before it would slip away. We circled counterclockwise, pitching and chucking, lumbering through pits and holes to safer ground, on and on, until you could see across the whole pine-scented Kulu Valley and to little McLeod Ganj, twinkling cozily and incandescent through the rain.

At the verge we had to wait and let an official car coming up the other way pass by. Our headlights reached like beacons. "Dalai Lama!" the driver cried excitedly. "Coming home! Coming home!"

I rolled the window down. "Me, too." I smiled at last. "Me, too."